I0643183

THE BLACKMAILER

BOOK 3 OF RIAN KRIEGER'S JOURNEY

ROGER A. SMITH

MILFORD HOUSE

an imprint of Sunbury Press, Inc.
Mechanicsburg, PA USA

MILFORD HOUSE

an imprint of Sunbury Press, Inc.
Mechanicsburg, PA USA

NOTE: This is a work of fiction. Names, characters, places, and incidents either are the product of the author's imagination or are used fictitiously. While, as in all fiction, the literary perceptions and insights are shaped by experiences, any resemblance to actual persons, living or dead, events, or locales is entirely coincidental.

Copyright © 2024 by Roger A. Smith.
Cover Copyright © 2024 by Sunbury Press, Inc.

Sunbury Press supports copyright. Copyright fuels creativity, encourages diverse voices, promotes free speech, and creates a vibrant culture. Thank you for buying an authorized edition of this book and for complying with copyright laws. Except for the quotation of short passages for the purpose of criticism and review, no part of this publication may be reproduced, scanned, or distributed in any form without permission. You are supporting writers and allowing Sunbury Press to continue to publish books for every reader. For information contact Sunbury Press, Inc., Subsidiary Rights Dept., PO Box 548, Boiling Springs, PA 17007 USA or legal@sunburypress.com.

For information about special discounts for bulk purchases, please contact Sunbury Press Orders Dept. at (855) 338-8359 or orders@sunburypress.com.

To request one of our authors for speaking engagements or book signings, please contact Sunbury Press Publicity Dept. at publicity@sunburypress.com.

FIRST MILFORD HOUSE PRESS EDITION: March 2024

Set in Adobe Garamond Pro | Interior design by Crystal Devine | Cover by Lawrence Knorr and Ashley Nichole Walkowiak | Edited by Sarah Peachey.

Publisher's Cataloging-in-Publication Data
Names: Smith, Roger A., author.
Title: The blackmailer : book 3 of Rian Krieger's Journey / Roger A. Smith.
Description: First trade paperback edition. | Mechanicsburg, PA : Milford House Press, 2024.
Summary: **1838.** In St. Petersburg, Russia, thirteen-year-old Rian Krieger finds herself dangerously close to the intrigue that infests the court of Tsar Nicholas I. And no one there suspects she is a girl posing as a boy. In Philadelphia, self-emancipator Jules Freeman is asked to put his Underground Railroad activities on hold and take on a challenging new project.
Identifiers: ISBN : 979-8-88819-199-6 (softcover).
Subjects: FICTION / Historical / General | FICTION / LGBTQ+ / Transgender | FICTION / African American & Black / Historical | FICTION / Historical / Civil War Era.

Designed in the USA
0 1 1 2 3 5 8 13 21 34 55

Continue the Enlightenment!

For
Susan, my muse
Matt, my rock
Alex, my inspiration
and Courtney, my blessing

CHARACTERS

In St. Petersburg, Russia

Rian Krieger: Thirteen-year-old tomboy, currently posing as a coachman for her Uncle Adrian in St. Petersburg

Adrian Krieger: Rian's uncle; owner of Krieger Locomotive, in Russia to build the Tsar's railroad

Seamus Gallagher: Rian's Irish cousin, in Russia to assist Adrian

Count Vladimir Sheremetev: the man who brought Adrian and Seamus to Russia

Colonel Alexander Malkovich: Sheremetev's partner

Second Captain Anton Zaitsev: Acting head of the Tsar's Imperial Horse Guards

Lev of Tsarskoye Selo: Woodcutter

Mikhail Stepanov: Captain of the Tsar's Imperial Horse Guards (deceased)

Prince Pyotr Volkonsky: Minister to the Imperial Court; the Tsar's gatekeeper

General Alexander von Benckendorff: Head of the Tsar's Third Section, which includes the Secret Police

Kiserev: Benckendorff's operative

George Mifflin Dallas: American ambassador to Russia

Henry Sommes: Manservant to Adrian and Seamus

Nicholas Pavlovich Romanov: Tsar of All the Russias

Grand Duke Alexander Nikolaevich Romanov: At age nineteen, the Tsar's oldest son, nicknamed Sasha

Grand Duchess Olga Nikolaevna Romanov: The Tsar's fifteen-year-old daughter

Grand Duchess Alexandra Nikolaevna Romanov: The Tsar's twelve-year-old daughter

Grand Duke Konstantin Nikolaevich Romanov: The Tsar's ten-year-old son, nicknamed Kostya

Madame Parshakov: In charge of the grand duchesses' virtue

Fyodor Litke: Tutor to Grand Duke Konstantin

In Philadephia

Otto Krieger: Rian's father; owner of Krieger Coach, partner in Krieger Locomotive and Krieger Rail

Kurt Krieger: Otto's younger brother and Rian's uncle; ship's carpenter

Hilda Krieger: Otto's half-sister

Maria Krieger: Otto's half-sister

Oskar Becker: Hilda's fiancé

Klaus Ritner: Maria's fiancé

Mila Krieger: Adrian's wife

Jabez Howes: Son of the late sea captain Levi Howes; Adrian and Mila's ward; Rian's cousin

Conor McGuire: Rian's best friend who sometimes lives with the Kriegers

Jules Freeman: Owner of Freeman Hydraulics, one of the few Black-owned companies in Philadelphia; foreman at Krieger Coach; formerly enslaved, but self-emancipated in 1820

Maddie Freeman: Jules's wife, founding member of the Philadelphia Female Anti-Slavery Society

Martha Freeman: Jules and Maddie's older daughter; in love with Logan Gallagher

Grace (Gracie) Freeman: Jules and Maddie's younger daughter

Rufus Freeman: Jules and Maddie's eldest son

Logan Gallagher: Seamus's younger brother; in love with Martha Freeman

Cee-Cee Porter: friend of Grace Freeman's; hired to work on Pennsylvania Hall

Penny (Pepper Pot Penny) Porter: Cee-Cee's mother

Frederick Hinton: Chairman of the Construction Committee of the Pennsylvania Hall Association

Marcus Edes: General contractor at Pennsylvania Hall

Randy Buck: Carpenter at Pennsylvania Hall

Emil Harberger: Carpenter at Pennsylvania Hall; afflicted with a weepy eye

Jonas Longstreth: Co-owner of Ellis & Longstreth Lumber

Rudolf Bartle: Plastering subcontractor at Pennsylvania Hall

Erasmus Shetzline: Painting subcontractor at Pennsylvania Hall

John Hunnecher: General contractor at the Shelter for Colored Orphans

William Rowland: Owner of Rowland Saw Works

Homer Good: Self-emancipator, hired to work on Pennsylvania Hall

Coffey Good: Homer's wife

Fred Hailer: Night watchman near Freeman Hydraulics

Lucretia Mott: Outspoken Quaker abolitionist; Otto and Rian's next-door neighbor

James Mott: Lucretia's husband and fellow abolitionist

Tom Mott: James and Lucretia's son; friend of Rian's

William Lloyd Garrison: Publisher of abolitionist newspaper *The Liberator*

John Greenleaf Whittier: Quaker, poet, abolitionist

Angelina Grimké: Daughter of slaveholders and radical abolitionist; betrothed to Theodore Weld

Theodore Weld: Radical abolitionist; betrothed to Angelina Grimké

Hugh Callaghan: President of the Moyamensing Hose Company and Seamus's nemesis

Siobhan Callaghan: Hugh's daughter and Seamus's sometimes girlfriend

Dylan Kennedy: Employee at Krieger Coach and President of the No Name Fire Brigade

Mikey McGuire: Conor's older brother; Seamus's rival for the love of Siobhan Callaghan

George Shippen: Bank of Industry Chairman of the Board; railroad entrepreneur

Edward Schiffler: Bank of Industry president

Billy Schiffler: Edward's son; a bully and one of Rian's antagonists

Austin T. Slatter: Slave catcher

Landon Slatter: Austin's younger brother

Hans Schmidt: Slatter's right-hand man

Ernst Winther: Krieger Coach employee

Harry Vogel: Krieger Locomotive foreman

James Forten: Perhaps the richest Black man in America; owner of a sailmaking loft on the Delaware waterfront

Thomas Forten: James Forten's son

Robert Purvis: Wealthy Philadelphia landowner who finances numerous abolitionist and Underground Railroad initiatives; James Forten's son-in-law

Braden McSweeney: Owner of McSweeney's Saloon

Ruben Hasselbach: Whiskey distiller

On Rian's return trip to America

David Winter: Portrait painter

Delilah Winter: David's wife

Dunworthy: British businessman aboard the *George IV* from Stockholm to
    London
Dewey Percell: British businessman aboard the *Great Western* from Bristol to
    New York
James Hosken: Captain of the *Great Western*

Notes to the Reader

Catherine the Great wrote numerous memoirs, one of which implied that the father of her son, Paul, was not her murdered Romanov husband, but a military officer named Sergei Saltykov. The memoir was kept under lock and key for decades, for its implications were explosive: *Not a drop of Romanov blood flowed through her son, Paul, and therefore not through Paul's sons Alexander, Konstantin, and Nicholas.*

Nicholas assumed the Russian throne in 1825 and became Nicholas I, Tsar of All the Russias. He had seven children, three of whom—Grand Duke Alexander, Grand Duchess Olga, and Grand Duke Konstantin—play prominent roles in this story.

In this era, Tsarist Russia adhered to the Julian Calendar, which differed from much of the rest of the world's Gregorian Calendar by twelve days. The dates in Russia are denoted in the Old Style (O.S.).

1838

1888

FRIDAY, FEBRUARY 16
(FEBRUARY 4 O.S.)

St. Petersburg, Russia

· RIAN ·

She knows.

Thirteen-year-old Rian Krieger rode Franklin counterclockwise around the Great Riding Hall of the Manege, the mammoth home of Tsar Nicholas I's Imperial Horse Guards. Doing laps in the hall on this day was a godsend. Frank's rhythmic canter, muffled by a thick layer of sawdust, gave Rian time . . . time to think.

Olga Nikolaevna knows.

Torchieres lined the perimeter of the hall, providing light and a modest plume of heat every twenty feet. Rian barely noticed.

The grand duchess knows I'm a girl.

For the past month, Rian had been living in two worlds. Long before sunrise and well after sunset, she exercised her Uncle Adrian's two black geldings in the Manege. Between times, she was the companion to the Tsar's son, ten-year-old Grand Duke Konstantin. But Konstantin wasn't at the top of her worry-list at the moment. That distinction went to Konstantin's sister.

Rian rode Frank past other grooms and a few guardsmen as they walked their horses from the stalls into the Great Hall. She gave them a polite nod. Count Sheremetev's words echoed in her ears: *Little girl, you are like a moth circling a candle. I warn you; before long your wings are going to get burned.*

Horse and rider cantered by the empty viewing stands to Rian's right. On other occasions Rian had envisioned the Tsar reviewing his troops from his box in the middle of the stands, but this evening she was too preoccupied.

And Grand Duchess Olga Nikolaevna Romanov, daughter of Tsar Nicholas I, is one huge, unsolvable wing-burner of a problem.

Rian put aside her cogitations when she spotted her cousin Seamus Gallagher standing with a young guard named Yuri near the Manege's Grand Foyer. She reined Frank to a halt. "Seamus, what are you doing here?"

"Good afternoon, Cousin," the twenty-two-year-old said. "Could you please tell this nice gentleman that I'm a friend of yours and it's okay for me to be here?"

Rian dismounted and casually stroked Frank's neck. "I'm amazed you got this far. How did you get past the guards?"

"I used your name. You're like the Imperial Horse Guard's little pet. Rian, we're in a hurry. Could you please get rid of this saucebox? We've gotta talk."

"*Vse normal'no, Yuri. YA voz'mu na sebya otvetstvennost' za etogo cheloveka.* [It's okay, Yuri. I will take responsibility for this man.]" Rian assured the guard.

Yuri gave a polite nod. "*Konechno. Spasibo, Rian* [Certainly. Thank you, Rian]."

After weeks of correcting him, Yuri finally pronounced her name correctly when he said REE-in. She smiled and bowed playfully to acknowledge his success. "*Ideal'nyy* [Perfect]," she said.

Yuri beamed, turned, and faded away.

Rian shifted her attention to Seamus. "What's the hurry?"

"Uncle Adrian's been arrested."

Rian felt a spasm of dread. She started leading Frank toward the stalls. "Arrested? Why?"

Seamus shook his head as he matched her pace. "For bribery, which is interesting since we decided last night that we weren't going to pay any bribes. It's all hogwash."

"Where is he? Is he okay?"

"They took him to the prison in the Peter and Paul Fortress. I think Prince Volkonsky is behind this."

Volkonsky. The Minister of the Imperial Court. The Tsar's gatekeeper. "This is bad. This is really bad."

"That's why I need you. I've got an appointment. I need an interpreter. Ambassador Dallas is in Moscow, so it's got to be you."

"Seamus, my Russian isn't good enough to meet with Volkonsky. What about Count Sheremetev? Can't he be the interpreter?"

"Volkonsky's arrested him too."

"Colonel Malkovich?"

"Arrested."

"Jaysus." Rian led Frank into one of the corridors that was flanked by scores of horse stalls. "Let me feed the horses. It'll take me two minutes. When's the appointment with the Prince of Darkness?"

"It's in an hour. I think he was expecting me to contact him."

"I can't meet him dressed like this. I should go to the apartment and get a change of clothes."

"I've got them right here. You can change in one of the stalls. Volkonsky doesn't suspect you're a girl, does he?"

"No, no one in the Imperial Court does." *We've got bigger things to worry about right now. Seamus doesn't need to know about my problems with Olga Niko-laevna Romanov.*

* * * * *

· SEAMUS ·

Seamus and Rian emerged from the Manege into the cold St. Petersburg twilight, both lost in their own thoughts. They passed the Admiralty Gardens and took a right on Nevsky Prospekt, heading for the Tsar's new residence, the Anichkov Palace. Seamus noticed neither the restaurants and cafés that lined the street, nor the houses of commerce, nor the opulent homes, nor the baroque government buildings.

An officious flunky escorted Seamus and Rian through seemingly endless palace corridors to Prince Volkonsky's office. Seamus was grateful for his cousin's presence as interpreter but nevertheless entered with trepidation.

"Prince Volkonsky, thank you for seeing us so promptly," he said in English. As he waited for Rian to translate, he couldn't help but glance around Volkonsky's office. Books, ledgers, and files were stacked on boards placed atop sawhorses and on the floor beneath them. On window sills. All around the perimeter of the room. The desk of the Minister of the Imperial Court was covered with more files. Files inches thick. Files piled upon files.

Volkonsky noted Seamus scanning his office. "Please forgive the disarray of my new office." The prince spoke in Russian, but even so, Seamus could detect the oily self-importance in his voice. "Seven weeks since the Winter Palace burned, and I still haven't settled in. Sadly, every available craftsman is now rebuilding the Tsar's home. There has been no one to make new cabinets for the new seat of government. Enough about my troubles. I hear you have troubles of your own. I assume you are here to speak on behalf of your business partner."

"Well, technically, he is my employer, but yes. You know this charge is a pile of hogwash." Seamus noted that Rian hesitated when she got to the word *hogwash.* He assumed she substituted a more diplomatic word for it.

"Your employer bribed an imperial official."

Seamus shook his head. "The head of the Architectural Commission didn't bother to pretend the payment he was asking for was a fee. It was an out-and-out bribe. We decided not to do it"

"We? So you were involved in this decision as well?"

Seamus hesitated, then plowed ahead. "There was no decision to be made. When we're told we have to pay a fee, we pay a fee. When it's a bribe, we don't pay it, which apparently is quite unusual. From what I hear, everyone pays bribes in this country."

Unexpectedly, Volkonsky responded in fluent, British-inflected English. "Let's cut the hogwash, shall we, Mr. Gallagher? Your uncle has been arrested because he has been a thorn in my side for four months. I have been waiting for him to succumb to the temptation of bribing someone for weeks now. Your sanctimonious uncle has refused to do so. And then this morning, he forced my hand by going to Grand Duke Alexander. Unfortunately for him, that was a grave mistake, because the grand duke came straight to me."

Seamus felt all the wind leave his sails.

"And what did your uncle reveal to Grand Duke Alexander?" Volkonsky continued. "That he planned to approach General Benckendorff about becoming a partner in the construction of the railroad from Moscow to St. Petersburg."

"Who the partners are in that project is none of your affair, Mr. Minister," Seamus shot back. "Your brother-in-law didn't get the contract. Count Sheremetev and Adrian Krieger did. You lost. They won."

Volkonsky turned and gazed out his window, as if he was hardly listening to Seamus. "Then it occurred to me that I don't need to catch your uncle or the count bribing an official. All I have to do is accuse them of doing it. Now Adrian Krieger, the count, and the colonel will rot in jail for years before we finally get around to a trial. I believe my solution is quite tidy. Don't you agree?"

"But they have done nothing wrong."

"That is subject to interpretation."

"Why are you doing this?"

"I could cite numerous reasons: because foreigners should not be involved in Russian business; because I do not believe your uncle is competent to do the job; because I think that giving the contract to Count Golitsyn was a better deal for the Tsar. But when you strip my motivations down to their core, I do this because I have the power to do it. Unless you care to join him, it is time for you and your little interpreter to leave my office. Say not one more word."

"But I have broken no laws."

Volkonsky stiffened. "I guess that will have to be determined. Guard, seize this man."

Seamus struggled with two guards who manhandled him toward the door. From behind, he heard Volkonsky utter words that he knew weren't good: *Peter and Paul Fortress.*

* * * * *

· RIAN ·

Rian sat frozen on the chair in front of Volkonsky's desk.

The Minister of the Imperial Court belatedly noticed her. "Ah, the gnat. It seems your days of irritating me are over. I am sure the Tsar will not approve of his son consorting with a relative of known criminals. Do not bother coming to the palace on Monday. Do not try to contact Grand Duke Konstantin Nikolaevich. I assume you can find your way out of the palace."

In shock, Rian rose.

"Shut the door on your way out," Volkonsky said dismissively.

Rian shut the door as she was told. But she didn't leave the palace directly. She detoured toward the classroom, which had been a drawing room before the Winter Palace was destroyed and the Romanovs relocated to the Anichkov Palace.

All of a sudden, being exposed as a girl pretending to be a boy isn't my biggest problem. My family and friends have been thrown into prison. The second most powerful man in the world hates us. He's cut me off from the Imperial Family. My only advantage is that he thinks I can't do anything about it.

She pulled a lighted taper off a wall sconce outside the door, entered the darkened classroom, and opened the drawer to Grand Duchess Olga Nikolaevna's library table. As she hoped, the manuscript, wrapped in heavy brown paper and bound with twine, was there. She withdrew the packet and read the words that Catherine the Great had penned in French more than forty years ago:

"To his Imperial Highness, Tsarevich and Grand Duke Paul Petrovich, my beloved son."

And next to that was Paul's signature and then the date: **13/11/1796**.

Beneath that:

Alexander I – 20/03/1801

And beneath that:

Nicholas I – 19/1/1826

Rian glanced at the doorway. *No footsteps.* She took a deep breath, untied the twine, and opened the wrapper to confirm that she held what she had come for. There it was, penned in French, in the Tsarina's own words:

The Memoir of Catherine the Great

She retied the twine, shut the drawer, and walked out the Anichkov Palace into the bitter cold of St. Petersburg.

Fook you, Volkonsky.

WEDNESDAY, JANUARY 3
(DECEMBER 22 O.S.)

Six weeks earlier

· RIAN ·

Rian and Seamus were walking along the promenade above the granite-sheathed banks of the Fontanka River. A steady stream of broughams, carts, landaus, freight wagons, phaetons, and coaches passed by on the street to their left. It was a cloudless, subfreezing St. Petersburg day.

"Cousin, we need to keep your secret for nine or ten more weeks," Seamus said. "As soon as the ice breaks in the Gulf of Finland, we're on the first steamship out of here."

Damn it, Rian thought to herself. An icy wind scudded off the Fontanka, prompting Rian to pull her coachman's top hat tighter on her head. *But I don't want to go home. If they make me get on that steamship, I'll get off in London. I can do a better job of surviving there than Oliver Twist does.* Then she stopped walking as her cousin's words sunk in. "We? Who's we?"

"You and me. Uncle Adrian is afraid you'll jump ship in London rather than sail all the way back to Philadelphia, so I'm going with you. Adrian will stay here to get the railroad project going with Count Sheremetev and Colonel Malkovich."

Rian crossed her arms and turned her back to the wind, heedless of the expansive neoclassical grandeur of the Naryshkin-Shuvalov Palace across the street. "No, we've got to stay here. Tsar Nicholas has ordered me to become a companion to Grand Duke Konstantin. I've got a chance to change Russia."

Despite the wind, Seamus turned to face Rian. "Cousin, it's only you and me here. Let's be honest with each other. Put aside the Tsar and his little boy and Russia for the moment. The reason that you don't want to go home is that everyone here thinks you are a boy."

Damn, he's been talking to Uncle Adrian. "Well, that's true, but. . . ."

"Adrian and I were willing to go along with that lie when we first came here because you were our coachman, beneath the notice of anyone who mattered."

"Yes, but. . . ."

Seamus held up his hand to shush Rian. "But then the three of us distinguished ourselves—you as much as Adrian and me—when the Tsar's palace burned down. That one night changed everything. The Tsar decided he wanted Adrian and me to build his railroad and you to become a companion to his ten-year-old son."

"Yes, but. . . ."

"Rian, we have a powerful enemy now."

The reference to Prince Pyotr Mikhailovich Volkonsky, Minister of the Imperial Court, chilled Rian more than the wind coming off the Fontanka.

Seamus continued. "He's got it in for all of us. You saw Volkonsky kill Captain Stepanov and three soldiers during the fire. That's a loose end that Volkonsky won't ignore. Then the Tsar changed his mind and gave the railroad project to us instead of Volkonsky's brother-in-law. That surely curdled his milk. So all three of us are in his sights."

"I'm going to be the grand duke's companion. Volkonsky wouldn't dare touch me, would he?"

A man dressed in a heavy overcoat and wearing an ushanka[1] with its earflaps turned up stopped nearby to watch three boys tentatively testing the ice on the river. Seamus indicated with a flick of his head that he didn't want to continue their conversation near a potential eavesdropper. He grabbed Rian by the crook of her arm and started them walking again. "Volkonsky is the Tsar's gatekeeper. He personally okays every document Nicholas reads, every visitor he sees. What do you think will happen if Volkonsky finds out you're a girl?"

Rian gave passing notice to a coach-and-four that rumbled and clopped by them on the cobblestone street. "He won't find out. I'm not going to tell anyone."

Seamus put his arm around her shoulders as they walked. "Let's play a little question-and-answer game. How many people in St. Petersburg know you are a girl?"

Rian welcomed the warmth of her cousin's closeness . . . *but I'm not enjoying this conversation.* "You and Uncle Adrian are the only ones who know."

"You're wrong already. Ambassador Dallas knows. Your father wrote to him from Philadelphia and spilled the beans. Dallas wasn't happy when he learned

---

1. A ushanka is a mink-lined hat.

about it, and that was when you were our coachman. What do you think his reaction is going to be when he finds out about you becoming companion to the grand duke?"

"I dunno. Probably not good."

"What about Count Sheremetev and Colonel Malkovich? Do they know?"

"Nope, they don't suspect anything, and I've been with them a lot. We've spent hours playing cards together. Do they know you plan to send me home?"

"Not yet." Seamus steered Rian to take a right onto Nevsky Prospekt, St. Petersburg's busiest street. "What about Henry, the manservant? Does he suspect anything? You've been sharing a bedroom with him on and off since we picked him up in London."

"No. I've been careful."

"So three people, not counting you, know you're a girl. What did Ben Franklin say about people keeping a secret?"

Rian kicked an errant chunk of snow that had found its way back onto the shoveled sidewalk and watched it skitter ahead of her. *Now I hate this conversation.* "Three people can keep a secret if two of them are dead."

Now safely away from any potential listeners, Seamus stopped on the Anichkov Bridge, wheeling Rian around so they could observe the graceful arc of the river as it meandered through St. Petersburg. He spent a moment eyeing the kids on the river, who were strapping ice skates onto their shoes. "So you don't think anyone else will figure out you're a girl, even by accident?"

"Seamus, I'm really good at this. I've been a boy since we left home. That's six months." *And if I play my cards right, I'm going to make myself so important as the grand duke's companion that no one would consider sending me back to America. I don't want to go home. I like it when everyone thinks I'm a boy.*

"Okay, let's get back to the count's place. I'm hungry."

"You go. I'm going to check in the post offices. Then I've got to go feed the horses."

* * * * *

Okay, Eena, sooner or later you've got to try it, Rian said to herself. *Eena* was the name her cousin Jabez called her when they were toddlers because he couldn't say *Rian.* She still referred to herself that way in her thoughts.

Rian entered the Imperial Post Office Building on Nevsky Prospekt—her third post office of the day—and approached the same window she had visited a dozen times before. This time, however, the window was occupied by a clerk she had never dealt with. The clerk ignored her.

"*Privet* [Hello]," Rian said, then continued in her fractured Russian, "I'm here to see if there is any mail for Rian Krieger, Adrian Krieger, or Seamus Gallagher. We lived in the Winter Palace for a few weeks before it burned down."

With the mention of the Winter Palace, the clerk looked up from his boredom. He assessed her coachman's duds, seemed to weigh the consequences of irritating some powerful person, then established his ground. "Winter Palace mail is now being sent to District 6. You are at the wrong facility. Go away now."

New guy, same response. "I have already checked the post office in District 6. They have nothing. We now live with Count Sheremetev, but we have received no mail since we arrived in Russia, and that was more than two months ago."

"Sheremetev, of the Palazzo Sheremetev?"

Rian nodded. *Perhaps the count's name can help me.*

"The Palazzo Sheremetev is across the Fontanka River. That's District 4. Try there."

"I just came from there. They have nothing."

"I can't help you."

Okay, Eena, this is it: your first bribe. Rian fished a kopek out of her pocket and slid it across the marble surface of the counter. "Really? The names would be written in English, not Cyrillic. I thought it might have been delivered here and gotten stuck."

The clerk peered at Rian for a long moment, checked behind her to note there was no one in line. "Tell me the names again?"

"Rian Krieger, Adrian Krieger, Seamus Gallagher."

The clerk pocketed the kopek, walked away from the counter without another word, and was gone for about five minutes. When he returned, he carried a handful of letters and two slim packages. "Seven kopeks."

Rather than argue with the clerk about his greedy extortion, Rian fished seven kopeks from her pocket and handed them to the clerk. He shoved the pile toward her. "Come to me next time. There may be more in the future."

Before she left the window, Rian examined the bundle. The packages were from Hatchards Booksellers in London—the final installment of *The Pickwick Papers* and the November issue of *Bentley's Miscellany*, which contained Chapters 16 and 17 of *Oliver Twist*. Both had been opened and carelessly rewrapped and tied. Someone had stamped the wrapping paper.

"What is this?" Rian asked, pointing to the stamp.

"That is the stamp of the Third Section. That means they have read your magazines. They like to know what printed matter is coming into Russia.

Apparently, they did not find them to be subversive. You have taken up enough of my time. Next!"

The next person in line shouldered into Rian's place. As she walked toward the post office door, she found a letter from her father that was written entirely in German.

* * * * *

21 October 1837

Liebling,

Yesterday I received your letter dated 15 September. I assume that the Elizabeth *met a westbound ship somewhere on the Atlantic and exchanged mail. I am very angry with you for running off, but grateful to receive confirmation that you are safe and in the care of my brother. If in fact he is unable to arrange passage for you back to Philadelphia and you continue on with him to St. Petersburg, so be it. I understand that your intention is to masquerade as a boy during this adventure of yours. I hope you will soon tire of your subterfuge and return to me of your own free will.*

You will be pleased to know that I kept two people—Jules would call self-emancipators—out of the clutches of that odious slave catcher Austin T. Slatter. I didn't know what to do with them, so I took them to Jules's house, and he quickly got them aboard his Underground RR and on their way to safety.

That event precipitated a reconciliation between Jules and me, and I have asked him to return to Krieger Coach as foreman. He is inclined to do so, but only part-time, as he is so busy getting Freeman Hydraulics going. As this depression is not easing, he is probably doing better selling steam-driven fire pumps than we are selling railroad cars, because fire companies don't seem to be feeling the pinch the way honest businesses are.

I am still angry with your cousin Jabez for switching places with you. Ironic that he didn't want to go to Russia and you did, because he does not make good use of his time here in America the way you used to. He continues to defy his Aunt Mila at every turn. She told me he skips his schooling and instead gallivants off with friends who are up to no good.

I have written to Frau Gilbert in Switzerland and told her that your matriculation in her finishing school is now unlikely. Rian, I have never been to Russia, but as you know, your grandfather fought against the Russians during Napoleon's invasion and again during his retreat. He described them as brutal and vindictive people. Please do not remain in Russia if you believe you are in jeopardy. My half-sisters Hilda and Maria live in Stuttgart, which is more than a thousand miles from St. Petersburg but a lot closer than here.

Come back to me safe and soon. I cannot promise that all will be forgiven, but somehow we will reconcile.
Your loving
Vater

* * * * *

Twice a day for eleven weeks, Rian had walked to the Manege to feed and exercise Franklin and Washington, a matched pair of black geldings named after her favorite squares in Philadelphia, but affectionately referred to as Frank and Wash.

"*Privet* [Hello]," she said to Yuri, the guard at the portico entrance to the Manege. As he always did, Yuri gave her a slightly deferential nod, but this time, he uncharacteristically smiled and opened the door for her.

Rian walked through the riding hall, which could accommodate a hundred horsemen riding in formation at a time. A dozen torchieres placed around the perimeter cast a dusky glow about the cavernous room. More than the usual number of Imperial Horse Guardsmen were exercising their horses, but she thought nothing of it. Despite the muffling effects of a generous layer of sawdust, the sounds of horses at a canter echoed off the ceiling.

She gave a subtle wave to Second Captain Zaitsev as he rode his muscular charger around the ring. Since the death of Captain Stepanov, Zaitsev had been in command of the Tsar's Imperial Horse Guards. During morning workouts, when the chasm between the Horse Guards and the grooms relaxed, Zaitsev was quite friendly to Rian. They occasionally did laps together, and communicated using a mélange of German, French, and Russian that amused them both and seemed to work well enough. But like Stepanov before him, when in charge of the men, Zaitsev became stern and distant.

Today, Rian gave Zaitsev no further consideration as she walked between the torchieres and the review stands on the south side of the riding hall.

* * * * *

Rian saddled Wash and walked him past stall after stall down the corridor. As she emerged into the riding hall, she was forced to stop. Before her, an arc of twenty-five Imperial Horse Guards sat astride their steeds. The men were obviously waiting for her.

Second Captain Zaitsev dismounted. A guardsman handed something down to him.

Dark, was all Rian could see in the torchiere light. *Fabric. Heavy.*

Zaitsev turned and strode to Rian. Having no idea what was happening, Rian reflexively took a step back. Wash snorted.

He's holding a coat. Navy blue. What is going on?

Zaitsev held the coat out to Rian. "This is the greatcoat that Captain Mikhail Sergeyovich Stepanov wore when we accompanied the Tsar," Zaitsev said in his mixture of Russian, French, and German. "It is heavy, built for the cold of our Russian winters. You can see it has a small burn from the night the captain died. It is no longer suitable for service. The captain was fond of you. You tried to save his life. The men voted. We want you to have this. It will be much warmer than that English rag you bought in London."

Rian dropped Wash's reins and held out her hands to receive the coat, which Zaitsev draped across her outstretched arms. It was indeed very heavy, made of a thick worsted wool. Rian held the coat to her nose. It smelled of smoke. She examined the burn that Zaitsev had pointed out. It was almost imperceptible.

"Captain Stepanov would never have tolerated even such a small flaw to be worn in the presence of the Tsar. My wife cleaned and brushed it as best she could. Even with the burn it will last you for years. We think the captain would be pleased."

Rian fingered the red epaulets that graced each shoulder, then shrugged herself into the coat. Her arms slid effortlessly down the silk-lined sleeves. She felt the coat's heaviness envelop her. It was far too big. The sleeves extended inches below her fingertips. Its hem brushed her boots. Its brass buttons glistened in the torchiere light. She wrapped its double-breasted voluminousness tightly around her and burst into tears.

* * * * *

· ADRIAN ·

Adrian Krieger paced the drawing room of Sheremetev's palazzo while the count read correspondence at an ornate Louis XVI writing desk set at a window that looked out on the Fontanka River. "Count Sheremetev, tell me again why you think the Tsar is weak."

Sheremetev put down his letter, watched Adrian pace for a few moments, then returned his gaze to his letter. "I didn't say *weak.* I said *weakened.* Tsar Nicholas is an autocrat. He considers himself to be the paterfamilias of all of Russia. The people are his children. He must care for them, discipline them, and inspire them. When his brother died and he became Tsar, the Decembrists revolted and tried to bring about the same liberal reforms that were occurring in Western Europe. Nicholas put down the revolt in bloody fashion and, since that time, has leaned heavily on discipline. To the peasants, the serfs, the Tsar is a frightful half-god, half-man. To the nobility, he is the first among us."

"That doesn't sound weak to me."

"Ah, but we live in a very superstitious country, and not only in the rural areas. From the Imperial Family on down, superstition provides an undercurrent to all that transpires in Russia. And four days ago, the Tsar's Winter Palace—the symbol of his might, the legacy built by Peter the Great himself—burned to the ground. How do you think the superstitious amongst us would interpret that?"

"I don't know. As a bad omen for the Tsar?"

Sheremetev nodded. "Yes, it has weakened him significantly. And that is where our railroad comes in. A railroad from St. Petersburg to Moscow will give the Tsar something grandiose to point to. A sign of progress to counterbalance the embarrassment of the burned-out shell of his palace."

"So are Seamus and I here to modernize Russia or to make us rich?"

"Both. By building a railroad from St. Petersburg to Moscow, we will start the modernization of Russia. In the meantime, all four of us—you, Seamus, Colonel Malkovich, and I—will become very rich."

"You are already very rich."

Finally, Sheremetev put the letter down and gave his full attention to Adrian. "This is a different kind of rich. The kind of rich that will bring real power. And in this case, we will use that power to change the face of Russia. To bring about the liberal reforms that the Decembrists wanted a decade ago. We admit there is some risk. But all we are asking is for you three Americans to be Americans."

"Three Americans. Seamus, me . . . and Rian?"

"Yes, I definitely include Rian in this. I want you to do what you have already been doing: show initiative; think creatively; amass your own information; hire people based on their competence, not their breeding. We know this change is going to take decades. Think of it as change coming from the bottom up. If that is all we did to help Russia become a modern society, it would be enough.

"Rian will not be in a position to demonstrate any of those things."

Sheremetev broke into a broad, knowing smile. "You and Seamus will be working with Grand Duke Alexander on the railroads. Rian will be his younger brother's companion. These relationships are opportunities to bring about change from the top down. Our goal is to plant the seeds of change in the future Tsar of All the Russias and his loyal brother. Once again, change that may not be measured in years, but decades."

"You think Konstantin will be that influential when the grand dukes grow up?"

Sheremetev shrugged. "Their father was third in line to become Tsar. His brother Tsar Alexander died without an heir. His next brother didn't want the job and abdicated to Nicholas. You never know."

"What could Rian do that would be so important?"

"We think your nephew could be very important to this top-down endeavor. You must recognize this: Rian possesses abilities that are unique for his age. He speaks three languages and is rapidly learning Russian. He is knowledgeable about horseflesh and can drive a team like a man twice his age. He has a winning way that sees no class; he drew the late Captain Stepanov to him as well as that woodcutter who helped during the palace fire."

Adrian smiled for the first time in two days. "Is that all?"

"No, not in the least. He is only thirteen years old, yet a month ago he single-handedly led a crew of serfs to assemble sixty-four feet of track in one morning. He is courageous; he repeatedly disregarded his own safety to save imperial treasures in the fire. He plays cards like a professional gambler. And, as evidenced by that passport document he forged, he is highly creative."

Adrian was overwhelmed by Sheremetev's accolades, but still not convinced. "Do you have any reservations about a thirteen-year-old influencing the future of Russia?"

Sheremetev smiled. "We would prefer that he not stab anyone."

"You heard about that?"

"Malkovich and I were wondering if it was really true. Thank you for confirming it. The three of us were playing cards during our trip across the Atlantic. Rian lost a hand at durak. As you know, when you lose, you have to pay a penalty, but the penalties are always frivolous. Malkovich made him tell us something about himself that we didn't know before he dealt the next hand."

"And he told you he stabbed a man?"

Sheremetev nodded. "According to him, quite justifiably. Who better to influence the boy who is the brother of the future Tsar of All the Russias?"

"Count Sheremetev, I fear that Rian will be too close to the royal family. That alone will make his life dangerous."

"Adrian, a request from the Tsar is not a request. It is an order. You have no choice until Rian returns to America, whether that be a year or five years from now. We aren't asking that he nudge the grand duke toward the Enlightenment. We think he can have a long-term impact on the grand duke by being himself. That will be more than enough."

Himself, Adrian thought. *How can he be himself when he is a she?*

* * * * *

· RIAN ·

Rian had exercised Frank and Wash, thrown a scoop of oats into each of their feed boxes, and was brushing Frank while he ate. She hadn't taken Stepanov's greatcoat off in all that time.

Second Captain Zaitsev approached the stall and put his forearms on the top board. "I guess you like the coat."

"Very much. I will wear it for the rest of my life. Thank you."

"You weren't the only one who saw Captain Stepanov die. We know that Volkonsky killed him."

The mention of the Minister of the Imperial Court sent a chill down Rian's spine. "I hate him."

Zaitsev nodded, which implied that he hated Volkonsky as well. "Be careful. Do not share your sentiments with anyone, even here. Even in the Imperial Horse Guards, the desire to advance one's career could be more important than protecting one's friends."

"Even with you?"

Ziatsev smiled, glanced over his shoulder. "We are safe at the moment, but not while anyone else is around. Rian, Prince Volkonsky is a vindictive man. We can protect you here. I suggest you be careful while you are walking the streets of St. Petersburg."

* * * * *

Philadelphia, U.S.A.

· OTTO ·

Otto collapsed his umbrella and walked through Jules Freeman's factory, noting the bustle of a healthy business. He counted four men working on the chassis of two fire pumps and spotted Jules's son Rufus carting materials to one of the workers. *Rufus is a year older than Rian. That would make him fifteen or so. A son who will one day join his father as a partner.*

He entered the shop office without knocking and placed his umbrella near the door. Jules was alone in the room, which was unusual. *Where's Maddie?*

Otto dropped a leather envelope on Jules's desk. It contained so many gold eagles that it hit the desk with a heavy, jangly *thunk.* "Payment in full for the fire pump that I delivered to New York City."

Jules unbuckled the envelope's strap and peered inside. "They paid cash? I expected a bank draft."

Otto took a chair that sat before Jules's desk. "*Wo ist deine Frau* [Where is your wife]?" Otto asked in his native German. As Jules spoke passable German, the two conversed comfortably in either language, sometimes a mixture of both. "I was looking forward to seeing the smile on her face when she heard the tinkle of cash money."

"Uh, Maddie's still not talking to me."

"*Ausch* [Ouch]." Otto shifted his gaze to a wall calendar behind Jules that advertised *Jos. H. Humphrey & Sons Lumber.* "It has been eleven days since you burned the slave ship."

"Since Jabez burned the ship," Jules corrected him. "I went to the pier to torch it, but your nephew beat me to the punch."

"There were a number of us involved in the shenanigans that evening."

"Maddie doesn't care about the others. You were breaking a Black family out of jail and sending them North. So her ire—and her silence—are directed at me. How was New York?"

"It seems that the only businesses that are doing well in the midst of this depression are the criminals. I would put the Five Points Fire Brigade in that category. Like here in Philadelphia, fire companies are equal parts gangs and social clubs that occasionally put out fires. I daresay I did you a bigger favor than merely delivering your pump. I do not think those men would have taken well to doing business with a Black man.[2] I suspect they wouldn't have paid you and probably would have given you a good thrashing."

Jules sat back in his chair and smiled. "Then I am doubly in your debt. Did they like the pump?"

"Loved it. First steam-driven fire pump in New York City. I suspect there will be other orders from New York. Maybe hire a white man to make the delivery, though."

"How did the rest of your trip go?"

"New York has been hit hard by the depression, same as here. Erie Canal traffic is down. Some of the banks are still closed. Vacant shops. Quiet factories.

---

2. A note to readers: With the wish to keep this narrative as historically appropriate as I can, I have injected into the narrative three terms that African Americans used in the 1830s to describe themselves. In order to justify the use of terms that have since gone out of fashion or even become offensive, I cite African American civil rights icons who used those terms with dignity. James Forten identified himself as colored, W.E.B. Dubois called himself a Negro. Martin Luther King used that term as well and also called himself black. In recent years, the term *black* has been capitalized to *Black*. I have chosen to use that more modern form throughout *Rian Krieger's Journey*.

I estimated that a third of the wharves were idle. I stopped in at the *Camden & Amboy Railroad* office in Hoboken. Stevens says his traffic is down, and of course he isn't interested in any new locomotives or rolling stock. He sees no end in sight."

Jules shook his head. "How did Jabez like New York?"

Otto shrugged. "My nephew is hard to impress. In his young life, he has walked the streets of every port city from here to Guangzhou. We met with his father's attorney. I hoped that seeing some of Levi's real estate holdings might spark . . . something. Jabez will be a wealthy young man when he turns eighteen. Hearing that didn't change his attitude a bit."

"And?"

"He still says he wants nothing to do with riches that were made through the slave trade. He told the lawyer he wanted to give everything away."

"Good lad. Gotta admire his attitude."

Otto shook his head. "There are complications. Levi's estate is a botch. If the *Bridger* had sunk in the middle of the ocean, that would be one thing. But Levi committed suicide and his body was buried at sea. We have no proof that he is actually dead except that's what the first mate told Jabez and me. And now of course, the first mate has disappeared, as have the other crew members."

"So your word isn't good enough?"

"So says the attorney. Ironically, what would have helped resolve things is the ship's logbook."

Jules rolled his eyes. "Which was destroyed the night we burned the ship."

Otto nodded. "Jabez's situation gets even more complicated. Adrian is Jabez's legal guardian, but he's in Russia. Mila has no legal standing. The lawyer said it may take seven years until Levi can be declared dead. If it occurs sooner, Jabez will inherit it all when he turns eighteen in four years. Then he can do whatever he wants to with the estate."

"So he waits. Maybe he'll change his mind by that time."

"The boy is an enigma. He switched places with my daughter because he didn't want to go to Russia. He took it upon himself to burn his father's ship because it was involved in the illegal slave trade. But aside from his hatred towards my late brother-in-law, I see nothing. No motivation. No passion. No desire to work or go to school. I tell you, Jules, I always wanted a son, but if this is what it's like. . . ."

"Any word from Russia?"

"No. Not a word. I don't even know if they arrived there. I know Rian planned to masquerade as a coachman and she is learning to play cards. Other than that, I have heard nothing. Nothing from London. Nothing from St. Petersburg. So, is Maddie coming in to work today?"

"Oh, she'll be in. But she waits until she knows I've left for Krieger Coach. Hopefully, we'll have it out soon."

* * * * *

· JULES ·

Jules tried to ignore the silence. Tried to act as if his wife hadn't been as cold as the January weather for eleven days. He placed his dish next to the washtub.

"You still smell like smoke," said Maddie. She agitated the hot dishwater again with a cake of lye soap.

Well, at least she's talking. "It's rained every day since we burned the ship. I couldn't exactly hang my clothes out in the wet weather."

Maddie scrubbed a plate with more intensity than it deserved. "You went too far."

Here we go. "Maddie, it was a slave ship. It smuggled a hold full of our brethren into Cuba, then came here to reprovision so it could sail back to West Africa and do it all over again."

Maddie dropped the plate back into the hot water and turned to him. "You could have been killed!"

Maddie's words were not a surprise, but their intensity was. Jules felt like he had been punched. "Can you please keep your voice down? The kids will hear us."

"You think that Martha doesn't know? Grace? Rufus? Even the littles know!"

"Well, then how about the neighbors?"

"I don't care about the neighbors! I want to keep yelling until you promise me you are going to stop taking such risks."

Jules retrieved the sweet potato bowl from the table and placed it on top of a dirty dish. "The rain has stopped. We haven't taken our evening constitutional since . . . since before that night. May we continue this conversation as we walk?"

Maddie placed both hands on the washtub and hunched toward the soapy water. She nodded.

Relieved that they were finally talking, Jules didn't want to give Maddie an opportunity to change her mind. "I'll tell the kids to finish the dishes."

He walked into the parlor to find Grace, Rufus, Jeremiah, Missy, and Gladys all reading by candlelight. "Where's Martha?" he asked, referring to his oldest child.

Grace glanced up from the latest issue of *The Liberator.* "She went out for some fresh air."

"Grace and Rufus, your mother and I are going out for a walk. Would you finish the dishes, please?"

Grace set the newspaper on a side table and picked up her candle. "Pop-Pop, we're proud of you for burning the ship."

Jules noted that all the kids were looking up at him. "You haven't told anyone, have you?"

Grace rolled her eyes. "About what? About the hidey-hole upstairs? About the steady stream of fugitive self-emancipators who come to our house? About you teaming up with a man who hates our people to burn a slave ship? We've kept those kinds of secrets to ourselves since we knew they were secrets."

* * * * *

After they descended the front porch steps, Jules offered his arm to Maddie to link into him. His wife folded her arms in front of her instead.

Moyamensing, called Moya by its residents, was fifteen blocks west-to-east, eight blocks north-to-south, and the poorest political district in Philadelphia. The Freemans had built their house on Twelfth Street when the western blocks of Moya were still undeveloped. The homes that had been built since that time were like theirs: modest, well constructed, on a quarter-acre plot that allowed room for a front and back yard, a privy, a garden, and a small barn to house their cow at night.

This relative spaciousness was not the norm in the older, eastern sections of Moyamensing. Recent Irish immigrants, free Blacks, and Germans crammed cheek-to-jowl into a hodgepodge. And now, with the Panic of '37 well into its second year and still deepening across the United States, probably a third of Moya's residents were unemployed. It was a volatile mix. Poverty, distrust, and resentment were bitter ingredients in the stew that was daily fare in Moya. During the heat of summer, when tempers shortened and the moon was full, the stew occasionally boiled over.

But this is the beginning of January, thought Jules. *The first non-rainy night in more than a week will bring out strollers, not brawlers.*

Jules and Maddie walked in silence. Smoke from a hundred wood and coal stoves gathered into a cloud above them and eliminated any chance of seeing stars. Rainwater dripping from the trees pattered onto the brick sidewalk.

They walked toward an aura of light cast by a recently installed gas streetlamp, past other homes dimly lit by candlelight or perhaps a whale oil lamp. They turned east on Fitzwater.

"I don't want to become a widow," Maddie finally murmured, her voice still hard-edged.

"Maddie, no one was killed. None of us. None of the slavers. That was the plan: no one dies."

"But he almost did."

"And I saved him."

"I don't trust that man."

That man was Hugh Callaghan, head of the all-Irish Moyamensing Hose Company, the largest fire company in Moya, which also dominated crime in the district.

"Neither do I, but we found common cause for an evening."

"He hates our people because of the color of our skin. His men harass us, vandalize our homes."

"And Hugh told me in that respect nothing's changed. But now at least we talk. And he's buying a new fire pump from Freeman Hydraulics."

"Make sure we get his money up-front."

Jules heard in Maddie's comment the sliver of a lighter note in their conversation. He again held out the crook of his arm.

Maddie slipped her arm into his. "I want you to promise me. No more violence. You do enough."

"*We* do a lot. Both of us. But it doesn't seem to be enough." Jules noted another couple walking toward them as they passed beneath the light of a streetlamp half a block away. "I will make this promise. I will only engage in such behavior after I talk with you."

"And no guns."

"I agree."

The other couple met them halfway between gas streetlamps. "Well, if it isn't Mr. and Mrs. Freeman," said a familiar voice from the darkness.

Of all the strollers we could bump into, it had to be him, thought Jules. "Good evening, Hugh. We were just talking about you. I don't believe I've had the pleasure of meeting your wife."

"Nice to meetcha, Mr. Freeman," said Hugh's wife in a thick Irish brogue. "I believe I owe you a hefty debt for saving me husband's life."

"Jules did *not* save my life," Hugh interjected from the darkness. "I could have gotten myself out of that fix."

Undeterred, Hugh's wife continued. "Hugh was just saying that if all the coloreds were like you, he wouldn't have a problem being neighbors with you all."

"That's not entirely true," said Hugh. "I said I wondered what it would be like if they were all like you. Would there still be a race problem?"

Maddie held tight to Jules's arm. "Seems to me, then, that the problem is poverty—Irish poverty, Black poverty. Solve that, and maybe we make the world a better place."

Hugh snorted. "I might be able to see my way past the issue of color, but my lads can't. So, like it or not, that's the boat I'm rowing."

Jules noted that Hugh, notorious for speaking in an Irish brogue when in public, addressed Maddie and him in the Queen's English. *He hates me because I'm Black, yet he honors me with proper speech. Is he crazy or sly like a fox?*

"By the way," said Hugh, "there's a bit of an unforeseen consequence of Otto Krieger's little foray up in Kensington the night we burned the ship. Magistrate Stone was a tad vexed when he found the rear of his jail destroyed and that slave family missing. He blamed Austin T. Slatter. Figured he had busted the family out so he could spirit them back into slavery in Delaware. He threw Slatter in jail, but he got out on bail, then disappeared. Stone has put out a warrant for Slatter's arrest. I don't think we'll be seeing him for a while."

If Hugh Callaghan was an adversary and occasional ally, Austin Slatter was a mortal enemy. A devil. A slave catcher who hunted down self-emancipators and returned them to enslavement. He had been a part-owner of the slave ship *Bridger* before it burned. Jules and Hugh's act of arson had ruined him.

Jules pondered the thought of Slatter on the lam. "*Schadenfreude,*" he muttered.

"What's that? Never heard that term before," said Callaghan.

"Schadenfreude. It's a German term. I learned it from Otto. It's the sense of pleasure that you feel when you hear about someone else's misfortune. I don't ever recall experiencing it until this moment. Thank you for telling me the news."

"You speak German?"

"Of course. Had to if I was going to run an all-German shop."

"You keep surprising me, Jules. I'm glad we bumped into you. Happy to have brightened your evening a little."

Callaghan's compliment, backhanded as it was, still gratified Jules. "Slatter's a bad penny. He'll turn up doing his mischief soon enough. That's going to be interesting, since he knows your boys divested the *Bridger* of all its coffee before it was burned by perpetrators unknown."

"Yeah, that aspect was a bit of a bollocks. If and when he returns to Philadelphia, Slatter will have it in for me. But on the other hand, until then there's one less man catching your fugitive brethren and getting them out of my neighborhood."

"It's not your neighborhood, Hugh. We share it."

"For now, Jules. As you know, I'm doing my best to change that."

Enough of this. Jules squeezed Maddie's arm with the crook of his elbow to steer her back to their stroll. "Your new pump will be finished by the end of the month. I'll send you a note when it's ready," he called back into the darkness as he and Maddie walked away.

* * * * *

Jules and Maddie were passing the vacant lot next to their house when a breeze parted the layer of chimney smoke above them. Light of the waning crescent moon briefly illuminated the large rock in the middle of the lot. Jules saw two figures standing by the rock. A flicker of a passing thought: *One of them looks like Logan Gallagher.* Logan was Seamus Gallagher's little brother, who had been in love with Martha until Maddie and Jules broke them up.

Jules and Maddie reentered the house with their eleven-day-old dispute now put to bed. "Is Martha back yet?" he asked Grace as he shed his rain slicker.

Grace put down her newspaper. "Nope, not yet. But you have visitors. Mr. Forten and Mr. Purvis are waiting for you in the kitchen."

* * * * *

· LOGAN ·

"Do you think they saw us?" Martha whispered into the darkness.

Logan shuddered. The blanket that insulated them from the rock's coldness had fallen off their shoulders and lay in a wupse behind them. Logan didn't know if his shudder emanated from the cold or the thought of Jules and Maddie learning that he had broken his promise. *We had broken our promise.*

"I don't think so," Logan responded.

"What are we going to do?"

"Same thing we've been doing for six weeks. Meet here when we can and never tell anyone."

"No, I mean *what are we going to do about us?* I still love you."

"No, we can't do that. If we do, it won't just be me who gets beat up. They'll hurt you. The people of this town don't abide an Irish boy and a Black girl being in love. It's amalgamating."

Martha reached behind her and pulled the blanket up around their shoulders again. "What if we left Philadelphia?"

"Do you think the rules would be any different someplace else?"

"I don't know. Maybe."

"No, we can't do anything more than meet at this rock. We talk. That's it."

Martha remained silent. She didn't move away from him. Didn't pull her warmth from his side.

"I've made a decision," said Logan. "I'm going to go with No Name."

No Name Fire Brigade was an upstart hose company started by Logan's older brother Seamus, in part to help put out fires in Black houses in Moya-mensing—something Hugh Callaghan's hose company made a point of not doing.

"Good. What about the other stuff? Stealing things off the docks?"

"That's part of the deal. Between putting out fires and me dockside activities, I should be able to scrape by; keep food on me family's table and enough coal to keep the fire going all night."

"Are you going to tell Hugh Callaghan? He's not going to like it."

"I think he already knows, but I'll tell him."

"Be careful. His Moya boys'll beat you up a second time."

"They beat me up the first time because of you. The truce between Moya and No Name is still holding, even after that brawl at the ship fire. I'll be all right."

"You should go back to work at Krieger Coach. They haven't hired anyone to replace you yet."

"I quit because I couldn't look your father in the eye. Because every moment I spent with him was a lie. We promised your folks we wouldn't see each other."

"But we only talk."

"And yet two minutes ago, you talked about running away from Philadelphia."

* * * * *

· JULES ·

Jules and Maddie entered their kitchen to find James Forten and Robert Purvis.

Forten, age seventy-two, was probably the richest Black man in North America. Although the history books of the day never mentioned him, he was a heroic veteran of the American Revolution. He owned the largest sailmaking shop on the Delaware. He frequently contributed to William Lloyd Garrison's

Pennsylvania Hall. (Courtesy of the Library of Congress.)

The Liberator, and served as a prominent member of numerous anti-slavery societies.

Purvis was only twenty-seven. *A youngster*, thought Jules, who wasn't sure of his own age but figured it was around thirty-seven.

Purvis was James Forten's son-in-law, also wealthy and involved in the abolition movement. Although one-quarter Moorish, Robert was light of complexion, a fact that could have prompted the unwitting to allow him access to the city's best hotels, restaurants, and theater seats. Instead, Robert chose to embrace his Black ancestry and deny himself those prerogatives.

Forten and Purvis rose as Jules and Maddie entered the kitchen. "Jules, Maddie," said Purvis. "We apologize for barging in on you unannounced. . . ."

"No," said Jules, "we are happy to see you both. Please sit. Given the hour, I assume this is a business call, not a social visit."

Both Forten and Purvis nodded and took their seats.

Maddie replenished the kitchen stove with a few more sticks of firewood, then turned to leave. "Then I will leave you men to your business."

"No, Maddie. Please stay," said Purvis. "This matter will impact you as well." When Maddie had settled in, Purvis laid a roll of what Jules recognized as architectural drawings on the table. "You know Mason Edes died last month."

"Mason Edes . . . ?" responded Jules.

"He was the general contractor in charge of building Pennsylvania Hall."

Pennsylvania Hall was the Pennsylvania Anti-Slavery Society's new "Temple of Freedom," under construction to eventually house anti-slavery meetings and conventions. Jules and Maddie had purchased a few shares of stock in the corporation to help finance the project.

Robert took out a pipe and tamped down some tobacco. "We hoped that Edes's son would be able to fill his shoes, but it's been a disaster. James and I just left a meeting of the Board of the Pennsylvania Hall Association. The board was unanimous. We would like you to take over the project."

Jules looked at the unrolled drawings on the table. "Me?"

Forten and Purvis nodded.

"James, Robert, I'm already working six-and-a-half days a week. I don't know where I would find the time. I am trying to do my best at two jobs. I'm barely keeping Freeman Hydraulics afloat. I arrive there long before sunrise and line up ducks for the day. Then I walk to Krieger Coach and take over as foreman for the middle of the day. Then I return to my own business to make sure that the tasks that I assigned were carried out. And then there's committee meetings, Vigilant Committee missions that arise at the drop of a hat, not to mention the stream of self-emancipators that flow through this house."

Robert took a few moments to light his pipe, and the sweet aroma of tobacco wafted around the room. "James and I talked about that on the way over. We would be happy to relieve you of all your committee responsibilities. Vigilant Committee missions as well. We will recruit others to come to the aid of recaptured self-emancipators. As far as your Underground Railroad houseguests go, perhaps James and I can take some of them off your hands. Others of our brethren will step into your shoes."

"But I'm still working seventy hours a week keeping two businesses afloat."

Maddie stirred in her chair. "I can fill in at Freeman Hydraulics."

Jules turned to his wife but kept his mouth shut. He already knew what she was going to say.

Maddie smiled that knowing smile of hers and addressed Forten and Purvis. "I already keep the books. I run the place when Jules isn't there. We have only eight employees and four of them are our own children. We're in the midst of a depression. Business isn't exactly flooding in. Freeman Hydraulics can get along for a few months without my husband."

James smiled. Robert nodded deferentially to acknowledge the generosity of Maddie's offer. "Jules, the Hall is under roof. Everything that is left is finish work. When you were enslaved, you were trained as a carpenter." Robert opened his arms, calling attention to the fine woodwork around the kitchen. "The craftsmanship of this whole house is a testament to your skills."

I would be leading the crew that finishes the building that will become the epicenter of the abolition movement in Philadelphia, thought Jules. "You should be hiring a contractor, not a lead carpenter. No one in charge of a project that large should spend much time banging nails. His job is to do whatever it takes to keep the work flowing."

Purvis brightened. "Exactly. You can oversee the work of all the craftsmen. The quality has fallen off since Edes died. Materials aren't arriving on time. The men take long breaks or disappear altogether. The project is woefully behind schedule."

I'm missing something here. What are they not telling me? "Edes. Did he run a white-only shop?"

"Of course," said Purvis. He looked down at his hands. "Hiring our brethren was not a consideration when the Association was interviewing contractors."

"So all of his men are white. They won't take well to being ordered around by a Black man."

"You oversee whites at Krieger Coach," Forten said

"With some difficulties. Edes's son won't like being replaced."

Purvis waved his pipe as if to dismiss Jules's apprehension. "The board president has already told him that his whole outfit is close to being fired. We're in the midst of a depression. There's no other work to be had. He will knuckle under."

"There must be twenty contractors in the city who would jump at this job. Everyone needs work."

Purvis shifted in his seat and glanced at James Forten, who gave him a nod. "Jules, you aren't the first person the board has asked to take on the job."

The pieces of the puzzle began to fall into place. "How many others?"

"Nine. All said no because they didn't want to be associated with us. Ninety-five percent of the people in this city still support slavery, either because they find it acceptable or because they fear that if the slaves were freed, two million Negroes would flee to the North. Mason Edes was an abolitionist. His son is less enthusiastic. We should have asked you earlier, but the white members of the board . . ."

"Didn't even consider hiring a Black man until there was no alternative. I understand," said Jules. "When does the job have to be finished?"

"Dedication is set for Sunday, May 14. The next day starts the Anti-Slavery Convention of American Women. We expect three thousand people to be here."

Jules checked the calendar on the kitchen wall. "What needs to be accomplished in the next four-and-a-half months?"

While Purvis unrolled the plans on the table, James Forten took a sheet of paper out of the inside pocket of his frock coat. "Like we said, the building is under roof. The doors and windows have been installed, but pretty much everything else is wanting."

"Lath and plaster?"

Forten nodded.

"So, flooring? Trim work? Interior doors? Paint?"

Forten nodded at each as he ran his finger down at his paper. "Plus coal gas lines for lights. That should be it."

"What about exterior? Brick sidewalks?"

"Yes, that isn't on my list, but it has to be done."

"What would I be paid?"

Forten folded the paper and returned it to his pocket. "Edes cut a deal with the board. They had to pay him enough so he could pay his men and buy materials, but he took his own payment in the form of shares of stock. We have created a business plan that I am very proud of, Jules. We have no mortgage, so we only have to pay maintenance and upkeep. Rent from the Free Produce[3] store, the bookstore, and the newspaper, plus whatever we make when organizations meet in the building will produce a tidy profit every year. If you take the same deal Edes had, you won't get rich, but you will have a sizable nest egg once it comes time for your retirement."

Jules eyed Maddie. She gave him a subtle nod.

"I'll take the job on one condition."

"And what is that?"

"My suspicion is that when Edes's men find out they are going to be taking orders from a Black man, some of them will quit."

Purvis turned to Forten. Forten's shrug implied that he had also considered the possibility. Purvis returned his attention to Jules. "Not unlikely."

"If they quit, I hire their replacements."

"And . . . ?"

"And if they are qualified, I'll hire our brethren."

Forten smiled. "Robert and I talked about this possibility. I'm afraid we'll have to take this back to the board. Some of them aren't going to like it."

"Those are my conditions."

---

3. Free produce during this era meant products like cotton cloth, molasses, sugar, and rice that were untainted by the sin of slavery. The Free Produce Movement was a difficult "sell" because the products were significantly more expensive than their slave-produced alternatives.

"Good man," said Forten. "But I have a word of caution. Remember, twenty years ago I tried to start an all-Black fire company in Moyamensing. That generated a huge backlash. Most newspapers in Philadelphia had a field day with it. We barely lasted a year before we disbanded for fear of one of our men getting killed. Be smart about this. Hire a white man every once in a while."

Jules nodded, tacitly accepting Forten's advice. "Now I'd like to see these plans."

SATURDAY, JANUARY 6
(DECEMBER 27 O.S.)

· ADRIAN ·

Colonel Malkovich and Count Sheremetev set up a session to tutor Rian about life in the royal apartments in the Anichkov Palace. Adrian asked to sit in.

Malkovich held a riding crop as a pointer. "Rian, you start as the grand duke's companion in five days. We're holding these sessions to familiarize you with the doings of the royal family. We want you to avoid missteps. However, much of what I am about to tell you is conjecture now that the Tsar has moved the family to his new residence. The royal offices are still in a state of upheaval. There is simply no room in the smaller Anichkov Palace to put everything. Files, papers, reports, edicts—they are stacked willy-nilly in half the rooms of the palace with little organization. Whether that sort of disorganization has filtered over into the royal apartments, we have no idea."

Adrian watched Rian as she sat attentively in her chair. He had to admit that his niece certainly looked like a boy. She was solidly built, with green eyes and light brown hair, wide shoulders, a strong jaw, high cheekbones, and slightly olive skin. Most notably, like himself, his two brothers, and their father, she sported a wide gap between her two front teeth.

Malkovich continued. "The Tsar has a routine that he adheres to every day. He rises early and attends to dispatches that have arrived at his desk from the world and the eastern part of his empire since the previous night. The grand dukes and duchesses start their days a bit later. You and Grand Duke Konstantin will meet your tutor at 7:30."

"I'll have to feed and exercise Frank and Wash before then," Rian said.

Malkovich cocked his head at Adrian in silent question. *Can Rian do it all?*

Adrian nodded to Malkovich.

Malkovich took his cue from Adrian. "Yes, I suppose you will. Promptly at ten o'clock, the Tsar eats breakfast with the Tsarina and his children. You will not join them. The Tsar conducts *la revue de la famille*, in which the grand dukes and grand duchesses, no matter their age, report about their mornings and progress on their studies."

Adrian watched Rian as Malkovich spoke. Her eyes never left the colonel. *Amazing what the belief that you could affect the course of world events does for your focus. She was dismissed from formal schooling in Philadelphia in part because she couldn't sit still. Now she hangs onto Malkovich's every word.*

Malkovich continued. "Then the children return to their tutors and work with them until four o'clock, when the Tsar returns to the royal apartments to take dinner with his family and one or two members of his inner circle. You of course will not be part of this."

Malkovich turned to an easel and pointed with his riding crop. "Here is a list of the Tsar's children." He drew a line under the first two names.

Grand Duke Alexander Nikolaevich – age 19
Grand Duchess Maria Nikolaevna – age 18

"You are unlikely to see either of these two. Alexander returned from his tour of the empire a few days before the palace burned. He is assuming more responsibilities outside the palace"—Sheremetev nodded to Adrian—"such as working with your uncle and cousin. His family calls him Sasha, but you should never use this familiar term. The grand duchess has her own tutor and is being prepared to be married off in the next year or two, most likely to a prince of one of the many German principalities."

The count circled the next three names with his riding crop. "These are the three children whom you are likely to be spending the most time with, Rian."

Grand Duchess Olga Nikolaevna – age 15
Grand Duchess Alexandra Nikolaevna – age 12
Grand Duke Konstantin Nikolaevich – age 10

"The two grand duchesses are inconsequential. They are rarely seen outside the palace and spend little time in the company of men. By all means, pay deference to their rank, but they will never make any decisions that affect the future of Russia. It is Grand Duke Konstantin whom the Tsar wants you to spend time with. You are three years older than him, and he will undoubtedly be very impressionable. When you are alone with him, it will be acceptable to use his nickname, Kostya. Always refer to him as 'grand duke' when in the presence of adults."

His presentation drawing to a close, Colonel Malkovich put his hands behind his back but still held his riding crop. "Don't worry about the youngest two children. They also have a separate tutor. I doubt you will ever encounter them. Questions?"

"What am I to do with Grand Duke Konstantin?"

"Whatever he is doing, you should do. Apparently, Konstantin is quite the willful child. His previous governess couldn't handle him, so his father hired an older man who he wouldn't be able to bowl over. Fyodor Litke is an accomplished mariner and scientist. He has sailed around the world twice. He is a respected member of the Russian Academy of Science. I believe you will learn much from him."

A maid knocked on the door and addressed Count Sheremetev in Russian. Adrian heard his name mentioned.

Sheremetev turned to Adrian. "It seems the American ambassador is here to see you."

This can't be good, Adrian thought to himself. *The ambassador knows Rian is a girl. He didn't kick up much of a fuss when Rian was a lowly coachman, but now that she's going to be a companion to the grand duke. . . .*

George Mifflin Dallas, American ambassador to the Russian Imperial Court, entered the room with a full head of steam. "I'm sorry to interrupt your morning, gentlemen, but I have some urgent news that I believe you should know."

"Mr. Ambassador," said Sheremetev. "It is good to meet you. Please sit down."

"I would prefer to stand, thank you. An hour ago, General Benckendorff, the head of the Third Section, paid me a visit at the embassy.""

"What is the Third Section?" asked Adrian.

Colonel Malkovich shook his head. "Benckendorff is a man whose attention you would prefer not to attract, but we have nothing to worry about."

Adrian noticed that as Malkovich was speaking these words, he was really addressing the count.

Malkovich laid his riding crop on the tray of the easel. "The general founded the Third Section after the Decembrist Revolt to root out the remnants of those still disloyal to the Tsar. Most people think of the Third Section as the Secret Police, but they also are responsible for censorship of all publications and the arts in Russia." He turned to Dallas. "What did Benckendorff want?"

"The Tsar informed him that he has embraced the idea of you Americans overseeing the creation of a railroad from St. Petersburg to Moscow. He wanted to know what I knew about you and Mr. Gallagher. Fortunately, I was able to tell them much about the Krieger family that I knew from my time in Philadelphia."

"It seems then that there should be no problem," interjected the count. "Seamus and Adrian are not revolutionaries. They are no threat to the Tsar."

Dallas straightened to his full height. "He also asked specific questions about young Rian here."

"And what did you tell him?"

"I lied, of course."

"What do you mean?" asked the count.

"You really don't know, do you?"

"Know what?"

"That the young man you are about to send into the Tsar's inner sanctum is an impostor. Rian Krieger is a female."

* * * * *

· RIAN ·

Humiliated, Rian sat in her room, awaiting the judgment from the adults. Through the door she could hear angry words flying back and forth. *Betrayal... Lies... Deception... Jeopardy.* Ambassador Dallas left, slamming the door behind him. At one point, she heard heated words between Sheremetev and her uncle.

"*Adrian, this is your fault as much as it is your niece's. You should have told us.*"

"*When she appeared on the* Elizabeth, *we decided she was going to be our coachman. Her role was to take care of horses. How could we have anticipated this? I never dreamed she was going to become the grand duke's companion. What if we say no to the Tsar?*"

"*No one says no to the Tsar. He will know something is amiss. He will assign Benckendorff to find out what. Benckendorff's Secret Police are relentless.*"

"*We tell Benckendorff the truth. You can honestly say you were deceived.*"

"*Volkonsky will love that. He will throw all three of you deceivers into prison. He will make sure the railroad contract reverts to his brother-in-law.*"

"*What do you care, as long as a railroad gets built?*"

"*That's what I'm telling you. The railroad won't get built. It will become bogged down in petty squabbling and be stripped of its momentum by one bribe after another. No, Krieger Locomotive is the key to changing the face of Russia.*"

"*What if we send her back to America?*"

"She can't leave right away. The Baltic will be frozen shut until March. The overland route is grueling during the winter."

"Okay, so all we've got to do is make it through the next eight weeks."

After half an hour, Adrian opened her door without knocking. "Rian, come with me. We have made some decisions."

Sheremetev stood near a window. "Rian, unfortunately you and your uncle and cousin have boxed us in with your deceit. We are forced to have you go forward as the grand duke's companion. However, you will spend as little time with Konstantin Nikolaevich as possible. Arrive late. Depart early. Tend to the horses, which unexpectedly need an inordinate amount of attention. Take many days away from the palace because you become mysteriously sick. Remain as reserved and as reticent as you possibly can. Do not speak unless spoken to. Never offer an opinion."

"So I'm not going to be myself? That's what you wanted me to do before, be myself."

"That was before we found out the truth about you. You are a naive little girl. You have been one big lie since you insinuated yourself into this enterprise."

Adrian stepped from his position at the fireplace. "Now hold on, Sheremetev. Three days ago, you said many laudatory things about Rian. She speaks three languages. She's learning Russian. She knows horses. She led the peasants to assemble the railroad track. She ran into the fire. Now, you disparage her because she deceived you about her sex? Think about it. That's what this entire mission has been so far . . . one big deception. We're not rich Americans. We're a couple of—"

The count held up his hand to stop Adrian. "I am fully aware of the nature of our collective deception. The problem is not the deception. The problem is that Rian is a girl. No attempt to deceive can change that." Sheremetev returned his attention to Rian, bending down so that his face was a few inches from hers. "Your job now is to get through the next two months and attract as little attention to yourself as possible. Do you understand?"

Rian hung her head. "Yes, sir. I understand."

"Good." Sheremetev stood back up to address all three Americans. "Fortunately, this has been a light winter. When the ice on the Gulf of Finland breaks in early March, Rian will be on the first ship out of Kronstadt. You two must figure out who will accompany her."

MONDAY, JANUARY 8
(DECEMBER 28 O.S.)

· RIAN ·

It was Rian's first day acting as companion to Grand Duke Konstantin Nikolaevich. *This isn't what I expected,* Rian thought to herself. *The Anichkov Palace is a wreck.*

Rian and the grand duke—age ten and dressed in naval attire—sat at a library table at one end of a drawing room that had been commandeered to become a classroom. Thirty feet away, at the other end of the room, Grand Duchesses Olga Nikolaevna, age fifteen, and Alexandra Nikolaevna, age twelve, sat at a similar table.

In the corner by the door, an old woman sat in a chair and read a book. She looked up when Rian first entered the room, but didn't rise, didn't smile, and didn't introduce herself.

Their "classroom" was a mess. The students shared the room with a farrago of items rescued from the palace fire less than two weeks ago. In the middle of the room lay a jumble of twenty identical dining chairs, a globe, a butcher block table, a chandelier, statues, busts of unidentified people without pedestals, pedestals without busts, and a disassembled armoire that may or may not have all its pieces. The perimeter of the room was equally chaotic. Five stacks of framed paintings leaned against one interior wall. Along the other three walls were pile after pile of papers-of-state, many slumping into their neighbors.

Their tutor, forty-year-old Fyodor Litke, had left Rian and Konstantin fifteen minutes ago to attend to the grand duchesses. "The grand duchesses' tutor has been ill since the fire," Litke had announced, "so I must divide my time among all of you."

Rian noticed that every time Litke got close to either of the two grand duchesses, the woman sitting in the corner cleared her throat and gave Litke a scowl and a shake of her head.

Rian and Kostya were supposed to be reading a nautical map of the Gulf of Finland, but the grand duke was more interested in practicing his English with Rian. "Gospodin[4] Litke is a great explorer. He has sailed around the world twice. He is an expert on the Arctic Ocean. He hates being my tutor, but he hates teaching my sisters worse."

"We should study the map like Mr. Litke said."

The grand duke ran his finger in a circular motion around Neva Bay, the water between St. Petersburg and the deepwater port of Kronstadt. "I already know this part pretty well. I sailed all around it the last two summers."

"With Gospodin Litke?"

"At first. My father gave me a yacht when I was eight. It's not very big, but you and I can sleep on it next summer. Gospodin Litke gave me lessons, then he said the best way to continue to learn was to do it by myself."

"Your father didn't mind?"

"No, Father wants me to take over the Navy one day. That's why he hired Gospodin Litke. He told him to do what he thought best. And like I said, he doesn't like being my tutor, so he lets me go out on my own a lot."

Rian again perused the map. *St. Petersburg to Kronstadt must be twenty miles.* "That's pretty adventurous."

"Neva Bay is also called the Marquis Puddle. It is very shallow. Gospodin didn't think I could get into too much trouble."

"Show me some things on the map that I should know. I don't want Mr. Litke to think I'm a bad student."

"He won't. He knows that you speak German, French, and English. He hopes you can teach me those languages, so that means he won't have to."

Litke left the room and shut the door behind him. Olga immediately rose from the table, went over to a stack of papers-of-state, and started perusing whatever file was on top using the light that came streaming in the window. The old woman in the corner put down her book and watched her but didn't say anything.

"Who is that?" Rian asked, pointing subtly at the old woman.

"That is Madame Parshakov. She is in charge of my sisters' virtue. She came from Siberia. Her only job is to make sure that my sisters are not touched by a man until they are married. She doesn't talk very often, and when she does I can barely understand her."

Konstantin returned his attention to the map. "My sister is bossy."

---

4. Gospodin is a Russian term of respect, like *mister* or *sir*.

"Which one?"

"Olga. I shouldn't have to listen to her. I'm a general admiral in the Russian Navy."

"How did you become a general admiral?"

Kostya shrugged. "My father gave me that rank when I was four. Olga's a stupid girl. All girls are stupid. They are only good to marry off to some German prince and form alliances."

"I don't think all girls are stupid."

"Really? Name one."

"Uh, there's a girl who used to live in Philadelphia who I knew pretty well. She rides horses. She plays the violin. She helped a slave escape to freedom. She stabbed a man who was attacking her."

"What was her name?"

Now what do I say? Rian thought to herself. "Her name is Eena."

Rian felt pretty safe using her childhood name. Her cousin Jabez was the only one who still called her that. *And Jabez is in Philadelphia.*

"How old is she?"

You're getting in deeper, Eena. Don't make this lie any more complex than it already is. "She's the same age as me."

"Where is she now?"

"Uh, she ran away because her father was going to make her wear dresses all the time and send her to a finishing school in Switzerland."

"Where did she run away to?"

End this, Eena. End it now. "Uh, I think she ran away to sea, but I don't know for sure."

* * * * *

Philadelphia

· JULES ·

Pennsylvania Hall occupied the entire lot bordered by Sixth and Haines Streets and two alleys. Jules entered the building through the double door on Sixth and found himself in a large, unfinished foyer. He could see all the way to the back of the building—six or so rooms divided by a central corridor—through walls that were framed but not sheathed. *No activity down here. No workers moving material. No banging of hammers. No rasp-rasp-rasping of saws.*

The sound of men talking and laughing echoed from the floor above. Jules climbed the right-hand set of roughed-out seven-foot-wide stairs to the second floor. When he entered Pennsylvania Hall's Grand Saloon for the first time, the conversation and laughter immediately stopped.

The room was more than two stories tall with a soaring ceiling. The U-shaped Gallery on the third floor wrapped around three sides of the saloon, giving a hint to the magnificent potential of the building. Like the street-level floor, nothing was finished. The ceiling above the Gallery had been sheathed with lath[5] strips, but the work had stopped there. No railing or knee wall had yet been installed around the Gallery.

The ceiling above the main floor was unclad, and Jules could see between the trusses up to the roof. The bricks that supported Pennsylvania Hall's exterior marble sheathing were visible between the studs along the outside walls. The posts that held up the Gallery were rough-cut 4x4s, which at some point would have to be replaced by stately round pillars.

Purvis and Forten had told Jules the job was in trouble. His first walkaround confirmed it. The place was a mess. Board ends littered the floor. A wheelbarrow with a broken handle sat canted on its side. *No one has swept up in weeks.*

In the center of the room, two men stood atop a wooden scaffold about fifteen feet square. To Jules's left, a group of six men sat in a circle around a crate turned on end. All of them were staring at him. One man slept on the floor over by the far wall.

Jules walked to the circle of men. They were playing cards. "I'm here to see Marcus Edes," he said to the group.

Most of the men returned their gazes to their cards. One man threw a card onto the crate and replied, "He's the tall one up on the scaffold."

"How come there's nothing going on here?" asked Jules, trying to keep his voice as non-accusatory as possible.

The man who answered Jules's first question rose and approached him, his posture mildly threatening. He had a weepy, guck-encrusted left eye that caused his face to contort into a constant squint. "Who wants to know?"

Jules could feel the resentment radiating toward him. Conflicting urges assaulted him at the same time. He could turn on his heel right now and leave the

---

5. Until the 1940s, a common wall covering was lath and plaster. Wall studs and ceiling joists were sheathed with lath—thin strips of wood about a ¼-inch thick and 1½ inches wide. They were nailed to the studs horizontally, separated by a ⅜-inch gap. Excess plaster from the first coat, forced through the gaps, would expand on the other side and form locking "keys" that held the dried plaster tight to the lath. Horsehair was frequently mixed into the plaster to provide flexibility and durability.

building. He could pummel the man, taking out the top dog, and see who else walked out the door. But Jules had learned long ago to keep his feelings—his fear and his rage—tamped down tight. He wasn't about to let this man's hostility deter him from his plan. Instead . . . "Answer my question."

The man took another step toward Jules, and Jules girded himself for a fistfight. Rather than step backward in a defensive stance, he extended his left foot slightly forward but kept his hands at his side.

"None of that, Emil," said one of the other card players, who rose and walked toward Jules. This man was tall and lanky and had a smile that appeared genuine. "We ran out of materials. We've got no more lath, no nails."

"Is any new stuff coming?"

"Afraid you'll have to ask Edes," said tall-and-lanky.

"Where are the others? There should be two dozen men on a job this size."

"Some are sick. Two got hurt yesterday. Some quit when they heard you was going to be the new strawboss."

Jules turned and gave a quick glance at the card players, all of whom were making a poor show of concentrating on their cards. "But you men didn't quit," he said to tall-and-lanky.

"Well, for myself, I wanted to make sure the rumors were true first."

"If the rumors were that you would have a Black man as a foreman, they were true. My name is Jules Freeman. People I work with call me Jules."

Tall-and-lanky stood there but didn't offer his hand. "My name is Randy Buck."

"Well, Randy, if you are going to quit because I'm Black, now is the time to do it."

Randy snuck a quick peek at the card players, got no reaction, then turned back to Jules. "I think I'll see how you make out with Marcus first." He shifted his attention to the scaffold. "Hey Marcus!" He then pointed to Jules with his thumb.

The taller of the two men on the scaffold turned, then turned back. "Tell him I'm busy," he said, his voice echoing off the far wall. Then he returned to his conversation.

My next test, Jules thought to himself. *I can't yell up to him and demand that he come down. There's no ladder up to the scaffold. Forcing me to climb the scaffolding to talk to him will be humiliating. I sure as hell am not going to wait until he comes down. Okay, I'm already in a hole here. I need something . . . something dramatic . . . something to get their attention. Randy. Randy is the key here.*

Jules scanned the Grand Saloon and saw an unused scaffolding board—a stout twelve-foot plank— lying on the floor. He strode to the board, noting as he walked that the floor sloped gently toward the front. *Like it would in a church.*

He picked up the plank and leaned it against one of the posts that supported the Gallery. Before he turned back to the men, he closed one eye and visually lined up the posts, assessing their placement. *Straight as a die.*

He returned to Randy. "Do me a favor. When I get up to the Gallery, hand that plank up to me."

Randy didn't say he would or he wouldn't, but he looked at the other card players and got a *do-what-you-wanna-do* shrug from a couple of them.

Jules returned to the stairs and climbed to the Gallery level. *Come on, Randy, do this one thing for me.* He emerged to more construction mess. A bundle of lath strips—*nowhere near enough to finish the ceiling, let alone the walls*—lay under a window.

Jules walked to the unwalled edge of the Gallery and looked down at Randy. "Okay, Randy, hand it up, please."

Randy hesitated. He grabbed the plank with one hand and Jules feared for a moment that he was going to tip the board over. The hesitation lasted for five more seconds, then Randy did as Jules requested.

Jules pulled the plank up to his level and grabbed it in the middle so its weight balanced. He walked along the edge of the Gallery until ten feet separated him from the scaffold in the middle of the saloon.

Jules, he said to himself, *this is either going to be a brilliant move or you are going to appear the fool.*

With a 1-2-3 heave-ho motion, he lofted the plank toward the scaffold. The far end of the board landed with an inch to spare and a loud wood-on-wood clatter. The plank's momentum threatened to carry it too far, but Jules stomped his foot on the bouncing board and stopped its forward motion. It came to rest, perfectly bridging the ten feet to the scaffold with a foot on either end.

Okay, whether brilliant or lucky, you did it.

Marcus Edes, who had been pointedly ignoring Jules's activities up to this point, turned at the sound of the clattering board.

In four purposeful strides, ignoring the void below him, Jules walked along the plank to the scaffold. Someone offered an impressed whistle from down below, but the whistle was truncated by someone else's sharp "Shut up!"

Edes greeted Jules with folded arms. "You could have waited."

"I don't much like waiting. Tell me what's going on up here."

Edes turned his gaze to the bare roof truss above. "Project's stalled until we can figure some things out."

"What things?"

Edes turned his gaze to the ceiling, sighed, then turned back to Jules. "The architect. It's his first commission, so he came up with some fancy-pants ideas to show off how talented he is. In the ceiling, right here, we're gonna have to install a convex mirror that will reflect light from the gas lights back down to the audience. He says it's going to be all sparkly, like a diamond. We have to figure out where to put additional nailers to hold up the mirror. Can't proceed installing lath until we figure out about the nailers."

Jules surveyed the Grand Saloon from this new lofty vantage point. *The bones of this building are perfect. Every line is straight and true. Edes-the-elder knew what he was doing. The carpenters did their jobs well. The talent is—or was—here. If I can get this project back on track, we'll be fine.* "I would like to talk to you in private."

"After I solve this problem."

Jules bent down, picked up a lath strip that was lying on the scaffold, and used it as a pointer. "Put the nailers here and here. When this project is finished, the mirror is going to be the center of a nine-foot sunflower with gold rays in the ceiling. The house manager will be able to crack open the rays of the sunflower during the hot summer days to provide ventilation through the roof."

"How do you know that?"

"Thomas Stewart—your fancy-pants architect—created a detail on the fifth page of the architectural drawings. He anticipated the problem and solved it for you. By the looks of it, he got it right." Jules turned his attention to the shorter man on the scaffold. "Now, I would like to talk to Mr. Edes in private."

Shorter-man looked at Edes. Edes gave him a curt nod. Shorter-man monkeyed down the side of the scaffold.

Jules watched the man awkwardly descend. "You should have a ladder to get up and down this scaffolding."

"Used to. Somebody stole it."

"You know why I'm here?"

Edes nodded. "Webb told me. I never wanted this job. My father was the master carpenter. He was bringing me along slow, giving me tasks with each new project that we did. He said in a few more years we would be partners. Mason Edes & Son. We'd built houses and a couple of commercial buildings on Market up until this point. We were doing powerful well until the Panic. Dad was real happy when he landed this job. It was going great. Then he died."

"What are you trained to do?"

"Oh, I can pretty much build a house from the ground up once the foundation's laid. I can't do brickwork. Not crazy about laying shingles, but I'll do it."

"Ever led a crew before?"

"Only a framing crew a couple of days when the foreman got sick. Finish crew generally knows what they're doing, so I never had to do that. But I've done a lot of finish work."

"Ever read a set of architectural plans?"

"No."

"Ordered supplies? Worked with subcontractors?"

"No, my father did all that."

"Okay, Marcus, here's what I see." Jules used the lath to point to the expanse of the Grand Saloon with a sweeping motion. "Everything that's been done so far on this project has been done well. Your walls are straight as a die. The main floor of the Saloon slopes gently toward the front, just the way it's supposed to. That must have been a bitch to get right, so your daddy knew what he was doing and your men did it perfectly. I would be pleased to have you continue with this project."

"Your name is Jules, right?"

Jules nodded.

"Here's the problem. People in this town don't forget. If I decide to take orders from you, I'll never get another carpentry job in Philadelphia."

"But you are already building a hall that is going to house the Pennsylvania Anti-Slavery Society. What's the difference?"

"This was my father's project. He leaned in that direction. My understanding is that no one else would take the job anyway. Hell, Dad had never built anything this big before. This was a leap for him. He assumed his future was bright, because he was going to be the guy all the abolitionists in this town hired. But now the depression's hit and no one's building anything. The abolitionists aren't going to hire me because I couldn't finish the job. Anyone else won't hire me because of you."

Jules stuffed down his irritation because he knew he might get better results by not showing his true feelings. "I'll tell you what—how about if I give you until tomorrow to give me your final answer?"

"Not sure I'm inclined to change my mind, but I appreciate the offer."

Jules jerked his thumb at the card players below. "Who of those men do you think will stay with the project?"

"Dunno. It's up to them."

"Who among them could lead a crew?"

"Not sure any of them has ever led a crew before."

"Your supplies—lumber, nails—where did your father order them from?"

"The boards came from Ellis & Longstreth. I don't know the rest. It just showed up."

"Did you order for the next phase? Those men could be installing lath downstairs right now."

"Uh, no. We finished building the Gallery last week. I hadn't thought about the next step yet."

"You built the Gallery after your father died?"

"The men and I did, yes."

"You—and they—did a great job. Come on, Marcus. If you come back to work tomorrow, you will be the foreman of the crew. You and I will meet first thing every morning and we'll figure out what the priorities are."

"How much would I get paid?"

"Foreman's wages. Less than your father was making as the general contractor but still good money, especially these days."

Edes glanced up at the place where the convex mirror would eventually be installed. "Let's go down and talk to the men." He turned and walked across the plank to get to the unfinished Gallery. Jules followed him, and they took the stairs to the second floor. When they emerged back into the Grand Saloon, the workers were standing and waiting for them.

Edes addressed the men before Jules had a chance. "Fellas, this man is going to be running the place. He seems to know what he's doing, so I don't think you should quit because he's Black. I'm going home to think about it for the rest of the day. I suggest you do the same. I may be back tomorrow, or maybe I won't."

"Gentlemen," said Jules. "If you know you are going to stick with me, there's no need to go. There's a day's worth of redding up here to get this place organized before we start installing the lath. If Marcus comes back tomorrow, he will be your foreman."

The men hesitated, staring at each other for a few moments. When the first man got up, he grabbed his tools, then walked down the stairs to the foyer. The rest followed suit. Within three minutes, the only useful things in the Grand Saloon were the broken wheelbarrow and a few oil lamps.

* * * * *

At six o'clock in the evening, Jules was sitting on an empty nail keg, making calculations on a scrap of cedar shingle by the light of a whale oil lantern. He heard the door to the street open and close downstairs and the sound of someone fumbling their way up the steps in the dark.

"Jules? Are you here?"

Jules recognized the voice of Frederick Hinton, a member of Pennsylvania Hall's Board of Managers whom he had served with on numerous Pennsylvania Anti-Slavery Society committees. "Up here!"

Hinton emerged at the top of the stairs, surveyed the ill-lighted expanse of the Grand Saloon, and walked over to Jules. "I came to see how your first day went."

"Well, all the men left, and they took their tools. I don't think that's a good sign. I'll know more tomorrow morning. Maybe I've lost the whole crew. Maybe some of them will have a change of heart when they realize there's no other work to be had in the city."

"That doesn't sound good."

"Could have been worse. No fisticuffs. No yelling. I needed some planning time anyway. Got my lath order ready. I stopped by Ellis & Longstreth. They'll have all the lath we need by noon tomorrow. I think I've got a plastering crew lined up. Robert Purvis has given me the names of some of our Black brethren who will be eager for a job, but they likely have little in the way of skills, and doubtful any tools."

"We gonna make the deadline? We've got eighteen weeks 'til dedication."

"That's what I'm working on now. It's going to be tight, no matter what. A lot of variables. How many workers show up tomorrow. How skilled the replacements I hire are. If the plastering crew shows up in time. How long it takes the plaster to dry. If I can find a painting outfit that will work with us." Jules showed his cedar shingle to Hinton. "Here's how I've mapped it out."

Lath installation	2–4 weeks
Plaster	2–5 weeks
Build stage	1 week
Install columns	1 week
Finish carpentry	8–12 weeks
Paint	2–4 weeks
Gas lighting	1–2 weeks
Furnace/Boiler/Heat	2–4 weeks
Move in	1–2 weeks

"Appears to me that if everything goes right, you're already running over by two weeks. What does 'install columns' mean?"

Jules pointed with a sweeping gesture toward the posts that held up the Gallery, barely visible on the periphery of the oil lamp's aura. "All those posts are temporary. The columns are being built off-site by E.E. Flury & Sons. When the time comes, we'll jack up the Gallery a quarter inch or so, slip out the post, and slip in the column. It's not hard."

Hinton cocked his head as if to say *not hard for you, maybe.* He then pointed to Jules's list. "I'm a barber, not a contractor, so I really don't know what I'm talking about, but I've gotta ask: two to five weeks for plastering?"

"Plaster takes three coats. Each coat is about a quarter-inch thick. If you're lucky, each coat takes about three days to dry. But, if it's cold—this place isn't heated yet—or if it's rainy outside, or if the sun doesn't shine, it can take a lot longer. The way I figure it, it'll be late January or early February when the plasterers start—the worst possible time."

"What are you going to do?"

"What am I going to do? I think I'm going to put a locomotive in the basement."

TUESDAY, JANUARY 9

· JULES ·

The next day, Jules—toolbox in hand—arrived at Pennsylvania Hall an hour before sunrise. His hope was that at least one or two men would be there waiting for him to unlock the door. *Putting aside their hatred in order to put in an honest day's labor.*

No one.

He started cleaning up debris that littered the future rooms of the ground level. *Free produce store, abolitionist bookshop, newspaper office, two committee rooms, a lecture hall in the back. When this place is up and running, the ground floor alone is going to be worth it.*

Tall-and-lanky Randy Buck showed up about an hour later. His talkative mood was gratifying, although Jules quickly concluded that Randy found it difficult to talk and work at the same time.

"Gotta tell you, Jules, I wasn't inclined to come today, but my missus laid into me good. She said this is a good job and there's no other carpentry work to be had. She said that if I didn't feel like doing the job I was trained to do, I could help her doing laundry for the richies. Well, truth be told, that woman works harder than I do for a quarter of the money. Course, I'd never tell her that, but I sure didn't want to spend the day cartin' hot water."

By ten, all three floors of the hall were cleared of debris and swept. No one else had shown, but a boy on a wagon from Crank's Hardware arrived with two kegs of nails for the lath.

By eleven, Jules and Randy had repaired the wheelbarrow, built a pair of sawhorses, and thrown together a passable sixteen-foot ladder out of 2x4s and wood scraps. As they were leaning it up against the scaffold, Jonas Longstreth himself delivered the first wagonload of lath.

"You put a smile on me and my partner's faces yesterday," said Longstreth as he unlatched the rear gate to the wagon. "We started sawing lath for this project a month ago, then Mason Edes died and no one ever contacted us. Figured the board of managers had gone someplace else."

Jules picked up a lath strip, eyeballed it for straightness, and nodded in approval. "How come you're doing the delivery?"

"Doing everything these days. We're down to two workers, so I'm doing chores I haven't done in years: picking up wood at the sawmill, running the machinery, making the deliveries. You should get your men out here to unload this wagon so I can get back to the shop. I'll be back in an hour with another wagonload. This is a big order. We'll be at it most of the day."

"I've only got one worker. Apparently, everyone else quit."

Longstreth laid his arms on the stack of lath and bowed his head momentarily, then turned to Jules. "Ellis and I are both supportive of the abolitionist cause. I can get the word out to some of the boys I let go when things got bad. The men who worked for us knew our sentiments. Some of them would be happy for the work."

Jules, Randy, and Longstreth had the wagon halfway unloaded when Mason Edes and three men showed up with their toolboxes. One of them was weepy-eyed Emil Harberger, the man who was so aggressive toward Jules the previous day. *That makes five. If I'm going to finish this project on time, I need twenty more men.*

* * * * *

Jules arrived home long after the rest of the family had eaten supper. Seated at the kitchen table, he updated Maddie on the rest of his day. Robert Purvis and James Forten had ridden uptown in Forten's buggy to check up on him. They thought they could supply ten free Blacks who would be suitable. Jules was gratified to hear that half of them already had some carpentry experience. Late in the afternoon, Jules had walked a mile to the northwest to visit the construction site for the Shelter for Colored Orphans, a second significant project that the city's reformers had chosen to take on at the same time as Pennsylvania Hall. The building was barely under roof but had a full crew of workers. *All white*, Jules noted. The contractor told Jules he was not inclined to share any workers with him.

His last stop of the day had been the Krieger factories. It didn't take much convincing to get Otto Krieger to agree to fabricating a furnace and boiler to be installed in the basement of the Hall. The Krieger Locomotive factory was designed to build locomotives, but the market for new locos was almost nonexistent. They were already building the hardware for Freeman Hydraulics's steam-driven fire pumps; why not build a furnace? If they could get it up and running before the plaster was laid, the furnace could shorten the drying time considerably.

Maddie placed a bowl of leftover stew on the table in front of Jules. "Is that Emil character going to cause any problems?"

"I'm not sure. Probably. Right now, Marcus Edes is the foreman, so it's his problem. It only gets to me if Edes can't handle him."

Jules and Maddie's daughter Grace entered the kitchen and sat next to Jules. "Pop-Pop, Mother says you're hiring Black folks to work up at Pennsylvania Hall. I know someone who wants a job and would be a good worker."

"Black?"

"Of course. Knows reading and writing as good as me, but wants to learn how to be a carpenter."

"How old?"

"Sixteen. Same as me."

"This job is going to be difficult. I don't want some young hothead coming in who can't handle a bunch of whites who don't want anything to do with him. It's going to be a challenge mixing our folks with those white men."

"Oh, she's a tough cookie. She'll be able to handle it."

"She?"

"Yeah, her name is Cee-Cee and she wants to bang nails."

· RIAN ·

Gospodin Litke had been attending to the grand duchesses for ten minutes, then left the room. As soon as he closed the door, Grand Duchess Olga rose from her table and traversed the thirty feet to Rian and Konstantin's table. Madame Parshakov put down her book and stood, but watched from a distance.

Grand Duchess Olga Nikolaevna crossed her arms and hovered above them. "What are you doing?" she asked in Russian, her tone dripping with imperiousness, even to Rian's untrained ear.

"Nothing," Konstantin snorted at his older sister. "You should go back to your table. Madame Parshakov is giving you the evil eye."

Rather than respond to the grand duke, Olga shifted her gaze to Rian.

Rian fidgeted for a moment, not wanting to alienate either Konstantin or Olga. "I'm reading a novel in English to Kostya."

Olga stamped her foot. "When in my presence, you will refer to my brother as Grand Duke Konstantin."

Wow, she is bossy, thought Rian. "Then that is what I will do. Thank you for telling me."

"Tell me about this novel."

Rian showed Olga the cover of the February 1837 edition of *Bentley's Miscellany* that contained Chapters 1 and 2 of *Oliver Twist*. "There's an Englishman named Charles Dickens who is writing a novel in installments. A bookshop in London sends me new installments every month. I got Chapters 16 and 17 the other day, but I'm starting Kost—the grand duke—on Chapter 1."

"I want you to read it to me," ordered Olga.

"I can't. I have to stay here with the grand duke."

"I order you to come to my table and read it to me. I am Grand Duchess Olga Nikolaevna Romanov. I am five years older than my brother. I am in charge when Gospodin Litke is not present."

Konstantin sat up straight in his chair. "No, you can't order Rian around. He is my companion. Father says—"

"Father isn't here, nor is Gospodin Litke."

Count Sheremetev told Uncle Adrian he wanted us Americans to act like Americans. I'm not sure what that means, but . . . "I'll tell you what. If you and your sister—er, Grand Duchess Alexandra—bring your chairs down here, I will read to all of you."

Olga turned toward her sister, then returned her attention to Rian. "Romanovs don't carry chairs."

"Father did," said Konstantin. "He carried the Throne of Peter the Great out of the Great Hall during the fire. Rian helped him. That is why he is here."

Olga glared at Konstantin. "What I meant to say was that Romanov grand duchesses do not carry chairs."

Rian saw her opening. "But American companions to grand dukes do, and I bet Romanov grand dukes do as well."

The grand duke nodded.

Olga put her hands on her hips. "So you should bring your chairs to our end of the room."

"If I do that, we'll be closer to Madame Parshakov's evil eye. What if the Grand Duke Konstantin and I go get your chairs and bring them here?"

Olga considered the proposal. "You must start reading the book from the beginning."

Rian glanced at Konstantin, who nodded. Rian smiled up at Olga. "I think we have a deal."

When Gospodin Litke returned to the classroom, Rian was reading to Olga, Alexandra, and Konstantin. Madame Parshakov had moved her chair halfway down the room to better keep an eye on the youngsters. Litke approached the students, heard what was going on, returned to his own desk, and started reading a very large book. By the time Rian quit reading, Oliver Twist had asked for more gruel and consequently was about to be banished from the workhouse.

"Do you have more chapters of this novel?" asked Olga, who was sitting next to Rian.

"Yes, I bought six more issues like this in London. Two more issues came in the mail the other day. One was more chapters of this book, the other was the last chapter of a book that Dickens was writing at the same time."

Grand Duchess Olga Nikolaevna gently pried the *Bentley's Miscellany* out of Rian's hands, which elicited a cautionary clearing of the throat from Madame Parshakov.

"Tomorrow, you will continue reading this novel to us." When she slid the magazine back toward Rian, her hand grazed Rian's elbow. Madame Parshakov again cleared her throat.

The grand duchess stared defiantly back at Madame Parshakov, turned her gaze toward Rian, and sniffed. "You smell like horses."

* * * * *

· RIAN ·

The sun had already set when Rian, wearing her new greatcoat, left the Anichkov Palace. She spotted the serf named Lev, who was delivering a wagonload of firewood to the Palace. Lev was a woodcutter whom she had become friendly with during the few weeks the Americans had lived in the Winter Palace before the fire. He had helped her assemble railroad ties and track for a demonstration to the Tsar that never happened. The two of them had fought the Winter Palace fire together, but she hadn't seen him in the two weeks since then.

"*Privet, Lev. Chto ty zdes' delayesh'* [Hello, Lev. What are you doing here]?"

Lev turned to Rian, a bundle of firewood in his arms. "Ah, Master Rian," he said in Russian. "I am delivering firewood to the Tsar, same as always. Your Russian is improving."

"Thank you. May I help you?"

Lev gave Rian a long regard. "I think not. I see you are no longer dressed as a coachman. You look like a member of the Tsar's Horse Guards. Very impressive. My aunt tells me you spend time with the grand duke. I do not think it would be appropriate for a young man of your station to help with the firewood."

Rian hadn't thought about Lev's aunt since the fire. She used to work in the bakery of the Winter Palace. Apparently, she had been moved over to the Anichkov Palace. *And same as in the Winter Palace, stories about the royal family make their way downstairs.* Rian laughed. "I would be happy to help you. Honest. Your wagon is almost empty. Is this your last trip of the day?"

"It is. There are fewer fireplaces for us to feed now that His Imperial Majesty has taken up new quarters."

"Are you going home after you finish?"

"I am. A rare early night. I intend to sit by the fire and play my balalaika."

"Since you are passing right by the Manege, how about if I help you with the wood and you give me a ride to the stable?"

* * * * *

On the wagon ride to the Manege, Rian wanted to show off her growing Russian vocabulary. "Are you married?"

"No, I live by myself. My parents were servants of the Tsar as well. They both died of cholera seven years ago."

"The same epidemic that took my mother in Philadelphia. Did you grow up in St. Petersburg?"

"No, I grew up on the Tsar's estate in Tsarskoye Selo, but I live here in town now. In the same neighborhood we visited on the night of the fire."

"Do you like supplying the Tsar with firewood?"

"It is what I have been told to do. I have no choice."

"You belong to the Tsar?"

"No, I belong to the land. The Tsar owns the land."

Rian didn't understand the difference, but what she did understand was that Lev had no choices in his life.

They arrived at the Manege, and Rian hopped out of the wagon. She was about to thank Lev for the ride and bid him adieu when she noticed that some of the boards in the bed of his wagon were rotted almost all the way through. "Lev, you must lose a lot of firewood out of your wagon. You need new boards."

"Of course I do, but the estate manager does not allow serfs to make use of the Tsar's forests. I cannot afford to buy new boards."

"If you had the wood, would you be able to make new boards?"

"Of course, I am a woodcutter."

"So what if I can get you some wood?"

"Then I would be able to make a fine new wagon bed."

"And perhaps I would be able to help you."

Two evenings later, with Adrian's blessing, Lev and Rian carted two of the railroad ties that were no longer needed for the locomotive demonstration to Lev's neighborhood.

"This section of the city can be dangerous," said Lev as they turned onto his street. "If you ever come back here without me, make sure you watch out behind you."

Under a lean-to behind Lev's one-room lachuga,[6] they sawed the ties lengthwise by candlelight using a two-man saw. Partway through the evening, three of the men who had helped with the railroad demonstration joined them. Everyone took turns with the saw.

---

6. Shack.

The men shared a bottle of vodka. They offered a swig to Rian, which she tried, but it burned so much on the way down that she shook her head when the bottle was offered after that.

She helped to smooth rough board edges and straighten lines with a hand plane. Lev drilled holes in the boards and the wagon's cross beams. Lev and Rian whittled pegs to insert into the holes to secure the boards to the wagon.

The job complete, the four peasants and Rian retired to one serf's lachuga, which was warm but so sparsely furnished that two men had to walk to their own homes to bring extra chairs to be able to sit by the fire. Three balalaikas appeared. Music lulled Rian. The wife of the house served fish stew. The men drank more vodka.

A deck of cards appeared, and the group played durak. Penalties for losing a hand were always frivolous. One time, Rian's penalty was to pluck out a tune on the balalaika. The men were impressed that she played it as well as she did.

That first evening with the serfs led to another, and then another, and then another. Adrian and Seamus were so preoccupied with their efforts with the railroad that they barely noticed. Lev always cautioned her to be careful on her walk to the neighborhood. Rian told Lev that she was used to rough neighborhoods in Philadelphia. "I've got some eyes in the back of my head," she said in her best attempt at her growing facility with Russian. Her translation didn't work well, which caused great merriment with the men.

Rian always arrived with a gift—usually food. Sometimes she and Lev played cards with the other men. Sometimes they only talked, mostly in Russian, but at Lev's insistence, Rian introduced him to basic English. He told her stories of growing up on the Tsar's estate in Tsarskoye Selo. She told him tales of America, of helping a slave escape to freedom, of stabbing a man who tried to rob her and a friend, and of stowing away on the *Elizabeth*.

* * * * *

· JULES ·

Lantern in hand, Jules peered out through the kitchen door to find Robert Purvis. "Is this visit good news or bad news?" he asked as he extended his hand to pull Purvis into the kitchen.

Purvis resisted the pull and instead tugged Jules down into the backyard. "Little of both, I'm afraid." Purvis turned, revealing a man and an obviously pregnant woman.

As was long-established practice, stationmasters and conductors on the Underground Railroad did not use their names when in the presence of self-emancipators. Jules turned to Robert. "You told me I would be relieved of these responsibilities while I'm involved in my new project."

Behind him, Maddie spoke from the kitchen door. "Husband, it's below freezing out there. Quit fussing and bring those people in. You know you're going to do it anyway."

* * * * *

Jules, Maddie, Purvis, and the two self-emancipators, whose freedom names were Homer and Coffey, sat at the kitchen table. The couple had been on the run from Virginia for four weeks. They ate bread and sipped steaming mugs of a stew that Maddie had thrown together by heating a pan of milk, butter, and oysters.

"The tempo on the Underground Railroad has picked up considerably since New Year's," said Purvis. "I have no more room, nor does any other stationmaster I know of."

Jules was mildly irritated that he had to deal with these people. He had intended to spend the evening figuring out how to find and hire—and train, if need be—enough craftsmen to stay on track at Pennsylvania Hall. "What's going on?" he asked, but without much interest.

"The depression is what's going on. The price of cotton in New Orleans is down to seven cents a pound. No one in the South is buying slaves except in the Texas Republic. Meanwhile, slaveholders just below the Mason-Dixon Line have checked their ledger books and done their calculating. They can't afford to feed their chattel. So, our enslaved brethren are being either slowly starved or loaded aboard ships to Galveston. With nothing to lose, many of our people run away. Those that succeed find us."

Jules turned his attention to Homer. "We will outfit you with new clothing and keep you moving north."

"Husband, no we won't," interjected Maddie. "Look at this woman. She is ready to give birth at any moment."

To validate Maddie's words, the exhausted Coffey, her hands wrapped around her mug of stew, merely stared vacantly at her mug and nodded.

"Wife, these people have to stay ahead of the slave catchers. Besides, neither one of us has time to care for them."

Purvis halted the disagreement by holding up his hand. "My friend, ask Homer what he did in Virginia."

The way Purvis framed his directive got Jules's attention. "What did you do when you were enslaved, Homer?"

"Master brought me to Loudoun County to see after Oak Hill when he bought it."

"See after it?"

"The president hadn't lived there for a couple of years, so it needed some work."

"The president. What president?"

"President Monroe."

"Oak Hill was President Monroe's home?"

Homer nodded.

"And what did you do to take care of it?"

"I'm a carpenter. It needed a lot of fixing."

"Are you any good?"

"From what I could see, I was the best carpenter in Loudoun County."

TUESDAY, JANUARY 16
(JANUARY 4 O.S.)

· RIAN ·

This morning, Gospodin Litke had seemed less interested in teaching them than usual. *The world is your classroom!* he had told Rian and Kostya. *Make your own adventures and be back here by one o'clock.*

The fifteen-mile-long *St. Petersburg to Tsarskoye Selo Railroad* was the only railroad in Russia. It had been operating for two months. The youngsters walked to the train station on Zagorodny Prospekt to examine the steam locomotives, which only operated on Sundays. The other six days, the train to Tsarskoye Selo was pulled by a horse.

Most times Rian and the grand duke spoke Russian to one another, but when Rian got stuck, she sprinkled her sentences with French, German, or English, as the grand duke was being tutored in all three.

"I see this engine was built by Robert Stephenson in Great Britain," Rian told the grand duke, proud that she was able to convey most of the sentence in Russian. "That company supplied a few locomotives to America before we started building our own. The English engines are more temperamental than the ones we build in America. That's why Count Sheremetev asked my uncle to come to Russia. Russia needs locomotives that are ruggedly built, like the ones in America."

"Which is more important," asked Kostya, who apparently had no interest in locomotives, "to have smart men work for you or loyal ones?"

Rian was a little disappointed that the grand duke wasn't interested in her lecture about locomotives. "What are you talking about?"

"My father asked my brother this question at the dinner table last night. What do you think?"

Rian had never thought of such a question before. "I'd go with smart. What about you?"

"Definitely smart. Sasha said 'loyal.' But he only tells Father what he thinks he wants to hear. I don't think that is right."

"How do you know he does that?"

"I heard Sasha talking with my Aunt Elena. There's a commission studying whether Father should free the serfs. Sasha told my aunt he hoped the commission would say that freeing the serfs was a good thing. My aunt agreed with him. Then at dinner, Father said his commission reported that freeing the serfs was a bad idea. He asked Sasha what he thought. I could tell Sasha didn't know what to say, so he said what he thought Father wanted to hear. He said the serfs are happier the way they are."

"Did you say anything?"

"I did. I said I thought they should be freed. Father said he hadn't asked me, and I was too young to have an opinion."

"I think you were right."

"Right about the serfs, or right to say it to Father?"

"Both."

* * * * *

Rian and Kostya returned to the Anichkov Palace to find that Grand Duchess Alexandra Nikolaevna wasn't feeling well and had returned to the imperial apartments. They joined Olga at her table, but shortly thereafter, the grand duke was called to his cello lesson. Then Gospodin Litke rose to leave the room. He turned at the door and told Rian and Olga to attend to their reading assignments until he returned. Madame Parshakov sat in the corner, ever vigilant for an errant touch.

As soon as Litke left the room, Grand Duchess Olga Nikolaevna opened the drawer to her table and pulled out some papers. She read studiously for ten minutes before speaking to Rian, who was sitting across the table from her. "Do the women of genteel society in your Philadelphia wear pants?"

Rian welcomed the interruption because it allowed her to stop concentrating on her reading. "Only one that I know of."

"Do you know her?" Olga asked.

That got close to home pretty quickly. Careful, Eena. "Pretty well."

"Does she ride horses like a man?"

Rian smiled to herself, but the smile escaped and made itself known to Olga. "Yes, she does. Why do you ask?"

"My great-grandmother rode a horse like a man. She even wore men's clothing."

"Who was your great-grandmother?"

"Catherine the Great, of course. You really aren't very well educated, are you?"

Back when Sheremetev was speaking to Rian, he tried to teach her about the Romanov dynasty. He had made a chart of Grand Duke Konstantin's ancestors that went all the way back to the 1600s. Rian remembered that Catherine the Great had expanded the Russian Empire significantly, but few other details. *I should have paid closer attention.* She shut her eyes and pictured Catherine II's position two rungs down from Peter the Great. "Oh, I didn't know which of your great-grandmothers you were talking about. I know all about Catherine the Great. She was Peter the Great's granddaughter."

"You're so stupid. She wasn't his granddaughter. She married his grandson, Peter III. She was a German princess from Prussia."

"That's what I meant."

"She was a great leader. My great-grandfather Peter III was a weak leader, so she wrested the throne from him. She controlled the men around her by force of will. I think all women should have that right. I think women are smarter than men anyway."

"I agree with you."

"You do?"

"Certainly."

Madame Parshakov harrumphed, indicating there was too much talking and not enough reading going on.

Grand Duchess Olga lowered her voice. "Prince Volkonsky doesn't. He thinks women are stupid. He thinks the only thing my sisters and I are good for is to marry off to some German prince. I hate him."

Rian thought it would be indiscreet to acknowledge their mutual dislike of the Minister of the Imperial Court. "How do you know all this about your great-grandmother? I didn't know these things."

Olga lifted her papers slightly off her desk. "It's all here," she whispered. "In her memoir."

"Where did you get that?"

Olga surreptitiously pointed toward a stack of papers-of-state by the wall. "From over there. All those files were brought here willy-nilly the day after the palace burned. There are whole rooms filled with nothing but papers. I think some of them were supposed to be locked back up, but things got so confused that they didn't get put into the vault. Father is usually so organized, but since the fire everything has been a jumble. I think it drives him crazy."

"Is your great-grandmother's memoir that important? That it has to be locked up?"

"I don't know, it's mostly in French. Can you read French as well as you speak it?"

"I think so."

"Could you help me translate it?"

"Sure, if I have time."

"You can't tell Sasha or Kostya. They would tell Papa." Olga read her book for a few moments, then said, "You speak Russian like a peasant."

* * * * *

· JULES ·

Otto stopped writing when Jules entered the office of Krieger Coach. "*Du siehst scheiße aus* [You look like shit]."

Jules slumped down heavily in his chair. "You try running two and a half operations, see how you look after a week."

"Well, I am grateful every time you walk in the door. I know it is hard for you to interrupt your day to keep things running smoothly here."

"I think our Krieger Coach arrangement is working out. Ernst seems to be doing well here in the shop with a little bit of hand-holding from me. And it's only until May. Then I return to my old schedule."

"How are things going at Pennsylvania Hall?"

"We are bumping along. I've hired a dozen men and one girl. Some experienced, some not, some Black, some white. No fights yet."

"How is the young girl doing?"

"She's a bit like Rian. Fearless. Game to try anything. Doesn't let the men push her around any, either Black or white. They can be pretty hard on her."

"Where did you find her?"

"She is a friend of Grace's. She's a quick learner."

Otto signed a letter, blotted it, and pushed it aside. "We have all the materials for your furnace across the alley. We will fabricate the parts in the shop, but the final assembly will have to occur in the basement of Pennsylvania Hall. I must say, this would have been a lot easier if we had been able to deliver it before the first floor was laid. Block out the first week in February for us. Be prepared. We may have to tear out some flooring to get it into the basement."

"How will you rivet it together without a steam riveter?"

"We will install a temporary forge in the basement. Vent it through the chimney. Heat the rivets and hammer them into place the way Adrian used to do it in the old shop."

Jules shook his head. "I wish they'd asked me to take over this job a lot earlier. I could have foreseen this kind of problem. I set the project back a week in order to buy two weeks of drying time down the road."

"Do you still need more people?"

"Seems like half the city's unemployed, but no one will work with us. Same goes for the Shelter for Colored Orphans, I'm told. I need at least ten more, whatever their skills. I'll take any color. At this point any sex."

"How is Maddie doing as the temporary boss of Freeman Hydraulics?"

"Taking to it like a duck to water. I get home after dinner, sometimes even after the kids have gone to bed. She talks about her day. I talk about mine. She's had a busy week. Bunch of inquiries have come in from New York. I assume because the Five Points boys are showing off that pump you delivered. Like you said, the only ones who seem to be doing well in this depression are the criminals."

"Well, I am no longer sure about that. I had lunch with the president of the *Philadelphia & Columbia Railroad* this afternoon. Remember the rail that we replaced up to the top of the Belmont Incline?"

"Vaguely. I never paid much attention to Krieger Rail's side of the business."

"Last May, the *Philadelphia & Columbia* replaced both tracks to the top of the incline with Krieger Rail. It was an experiment. Less than a mile. They wanted to see how it did. Well, apparently they liked what they saw. They want to replace the rest of their strap metal and wood rail with our T-stock."

Jules did a quick calculation. "That's almost 320 miles worth of rail. Quite a coup. Did he bargain with you?"

"Yes and no. They're paying full price, but a quarter of the payment is in *P&C* stock."

"Are you sure that's a good idea?"

"It's a gamble, I suppose, but if the gamble works, I will become a rich man."

"What did Aaron Bassinger say about it? He's the Krieger Rail president."

"Aaron didn't like the deal. He and his shareholders are taking the cash. I am taking the stock."

"Your brother wouldn't approve of this, Otto. He would have held out for cash."

"Jules, we're in a depression. This is a way all the railroads have to operate in order to expand and modernize."

"You should write to Adrian and tell him about this."

"Oh, I will. But right now, hopefully Adrian is making us rich in Russia and making sure my daughter stays out of trouble."

THURSDAY, JANUARY 18
(JANUARY 6 O.S.)

· RIAN ·

We really shouldn't be doing this, Rian said to herself.

Grand Duke Konstantin had been called to his cello lesson. Without Konstantin to attend to, Gospodin Litke stepped out of the classroom. Once again, he had left Olga and Rian to study by themselves under the silent scrutiny of Madame Parshakov. The door had no more than closed when Olga withdrew Catherine the Great's memoir from the library table drawer and unwrapped its brown paper covering.

The farther they plowed through the French manuscript—Rian doing the bulk of translating from French to Russian—the more uncomfortable Rian became. "Grand Duchess Olga Nikolaevna, we should stop reading this. It is none of our business."

"I think you don't like the fact that Catherine was a strong woman who made men do what she wanted them to do."

"No, that's not it at all. Catherine is writing about some things that she wants to be kept secret."

"How do you know?"

Rian retrieved the heavy brown paper wrapping. "Here, this passage says, 'To his Imperial Highness, Tsarevich and Grand Duke Paul Petrovich, my beloved son.' Here's his signature. That means that your grandfather read this after Catherine died and still felt it should be kept secret. You said yourself, these papers were locked up before the Winter Palace burned."

"No, I want to read this. You know French so much better than I do. I can't do this without you. You will help me translate."

The pressure to comply and Rian's own curiosity got the better of her. With Rian doing the bulk of the work, they continued translating.

They read about Catherine's childhood as Princess Sophie in the Kingdom of Prussia.

Mere pages later, Catherine described her arranged marriage at age sixteen to Grand Duke Peter Romanov, an immature boy one year older than she who still played with toy soldiers and treated her with indifference. "She was only a year older than I am now," commented the grand duchess.

They slogged through the unhappy first years of their marriage and her growing awareness that her husband was a feckless, inept, erratic drunkard. On one occasion Peter executed a rat that had the temerity to eat two of the miniature papier-mâché soldiers he had placed on guard in front of a tabletop fortress in a room off his bedroom. He hung the rat for three days as an example to other rats. "Peter was my great-grandfather. I don't think I would have liked him," said Olga. "He wasn't the Tsar yet. Catherine stood up to him. She was so young, but she was strong even then. Stronger than he was."

They read about the frequent rebukes of her mother-in-law, Empress Elizabeth, who chastised Catherine for not bearing an heir to the Romanov throne. "Empress Elizabeth says Catherine didn't conceive because she rode horses like a man," observed Olga. "But this memoir says they have been married for six years and they have not yet shared a bed."

They learned about Catherine's dalliance with the dashing chamberlain Sergei Saltykov, who told her he loved her passionately. "I don't blame her for being attracted to him. My great-grandfather was a terrible person. He ignored her. He had affairs with other women. I would have given myself to Saltykov."

They read about the increasing pressure from the empress to produce an heir. Olga became indignant. "Catherine should bed Saltykov. He should be the father of her child, not the dimwitted Peter."

Olga despaired over Catherine's continued rejection by Peter, then Catherine's pregnancy and the birth of Paul, the future Tsar of All the Russias. "She did it. I am so happy. The doltish Peter is not my real great-grandfather. I am the descendant of Catherine the Great and her great love, the handsome army officer Sergei Saltykov!"

Rian sat back to regard the immature, sheltered, romantic Olga. *What this story means to you is that Catherine the Great returned the love of the man who loved her, even though he was not her husband. She did what she needed to do to bring an heir to the Romanov throne. But Olga, you have missed the most important part of this memoir. Paul—your grandfather—was Sergei Saltykov's son, not Peter III's. Your grandfather was not a Romanov.*

Rian surreptitiously turned over the sturdy brown paper which had held Catherine's memoir. She again read the words: "To his Imperial Highness, Tsarevich and Grand Duke Paul Petrovich, my beloved son." Next to that was Paul's signature and the date: 13/11/1796.

Beneath that: **Alexander Romanov 20/03/1801.**

Paul's oldest son, thought Rian.

And beneath that: **Nicholas Romanov 19/1/26.**

Alexander's younger brother who assumed the throne when Alexander died— the current Tsar, and Olga's father. My God, they all signed it. Every Tsar since Catherine has known the same secret: There is not a drop of Romanov blood in the Romanov dynasty.

* * * * *

· JULES ·

It had been an eventful week in the Freeman home. Coffey had given birth to a healthy baby boy in the girls' bedroom upstairs. Maddie had forged new papers for Homer and Coffey stating that Homer had purchased the couple's freedom in 1835. With 150 miles between them and their enslaver, the couple had decided to remain in Philadelphia rather than keep on running. Homer had agreed to start work at Pennsylvania Hall as soon as Coffey was able to stay at the Freeman house by herself. Using the resources of the Philadelphia Vigilant Committee, both had been outfitted with two sets of clothing, including a beaver hat for Homer.

On Homer's first day of work, he and Jules walked to Pennsylvania Hall before sunrise. Jules loaned Homer his tools for the morning and kept one eye on him as he installed lath under the Gallery in the Grand Saloon. What Jules observed was the efficient, precise work of a skilled artisan. By midmorning, he had seen enough, and he and Homer left Pennsylvania Hall to purchase new tools for Homer.

It was the first time the self-emancipator had been out on the streets of Philadelphia during daylight. White men and women, singles and couples, and gaggles of street urchins bustled along the brick sidewalks. A white scissors grinder, his cart parked at the side of Filbert Street, glanced up from his wheel and gave Jules and Homer more than a passing glance as they walked by. Homer looked anxiously behind him.

He's skittish. Same as I was when I first arrived here eighteen years ago. "Relax, Homer. Maddie did a great job of forging your emancipation paper. You'll be fine as long as you stop walking like some yokel who's never been in a city before."

"Oh, I did jobs in Washington a bunch of times. It's smaller, but it's still a city. But white folks look at me different here."

"How do you mean?"

"In Washington, they didn't see me. If I was walking along a sidewalk and met a white couple coming the other way, I stepped out into the street. They paid no more attention to me than they would a stray dog. Here, people look at me all right, and what they see is a dog that could be rabid."

"They're not all that way." A gentleman and lady approached them arm in arm. "Okay, here comes a good opportunity. When we meet this couple, do not step out into the street. Walk ahead of me. We have as much a right to be here as they do. Give the lady a polite tip of your hat and give them both a smile as we pass by, but look mostly at him."

The couple walked past Jules and Homer. The man acknowledged each tip of the hat with a polite nod.

Homer looked behind him as the couple continued down the street. "Sweet Jesus, I would have been throttled in Washington if I had tried that."

"There may be times that you'll find it's still wiser to walk out into the street. Your instincts will get sharper with time."

"Right now, my instincts are telling me I'm walking on thin ice."

* * * * *

A bell tinkled as they entered the sales room of Rowland Saw Works, prompting a man to come out of an office and take his place behind the counter. "Jules Freeman," he said with a smile, "back again, I see."

Jules gestured to the man behind the counter. "Mr. William Rowland, I'd like you to meet Mr. Homer Good. This is his first day on the job, and he needs some new tools."

Rowland shook Homer's hand. "Glad to meet you, Mr. Good. Construction at Pennsylvania Hall's been a real boon to my business lately. I've sold a dozen saws since Jules took over the job." He turned his attention to Jules. "How is it going, teaching carpentry to your new hires, Jules?"

Jules smiled. "Some are taking to it, some are struggling. A lot of banged-up thumbs and the swearing that goes along with them."

Rowland turned his attention to Homer. "And how can we help Mr. Good here?"

Homer surveyed an array of saws hanging from pegs on the wall behind the counter. "I'd like to get a feel for that crosscut saw right behind you."

Rowland raised one eyebrow. "Very discerning." He turned and pulled the handsaw off the wall. "Twenty-four-inch blade, seven teeth per inch. This is a tool for a skilled craftsman, not like the apprentice saws I've sold to Jules up until now."

Homer accepted the saw, turned it upside down, and stared down the length of the blade to eye the set of the teeth. Satisfied, he said, "And the 24-inch ripsaw over your right shoulder."

"Whoa-ho! Congratulations, Jules, you finally found a man you don't have to train!" Rowland pivoted to pull the saw off its peg, hesitated, then turned back to his two customers. His tone became more conspiratorial. "When did you arrive in town, Mr. Good?"

"Last week."

"I figured. Where did you start running from?"

Homer stiffened. "I'm not running from anyplace. I bought my freedom. I've got the papers to prove it."

Rowland turned to Jules. "Jules, no skilled carpenter would move to a new community and leave his tools behind unless he had to travel light. Mr. Good, I shouldn't sell you these saws. There are white men on that crew at Pennsylvania Hall who would know right away you are a fugitive slave."

Jules sensed Homer's discomfort. *Easy, Homer. You're going to have to get used to this if you are going to stay in Philadelphia.*

Rowland put up his hand. "However, one of my best friends—a longtime carpenter—recently died. His wife stopped in two weeks ago and sold me his entire toolbox: Level, hammer, squares, a couple of screwdrivers, brace and bits, and two saws made in this shop just a few years ago. All well cared for but properly nicked up. I'll sell you the entire kit for less than the cost of the two saws you were interested in."

* * * * *

"See?" Jules said as they left the store with Homer's new toolbox. "Not everyone is a threat here."

Homer turned again to see if anyone was stalking him from behind. "What percentage?"

"That's a good question. Allies like William Rowland? Five percent. Those who don't much care one way or another as long as you don't do something to ire them? Eighty percent. The rest would just as soon kill you as look at you."

"That's fifteen percent. That doesn't make the ice feel any safer right now. What about the guy with the weepy eye?"

"Emil? I'd put him strongly in the fifteen percent. I haven't had any trouble with him yet, but I think you'd best keep your distance."

"I suspect I can fix his eye. There's probably something in there. A speck of wood or something."

"How do you know that?"

"When you live fifteen miles from the nearest doctor, you learn to do a little bit of everything. Sewing up cuts and taking out slivers and getting shit out of the slaves' eyes sort of came natural to me. I even worked on master's family a couple of times when the doctor couldn't come."

"Emil's eye. How would you fix that?"

"When you were a kid, did you ever turn your eyelid inside out?"

"Uh, no. But one of the boys I knew used to do it with both his eyelids and then chase the girls around. He was never right in the head, though."

"Well, one way or another, I'd have to turn Emil's eyelid inside out."

"Like I said, I think you better stay away from that one."

* * * * *

When Jules and Homer were about to cross Sassafras Street, Jules spotted Hugh Callaghan standing in front of Pennsylvania Hall with his hands in his pockets. It appeared that Hugh had been watching them for a while.

"Okay, as happy as I was to have you meet William Rowland, I'm not happy with this gump. Hugh Callaghan is the head of an Irish hose company and a gangster. He's no friend of the Black man. Keep sharp."

"Sweet Jesus," said Homer. He reflexively checked behind him.

Jules and Homer halted when they got to Hugh.

Hugh paid no attention to Homer. "I heard you were the new strawboss up here. Came to see how you were doing."

Jules gave a flick of his thumb to Homer. "You should get back to work. I'll be there in a minute."

Hugh watched Homer as he ascended the three steps to the Hall's portico and entered the building. "Jules, you and I had an unwritten agreement. I don't harass you in your evening activities as long as you keep your African brethren moving north. That yokel acts like he just arrived yesterday."

As was often necessary when one consorted with self-emancipators, Jules layered one lie neatly on top of another. "That yokel is my half-brother. He bought his freedom three years ago in Washington. He's living with Maddie and me now."

"And how long has he been here?"

"He arrived last week."

"Is he going to stay very long?"

"Not sure. He just started. He's a master carpenter. We'll see what happens once the Hall is done."

"When is that?"

"The dedication is set for May 14."

"Hmm," said Hugh. His gaze rose up three stories to the triangular pediment that sheltered the portico. He read the words: Pennsylvania Hall. "How long do you think your Temple of Liberty is going to last?"

* * * * *

When Jules entered the foyer of Pennsylvania Hall, he found Homer digging a sliver out of a white worker's hand with a pair of tweezers. He never asked where the tweezers came from, but assumed they must have been in the toolbox they had purchased half an hour ago.

* * * * *

• LOGAN •

Logan leaned into the rock in the vacant lot, the blanket draped over his shoulders. *Come on, Martha. Please come. Please, please, please.*

After half an hour of waiting in the cold and dark, Logan heard Martha's footsteps approaching. He held out the blanket and she snuggled in.

"Where were you last night?" she whispered.

"We had to put out a fire. No Name got there first, so we'll get the bounty from the insurance company. It was a good night, but it was midnight before we were done. How late did you stay here?"

"An hour. I didn't have a blanket. I froze."

"I'm sorry. We need a better system. I wasn't even sure you were going to come tonight."

Martha put her arm around Logan's waist. "We need someplace warm to meet."

After a long pause, Logan said, "There's a grog shop on Catherine Street that serves both your people and mine."

"But I bet they don't serve women."

Logan shook his head. "Pff, not women like you. Prostitutes, maybe."

A gust of wind whipped by them, forcing Martha to bury her head into Logan's chest. "At least someplace we can get out of this wind."

"We can't go to my place. Me mum wouldn't like it, but worse, me brothers and sisters would blab it all over the place. Then there'd be hell to pay."

"I've got an idea. My parents' factory is seven blocks from here. The last one of us out for the night always banks the fire before we leave. It will be a lot warmer there than here, and no wind."

· RIAN ·

Grand Duchess Alexandra was still sick. When Kostya was in the classroom, Rian read *Oliver Twist* to Olga and him. Rian frequently joined Kostya for his music lesson, but as he was learning the cello and she played the violin, sometimes his tutor told her not to come. In those instances, Rian often found herself reading Catherine the Great's memoir to Olga under the watchful eye of Madame Parshakov.

Catherine was twenty-nine when the memoir ended in 1858. Her mother-in-law, Elizabeth I, still reigned as Tsarina. Catherine's husband, Grand Duke Peter, showed little interest in taking over the "family business." Catherine increasingly engaged in court intrigue.

Olga turned the last page of the manuscript and sighed. "It is okay. I know how the story goes from here. Tsarina Elizabeth dies. Peter rules for six months. He is as inept a Tsar as he is a husband. Catherine shoves him aside and throws him into prison. That is where he dies."

"Wow, and I thought my family was rough," Rian muttered, although she didn't think Olga was paying attention.

"Rian, I think I have a problem."

"What?"

"The real father of my grandfather was Sergei Saltykov. He was chamberlain—a soldier—not even royalty. That means my grandfather was not a real Romanov. That means my father isn't, so neither am I."

Rian turned in her chair and faced Olga. "I know."

"You figured that out?"

"Right away."

"Do you think less of me, knowing that I am not a Romanov?"

"You are the great-granddaughter of Catherine the Great. Isn't that more important? She ruled Russia for thirty years. She bent Russia and all her rivals to her will. She was a better Romanov than her husband."

"You didn't answer my question."

Rian reached toward Olga, but Madame Parshakov loudly cleared her throat well before any touch occurred. "No, I don't think less of you. I like you."

"You do?"

"Of course. At first you were a little bossy, but now we have shared secrets. I like being with you."

"Rian, I have never spent this much time with a boy. Not in my entire life." Olga hesitated for a few moments. "Of course, you are a lot younger than I am, but you have seen much more of the world than I have. America. London. Even more of St. Petersburg. I don't want you to go back to America. I want you to stay in St. Petersburg forever."

"I want to stay in St. Petersburg, too. I enjoy being tutored by Gospodin Litke. I love my sessions with you and Kost . . . er, the grand duke."

Olga laughed. "It's okay. You can call him Kostya. I have changed my mind about that. You have grown on me. I believe I like you a lot." Grand Duchess Olga Nikolaevna hesitated. She looked down at Catherine the Great's memoir. "I may even be in love with you."

A warning rang in Rian's ears as insistent as the bell of a fire pump racing down the street toward a fire.

"But Rian, you haven't shared any secrets with me. You know the most amazing secret I could ever have, and I know none of yours."

Stop this, Eena. Stop this right now. "I don't have any secrets."

"You must have something. . . ."

Rian was still reeling from Olga's "I may even be in love with you" declaration. *Eena, you've got to turn this around right now. Put on the brake.* "Well, I could tell you one thing."

"Yes, tell me your secret. Tell me anything."

"I stabbed a man once."

"You did? When? Was it here in Russia?"

"No, it was last year, in Philadelphia. The largest battleship in the world was about to be launched from the Navy Yard. A hundred thousand people walked to the docks to watch. A friend and I were climbing up stairs to get to the roof of a warehouse to get a good view and we were attacked by a pair of ruffians. I stabbed one of them in the leg with my jackknife as hard as I could. We held them off until help came."

Olga gazed back at Rian. "That is an excellent secret. You are a hero. I hope that someday I will be able to do something heroic. Now I know I am in love with you."

Brake! Brake! Put on the brake! "And I love being with you and Kostya."

The grand duchess noted Rian's response. She briefly shut her eyes. She looked back down at the manuscript.

I've hurt her.

Olga straightened in her chair. "Rian, you can never share the story of my grandfather's real father with anyone."

Rian spit on her hand and held it out to Olga. "In America, if you spit on your hand and shake hands, it is a solemn oath. A promise that can't be broken."

Olga was about to shake Rian's hand when the eagle-eyed Madame Parshakov bolted out of her chair and screeched, *"Nyet! Nyet! Nyet!"*

N° 131. Les montagnes de glace sur la place de l'Amirauté, pendant les fêtes de Pâques, à Saint-Pétersbourg. Par M. V. Timm.

St. Petersburg Ice Slide (Alamy Stock Photo)

SUNDAY, JANUARY 21
(JANUARY 9 O.S.)

· RIAN ·

What are you doing here, Eena? This is more of what the count told you not to do.

The Tsar and Tsarina, their five eldest children, and Rian were attending the first winter carnival of the season. The temperature was well below freezing, but Rian's Imperial Horse Guard greatcoat kept her warm. The sun, low in the sky, was shining on this cloudless day.

The group strolled past jugglers, tumblers, games of chance, and open-air theaters with short skits. Adults and children flocked to a merry-go-round type of contraption called the *Flying Horses*. They mounted carved wooden horses suspended by chains from the roof of the merry-go-round. As the contraption rotated ever faster, the horses flew out higher and higher, thus giving the riders the sensation of flying.

And right now, Rian and Olga were about to slide down a six-story-tall ice ramp on a two-person sledge, a primitive sled that wasn't much more than two wooden runners and a rope to hang on to.

For ten minutes, the Imperial Family had climbed the stairs, sledges in hand, along with a stream of other carnival-goers. The Tsar and Tsarina were clearly enjoying this casual interaction with commoners. Perhaps disarmed by Rian's childish appearance when wearing her greatcoat, they even relaxed the strict "no touching" regimen maintained when under the eye of Madame Parshakov.

As the royal party rose up each flight of stairs, Olga had manipulated the pairings so that she and Rian were going to occupy the same sledge.

As usual, Olga assumed an air of authority, as if she were out in the world much more often than she actually was. "This carnival is held in honor of the Holy Great Martyr Tatiana. Russian carnivals always honor some saint or martyr, but Father says he likes them because they keep the people happy. I attend every carnival of the winter. The ice mountain is my favorite ride. I do it at least once each carnival, but more often two or three times. Catherine the Great was the first in the family to go down an ice mountain. I think it is only fitting that we continue the tradition. Father usually assigns one of the Imperial Guards to drive my sled, but I convinced him you could do it. After all, you used to drive a team of horses back when you were a coachman."

Rian didn't respond. She could tell that Catherine the Great's memoir had affected Olga. She had started to think for herself and form her own opinions. She was becoming even more bossy. And willful. And flirty.

The farther up the stairs they climbed, the more apprehensive Rian became, but now not because of Olga's flirty behavior. This tower was very tall and the angle that they were about to drop was incredibly steep. Every once in a while an attendant would throw a bucket of water on the incline, and the water would freeze almost immediately. Rian leaned over the railing and watched sleds coming at them from the opposite tower. They were traveling faster than any train she had ever seen. *Maybe you shouldn't be driving the grand duchess's sled, Eena.*

Rian and Olga were the first of the royal party to get to the top of the tower.

A boy about Rian's age, shivering in his threadbare coat, greeted them. "Ever done this before?"

"Not yet," responded Rian.

"Well, it's easy. You sit in front. Put your feet up on this bar and hang on to the rope to steady yourself. Your lady friend"—the boy obviously had no idea he was referring to Grand Duchess Olga Nikolaevna Romanov—"straddles you on either side and puts her arms around your waist. I push you over the edge and you're off. You steer by leaning, but you can't really steer very much. Don't try to stop by digging your boots in. You'll go ass over teakettle."

Rian did as she was told. Olga climbed on behind. The boy shoved the sledge with a little more enthusiasm than Rian felt was necessary. Olga buried her head into Rian's shoulder and hung tight to her waist. They both screamed joyous screams.

* * * * *

Rian and Olga got separated from the rest of the royal party as they waited in line to climb the second tower.

Olga glanced back at her father and Kostya. "I hate my life."

"You do? Why?"

"My parents keep me cooped up in the palace. It is nothing but a huge, ornate cage that I am barely allowed to leave until I marry."

"Many people would love to live in the Anichkov Palace."

"But I never get to meet anyone. Not real people. Talk to real people. I want the life you have. You spend your day with Kostya and me, then you play durak with that serf in his home. You exercise horses with the Imperial Horse Guards in the Manege. You are living life as you wish with the people you wish. Peter the Great was like you. He hated life at court. He preferred to drink with regular officers in his Army. You are the only real person I know."

MONDAY, JANUARY 22

· JULES ·

The late afternoon sun was undetectable through thick winter clouds that made it feel like dusk. Jules walked up the steps of the unfinished Shelter for Colored Orphans with mixed emotions.

On one hand, it was impressive that a dedicated band of women, including Lucretia Mott and his own dear wife, Maddie, had been able to raise funds—during a depression, no less—for two massive building projects at the same time. Pennsylvania Hall and the Shelter had both been financed through the tireless efforts of a small band of reform-minded women.

On the other hand, Jules found himself constantly competing with the Shelter for men and materials. The Shelter project had progressed dramatically since his unsuccessful mission two weeks ago. It was under roof. A dozen workers were installing windows and a couple of exterior doors. Jules wandered through first-floor rooms, which were studded out but unsheathed with lath. *We're three weeks ahead of him. This might just work.* He found contractor John Hunnecher in what Jules guessed would be a kitchen and dining area big enough to serve perhaps forty orphans.

Hunnecher turned his attention from a set of plans that had been placed on two wide boards atop a pair of sawhorses. "Mr. Freeman, I was just about to pay you a visit."

Jules took this as good news. "I hope you have reconsidered my proposal that we share workers."

"Indeed I have. I've lost three men in the past two days."

"Why?"

"I'm not sure. There's something going on along the Canadian border. Two of my crew—brothers—up and quit and left town the next day. Took another man along with them."

Jules didn't much care what was going on up in Canada. "Well, I figure my folks have another nine working days before our lath is completely installed. I won't need any nail bangers while the plasterers or the painters are working. I can send you nine master carpenters and a dozen folks with lesser skills to support them for about seven weeks. That will keep my men employed for a little while longer and will speed your job along. I hope you would return the favor when they finish with the lath, because right about that time I'll need as many finish carpenters as I can get."

"The guy who used to be the general contractor—Edes. How has he done for you?"

"I meet with him every morning. He has a good eye. Keeps the men in line. He'll be fine as long as you lay out the day's tasks with him."

"Those folks who are helping the carpenters . . . I hear you're hiring Negroes like yourself."

Jules stiffened. "Eight of them are Black. Willing workers. Some of them are as skilled as the white carpenters, but the unions won't accept them."

"Any Irish?"

"One. And since I'm getting your drift, one of the Negroes is also a young woman."

"I'm afraid my men won't work with the Negroes, and I won't hire your Irishman. I'll take all the whites, no matter what their skill, as long as they're able to do an honest day's work."

"And when the time comes, when the plasterers arrive, you'll send your carpentry crew down to me?"

"When the plaster and painting crews are here, I'll have no need for carpenters. I'll be happy to do that, but like I said, a lot of them won't be interested in taking orders from you, much less working with members of your race."

Disappointed but not surprised, Jules turned to leave.

"Hey Mr. Freeman," Hunnecher called before Jules reached the hallway, "who's building those Doric columns for you?"

Jules turned. "E.E. Flury & Sons. I'm expecting delivery this week."

"I suggest you go check up on them. They went out of business last Friday."

* * * * *

As Jules walked back to Pennsylvania Hall, he noted the sky was darkening further. *Snowstorm's coming,* he thought to himself, but that wasn't his biggest worry. *If E.E. Flury is truly out of business, I'm screwed. There's not another factory in Philadelphia that can build columns. It will take too long to line up something in New York or Baltimore.*

He entered Pennsylvania Hall expecting to hear the sounds of sawing and hammering. Instead a chorus of "Ohhhhs!" echoed up from the basement.

What the . . . ? He walked down the corridor toward the basement door. He was greeted by two men who had just reached the top of the stairs. "Do not go down there," one of them said to Jules, but both men were laughing, so Jules merely became more curious. He picked his way downward, past men who were sitting on the stairs to get a better view of what was going on below.

"That is disgusting," one of the men uttered, but once again, the tone was jovial.

A ring of men had arrayed themselves in the middle of the basement, all facing inward and focused on . . . something.

The large convex mirror meant to be installed in the ceiling of the Grand Saloon had been stored in the basement since its delivery a week ago. Two men had removed it from its crate and were holding it high above them. Three other workers held lanterns in front of the mirror.

"No," Jules heard Homer say in a commanding voice. "Look down."

Jules shouldered his way into the circle of men.

Weepy-eyed Emil was lying atop two scaffolding boards that had been placed atop barrels. Homer was standing over him, using light from lanterns and mirror to aid his work. Next to Homer, lanky Randy Buck agitated the crowd by brandishing a brass syringe above his head.

Jules peered over Randy's shoulder. Homer had pulled Emil's eyelid up and inverted it over a looped piece of wire.

"I'm telling you, Homer, you mess up my eye and I'll kill you," said Emil. "You too, Randy."

"How can it be any more messed up than it already is?" responded Homer. "Get ready with the syringe, Randy."

Randy held the syringe aloft. Someone uttered, "Oh my God."

"Hurry up," said one of the men with the mirror. "This thing is heavy."

"Keep looking down at your feet like I told you," Homer said. "That will keep your eyelid in the peeled-back position." Then Homer lifted Emil's inside-out lid and exposed his entire eye.

"Ayeaow!" yelled Emil.

"Settle down. We're almost done. All right, Randy, shoot the water right into his eye. Empty the whole syringe."

Randy did as he was told. Water spurted.

"Ayeaow!" Emil yelled again.

Homer released Emil's eyelid from its tortured state, then picked up a half-inch sliver of wood that had washed from Emil's eye and onto his shirt.

Homer first showed it to the sputtering, blinking Emil, then held it aloft for the onlookers to see.

"Ohhh!!" screamed the crowd.

* * * * *

"Where did you get the syringe?" Jules asked as they walked home together that evening.

"The midwife had it in her bag when Coffey was having our baby. She loaned it to me."

THURSDAY, JANUARY 25
(JANUARY 13 O.S.)

· SEAMUS ·

Seamus Gallagher and Grand Duke Alexander, two years his junior, had just visited a vacant lot on the outskirts of St. Petersburg, a potential site for a locomotive factory. On the way back into town, Alexander had insisted that they eat their midday meal at a restaurant on Nevsky Prospekt. The two settled down to a warm dish of golubtsy—rolled cabbage leaves stuffed with beef and rice.

As the grand duke spoke English with a cultured British accent, Seamus was enjoying his day immensely. He put his napkin in his lap as the waiter served their meals. "That landowner seemed pretty eager to sell his property."

"I imagine he never thought he would ever come face-to-face with the future Tsar of All the Russias. After all, even in St. Petersburg, you don't meet a god all that often."

"A god. Is that what you are, Your Grace?" Despite his growing comfort with Alexander, Seamus adhered to strict protocol when addressing the grand duke. Sheremetev had warned Adrian not to call the grand duke by his given name, and certainly, never to use the familiar sobriquet *Sasha*.

Alexander cracked a wry smile. "To the peasants, at least half a god. To the nobility, probably not."

"Seems like a lot of pressure to me."

"I'm used to it by now. I was seven when my uncle died and my father became Tsar. During Father's coronation, 67,000 members of the Life Guard Regiment hailed me as I rode my Arabian to the Peter Palace."

"What do you think it will be like when you become Tsar?"

Alexander savored a bite of golubtsy while he pondered his response. "Hopefully, that will be a long time from now, but I think it will be different. Last year I toured the empire as part of my education. In Siberia, I encountered a village of exiles, mostly remnants of the Decembrist Revolt who were suffering terribly. It had been twelve years since they opposed my father when he assumed the throne. I wrote to Father and asked him to forgive them."

"What did he do?"

"He freed them from Siberia and reassigned them to the Caucasus. They are once again members of the Russian Army."

"At least they're not freezing their tails off. Congratulations. It sounds like your father listened to you."

Alexander shrugged. "That's what I thought at first, but now I'm not so sure. Russia is waging a bitter war against the tribes down there. The Chechens are brutal and our casualties are high. I now believe my father wanted to appear merciful, but in fact, he changed their fate from a joyless exile to likely death."

"Ouch."

"Your president, Mr. Van Buren—how is he doing?"

"He hasn't even been president for a year yet. Shortly after he took office, the American economy hit a rough patch. I don't think he's done much to improve things."

"Do you expect a revolution?"

"Not likely. More likely the people will vote him out of office and someone else will take his place."

"Ah, I have heard of your Great Experiment, leaving the fate of your country to the will of your common man. It sounds like you are not doing so well."

"It depends upon how you think about it. Right now, I would hazard that the common man isn't doing very well. But in Philadelphia, where I hail from, we have pipes that bring fresh water to every neighborhood and sewers that take our wastewater out of the city. We have gas lights on all our major street corners. We have railroad trains that leave stations daily, many of them using Krieger locomotives. Multiple times every day, they transport passengers and freight to the north, the west, and the south. America has laid a couple thousand miles of track in the last ten years. We've built canals to transport even more passengers and goods. I can travel from Philadelphia to Pittsburgh, a distance of over 300 miles—450 of your versts—in four days."

"If this is all true, it is quite impressive. To what do you attribute these many successes?"

Seamus stuffed down a twinge of anxiety. *What have you got yourself into, Boyo? You have no business being in this discussion. But when all else fails, give the grand duke a dose of good old Irish blarney.* "To many things. Plentiful resources. Access to markets. Entrepreneurship. Skilled labor that can move from job to job as they see fit."

"I was under the impression that your slave system prevents the free flow of labor."

"Slavery is mostly found in the South, although there are still remnants in the North. I have quite a few friends in Philadelphia who are working hard to bring all of it to an end."

"And how do you feel about it?"

Seamus knew he was addressing the man whose father controlled the lives of more than a million serfs. He also remembered Sheremetev's hopes that he could influence the future Tsar of All the Russias. He took a deep breath. "Your Grace, I don't think any man should have the right to own any other man."

Alexander moved some errant rice around his plate with his fork. "In Russia, the serfs belong to the land."

"Whoever owns the land controls the serfs, so what is the difference?"

The grand duke looked up from his plate. "Seamus, I have a request."

"And what is that?"

"When it is only the two of us and no other officials or family members are around, please call me Sasha."

* * * * *

· RIAN ·

Three weeks had passed since Rian, Adrian, Seamus, and the manservant Henry Sommes moved out of Count Sheremetev's palazzo. Their new home was a spacious apartment above a men's clothing store and a tobacco shop on Nevsky Prospekt.

It was the end of a long day. Rian left the cold of the Russian night behind her and climbed the stairs. She heard voices coming from the parlor as soon as she opened the door. *Count Sheremetev, Colonel Malkovich, Seamus, and Uncle Adrian. They're probably playing cards.* She lightened her steps and headed directly to her room.

Adrian called after her. "Rian, is that you? You're later than usual. Where have you been?"

Rats. She reversed direction and returned to the parlor door. "I had to exercise Frank and Wash."

"You always exercise the horses. What happened?"

"I left the Anichkov Palace later than usual."

"And why was that?"

Rian fidgeted, knowing that a storm was about to break over her head. "I ate dinner with the Imperial Family."

Sheremetev stood. "You stupid girl, this is exactly what you were instructed not to do."

Rian stood her ground. "It's kind of hard to say no to the Tsar, sir."

Adrian interjected himself into the conversation. "Count Sheremetev, could you please go a little easy on Rian? I'm sure she's doing the best she can."

Sheremetev wasn't interested in going easy on Rian. "Why were you invited to the Tsar's dinner table?"

"Grand Duke Konstantin and I drove a sleigh to Peterhof. The Tsar wanted to hear about our trip."

"What is Peterhof?" asked Adrian.

Sheremetev raised his hands to his head in obvious frustration. "It is a summer palace on the Gulf of Finland, built by Peter the Great. About thirty versts from here; twenty of your miles. That is a lot of ground to cover in one day. Who was with you?"

"No one. It was only the two of us."

Sheremetev stared at Rian for a long moment. "No guards. No tutor. Why did you go to Peterhof?"

"The grand duke wanted to show me his yacht."

"What are you talking about?" asked Adrian.

Rian turned to address her uncle. "Kostya's father gave him a yacht when he was eight. Last summer he sailed it by himself from Peterhof to Kronstadt and back and all over Neva Bay. He was nine. Kronstadt is seventeen miles from the palace. I could barely see it from the top floor."

Sheremetev tapped his foot. "Did the Tsar know about this expedition of yours before you left?"

"I think so. His tutor lets us do lots of things like that. The yacht is in drydock. Kostya showed me the yacht and then we explored the palace and came back."

"Forty miles for the horses in one day. Not a responsible decision for a former coachman to make," commented Sheremetev.

Rian shook her head. "They're Russian Dons. They have a lot of endurance. It was a troika—a team of three. Even so, we swapped them out halfway there so they could rest. The Tsar keeps a stable for that purpose, although I think the stablemaster was surprised to see us in the middle of the winter."

"Was anyone else with you when you dined *en famille* with the Tsar?"

"No, it was only us. But he had a meeting with General Benckendorff and Prince Volkonsky just before dinner. They don't like each other."

Sheremetev's shoulders sagged. "Benckendorff and Volkonsky. The head of the Secret Police and the Minister of the Imperial Court. I have heard enough. Adrian, apparently your niece is unable to follow orders or understand the gravity of her position." He turned his attention to Rian. "Little girl, you are like a moth circling a candle. I warn you; before long your wings are going to get burned. I will not be able to rescue you. In fact, your adventures may be our undoing—all of us. Come on, Malkovich. It is time for us to leave." Sheremetev and Malkovich exited the apartment. The count slammed the door behind him.

"I'm sorry, Uncle Adrian. I didn't want it to go like this."

Adrian gathered the playing cards off the table, neatened them, and placed them in a wooden box. "I suppose it was too much for us to ask that you minimize your involvement with the Imperial Family if the Tsar's whim dictates otherwise."

"I kind of feel sorry for them. Four weeks ago their house burned down. You should see the royal apartments. There is stuff piled everywhere. Sometimes I can hear the Tsar ranting about not being able to find documents that he needs."

"Yet Konstantin's education proceeds."

Rian nodded. "The Tsar wants him to become the head of the Russian Navy when he grows up. He's being trained for it. His tutor, Mr. Litke, he's kind of like *Vater* is with me. He lets Konstantin do a lot of things without much supervision. He says experience is the best teacher. That's why he lets him sail his yacht by himself during the summer."

"Ugh," said Adrian. He rose, walked to a settee, lay down, and covered his eyes with his arm, effectively taking himself out of the conversation.

Seamus, who had been silently sitting at the card table up until this time, asked, "The Tsar; he has no idea you are a girl?"

Rian shook her head. "Konstantin doesn't suspect either. A while back, you and I had a conversation. We didn't know if the Tsar is a good guy or a bad guy. I'm thinking he's a bad guy. Do you know that he doesn't know how many serfs he owns? It's over a million."

Seamus poured a splash of vodka into his glass. "He said that?"

"No, Konstantin told me that. But the Tsar did say at the dinner table that Poles and Jews are the cause of a lot of Russia's troubles. He hates all of them."

"Probably not a good thing to have the most powerful man in the world hate you."

Rian nodded.

"What about Volkonsky? Does he know you're a girl?"

Rian shook her head. "I hate him."

"What about General Benckendorff, the head of the Secret Police?"

"He scares me. He and Prince Volkonsky had a big argument. I could hear some of it from our classroom."

"What was it about?"

"I'm not sure. I think the general can talk to the Tsar without asking for the prince's permission first. The prince doesn't like that. I don't like either one of them. They talk about me in Russian and assume I don't understand what they are saying."

"Do you?"

"I get most of it. Benckendorff called me *novyy malen'kiy pitomets Tsarevicha*, the Tsarevich's little pet. Volkonsky thinks I'm a *komar*—a gnat. He's waiting for the *amerikantsy* to fail with the railroad project so good Russians can pick up the pieces."

"So one—the man who killed your friend Stepanov—thinks you are a gnat, and the other one thinks you are a pet. Do they meet with the Tsar very often?"

"Not together. Konstantin says they fight all the time."

"Well, apparently they agree on something. They don't like us. I wish the count hadn't left. He should hear this. Who else do you spend time with besides Konstantin?"

"His tutor. Mr. Litke teaches us French, German, and English. I'm better than the grand duke in all of them." She smiled. "Actually, I speak English better than Mr. Litke. Mostly, he teaches us naval science. It's all book learning right now, but after the ice breaks, our classroom will be on ships in the Baltic. Mr. Litke says that in a couple of years the grand duke will spend all summer on a ship. He'll start as if he was any other cadet."

Adrian, who had obviously been listening to the conversation from the couch, rose on his elbow. "Rian, you speak as if you are staying into the summer. I assure you: you are not. Who else do you spend time with?"

Rian wasn't surprised at her uncle's words. She sighed. "Kostya's music tutor. Kostya's learning the cello and I told the tutor I play the violin so now sometimes we practice together. He found me a better violin than the one I brought from home. He's a good instructor. I'm a lot better than I was when I left Philadelphia."

"Anyone else?"

"Sometimes with his sisters. It's different for them than it is for Konstantin. They're barely allowed out of the palace."

"What are they like?"

"Grand Duchess Alexandra—they call her Adini—she's a year younger than I am. She is very nice. She likes to sing."

"What about Olga, the older one?"

Rian fidgeted a bit and didn't answer.

"What's going on?"

"I told you that they don't let the grand duchesses out of the palace a lot. She's not even two years older than I am, but she already knows she's going to get married off to some German prince."

"So why did you hesitate?"

"She doesn't act her age. She seems to make excuses to interrupt our sessions. She's always ordering me around. She asks me questions about my life in America."

Rian stopped talking. Adrian noted her silence. "What?"

"I think I may have a problem."

"What is it? You already said no one suspects you're a girl."

"Except for her brothers, Olga doesn't have any boys in her life. None. I don't think she knows how to act around them."

"So why is that a problem?"

"I think she might be latching on to me because she thinks I'm a boy."

"Oh, no. Maybe it is a good thing that Sheremetev left. He certainly wouldn't want to hear this."

* * * * *

· JULES ·

Homer and Coffey had been living with Jules and Maddie for two weeks. Although Homer now felt safe enough to walk home by himself, on this occasion, Jules had asked him to stay after the other workers had left.

Two oil lamps were all that lit the Grand Saloon. Jules grabbed one, handed the other to Homer, and led him to one of the posts that supported the Gallery. "Ever built a pillar before?"

Homer nodded. "Remember I told you Oak Hill needed repairs when my old master bought the place? That's one of the things I had to do—replace the pillars. Why?"

"The outfit that was supposed to build our columns for us has gone out of business. I can't find anyone in Philadelphia to do the work, and it'll take too long to find a shop in New York or Baltimore."

Homer slowly pivoted 360 degrees, surveying pillars at the edges of the lamp light. "Can you find someone to mill and shape the pieces for us?"

"I could probably fit it in at Krieger Coach. I'll talk to my boss. We should be able to have all the milled wood you'll need here in a week."

"There's a lot of columns. I'll need some help."

"Who do you want?"

"Next best craftsman besides me on the whole crew is weepy-eyed Emil Harberger, except he ain't so weepy-eyed since I douched him out."

Jules shook his head. "When the lath work is finished here, Marcus Edes is taking all the white carpenters and journeymen to work at the Shelter for Colored Orphans."

"What're they going to be doing there?"

"Same thing. Installing lath ahead of the plastering crew."

"Then you should talk to Emil. He hates lath work. Says it's beneath a man of his skills."

"How do you know that?"

"We've been talking a bit since I fixed his eye. He's not such a bad guy."

* * * * *

· LOGAN ·

It was a moonless night with only a light wind. Temperature was well below freezing. Logan crossed Pine and turned north onto Twelfth Street. The Freeman Hydraulics shop was three blocks ahead. Somewhere in the distance, a night watchman called, "Ten o'clock and all's well!" Then he repeated the time in German: "*Zehn Uhr und alles gut!*"

I'll wager the night will never come that the watchman hollers the time in Gaelic, Logan thought.

Gas streetlamps at each intersection projected halos of light ahead of him. Smoke from a hundred chimneys occasionally wafted down into his path. Only rarely did he pass a house with rooms lit by either candles or lamps. *Most of the city's in bed.*

A figure passed through the halo at Spruce. *Martha.* Logan quickened his pace. Recently fallen snow crunched with each footstep. He didn't cross the street for fear of scaring her and dared not call out to her, which would call attention to the two of them.

As he drew abreast of her on the opposite side of the street, she heard his crunchy footsteps and turned. She stopped. He crossed. *Finally we'll be able to talk without freezing our arses off.* "Good timing," Logan said almost in a whisper.

"Good plan," Martha responded. Logan could almost hear the smile on her face.

They didn't speak further—nor did they touch—until they reached the shop. Martha pulled a key out of her pocket and unlocked the door.

"Did you steal your da's key?"

"Each of us has one. Pop-Pop, Mother, Grace, even Rufus. We never know who is going to get to the shop first, and Pop-Pop doesn't dare keep a key in a hidey-hole for fear that someone will see us."

They entered the shop, and Martha closed the door. It was a lot warmer in the building but pitch dark. "I can't see a thing," Logan said.

Martha found his hand and led him toward the office at the far end of the shop, fumbled a bit with the office door, proceeded into the room, bent slightly, and opened the door to a potbelly stove. Glowing embers cast a faint light.

Martha straightened, turned to Logan, put her arms around his neck, and kissed him. Logan pulled back momentarily, then he enthusiastically responded, pulling Martha close.

Martha broke their embrace, turned, and walked toward the office door. "I'll be back in a minute."

"What are you doing?"

"Conor McGuire used to sleep here when his brothers kicked him out and he had no place else to stay. Pop-Pop found him a straw mattress that he could lay out here in the office."

"So?"

"When Rian Krieger ran away, Conor moved in with your Uncle Otto, but the mattress is still out in the shop someplace. I'm going to go find it."

MONDAY, JANUARY 29
(JANUARY 17 O.S.)

· RIAN ·

Rian and Kostya had spent the day skating on St. Petersburg's rivers and canals, and the Tsar had again invited her to dine with the Imperial Family.

The late afternoon meal with the Tsar and the Empress was much different than what Rian was used to when she lived with her father. Here, the Tsar asked a question and the children answered. The Tsar asked his older son his opinion about matters of state, but asked the younger children what they did or accomplished during their day, never what they thought.

This afternoon, Rian found that despite these constraints, both Kostya and Olga were vying to stake out the territory of "closest to Rian-the-Companion."

"Rian is an excellent skater," said Kostya. "He is teaching me to skate backwards."

A little while later, Olga declared, "Rian is going to own a factory that makes locomotives when he returns to Philadelphia."

This caught Rian by surprise, as she had told Olga that *if* she were ever to return to Philadelphia, that is what she *would want* to do. "Uh, I don't think I'll be returning to Philadelphia any time soon," she said, *even though Seamus says we'll be on the first steamship out of Kronstadt in five weeks or so. And I've got to figure out how to get Olga to un-love me.*

"Tell Father about the gas lights that line the streets of Philadelphia, Rian," said Olga.

"No, tell Father about the girl who stabbed a man and ran away to sea," countered Kostya.

Rian froze. She had told Kostya and Olga different versions of the same stabbing story. To Kostya, it was about a girl; to Olga, it was about Rian Krieger, current boy companion to Grand Duke Konstantin.

"No," said Olga. "That wasn't a girl, that was—"

"Yes, it was," interrupted Kostya. "Her name was Eena and she was the same age as Rian."

A spasm of apprehension shot through Rian's body. Her heart raced. She gave Olga a pleading, wide-eyed shake of the head.

Olga regarded Rian for a long moment, then dropped her gaze. "Mother, all of a sudden I don't feel well. May I please be excused? I would like to go to my chamber."

* * * * *

· JULES ·

Jules found Dylan Kennedy running boards through the planer on the Krieger Coach factory floor. Dylan—also president of the No Name Fire Brigade—took over the hose company when Seamus left for Russia last year. Jules tapped him on the shoulder and signaled that he wanted to talk. Dylan nodded and pulled the lever that shifted the continuous belt from the drive pulley to the idler pulley. The planer wound down slowly as Dylan followed Jules to a place away from the cacophony of twenty other machines powered by the single shaft rotating near the shop ceiling.

Jules skipped the pleasantries. "I got a visit from Peter Jeffries at Pennsylvania Hall this morning. He was gilding some panels for the ceiling of the Grand Saloon."

"Jeffries. At the shop on Front Street, near Union?"

Jules nodded. "He'd finished with the panels ahead of schedule. All gold leaf. Once we install them, they're going to look like a 9-foot sunflower. Jeffries was pleased with his work." Jules paused, then added, "The panels were stolen last night. I'm checking with you to see if anyone from No Name was involved."

Dylan stooped, picked up a short piece of wood that hadn't made it into the scrap box, and tossed it in. "I doubt it. That's outside our territory, but I'll ask around. It's more likely one of the Ratters. I'll talk to Hugh. If it's one of Hugh's lads, he'd probably be willing to sell them back to you. Better get to them quick before all that gold is melted down. I'll send Logan up to the Hall if I learn anything."

"Logan. How's he doing? I haven't seen him since"—*since he stood lookout when I burned the ship*—"since he quit Krieger Coach."

"Yeah, I never understood why he left. He was only sweeping floors, but it was honest labor."

He left because Maddie and I made him break up with Martha. "I don't know. Thanks for checking up on those panels. And Dylan, we still need workers at the Hall. If any of your No Name boys are interested, tell them we'll hire Irish."

* * * * *

· LOGAN ·

Logan and Martha had finished their tryst in the Freeman Hydraulics office and were walking through the shop. Logan's left hand enlaced with Martha's right, allowing him to savor their last moments together for a week. His right hand held a candle.

"Twelve o'clock and all's well!" came the call of the night watchman as the man passed outside.

Logan reflexively turned to put his body between the candle and the front windows of the factory. "I still don't know how you can walk through the shop in complete darkness," he whispered to Martha.

Martha giggled. "Because I work here every day."

The candle faintly illuminated a steam-powered fire pump that was sitting near the front door. "Is this done?"

"It's been done for a week. Pop-Pop is going to deliver it to Baltimore, but he's been so busy with Pennsylvania Hall and Krieger Coach that he hasn't been able to make the trip yet."

"Baltimore. That's in a slave state. Does that make him nervous?"

"He and Mother had an argument about it. She doesn't want him to go."

"So how's he going to get the pump to Baltimore?"

"Good question. But he promised Mother that it wouldn't be until after Pennsylvania Hall is done."

"Too bad for your da. That's three months from now."

MONDAY, FEBRUARY 5

· JULES ·

Jules stuck out his hand to Marcus Edes, the carpentry foreman. "You're coming back, right?"

Edes shook Jules's hand warmly. "Hunnecher wants my crew at the Shelter for Colored Orphans until the lath is done. I figure that should take three weeks. Then we've got nothing until the painters leave here."

"Nothing at all?"

"I'm telling you, Jules, this depression isn't letting up. Nobody's even building an outhouse."

"Check in with me when your crew is almost done with the lath. Maybe we can start the finish work a little early here."

"The painters aren't going to like it. They tend to like a worksite all to themselves, same as the plasterers."

"Marcus, you and your men have done a great job here. I'll do what I can to bring you back here as soon as possible."

WEDNESDAY, FEBRUARY 7
(JANUARY 27 O.S.)

· RIAN ·

For more than a week, Grand Duchess Olga had studied at her library table at her end of the room. She had not said a word to Rian. Hadn't smiled. Hadn't walked over to Konstantin's end of the drawing room to listen to the latest chapters of *Oliver Twist*.

That changed when Kostya was summoned to his cello tutor, and everyone else was out of the room except for the austere, non-English-speaking Madame Parshakov. Olga rose from her table and walked back to Rian. Madame Parshakov took a new seat within easy throat-clearing distance from the two of them.

"Pretend you are telling me about *Oliver Twist*," said Olga.

Rian picked up an edition of *Bentley's Miscellany* from the corner of her table and offered it to Olga. "Is this good enough?"

"Are you a girl?"

"Yes."

"Is your real name Eena?"

"No. My name is Rian. Eena is a name I call myself. It's a nickname my cousin gave to me."

"Your cousin Seamus?"

"No, another one. He was supposed to be the one who came to Russia, but we switched places."

"Why did you run away?"

"It's the reason I told Kostya. My father was going to send me to a finishing school in Switzerland. I would have had to wear dresses."

"You shall refer to my brother as Grand Duke Konstantin Nikolaevich. You will never speak to me again. I suggest you get on the first steamship out of Kronstadt as soon as the ice breaks." With that, Grand Duchess Olga Nikolaevna turned on her heel and walked to her table at the other end of the room. Madame Parshakov scowled at Rian and returned to her usual seat.

* * * * *

It was not unusual for Rian and Lev to bump into one another as Rian was leaving the Anichkov Palace at the end of her day with Grand Duke Konstantin.

"My Aunt Yana speak at me," Lev said in halting English. "She want see you again."

Rian had not thought about Yana since before the Winter Palace fire. "Does she want to tell my fortune?"

Lev had exhausted his English and reverted to Russian. "Probably something like that. She is a soothsayer. She sees into peoples' souls. She is very strong. Very powerful. She says she has never felt heat come from anyone like she felt from you. She wants to know more about you."

That evening, Rian walked toward Lev's lachuga in the dark along her usual route. The night was moonless. Faint candlelight emanating from the occasional window gave minimal guidance as she navigated her way toward Lev's neighborhood. With about five blocks to go, she heard the faint, rhythmic crunch of snow behind her. The cadence matched her own. Her danger sense kicked in. She checked behind her but, with no streetlamps, could barely see a thing. She stopped abruptly. Two steps later, so did the crunch.

She picked up her pace. So did the crunch of snow behind her. The closer she got to Lev's neighborhood, the more vigilant she became. Lev promptly opened the door at her knock.

"I think someone was following me," Rian told Lev as he ushered her to Yana's lachuga a few doors down from his home.

"Come to my place after you are finished here. We can talk English and play cards. I'll walk you out of the neighborhood. You won't have any problem after that."

Yana greeted them, thanked Lev, and bid Rian into her home. *Dirt floor*, Rian noted. *Low ceiling. Smoky. Not much furniture. Same as the other lachugas in the neighborhood.* Then Rian spotted a low table near the fireplace that held a samovar, an urn for heating water for tea that seemed to occupy a place of prominence in every prosperous household Rian had been in. This was the first samovar Rian had seen in this neighborhood.

Yana gestured to Rian to take a seat by her fire. "My nephew says you can speak Russian better than when we met before."

"I am trying."

"No, I don't want any money from you."

"I didn't ask if you did."

"But you were thinking about it, *malen'koye solnyshko*."

Little sun. She called me "little sun." I like that. How did she know I thought she was going to ask me for money?

"Lev says you were foolhardy the night of the fire."

"A lot of us did things that were dangerous."

"You are thirteen years old, yet you were unafraid."

"I wasn't thinking about being afraid."

Yana drew up a chair facing Rian. "Give me your hand."

Rian complied.

"Still so hot. No less than the last time. The burning of the Tsar's home wasn't enough. Fire will follow you."

"What kind of fire? Fire like the Winter Palace?"

Yana nodded. "All kinds of fire. Fires that are out of control. Many of them. Fires that you think you control, but you don't. When were you born, *malen'koye solnyshko*? The date?"

"March 26, 1824, in America." *If you're any good at this fortune-telling thing, you should know about the date difference between Russia and the West.*

Yana shook her head. "Cursed calendars. Always causing problems. No matter. You are an *Obeh*, a fire sign. No surprise. Passion is also a fire." Yana turned Rian's hand over and examined her palm. "Interesting. Your life. It will be broken up."

"Broken up? How?"

Yana shrugged. "I'm not sure. Let's see what the tea leaves have to say."

Yana rose and pulled a porcelain cup out of a niche above the hearth. She removed the lid from a wooden box and spooned tea leaves into the cup. She leaned over the samovar and opened a spigot to fill the chipped cup with hot water. She handed the cup to Rian. "Ask a question about your future, then drink."

The teacup was chipped in two places. Rian blew over the surface of the water as she considered all the things she wanted to know about her future. *Will Olga tell anybody that I'm a girl? Can I become so valuable to the grand duke that I can remain in Russia?* She settled on her question that would give her a hint about both those questions. "Will I live in Russia for a long time?"

"Drink."

Rian took a sip.

Yana pushed the bottom of the cup gently toward Rian's lips. "No, the whole cup. Now."

Rian downed the hot, slightly bitter liquid. Dregs of tea leaves littered the bottom of the cup.

Yana held out her hand and Rian surrendered the cup. Yana peered at the dregs. "You will leave Russia soon, but because of forces that you are not even aware of." Her stare bore into Rian. "That was too easy. Ask another question. Make it a question of substance."

Rian reeled from the prediction that she would be leaving Russia soon. *I'm going home. Going home where* Vater *will force me to wear a dress.* The question she was dying to ask was, *Will I always have to wear a dress if I have to return to America?* but she couldn't bring herself to say those words to Yana. "My father and my uncle own a factory that builds railroad engines. Will I ever run Krieger Locomotive?"

Yana flipped the cup upside down on a plate and turned it around three times. She flipped the cup back over and studied the dregs that still remained in the cup.

"This is unusual. It is not uncommon for the tea leaves to be vague about the future. Not this time. They are quite definite, but this is still confusing." She gestured to the cup. "Here the answer to your question is *no.*" She gestured to the plate. "Yet here the answer is *yes.* I need to consult the beans."

Yana rose from her chair, moved it away from the fire, and signaled Rian to do the same. She knelt on the earthen floor and pulled a felt cloth out of her apron and spread it in front of the fire. "Forty-one beans," she said. "This may take a while."

Yana moved the beans around the cloth in motions that were indecipherable to Rian.

Finally, Yana pointed to the beans. "Here is your past. Here is your present. And over here is your future."

Rian could only interpret the jumble as three sets of beans arranged in a haphazard manner. "What do they say?"

"The beans tell me your past could have been easy, yet you took the harder path. You are unsettled. Something gnaws at you. You are surrounded by many who love you, yet they make demands on you that you find intolerable. You are impulsive."

Rian couldn't disagree with Yana about any of those. "What about my present?"

"These beans here are quite clear. You are not what you appear to be, although your deception does not come from an evil place."

Rian felt it was unwise to spend any more time talking about her present. "And my future?"

"Patience," responded Yana. She studied the present beans for two minutes longer. "More contradictions. Your appearance gives you peace. Your secret is safe with me."

"You know?"

Yana waved her hand dismissively, as if she were no longer concerned with the present. She stared intently at the future beans for minutes. She made the sign of the cross and sat back. "More heat. More fire. More passion."

"What else?"

"The beans tell me you are a good person, yet I don't understand how that could be."

"What do you mean?"

"I mean that I see no way but that your future is the work of the devil."

A tingle worked its way down Rian's back. "What is it? What do you see in my future?"

Yana shook her head. She shut her eyes, bowed her head, and was silent for at least a minute. "No, you go too far," she whispered, her head still bowed.

Rian couldn't tell if Yana was speaking to herself, to Rian, or to some unseen presence.

Yana shook her head, as if dismissing her thoughts, and raised her eyes to Rian. "We go on."

"What do the beans tell you?"

"Nothing that will do you any good to know. But there are two more things. You asked the question about your father's business. The beans say *no* and *yes*, same as the tea leaves." She pointed at the future pile. "*No* and *yes*."

"That's a stupid answer."

Yana shrugged, apparently unoffended. "The beans also answer the question you didn't ask out loud."

Dresses, Rian said to herself.

"You will do this thing that you find abhorrent for years, but then you will never do it again."

* * * * *

Rian walked to Lev's hovel in a stew of unease. *I'm leaving Russia soon. First I won't run Krieger Locomotive, then I will. There will come a time when I never wear a dress again. And there's something in my future I shouldn't know. What kind of fortune teller says that?*

Rian and Lev talked for a few hours. Rian told him about her session with Yana.

"My aunt draws her wisdom from many places," said Lev. "Her grandmother was a Romani; a gypsy. She taught her much, but Yana has since learned more from others and figured out some things for herself. Like she did with you, she can tell much about people by touch alone."

Lev donned his coat to walk Rian out of the neighborhood. Rian tried to wave him off. "It's been three hours since I arrived. No one would be willing to freeze that long to rob me of a few kopeks. I'll be fine."

Lev persisted. "No, I want more English lessons. You come often. Maybe I get so good that I visit America."

"Can a serf leave Russia?"

Lev shook his head. "Serfs run away all the time. Most are found and brought back. But others are successful. That will be me. I go to America. Get rich like your father."

When they arrived at the first street lantern, Lev gave Rian a friendly slap on the shoulder and reversed direction. "We play cards tomorrow night after I finish wood. Yes?"

"Yes," Rian responded. "Poker this time. Bring plenty of money."

Rian heard Lev laugh as he faded into the darkness. Her mood temporarily lightened by her joke, she walked toward the next street lantern. It wasn't long before she again detected footsteps behind her. She quickened her pace and the rhythm of the steps behind her did so as well. She started to run. The footsteps behind her matched her new pace.

Rian broke into a sprint. "Help! Help!" she yelled. She switched to Russian. "*Pomogi mne! Pomogi mne!*"

The huffing of a body in pursuit gained on her. She tried zigging and zagging, but her pursuer closed in. A hand grabbed the collar of her greatcoat and pulled down hard. The weight of a full human frame landed on her as she hit the snow and knocked the breath out of her.

A hulking man, easily six feet tall, his breath rotten, yanked her to her feet. "You little shit," he said in Russian. "You made me freeze my balls off for three hours. So I guess that makes you kind of lucky. I'm going to make this quick." He held Rian by her coat collar with one hand while he unbuttoned his coat. For a moment, Rian thought she might be able to slip out of her her greatcoat and start running again, but the man tightened his grip. He pulled a dagger out of his waistband.

Then someone whistled. A loud, piercing whistle like a person calling a dog. Rian's assailant loosened his grip slightly and turned toward the whistler. Under a street lantern stood a figure in a long civilian greatcoat, his hand in his pockets, his posture indicating that he didn't much care what happened next.

"Before you do that, Kuznetsov," said the man in the greatcoat, "look behind you."

In the darkness stood two other men.

* * * * *

The three strangers took Rian and her assailant to a forbidding stone building. The man in the greatcoat escorted her to a room with no windows, left, and locked the door behind her. Try as she might, she couldn't stop her body from shaking, which she knew was a combination of almost having her throat slit, fear of her current helplessness, and the fact that the room was very cold. Her thoughts looped around and around like the *Flying Horses* at the Winter Carnival. *Olga told somebody I'm a girl. Olga told. Olga told.*

The man in the greatcoat entered the room and shut the door behind him. "Empty your pockets."

Rian felt the menace behind his words. She stood and pulled out her pocket watch, a pocketknife, a few kopeks, and a deck of playing cards.

"Sit down," said the man in the greatcoat. Then he asked a flurry of questions.

"What were you doing in that section of St. Petersburg at eleven o'clock at night?"

"How do you know the woodcutter?"

"Did you steal anything from the Winter Palace on the night of the fire?"

"Why were you visiting the old hag?"

"What is your uncle trying to do here in Russia?"

"Has your uncle ever met with anyone to plot against the Tsar?"

"Why is your uncle working with Count Sheremetev?"

Rian answered the questions as best as she could. She revealed nothing about Sheremetev's wish to bring change to Russia. The man in the greatcoat left.

An hour after she first entered the room, she heard Uncle Adrian being interrogated in an adjoining room, but she couldn't hear the questions, and she couldn't hear Adrian's answers. *Olga told someone I'm a girl. Now Uncle Adrian's in trouble, too. Count Sheremetev said this would happen. It's all my fault.*

Rian rose from her chair and paced. Then General Benckendorff entered the room. "Sit down," he commanded. After she did so, he towered over her. "Do you know who I am, Rian?"

"Yes, Gospodin." Rian returned the man's stare. "You are General Benckendorff. I've seen you in His Imperial Majesty's residence."

"Do you know what I do?"

"You are the head of the Third Section."

"Do you know what the Third Section does?"

"You are the police."

"Not exactly. We investigate threats to His Majesty. Are you a threat, Rian?"

"No, Gospodin."

"Why would a man on the payroll of the Minister of the Imperial Court be interested in killing you?"

"Excuse me, Gospodin?"

"What have you done to ire Prince Volkonsky?"

The implications of Benckendorff's question washed over her. *This isn't about Grand Duchess Olga Nikolaevna.* "My friend Captain Stepanov. He was the head of the Tsar's Imperial Guards. He died the night of the fire."

"Yes, a true sadness. What of it?"

"I saw him die. I saw the prince strike the horses that pulled out the beam when Captain Stepanov was on it. He killed my friend and three other soldiers. I know he did it on purpose."

The general paused for a moment. "That is a wild accusation against a very powerful person. Why would Volkonsky want to kill the captain?" The tone of his voice implied surprise and interest.

Heartened for the first time since she had been escorted into the room, Rian relaxed a bit, but she was still shaking. "The prince had been trying to keep my uncle from meeting with Tsar Nicholas. The captain brought my uncle and cousin into the Winter Palace when it was burning. That's how they met the Tsar."

"Why would the captain do such a thing? Did he want the Tsar to meet your uncle?"

Rian suspected that was exactly Captain Stepanov's motivation, but she latched onto a sliver of truth. "No. My cousin—Seamus Gallagher—he was a firefighter back in Philadelphia. I think the captain thought Seamus could help."

"Ah, yes. And you were at the fire as well?"

"Yes, sir. I drove my uncle and cousin there. I was their coachman."

"Have you ever been in the rooms beneath Field Marshals' Hall?"

Rian did her best to match up the warren of rooms and hallways with what must have been above them. "Where the laundry rooms were? And the apothecary?"

Benckendorff nodded. "Yes, the apothecary."

"Yes, sir. I helped Lev bring some wood down there once. He took me to the bakery to meet his aunt."

"When was that?"

"I'm not sure. Probably six weeks before the fire."

"And what were you given during this tour of the workrooms?"

"Nothing."

"Nothing? Are you sure?"

"Uh, some bread. In the bakery. With butter on it."

"So you and this serf Lev ate freely of the Tsar's bread?"

"Yes, sir. The bread was a little burned. I doubt it would have ever been served to the Tsar or his family."

"Why would the Minister of the Imperial Court want to keep your relatives from meeting the Tsar?"

"I'm not sure, sir."

"Do not lie to me, you little pimple. I will squeeze the truth out of you before daybreak."

"No, I'm telling the truth." Her shaking became more violent.

Benckendorff abruptly left the room. Rian had a lot of time to think. By their questions, Rian could tell that the Third Section knew a lot about her and her uncle and cousin. They all had been watched for quite some time.

An hour later, Seamus, who Rian didn't know had also been gathered by the Secret Police, and Adrian were escorted into the room and offered seats.

General Benckendorff entered the room. "You are all free to go," he said in German. "Your stories all match up with one another, but please do not make any attempt to contact Count Sheremetev until we speak with him this morning."

Adrian spoke directly to Benckendorff. "What about the man who assaulted my nephew? Is he going to be charged?"

"That man is a valued operative of the Minister of the Imperial Court. He claims your coachman picked his pocket. We found no such evidence but saw no reason to hold him."

"If your men were following my nephew all night, you must know that isn't true."

"The Third Section is responsible for protecting the Tsar. What occurred this evening apparently has little to do with the Imperial Family's safety. To us, your squabble with Prince Volkonsky is of no consequence. You should be thankful that my man stuck his neck out and saved your coachman from being killed."

"I do thank you for that."

"Prince Volkonsky is a powerful man. Do you know what would have happened to his operative if he had run his knife through your coachman's heart?"

"I hope he would have been tried for murder."

Benckendorff shook his head. "Nothing would have happened."

"Then thank you. We owe you a debt of gratitude."

"Be careful, Mr. Krieger. I collect favors. I find they are more valuable than the bribes that lesser men think grease the wheels of the Russian state. But beware; sooner or later I ask for a favor in return."

"In that case, with great trepidation, I ask for another. Please pass the word on to the Tsar about this incident. Ask the Tsar to tell Volkonsky how displeased he would be if something happened to his son's companion."

Benckendorff frowned. "No one tells the Tsar how he should feel. However, my report is already written. It will be on the Tsar's desk when he reads his morning dispatches"—he checked his pocket watch—"in less than an hour."

"One last question, General Benckendorff. Why was my nephew being followed by your people?"

"The Third Section protects the Tsar by amassing information. A coachman who spends time with the grand duke by day and a woodcutter by night is noteworthy."

"Did your men learn anything this evening?"

"Yes, I think we did."

"And what is that?"

Benckendorff smiled for the first time. "American children are crazy. Why would anyone but a mad foreigner who spends the day with the richest family in the world also choose to play cards at night with the Tsar's serf? It makes no sense."

Adrian belatedly realized the general was making a joke. "I think you have identified one of the things that makes my nephew so unique. If you ever figure out the answer to the question, please let me know."

* * * * *

The three Americans paused on the street after they were escorted out of the Secret Police headquarters.

Adrian glanced back at the building. "Everyone okay?"

Rian was still shaking, and she knew the bitter cold was only partly to blame. "I just want to go home."

"I'm fine," responded Seamus. "But the poor rotter in the room next to mine was getting cuffed around more than a bit."

Adrian shook his head. "Did you see it?"

"Nope, but I sure could hear it. They weren't going easy on him."

A ruckus occurred at the front door of the station. Two Secret Policemen shoved a man out the door so violently that he fell into the snow at the bottom of the steps.

Rian ran to the man and knelt over him. "Jaysus, it's Lev."

Adrian and Seamus followed Rian and helped Lev to his feet.

Moments later, one of the policemen led Yana roughly out the door by her arm. He gave her an extra push toward the group.

"Now this is starting to feel a little more like home," said Seamus. "The upper classes get a little deference; the folks on the bottom get the fist. That's progress for me, though. First time the powers-that-be have gone easy on me."

* * * * *

British Troops Set Fire to American Steamship on Niagara River
One American Killed
The *Caroline* Was Being Used in Support of Canadian Rebels
Exclusive to the *Philadelphia Independent* by Harold Foote

Word has arrived in Philadelphia that hostilities have broken out along the Canadian border between American patriots and British troops. The Americans were acting in support of the Canadian rebel William Lyon Mackenzie, who spoke eloquently at an early-December meeting in Buffalo about the abuses perpetrated on honest Canadian citizens by the oligarchic colonial government of Upper Canada and their British masters.

On Navy Island, in the middle of the Niagara River, Mackenzie and his followers declared the Provisional Government of the Republic of Canada. Mackenzie's minions subsequently held informational meetings in Albany, New York; Burlington, Vermont; Cleveland, Ohio; Detroit, Michigan; and Rochester, New York.

Five hundred American patriots subsequently flocked to the newly declared republic, supplying food, gear, and guns. They were ferried to the island by the steamship *Caroline*. British marines crossed the international border, burst into the encampment, killed a watchman, seized the *Caroline*, set it ablaze, and turned it adrift above Niagara Falls.

I have spoken to Secretary of State John Forsyth, who stated that the situation is volatile, and calm heads on all sides are called for. Meanwhile, broadsides have been disseminated as far away as Philadelphia, Baltimore, and Washington to recruit more patriots to join the cause of the Republic of Canada and their American allies.

* * * * *

· LOGAN ·

It wasn't much of a rain, really more of a mist, but after walking for ten blocks, Logan could feel the wet seeping through his coat. *This better be worth it*, he said to himself.

He could hear banging coming from inside Pennsylvania Hall as he crossed Haines Street. *Settle down, Boyo*, Logan said to himself. *Jules is going to be happy to see you once he finds out why you're here.* He walked up the three shallow steps of the hall and under the portico, grateful to get out of the mist. A pile of sand, half as tall as he, spilled off the left side of the portico. Logan took off his coat, shook it, put it back on, opened the door, and entered the building for the first time.

A plasterer, strapped into a pair of stilts, yelled over his shoulder, "Shut the door!"

Chastened, Logan turned and closed the door. If it was a bit above freezing outside, it must have been twenty degrees warmer inside. He had entered a large foyer, fronted by four generous bay windows interspersed by three sets of glassed double-doors. There were similar double doors on both ends of the foyer. Wide stairs on both ends of the foyer led to the second floor. Although the foyer was far from finished, it didn't take much imagination for Logan to envision that someday soon this room would be a grand, inviting gathering place.

Logan had never seen a plasterer doing his job before, much less one on stilts. The stilts added more than two feet to the artisan's height and made it possible for him to easily reach the ceiling with his trowel. The foyer was sheathed in lath, and the plasterer was starting to lay a first coat onto the ceiling.

A pile of white powder that Logan assumed was quicklime—*How many wheelbarrows-full? Thirty? Fifty?*—covered most of the left side of the foyer, making access to that staircase difficult. A second man shoveled lime into a shallow, slope-sided tub that already held a good amount of sand.

Voices echoed down from upstairs. Banging of hammer on nails reverberated down a center hallway that was also covered with lath but no plaster.

"I'm looking for Jules Freeman," Logan said to the plasterer.

"Don't know," the man responded without diverting his attention from the ceiling. In his left hand, he held a handle that was screwed into the center of a one-foot-square piece of sheet metal. "He's around here someplace." He scraped a blob of plaster from the metal square with his trowel and made a broad sweep along the ceiling, leaving a swath of plaster smushed onto the lath and into the cracks. "Quit doggin' it!" the man barked, but Logan didn't think he was speaking to him.

"Keep your shirt on, Charlie," said the man with the shovel. "She can only carry two buckets at a time and she's feeding the men upstairs as well."

Logan surveyed the room. The air inside was as moist as it was outside. Beads of condensation occupied the trim at the bottom of every pane of glass in every window and door.

The front door opened and a young Black woman carrying two buckets entered the building.

"Shut the door!" yelled the plasterer.

The girl started to put her buckets down, but Logan said, "I'll get it," and she proceeded to the man with the shovel.

"This will do me for a little bit," shovel-man said to the girl. "Take care of the guys upstairs on your next trip."

"Excuse me," said Logan. "Do you know where Jules Freeman is?"

The girl turned to Logan while shovel-man emptied the first bucket into the tub. "Hear that banging down the hall? That's his crew. If you're gonna tell him something, it better be good. He's in a mood."

Shovel-man emptied his second bucket and set it down. "Get movin', Cee-Cee. Charlie doesn't cotton to you chinnin' when you should be workin'."

Cee-Cee picked up the buckets and shouldered her way back out into the elements. Shovel-man picked up a hoe and started mixing the lime, sand, and water.

Cautioned by the young woman's words, Logan walked down the hallway toward the banging. Sixty feet down the hall, three men—*two Black and one white*, Logan noticed— were on their knees hammering nails into wide planks. When the banging momentarily stopped, Logan stated, "I'm looking for Jules."

One of the men waved with his hammer toward a door and said, "Downstairs."

Logan weaved through the carpenters and arrived at a door to the basement. "Jules?" he called.

"Don't come down!" Jules yelled.

Logan could see Jules from the waist up. He was stripped down to an undershirt, nailing the basement stairs into place. Generous waves of heat flowed up from the floor below. Logan stood at the top of the stairs for five minutes until Jules called, "It's okay to come now!"

Before Logan reached the bottom of the stairs, Jules had turned his attention to another man.

"No, that's not what I said," said the man. He was obviously frustrated.

"Okay," said Jules. "Explain it again, because I don't understand it."

"Okay, the most important thing for you to hear is this: It was smart of you to install this furnace down here—"

"Thank you," said Jules, but to Logan it sounded like a cranky *thank you*.

". . . but you don't want the plaster to dry out too fast because it will crack."

"So, do we heat the building or not?"

"Yes, of course, but you've just fired up the furnace. This building has been unheated all winter. It's very humid in here. The heat will start to change the humidity very quickly. In a day or so, we'll probably have to throw some water around if it feels like the humidity is getting too low. No matter what, we'll mist the walls once or twice to slow it down a touch."

"Is that your job or my job?"

"You've done your job. The building is plenty warm on all three floors. Now you stay out of our way and let us do our work."

"Good," responded Jules. "That's something I can understand." Jules turned to Logan. "Haven't seen you since December."

Yeah, since I became your lookout when you and Jabez burned the ship.

"What are you doing here, Logan?"

That tone is about what I expected. I quit a good job at Krieger Coach because you found out about Martha and me, and you made us promise we'd never see each other again. Logan surveyed the basement. A new boiler and firebox were kicking out so much heat that he had to take off his coat. "Dylan sent me. We've got your golden rays."

"Who stole them?"

"I'm not supposed to say. It wasn't anyone from No Name. We had to pay the folks who purloined them from the gilder. Dylan says he'll give you the friends and family discount on the finder fee."

Jules smiled at Logan's phrasing. "How much total?"

"Thirty dollars. That includes delivery."

"Okay, I'll talk to the board and arrange payment. Please send my thanks off to Dylan. Hey, do you need a job? I'm still shorthanded."

Oh shit, Logan thought to himself. "Maybe. What would I be doing?"

"The plasterers got here yesterday. At least those who are willing to work on this project. Half their crew hasn't shown up. So their journeymen are now plastering in the out-of-the-way places. The craftsmen are doing the hard stuff. I've promised to get them people to haul water, wheelbarrow sand, move the scaffolds . . . that sort of stuff. I could use you."

"Hauling water? Like that girl I saw?"

"Don't be so disdainful. She volunteered for the job because someone needed to do it. She's been banging nails for three weeks, installing lath. Helped me tear out these stairs when we couldn't get the boiler parts down here. If you start hauling water with her, you will have a hard time keeping up with her."

"Since when are you hiring girls?"

"At this point, I'll hire anyone who's willing to put in a good day's work. Black, white, Irish, man, woman. Are you in or not?"

Logan hesitated.

"Listen," said Jules. "I know things were uncomfortable between us when Maddie and I forced you to break up with Martha. But that was months ago, and I respect you for staying away from our daughter. If there are any hard feelings, I'd like to put them behind us. Come on, Logan. I'm in a jam here. Help me out."

"I'll help you out for a while. At least until the plasterers are finished." *But this is not going to be easy, because I'm not staying away from your daughter. Martha and I rendezvous every Thursday night at ten o'clock in front of the potbelly stove in the office of Freeman Hydraulics. We tried to stop, but we couldn't. I'm in love with Martha, and she's in love with me.*

* * * * *

In no hurry to walk back to Moyamensing, Logan wandered through the construction site. Six plastering crews were bustling about the Grand Saloon, on the main floor, on scaffolds, and up in the Gallery. The plasterers were the crew bosses. They worked with practiced efficiency. *Now that is a job that I might like,* he thought to himself. *I think I would be good at it.* The plasterers yelled at the men who supported them when those guys didn't do something right.

"Hi, Logan. Have you seen my father?"

Logan turned to see Martha's little sister Grace. She was holding a basket. "Uh, yeah, he's down in the basement."

"Do you work here now?"

"I think so. Jules just hired me. I start tomorrow. What are you doing here?"

"Pop-Pop forgot his dinner. I'm delivering. Well, I better go find him. Things are busy at work. Mother gets tetchy when I'm gone too long. Good luck working for my father." Grace turned and descended the stairs.

Logan watched the plasterers for ten more minutes. When he left the building, he turned south on Sixth. Half a block away, he saw Grace walking with that girl Cee-Cee. They were both carrying two buckets of water from a horse trough and walking back toward Pennsylvania Hall. *I guess Grace isn't in that much of a hurry,* he said to himself.

FRIDAY, FEBRUARY 9
(JANUARY 28 O.S.)

· RIAN ·

Grand Duchess Alexandra had been called out of the classroom to take her pianoforte lesson, leaving Olga Nikolaevna alone at her library table.

Rian rose and walked to the other end of the room. "Your Highness, can we talk?"

"Go away. I told you never to speak to me again."

Rian laced her hands in front of her. "I owe you an explanation. I was my uncle's coachman. I liked doing it, and I was good at it. I never expected to be invited to become the grand duke's companion. I thought I would be good at that, too. And then I got to know you and I liked being with you. I'm sorry."

The grand duchess stared up at Rian. "You deceived me."

"Yes, I did. But I was trapped. You know what being trapped feels like. You told me that you hate your life. You're never allowed out of the palace. You don't get to meet people. That's how I feel when I wear a dress. I . . . hate . . . wearing . . . dresses."

"Go away."

· · · · ·

· LOGAN ·

Logan arrived for his second day on the job to find Charlie, the plasterer, using a hoe to mix quick lime and sand in the shallow, slope-sided tub. Cee-Cee was on her haunches, watching the process up close.

"There's four components," Charlie instructed Cee-Cee as he hoed, "quick-lime, sand, horsehair, and water. Each coat has a different mix, but what I'm teaching you today is for the scratch coat. Pay attention."

"Where's . . . ?" Logan realized he had never learned shovel-man's name. Yesterday, Charlie had kept Logan and Cee-Cee busy hauling water in support of all the plasterers all day long. Logan had had only sporadic interactions with shovel-man.

Charlie continued his mixing. "He's gone. Up and left for Niagara Falls. Gonna fight for the Republic of Canada."

"Who's going to take his place?"

"Cee-Cee, apparently. Woulda been you if you'd shown up earlier."

"Can I learn?"

"Can you count?"

"Sure," Logan replied confidently, although he was a little vague on his multiplication tables beyond five times five.

"You're Irish. You developed a taste for whiskey yet? I don't wanna waste time on somebody who doesn't show up because he's too drunk to work."

"I'll show up for work six days a week."

"Then no reason for you not to learn. The way men are leaving around here, I've gotta train who I've got. Now pay attention."

* * * * *

Charlie was a skilled and efficient craftsman. Strapped onto his stilts, he smushed the scratch coat into the cracks between ceiling lath strips and smeared it in practiced, arcing strokes of his trowel. When he finished the ceiling, he started working along the top parts of the walls, then he walked up and down the stairs—on his stilts, no less—to get to the high spots in the stairwells.

But Charlie couldn't work on his stilts and also do what he called *ground work*. "That's what you two idiots are for. You do everything to keep me moving. If I have to stop to wait for you to replenish my hawk"—that's what he called the sheet-steel square that held blobs of plaster—"you aren't doing your job."

So, the three of them became a team. Logan and Cee-Cee divided the groundwork, which meant:

- hauling buckets of water from the horse trough two blocks away.

- screening the sand to make sure there weren't any big particles. *Particles: That's a word I never heard before.*

- shoveling the proper ratio of quicklime and sand into the trough. *Ratio: Never heard that word before, either, but now I understand it.*

- throwing generous handfuls of horsehair into the mix. "Horsehair binds the plaster together and controls the shrinkage," Charlie had told them. "This building is going to be a showcase for the anti-slavery movement until slavery's abolished. I want Pennsylvania Hall to shine until the day its mission is complete. The proper amount of horsehair will make sure the plaster doesn't start to chip off years from now."

- mixing all the dry ingredients, then adding the right amount of water to make sure the plaster has the right plasticity. *That means that the blobs that I put on Charlie's hawk aren't too runny and aren't too stiff. Jaysus, that man can yell when it's not right.*

The problem was supplying the workers with enough water. Charlie wasn't the only plasterer. Teams of skilled craftsmen were working upstairs in the Grand Saloon. Cries for "More water!" frequently echoed down the stairwells. After his twentieth trip back from the water trough with two buckets of water, Logan felt like his arms were going to fall off.

* * * * *

· JULES ·

Jules left Krieger Coach, assured that things were running pretty well. The *Philadelphia & Columbia Railroad* had followed up their order for Krieger Rail with one for both passenger and freight cars. The rest of Philadelphia might still be battered by the depression, but in a couple of weeks Krieger Coach would be running with a queue of cars under construction for months to come.

Jules was a little perplexed when Otto revealed that a significant chunk of this new order would be paid in *Philadelphia & Columbia* stock. *Well, that's his problem, not mine. My stock is in Pennsylvania Hall. I've put my money where my mouth is, and it will pay me dividends for years to come.*

It was below freezing. The sky was cloudless blue. The sidewalks along Sassafras Street were shoveled. Plumes of condensed breath shot from the mouths of passing horses. Two years ago, this street would have been bustling with commerce. *It's better than a few months ago but still not good. I'm lucky. Inquiries keep coming in at Freeman Hydraulics.*

And perhaps most gratifying of all, Jules had finally wrestled the work at Pennsylvania Hall back on track. The white carpenters and journeymen left two days ago, replaced by an all-white plastering crew. Self-emancipator Homer Good and the formerly weepy-eyed Emil Harberger worked diligently on the Doric columns, trying to stay out of the way of the plasterers, arguing with one another about how best to go about the mammoth task. Jules had purposefully held one job back to keep the Black workers busy. There were enough competent carpenters to build the stage at the far end of the Grand Saloon.

But the problem is nobody likes anybody. Plasterers don't like carpenters. Whites don't like Blacks. Blacks don't trust whites. Homer and Emil can't figure out who's giving orders to whom.

As he approached Eighth Street, he saw Logan Gallagher dipping two buckets into the horse trough. *And I can't find enough men to haul water to keep the plasterers busy.*

Jules whistled. Logan straightened, then set his buckets down on the bricks and waited for Jules. Jules picked up a bucket, barely breaking stride. "Let's go. Can't keep Charlie waiting."

"I know," said Logan. "I've been thinking about that. We need more folks to carry water."

"Believe me, I've tried. I put the word out. Some kids show up. They work one day. They don't come back."

"Why?"

"Because Hugh Callaghan pays them more to work for him."

"I thought you two got along."

"That was when we had a common interest. He didn't want more Black people streaming into Philadelphia. I wanted to ruin the slaver Austin Slatter. So we burned his slave ship. Now things are back to the way they used to be: I don't like him, and he doesn't like me."

"Well then, I've got an idea. How about if we commandeer that fire pump that you're going to deliver to Baltimore some day and use it to pump the water to Pennsylvania Hall. There's a fire hydrant on the other side of Sixth Street from the hall."

Jules stopped walking, which prompted Logan to do the same. "Logan, that is a brilliant idea. I can have it here tomorrow." Then he thought for a moment. "How did you know about that fire pump?"

"Uh, Cee-Cee told me."

"How did Cee-Cee know?"

"I don't know. She's a friend of Grace's, right?"

"Yeah, it was Grace who asked me to hire her."

With that, Jules put aside any thoughts of Grace and Cee-Cee.

WEDNESDAY, FEBRUARY 14, 1838
(FEBRUARY 2 O.S.)

· RIAN ·

Gospodin Litke was out of the classroom in one of his many prolonged absences. The grand duchesses studied quietly at their end of the room. Olga had not spoken a word to Rian in five days. Rian and Kostya were sitting at their library table. He reached into his sack and slid a newspaper across to Rian. Rian read the ornate German typeface: *der Hamburger Versand* [*The Hamburg Dispatch*].

"I found this in the trashcan next to Gospodin Litke's desk," said Kostya. "There's an article about the Winter Palace fire. I thought you could help me translate it."

Rian translated the article from the German newspaper into Russian on the fly, and she found the account to be quite accurate. It described how workers in the basement apothecary had smelled smoke, worked on a defective heating pipe, and assumed they had solved the problem. Shortly thereafter, directly above the apothecary, the Field Marshals' Hall began to fill with smoke, and the Tsar was summoned from the opera. The Tsar took charge of the operation. Not yet aware of the direness of the situation, the Tsar was concerned that the smoke would damage the many valuable paintings in Field Marshals' Hall, and ordered the windows to be broken to clear the smoke. Vitalized by the fresh air, the fire . . .

Rian realized that the article was becoming increasingly critical of Tsar Nicholas and stopped reading aloud. She scanned the rest of the article. *Because of the Tsar's ill-advised decision, fire immediately raged through the Field Marshals' Hall. . . . Fire equipment, poorly maintained by the palace's fire brigade, broke down. . . . Early reports that no one died in the blaze were false, and at least thirty Army and Navy personnel died fighting the fire. . . . The Tsar acted bravely on numerous occasions. . . .*

"It says your father acted bravely on numerous occasions during the fire. There's nothing new here that you haven't heard about."

"Nothing about you?"

"No, nothing about me."

At that moment, General Benckendorff, head of the Third Section and the Russian Secret Police, entered the room without a knock. A shot of adrenaline coursed through Rian's body. *Olga must have told him I'm a girl.*

Madame Parshakov rose from her chair like someone had poked her in the butt with a needle. Benckendorff surveyed the room, ignored Madame and the grand duchesses, and strode toward the rear of the room, past all the junk in the middle, and stopped, towering above the grand duke and Rian. The grand duke, even at ten years old, aware that he had no need to stand, remained seated. Rian stood.

General Benckendorff bowed ever so slightly. "Your Highness, I would like to speak to student Krieger. It may take a while."

Rian froze. *He's going to throw me in jail.*

Benckendorff noticed that Rian was holding the *Hamburger Versand*. "Where did you get that newspaper?"

Rian avoided glancing at the grand duke. Instead, she looked directly at Benckendorff. "I brought it from the post office. It was in a trashcan."

Benckendorff grabbed the paper out of Rian's hands. "These rags are not to be trusted. They spread lies and misinformation about the Tsar." He addressed Rian. "This should never have gotten past the censors. You can get thrown into jail for possession of such documents."

The grand duke rose. "General Benckendorff, student Krieger was protecting me. I brought the newspaper to his attention and asked him to read it to me."

"And where did you get this newspaper?"

"I would prefer not to say."

"I will discuss this with your father later. Now I would like to speak to your companion." Benckendorff indicated with a sweep of his hand that Rian was to precede him out of the room. Rian momentarily considered running—*but where could I run to*? Once in the wide hallway, Benckendorff said, "This is far enough."

Rian gulped and turned to the general. It had been a week since he had interrogated her in the police station. *And that was when I almost had my throat slit.* The prospect of another session like that terrified her. *"Little girl,"* Count Sheremetev had said, *"you are like a moth circling a candle. I warn you; before long your wings are going to get burned." Well, here it comes.*

Benckendorff slipped the German newspaper in his inside coat pocket. "I understand that you have been loaning out copies of a magazine called *Bentley's*

Miscellany to various members of the nobility who frequent the Anichkov Palace."

Rian's eyes widened. *What the . . . ?* "Yes, I have. I thought they had been approved by the Third Section's censors. They have been stamped."

"Yes, I know. And you have charged these people for the privilege of reading your magazine?"

"Uh, yes, Gospodin. The first one—Baron Lvov—offered me a kopek, so I took it. Then others came to me and offered three times that to get bumped up in line. The amount kept getting bigger."

"What is the going rate to get bumped up to the top of the line?"

Rian looked quizzically at Benckendorff, unable to determine whether she was about to get arrested for pretending to be a boy or renting out Charles Dickens chapters. "Uh, the last person paid me ten kopeks for two chapters."

"How many magazines do you have?"

"I bought seven in London. I received another one in the mail from the bookshop early in January. I picked up another one at the post office yesterday."

"How many chapters is that?"

"Nineteen. In nine magazines."

"Please give me all nine."

"Yes, Gospodin. Did your censors change their minds?"

Benckendorff smiled for the first time. "No, not at all." He handed Rian a ruble—the equivalent of 100 kopeks. "This is a business transaction. I want to read this man, Charles Dickens. I want to know what all the hoo-ha is about."

Rian tried not to show the sense of relief that washed over her. But that was the moment she decided that she had changed her mind about heading back to America when the ice broke. *The pressure is killing me. Count Sheremetev is right. I'm too close to the flame.*

Impulsively, she handed the ruble back to Benckendorff. "Last week, you said that you found that favors were more important than money. I will get you all the editions of *Bentley's Miscellany* right away, except for the last one. They're in the classroom. But I want a favor in return."

"And what is this favor?"

"I don't know yet." *But if my secret gets out sometime in the next three weeks, it would be good to have you in my debt.*

Benckendorff was clearly amused by the bargaining. "What about the last edition?"

"I am going to loan that to Grand Duchess Olga Nikolaevna. She hasn't read it yet."

"But I will get it after she reads it?"

Rian looked at the general with a twinkle in her eye. "Yes, Gospodin, but that will cost you ten kopeks."

"Are all American children this cheeky?"

Rian smiled at Benckendorff. "No, Gospodin, but we do know how to bargain."

"Leave a note in my office when the grand duchess has finished reading." The general turned on his heel and walked away, then he stopped and turned again to Rian. "It was Gospodin Litke, wasn't it?"

"Pardon me, sir?"

"I assume the newspaper was Litke's. Subversive literature somehow finds its way into many St. Petersburg parlors. Litke has many friends abroad. The grand duke was protecting his tutor. You were protecting the grand duke. I applaud you both for your loyalty."

Rian noted that the general hadn't repeated his question. She thought she was off the hook.

"Never lie to me again," said Benckendorff. He turned and walked away, leaving Rian alone in the hallway.

* * * * *

Rian knocked on the door of Yana's hovel. Yana escorted her in and offered her a seat, but Rian detected no sign of the grandmotherly warmth that Rian had previously felt.

"I tried to visit Lev. There's someone else in his house."

"They sent him back to the emperor's estate in Tsarskoye Selo."

"Why?"

"Someone decided that Lev should no longer work in St. Petersburg. They sent him away."

"Have you heard from him?"

"His cousin told me he arrived at the estate. He is cutting wood. Then his cousin told me something that I don't understand."

"What is that?"

"Lev said he liked learning English with you. He wishes he could do it again."

A message, Rian thought. *He wants to run away to America.* "Maybe someday we will. Yana, I have a question for you. What was it that you didn't want to tell me last week?"

Yana shrugged. "A thousand palms, the tea leaves, my beans; they have never told a future like yours. Very clear, yet impossible."

"What is it? What is impossible?"

Yana shook her head. "No. You are too young to be burdened with this knowledge. Go back to America, child. That's what you have decided to do, isn't it?"

* * * * *

· LOGAN ·

The day after Logan made the suggestion to Jules, a freight wagon dropped off the fire pump, two hundred feet of hose, and two large wash tubs. As a member of the United No Name Fire Brigade, Logan knew how to couple a hose to a fire hydrant,[7] and there was one located across Sixth Street. Even though the fire pump was designed to be steam-powered, it could be operated without steam by pushing up and pulling down on levers on either side of the pump. Pumping up and down, up and down, Logan and Cee-Cee could get a hefty stream flowing into a tub in the foyer. When the tub in the foyer was full, they ran the hose up into the Grand Saloon to fill the second tub up there. With this new system, Logan and Cee-Cee could supply all the plasterers with water without hearing screams of "Quit doggin' it!" or "Faster! Faster!"

At the noontime break for dinner, the Black workers sat together on the main floor of the Grand Saloon and the white workers went to the Gallery, one story up. Logan and Cee-Cee climbed the stairs from the foyer and one of the Black workers waved Cee-Cee over to sit with them. Cee-Cee abruptly turned around and headed back down into the foyer. Logan gazed up at the men in the Gallery. None of them seemed much interested in him, so he turned around and followed Cee-Cee. She sat on the foyer floor and faced the windows, a small basket by her side.

Logan sat next to her. He took the first of two meat pies he had bought from a street vendor out of his cloth sack, momentarily considered offering a bite of the other one to Cee-Cee, but decided he was too hungry to share. "How come you didn't want to sit with your own?"

"That man who called me over? He's pretty handsy. Didn't want to give him a chance to get a cheapy in." Cee-Cee pulled a tin can out of her basket and removed its lid.

---

7. There were 185 cast-iron fire hydrants in Philadelphia in 1811, although fire hydrants didn't start to take on their modern appearance until the end of the Civil War.

Logan smelled the pungent aroma of pepper pot,[8] and all of a sudden sharing one of his meat pies didn't seem like a bad idea. "Where'd you get the stew?"

"My momma makes a big pot of it every morning. Sells it on the corner of Seventh and Cedar most every day during the cold months."

Logan turned to Cee-Cee. "'Pepper pot, smoking hot!' That's your ma?"

Cee-Cee nodded as she took a sip of her stew.

"Who made the lid for your can?" Logan asked. "That's downright handy."

"My daddy. He's a passable tinner. Does a lot of tinker work around Moya."

"I'll give you a bite of my meat pie for a sip of your pepper pot."

Cee-Cee smiled and handed the can to Logan. "Have as much as you want. I eat it every day."

Logan sipped. The soup wasn't very warm, but its fatty, spicy, chunky deliciousness made up for it. He handed Cee-Cee one entire meat pie. "You're a friend of Grace's, right?"

Cee-Cee took a bite of the meat pie and contemplated Logan's question. "Yeah, we know each other from church. She asked her daddy to give me this job."

"I've got a favor to ask. If Jules ever asks you how I knew that fire pump was sitting in his factory, tell him Grace told you and you told me."

"Why would I do that?"

"Well, we're friends, right?"

"Dunno," said Cee-Cee. "Never had no white friends, boy nor girl. Don't know anyone who does."

"Jules is friends with Otto Krieger."

"Grace says that's because Jules saved his life a long time ago. You haven't saved my life, and God knows I haven't saved yours."

"Well, you kind of did. I wouldn'ta been able to haul buckets all day yesterday without you spelling me every other time."

Cee-Cee chuckled. "Well, that's true. I'm still sore from all that hauling before you got hired. Grace said you used to be in love with her sister. I guess that's another example. How *did* you know the fire pump was there?"

"I can't tell you. But I wasn't stealing stuff or anything like that."

"Okay, I'll lie for you if needs be. Don't know if that means we're friends, but maybe it's a start."

---

8. Pepper pot stew, a favorite in Philadelphia since the mid-eighteenth century, had its origins in the West Indies and was probably brought to the city by enslaved Africans. *The Cries of Philadelphia*, published in 1810, described the stew as "made chiefly of tripe, ox-feet, other cheap animal substances, with a great portion of spice. It is sold very cheap, so that a hungry man may get a hearty meal for a few cents."

THURSDAY, FEBRUARY 15
(FEBRUARY 3 O.S.)

· RIAN ·

Rian had played hundreds of hands of poker with Count Sheremetev and Colonel Malkovich while crossing the Atlantic, in London, on the Baltic, and here in St. Petersburg. Then Ambassador Dallas spilled the beans about Rian, and the poker games ended.

Despite Sheremetev's ire, the two Russians still came to the Americans' apartment on Thursday evenings, but to play whist rather than poker. "Poker is not much fun with four," declared Sheremetev. "Whist, on the other hand, is a four-person game. We will play whist."

This evening, Rian sat lengthwise with feet up on a settee, an unobtrusive position to pretend to read the newly-arrived December edition of *Bentley's Miscellany*. It contained Chapters 18 and 19 of *Oliver Twist*, which Rian planned to read before she loaned it to Olga. *If she ever talks to me again, that is.*

However, instead of reading, she eavesdropped on the adults' conversation as they played cards—America versus Russia. Seamus and Malkovich had left the table between hands to search for a new bottle of vodka.

Adrian shuffled a deck of cards. "What are we going to do?"

"Pay the fee. We have no choice if we want to do business with him," Sheremetev muttered as he dealt a new hand with the second deck.

"Can we at least call it what it is? Fedorov is demanding a bribe."

"Bribe. Fee. In Russia the difference between the two tends to blur. It is the way things are done here."

"And you have already spoken to Volkonsky about it?"

"Of course. He claims that I must have misinterpreted Fedorov's request. There is no such thing as corruption in the imperial bureaucracy."

Adrian shuffled the cards one last time and set the deck to his right. "So he did nothing."

"Except probably go right to Fedorov and tell him to demand a larger bribe. The man is incessant. He does not want us to succeed and he is going to try to drain us of our capital."

Seamus and Malkovich returned to the table with a new bottle. As Seamus sat, he rejoined the conversation. "Then I say we go around Volkonsky. We've scheduled weekly meetings with Grand Duke Alexander. Why don't we just tell him and have his da solve our problem?"

Sheremetev considered the suggestion. "Go around the gatekeeper on a matter of state? He will be vindictive."

Seamus poured new glasses of vodka for the table. "How can he be more vindictive than he is now? He's already tried to have Rian killed. Our next meeting with the grand duke is tomorrow morning. I say we tell Alexander about the bribe. He goes to the Tsar. The Tsar tells Volkonsky to get Fedorov in line. It's time for the grand duke to grow some balls. He's going to run the family business someday, so start acting like it. And screw Fedorov. There's no way we should pay a bribe to that bastard."

"I agree," said Adrian. "We already know the Secret Police have been watching us. Who knows? Maybe Volkonsky's doing it, too. He could be waiting for us to pay a bribe so he can arrest us."

All four signified their agreement to the decisions by raising their glasses and then draining them.

Rian looked up from her magazine. "Excuse me. I have some information that might be valuable."

All four card players turned toward Rian. Sheremetev *tsked*, clearly perturbed by Rian's interruption.

Rian eyed the four card players over the back of the settee. "Prince Volkonsky and General Benckendorff don't like each other."

Sheremetev *tsked* again and started dealing a new hand. "That is well known at court. There is not a palace in the world that doesn't have intrigue."

"But General Benckendorff doesn't have to go through Volkonsky anymore. He meets with the Tsar every Wednesday. We could go through him."

Sheremetev stopped dealing. "How do you know this?"

"Grand Duke Konstantin Nikolaeovich told me. Volkonsky and Benckendorff had another argument outside the imperial apartment. The Tsar was trying to get away to supper. Kostya heard the whole thing."

"Benckendorff is a dead end," Sheremetev snorted. "He has no interest in the success of our railroad."

No, no. This can work. Come on, Eena. "But he could become interested. What if you sold him a share? He could get rich *and* poke Volkonsky at the same time."

The four card players looked at one another. They started smiling.

Seamus shrugged and spoke to the men at the table. "This could smooth out everything. We all become a little less rich, but we don't have to worry about the Dark Prince."

Sheremetev drained his glass, then savored the liquid for a moment before responding. "We would have to approach Benckendorff with a proposal. It will take weeks to get an appointment."

"I bet I can get an appointment," said Rian. "All I have to do is leave a note in his office. He owes me a favor."

Rian explained about her side business renting copies of *Bentley's*. How the price for getting bumped ahead in line had grown. How the general had been willing to pay a huge fee to get his hands on all the installments, but she asked for a favor-to-be-named-later instead. "Your appointment could be the favor. He'll do it. I know he will."

Sheremetev shook his head as he shuffled the playing cards. "Rian, I doubt your 'favor' has much value. My best guess is you amuse the general. When you try to cash in, he will no longer find you amusing."

"I'm not so sure," interjected Adrian. "He sounded pretty serious about favors when we were all being interrogated in the Third Section's headquarters last week."

Sheremetev started dealing the cards for the next hand of whist. "Then we should give it a try. Let's see how much currency this favor has."

Rian rose, putting her knees on the settee and her elbows on the back. "I will leave a note in his office tomorrow. But I'll only do it on one condition."

"And what is that?" asked Adrian.

"Let me play poker with you all."

Sheremetev swept all the cards on the table into a pile. "Adrian, your niece is becoming quite the wheeler-dealer." He started shuffling the cards. "I'm tired of whist. It's time to play poker. Rian, grab a chair."

* * * * *

· JULES ·

Jules pulled Cee-Cee aside before she left Pennsylvania Hall at the end of the workday. "Cee-Cee, your last name is Porter, right?"

"Yes, it is."

"Are you any relation to Pepper Pot Penny Porter?"

"Yes, sir. She's my momma."

"Homer and Emil have settled into a groove and are working well with each other. The rest of the men seem to have noticed. There have been no incidents, no fights. I'd like to give the men a reward—nudge things along a bit. Do you think your momma would be willing to make an extra kettle of stew and cart it up here for the men's noontime meal?"

"You paying, Jules?"

"Of course."

"In that case, I can answer for my momma. She'd be happy to make an extra kettle. When do you want it?"

"How about tomorrow?"

* * * * *

· LOGAN ·

Logan and Martha were lying on the meager straw mattress, heated more by their own passion than the glowing embers in the potbelly stove.

"We can't keep doing this. What are we going to do?" asked Martha.

Logan sat up. His coat, which had been covering both of them, fell away, revealing his bare chest. "We've said we're going to stop doing this twice, and it hasn't worked. If your parents find out about us, they are going to kill us."

Martha pulled Logan's coat back over her and gazed up at him. "They're too busy to notice. Pop-Pop leaves the house before any of the rest of us are up and gets home after we've all eaten dinner. Mother's covering for him here. I think she likes it. Business is good."

Logan felt around the floor in the dim emberlight for his pants, but couldn't find them. "Maybe you were right before. We could run away."

"Maybe you were the one who was right. Where would we go? Where in the world can a Black girl and an Irish boy live together?"

"I don't know. I've never even been outside of Philadelphia."

"That's not true. You were born in Ireland."

He located his shirt and fumbled with it until he found an armhole. "Well, yeah, but I don't remember it. Maybe we should go back there."

"That's your dumbest idea yet. The Irish are flowing into America for lack of jobs in Ireland. They're starving over there."

"Well, they're not doing very well over here either."

Just then, a loud clang sounded from the shop. Martha sat up. "Someone's here."

Logan stood and looked into the darkness for his pants. "Did you lock the outside door after we came in?" he whispered.

Martha grabbed her dress and started to slip it over her head. "I think so. I'm not sure."

Another clunk and the muffled sound of someone swearing.

Logan still couldn't find his pants.

A second voice, coming closer to the office, the words indistinct.

Logan finally found his pants on a chair. He stepped into one leg, then the other, and buckled his belt. Martha stood and the hem of her dress descended to her ankles. She turned to Logan in a frenzied attempt to help him button his shirt.

Faint candlelight visible from under the office door. A giggle. The door crashed open as two figures in an awkward, unbalanced embrace—one holding a candle, the other with both arms around the first one's neck—tripped across the threshold. More giggles.

Martha gasped.

Logan gently pushed Martha's hands away from his shirt buttons and turned to the intruders.

The two figures realized there was someone else in the office and separated.

"Gracie?" blurted Martha.

"Martha?" responded her little sister. "What are you doing here?"

"What are *you* doing here?"

Grace grasped the hand of the other intruder. "It's warm here. This is my friend Cee-Cee."

FRIDAY, FEBRUARY 16
(FEBRUARY 4 O.S.)

· ADRIAN ·

Adrian paced, walking the length of Count Sheremetev's drawing room and back. "I don't know. I just got a bad feeling when I told him."

The count sifted through papers at his writing desk. Colonel Malkovich stared into the fire from a nearby settee. Neither seemed particularly agitated by Adrian's report.

"What did you tell Grand Duke Alexander exactly?" asked the count without looking up from his papers.

"We met for coffee at the hotel, same as we do every Friday. I told him we intended to sell General Benckendorff five percent of our company stock."

"And what did the grand duke say?" asked Malkovich without looking away from the fire.

"That's when he became a little frosty—a little different. He asked me if we had talked to Benckendorff yet, and I said no. He said I should hold off for a bit. I said I saw no reason to. He said that since he's returned from his grand tour of Siberia, he's starting to get a feel for palace politics. He asked me to wait a day. We've got a date to meet tomorrow."

"So, we wait a day," said the count. "Adrian, this is going to be a decade-long project. It is important to get it started on a firm foundation. Our decision to include Benckendorff will pay dividends down the road. Be patient."

"But the way my meeting with the grand duke went still bothers me. Something's not right."

At that moment, Sergei, Count Sheremetev's Head Underbutler, entered the drawing room without knocking and babbled something in Russian that Adrian didn't understand. Then a man strode in behind him, in turn followed by three men in military coats armed with flintlock rifles. The man spoke rapidly to Count Sheremetev in Russian. Sheremetev rose and responded in an imperious, indignant voice.

A chill coursed up and down Adrian's spine. "What's going on?" he asked Sheremetev.

"We are being arrested," said Sheremetev. "We have been told to get our coats and come with these men."

* * * * * *

· SEAMUS ·

Seamus had taken a stroll to view the reconstruction of the Winter Palace. He was impressed that all the debris had been cleared away and hundreds of craftsmen were busy throughout the site. Joists for the first floor were in place in half the mammoth building.

He walked back to Count Sheremetev's palazzo to meet up with Adrian, the count, and the colonel. As he strode up the vast, granite front steps, the door suddenly opened and his three compatriots were escorted out of the building by four men, three of whom held rifles.

Seamus stepped out of the way. "Adrian, what's going on?"

"We're being arrested," responded his uncle as he was escorted down the steps. "They're taking us to the Peter and Paul Fortress."

This is bad, thought Seamus. The fortress was built to guard St. Petersburg from a naval attack, but that hadn't been a worry for a hundred years. *It's a prison now.*

He watched from the steps as the three arrestees were prodded into the back of an enclosed, windowless carriage. The three armed guards then followed them in. The fourth man—the man obviously in charge—latched the door and climbed aboard the front of the wagon to join the driver.

Seamus stared hard at the man in charge. *That's the man who I saw at the police station last week. He's the one who tried to kill Rian.*

* * * * * * * * * * * * * * *

Our narrative has now caught up to the book's opening scenes, in which Seamus finds Rian at the Manege and tells her Adrian, Sheremetev, and Malkovich have been arrested; the two cousins confront Volkonsky; Seamus is arrested; and Rian steals Catherine the Great's memoir.

* * * * * * * * * * * * * * *

· RIAN ·

Fook you, Volkonsky, Rian said as she walked out of the Anichkov Palace and back out into the bitter cold of St. Petersburg.

Adrian, Seamus, Sheremetev, and Malkovich are in prison.

She walked to the Black Eagle stationery store on Nevsky Prospekt and bought three hundred sheets of their finest rag paper, a large bottle of ink, and two steel-tipped pens.

I can't allow Catherine's memoirs to be found in my possession.

She walked to the Manege, the only place in St. Petersburg that she thought would be even remotely safe until the ice broke on the Baltic. She set up a makeshift desk next to Franklin and Washington's stalls. She wrote until after midnight, hid the stationery on top of a beam, and walked back to the apartment on Nevsky Prospekt.

At this rate, I'll be writing for the next three days.

* * * * *

· OTTO ·

One by one, Otto held three fried rashers of bacon over the cast-iron pan, letting the grease drip back into the pan before laying the bacon out onto his plate. Creaking floorboards above him indicated that Conor McGuire was stirring. Otto repeated the task, placing three more bacon strips onto a plate for Conor.

Otto cut two thick slices of stale bread and stuck a toasting fork into the bottom of one of them. He opened the door to the kitchen stove and held the slice to the fire.

As was his habit, Conor clumped downstairs into the parlor, walked through the kitchen without saying a word, and slipped out the back door to head for the privy.

Otto pulled the toasting fork out of the stove, noted with satisfaction that the bread was perfectly toasted on one side, flipped it over, and thrust it back into the stove. His slice properly toasted, Otto cracked two eggs into the pan, and the bacon grease sputtered.

* * * * *

Otto barely lifted his eyes from his morning paper when Conor joined him at the table with his plate. "Sorry I missed you last night."

"I was with Jabez. We learned a new card game called poker."

Jabez. A wave of sadness momentarily took Otto up short. *When Jabez and Rian switched places so she could run off to Russia, I vowed to watch out for him. I have failed miserably.* "How is my nephew doing? He has stopped coming into work."

"Okay, I guess. He doesn't go to school much either."

"And what does he do with his time if he is not working for me or going to school?"

"I don't know. He has made some new friends. They spend a lot of time down by the docks. Otto, I miss Rian. I wish she would come home."

The thought of his daughter half a world away caused a second wave of melancholy to wash over Otto. "Do you have any news of shipping on the Delaware?"

Conor worked as a messenger for the businessmen whose offices were housed in the Merchants' Exchange Building. He often delivered coded messages from the semaphore towers[9] to other Philadelphia businessmen. A day's advance knowledge of incoming ships or activity in New York gave the cartel that owned the towers a significant advantage over those who did not have access to their information.

Conor had broken the code and slipped Otto tidbits when they might be helpful . . . or interesting. "Did you hear about the *Printessa*?"

Otto shook his head.

"She sailed into Philadelphia a couple of days ago with a load of oranges, limes, and pineapple from the West Indies. Usually, when any fruit at all comes into port this time of year, the merchants in town snap it all up right off the boat, no matter what the price. This year nobody's buying because of the depression. The captain of the *Printessa* was going to leave with his cargo half unsold and head to New York, but he got word from New York that there was a ship up there that wasn't selling its fruit there either. The fruit was rotting, so he sold whatever he could to whoever showed up with a wheelbarrow. The word at the Merchants' Exchange is that he lost money on this trip."

Conor's story sobered Otto. *If it weren't for the* Philadelphia & Columbia Railroad, *I might be in a similar situation. As it is, I am doing quite well while merchants are struggling and people are starving. I should thank my lucky stars.*

* * * * *

· JULES ·

Jules was pleased to see his plan taking shape. Pepper Pot Penny arrived a few minutes before the noontime break. Logan and Cee-Cee helped her muscle

---

9. A string of optical telegraph (semaphore) towers from Cape May, New Jersey, to the Merchants' Exchange Building (MEB) in Philadelphia opened in 1809. Another chain of semaphore towers, built in 1834, extended from the MEB to a building on Wall Street in New York City. Moveable mechanical flags atop a tower could be seen with a telescope from an adjacent tower as much as ten miles away. Short messages could travel a hundred miles in less than fifteen minutes.

her cart up the three stairs onto the portico, through the double doors, and into the foyer.

The workers lined up, some with tin cups, some with tin cans, to receive a generous ladle of stew from Penny. Jules watched with satisfaction as the men sat down, not in their usual all-Black or all-white pods. Today, they sat randomly, backs to the walls of the foyer. *Probably hoping to be close enough to the kettle to get seconds*, thought Jules.

After all who wanted more stew had returned for seconds, or even thirds, Jules approached Penny as she was packing up her stuff. "The plasterers have worked hard to finish this job quickly. I suspect next Friday will be their last day. Any chance you can come back again with another kettle of stew?"

Penny nodded. "I can do that." Then she eyed Cee-Cee, currently sitting next to Logan Gallagher and exchanging words in hushed tones. "How's my daughter working out for you? She behaving herself?"

"She's one of my best workers. Why, what are you hearing at your end?"

"Barely see the girl. She works here ten hours a day, then most nights she doesn't drag herself back home until after I've set my kettle going at the hearth and gone to bed. Little worried, truth be told. That young man Logan. Is he anyone I need to worry about? I don't want Cee-Cee getting in trouble, but especially with no white boy."

Jules stole a glance at the two youngsters. "I believe they're both smarter than that, but if I get wind of anything, I'll let you know."

THURSDAY, FEBRUARY 22

· JULES ·

The plasterers were working on a punch list of touch-ups that would take them through the next morning. After tomorrow's noontime pepper pot stew celebration, they would pack up and leave on Friday afternoon. Jules and the crew boss Rudolf Bartle were finishing their walkthrough of the building, ending in the Gallery of the Grand Saloon. The finish coat, now mostly dry and white, gave more than a hint of the building's impending grandeur.

Despite the tasks that Jules knew lay ahead, he was in a good mood. "Your men have done a beautiful job, Rudolf. Congratulations. Where to next?"

"We're going up to the Shelter for Colored Orphans. Expect the job will take about three weeks. After that, there's nothing."

The news of no work beyond the Shelter didn't surprise Jules. The Hall and the Shelter were the two biggest projects going on in the city right now, and there wasn't much else happening in the construction trades.

"This depression's a fooler, Jules. Every time I think we're coming out of it, I check around and there's no work to be had. You can see it on the street. More panhandlers. Until three months ago, the baker near my house rented a storefront. Now he's peddling his bread out of a pushcart, and the storefront is still vacant. There's kids selling pineapples out of wheelbarrows, but nobody's buying. I'm afraid your brethren are bearing the brunt of it, Jules. And the Irish, of course."

"It's interesting that I would be happy to hire a few more skilled workers, but I can't find anyone who's willing to work here. They are so hateful. . . ."

"Sometimes I wonder. Is it hate or fear?"

"Who am I or what am I doing that they have to be fearful about?"

"Maybe it's not you but what you represent. Meetings in this building will try to bring about freedom for two million of your brethren. If that happens, they will be streaming into this city."

"The men who choose not to work for me—they are choosing to not put food on their family's plate. They will be old men by the time slavery is ended in this country."

Bartle shrugged and shook his head, signifying an end to the discussion. "Uh, Jules, a couple more things. That fire pump ended up being quite useful for getting water to my guys. Do you mind if we take it with us to the Shelter? Give me a reasonable price for the pump, hoses, and tubs and I'll rent them from you for three weeks, maybe four."

Jules pondered the offer. *Maddie will appreciate a little extra income for Freeman Hydraulics.* "Yeah, I can come up with something."

"Good," said Bartle. "And I don't know if you've noticed, but my guy Charlie has been working with two of your people, uh . . . Logan and the little colored girl."

Bartle's one of the good guys, but even he can't take the trouble to learn her name. "Her name is Cee-Cee. She's a friend of my daughter."

"Well, Charlie said they're as good a crew as he's ever had. He's teaching them some tricks of the trade, even though neither one of them will ever be able to join the union. He'd like to take them up to the Shelter while we're working up there. Are you okay to let them go with us for a bit?"

Jules was pleased that the two kids were learning some skills. He thought he was going to have to lay them off for three weeks while the painters did their work. Now they would have a job until it was time to come back to the Hall. "Hunnecher doesn't hire Blacks or Irish. He's not going to be pleased."

"I'm a subcontractor. Hunnecher doesn't get to tell me who I can bring along with me. Besides, they're only mixing plaster."

"Then, sure, take them if they want to go. But send them back when your job is done."

"Oh, that's going to happen for sure. Like I said, after that job's finished, I've got nothing. Oh, and by the way, I'm sorry about the news."

"What news?"

"You didn't know? The Constitutional Convention made its final vote this morning. They're done with their work. If the people of Pennsylvania ratify it, you're gonna lose your right to vote."

* * * * *

New State Constitution Ratified
Exclusive to the *Philadelphia Independent*
By Harold Foote

In Philadelphia today, delegates to the Pennsylvania Constitutional Convention voted on a final draft of the new state constitution that they have been laboring over since May of last year. The proposed constitution will be submitted to the voters for their approval. Citizens will vote on the revised document in October of this year.

The most controversial change to the new constitution is a resolution limiting voting eligibility to "white" freemen over the age of twenty-one who have recently paid taxes. This change specifically denies free Negro males the right to vote, which they have held for forty-eight years, since the ratification of Pennsylvania's Constitution of 1790.

The resolution to add "white" to the wording of the new document was originally defeated when the delegates were meeting in Harrisburg last spring. The most recent resolution, denying the franchise to free Black males, passed by a vote of 77–45. The fifty-eight Democrats who supported the measure were joined by nineteen Whigs and Anti-Masons.

Other changes to the new constitution include stripping the governor of his power to appoint local officials. . . .

* * * * *

Jules finished reading the article. Whatever good mood he had been in at the start of his day had long since disappeared.

FRIDAY, FEBRUARY 23

· LOGAN ·

It was the plasterers' last day on the job. Logan and Cee-Cee were mixing a last wee batch of plaster for Charlie's touch-ups when the fight broke out.

They rushed upstairs to see Jules and the plastering contractor Rudolf Bartle pulling men out of a Black vs. white melee. It took five minutes for them to separate everyone.

The last combatants were Homer, that Black man whom Jules claimed was his half-brother, and some white plasterer whom Logan didn't know. As the last swings were swung, the formerly weepy-eyed Emil Harberger stepped between the two and shoved Homer away from the plasterer. Rather than stick with his fellow whites, Emil stayed with Homer, talked to him, said words that were unintelligible to Logan but sounded soothing.

Moments later, Jules approached Homer and Emil. Logan moved closer to listen in on Jules's conversation.

"What the hell was that all about?"

"He's been riding me all day," said Homer. "Says 'Come constitution time, you Africans are gonna lose your rights. No votes. No nothing. Then we're gonna ride you outta town.' Jules, until yesterday, I didn't even know what a vote was. Never thought about voting. But I got sick of him. He wouldn't quit. Finally I popped him one good."

"Jules," said Emil, "Homer took it for a lot longer than I would have. He should have hit him an hour ago."

After things had settled down, most of the men returned to their tasks, but the tension was still thick. The plasterers continued with their touch-ups. The carpenters worked on the stage. Homer and Emil worked on the columns in silence.

At the noontime break, Logan and Cee-Cee stationed themselves next to Cee-Cee's mother and helped Pepper Pot Penny ladle her steaming deliciousness into the cans and cups of the workers.

This time, however, there was little mixing of Black and white. The white plasterers, each with his own can of pepper pot, walked upstairs to the Grand Saloon.

The Black carpenters remained down in the foyer.

Emil, who lately had been eating his dinner with Homer, watched the parade of plasterers as they left the foyer. He surveyed the carpenters, now sitting themselves around the perimeter of the foyer. "It's sunny out," he announced to no one in particular. "I think I'm going to eat out on the portico."

Homer rose and headed for the front door. Jules and Rudolf Bartle followed. Logan looked at Cee-Cee. She nodded and the two of them followed the others out onto the portico, where the sun streamed down and provided a modicum of warmth. The six of them sat on empty nail kegs and slurped their pepper pot.

Conversation was subdued. Logan was a bit surprised to find himself eating his dinner with his Black boss Jules, the white plastering contractor Bartle, Jules's half-brother Homer, the formerly weepy-eyed and hostile Emil Harberger, and Cee-Cee, Logan's secret girlfriend's sister's secret girlfriend.

Charlie, who had walked upstairs to eat with the other plasterers, came outside with a steaming second tin cup of pepper pot. "Penny says there's plenty more stew, and you should get it while it's still hot." Rather than return to the Grand Saloon, he eyed a seventh empty nail keg and sat down. "Nice out here."

Passers-by glanced at this motley group eating dinner together. Their glances became stares, and they weren't always friendly.

MONDAY, FEBRUARY 26
(FEBRUARY 14 O.S.)

· RIAN ·

For ten days, Rian felt like she was riding on a giant pendulum.

At one end of the pendulum's arc, shock and fear paralyzed her. She was abandoned, alone in an alien land with no one to support her. All the people she had relied upon had been ripped away. Adrian, Sheremetev, Malkovich, and Seamus were rotting in the Peter and Paul Fortress on the opposite shore of the Neva River. The morning after their arrest, she was evicted from their apartment. Although she had tried to enter the Anichkov Palace on Monday, Volkonsky had been right. The Tsar had banned her from entering, taking away any hope of assistance from the grand duke and even Gospodin Litke.

Then there were moments when the pendulum swung the other way, toward anger and resolve. *Quit feeling sorry for yourself. Do something about your situation.* She became focused, productive, vengeful. Last year—*a lifetime ago*—Rian had helped Robert Purvis and Seamus translate *The Art of War*, a book by the Chinese general Sun Tzu, from French to English. She pondered some of those two-thousand-year-old words of wisdom from memory.

It is the business of the general to be serene and inscrutable, impartial and self-controlled.

He changes his methods and alters his plans so that people have no knowledge of what he is doing.

At first, be shy as a maiden. When the enemy gives you an opening, be swift as a hare and he will be unable to withstand you.

Of all those close to the commander, none is more intimate than the secret agent.

After the troops have met, he cuts off their return route as if he were removing a ladder from beneath them.

That was her temper when the guard Yuri approached her as she was brushing Wash in his stall. "A gentleman is looking for you. He is waiting outside the main entrance."

Rian slipped into Captain Stepanov's large military greatcoat and followed Yuri. She was surprised to find Ambassador Dallas standing in the cold. "Good evening, sir," she said, offering politeness but no warmth.

"Rian, thank goodness I've found you. I understand that your uncle and cousin have been arrested and you were evicted from your apartment. I've been searching for you since I returned from Moscow. Are you all right?"

"What do you want?"

"I want to help you."

Rian stifled the urge to burst out crying but managed to croak out, "I don't need your help."

"You've been banished from the Tsar's palace? Forbidden to see the grand duke?"

Rian nodded. "They never even gave me a chance to say goodbye."

"Where are you living?"

"Here. I sleep in the carriage at night. No one bothers me."

"What about all the possessions from your uncle's apartment?"

"They're gone. They threw me out with what I was wearing. I grabbed a couple of things on my way out."

"No other clothing?"

Rian shook her head. "One coachman's outfit. One of the suits I used to wear to the tutoring sessions in the palace. This greatcoat. That's it."

"My Sophia is a little older than you. I can get you one of her dresses."

Rian stifled an urge to swear at the ambassador. "Like I said, I don't need your help."

"Where did you get the greatcoat you are wearing? It's a bit big for you."

Another urge to cry bubbled up. "It was Captain Stepanov's. His men gave it to me. They said he talked about me a lot. They said I made him want to meet more Americans."

"What are you doing for food?"

"I'm exercising some of the guardsmen's horses. They throw me enough kopeks to feed myself."

"Have you heard any news from your uncle or cousin?"

"No."

"What about the valet your uncle hired in London? What happened to him?

"One of the count's buddies snapped him up."

"A pity he didn't offer to hire you as well."

"He did. I said no. I had other plans."

"What plans?"

"Wait a few more days. Then meet with General Benckendorff."

"I wasn't talking about plans to gain the release of Mr. Krieger and Mr. Gallagher. Leave that to the adults. It became my highest priority as soon as I learned of their arrest."

"They're innocent."

"Apparently innocence doesn't matter much in this country. They have angered powerful men."

"That's why I'm going to meet with the general."

"The head of the Third Section isn't likely to meet with a child."

"He'll meet with me."

"And why is that?"

"He owes me a favor. I have something he wants. He just doesn't know it yet."

"Rian, my priority is to get you onto the first ship to England as soon as the ice breaks on the Baltic. We'll have you out of here in less than two weeks."

"I have to get my uncle and cousin out of prison. And the count and the colonel. Then I'll think about leaving."

"Leave your uncle and cousin to me."

"How long will it take you?"

"It is my job to look after the few American citizens who live in Russia."

"How long?"

"Weeks. Maybe months."

"And the count and the colonel?"

"I have no power to help them."

"That's what I figured. So I'm going to keep doing what I'm doing."

"And what is it that you are doing?"

"As soon as I finish with the horses, I'm working at the Winter Carnival in the Admiralty Gardens. This is the last day."

* * * * *

Even though this had been a mild winter by St. Petersburg standards, as far as Rian was concerned, it had been long and cold. To the Russians' credit, instead of hunkering down in their homes, they frequently played and socialized outside. As evidence of their hardiness, there seemed to be an outdoor festival every couple of weeks.

Rian scanned the crowd from the top of the ice mountain tower, a platform that was about fifteen feet square. *Olga said she comes to every carnival and always goes down the ice mountain. Well, she hasn't shown yet, and this is the last day of the carnival. If she doesn't show, I have to pare back my plan. I really don't want to do that. Of course, this has to be a goddamn Monday. Mondays are unlucky in Russia. Starting anything in Russia on Monday is especially unlucky. Damnit.*

Rian had been launching sledges at the top of the ice mountain for the past three days. One day had been bitterly cold. Although wrapped in Captain Stepanov's heavy military greatcoat, the cold seeped into her bones. The next day hadn't been as cold, but the wind coming off the Neva River had bitten right through the coat and chilled her once more. The third day had been both cold and windy. Now, on the fourth day, the sun was out and the temperature was above freezing.

Rian had dipped into her meager funds, paying off Mikhail, the boy who should have been giving sledders a push over the edge of the platform. Only on the second day did she learn that some people would pay a kopek to get an extra enthusiastic launch over the precipice. She had given the brief orientation about riding the sledge down the icy incline so many times that she could do it in her sleep.

Finally, Rian's patience and suffering paid off. Mikhail and another boy shouldered their way to the top of the platform. "She's here," said Mikhail. "She's on the stairs now." Rian peeked over the railing. *Perfect: it's Olga and Konstantin.* Rian scanned the crowd to find Madame Parshakov, the guardian of the Grand Duchess's virtue. *Even more perfect: Parshakov is standing outside the ropes. She's not coming up with them.*

Rian didn't reveal herself until fifteen minutes later, when the two siblings got to the top of the platform. "Olga, can I ride down with you?"

"Rian, what are you doing here?"

"Waiting for you. I need to talk to you. Hello, Kostya," Rian said to Konstantin. "Are you okay to go down with Mikhail here?"

"No!" yelled Olga. She shoved at Rian's chest with both hands. "I'm not going anywhere with you."

"Come on!" came a voice from the stairs. "You're holding up the line!"

The cold and her crumbling plans combined to start Rian shivering violently.

"We talk first," said Olga. "If you are honest with me, then maybe I will ride down with you."

Rian took a breath. She turned to Mikhail and the boy who had accompanied him on lookout. "Can you take over for me for a bit?" The boy nodded and greeted the next pair of sledders in line, asking them, "Have you ever done this before?"

Rian turned to Konstantin. "Kostya, I need to talk to Olga in private."

"No," said Olga. "Kostya knows everything. I told him."

"Everything?"

"Yes, everything. You talk to both of us, or he and I get on our sledge right now."

Rian ushered the two royals to the corner of the platform. Mikhail took it upon himself to stand guard, keeping others on the platform out of hearing distance.

Olga crossed her arms and faced Rian. "Did you take the memoirs?"

"Yes, that's what I want to talk to you about. . . ."

"Are you going to harm my family?"

Rian gazed out at the throng of carnival-goers below, then back at Olga. "Not if my plan works."

"What if it doesn't work?"

"Then I will have betrayed you and your family."

Olga turned away. "You don't care about my family."

Rian maneuvered around so that Olga was forced to look at her again. "You asked for my honesty. No, I don't really care about your family. I don't think I like your father that much. He owns a million serfs. That alone is reason enough to dislike him. But I care about you. I care about Kostya. I don't want Catherine the Great's memoir to be published, but I'm willing to risk that happening to get my family and friends out of prison."

"That's why you took it? To save your family?"

"Yes. They are innocent. Prince Volkonsky made up the charges against them."

"Why do you need me?"

"Well, that's the thing. I don't need you. My plan has already started. But if you *do* help me, I will get revenge."

"Revenge? Revenge against Volkonsky?"

Rian nodded. "I saw him kill my friend Captain Stepanov. This is the captain's greatcoat. His men gave it to me. You hate Volkonsky too. Come on, Your Highness. . . ."

"I do hate Volkonsky. He is dismissive of me because I am a girl. He thinks I am only useful because I will one day be married off to solidify some political alliance. He underestimates me."

"Exactly. And now you get to strike a blow. . . ."

Olga stared out to the east. "The Admiralty Building blocks any view of the Winter Palace, even from this height. My father decided that the Winter

Carnival would be set up here so the people wouldn't see the ruins. He was afraid they would be reminded that the palace burned on his watch. They would think less of him."

"You live in a superstitious country."

"If the people learn that he is not a Romanov by blood, it could be the end of us."

"I know," was all Rian could think to say.

"We are the descendants of Catherine the Great. Our family has ruled Russia for two hundred years. The Winter Palace will be rebuilt. The people's awe of my father will be rekindled." She turned and stared at Rian. "Nothing you can do to us will change that."

For a moment, Rian thought Olga was going to reject her out of hand. Then. . . .

"I will ride down the ice mountain with you. We will talk. If I don't like what you tell me, I will turn you in to Volkonsky myself. I'll tell him you have betrayed our family, and you are a girl."

Rian turned to Mikhail, who was still keeping people from eavesdropping on her conversation with Olga. "Mikhail, we're done talking. Are you still okay to go down with the grand duke?"

Two minutes later, Rian had settled onto the sledge, her feet on the front crosspiece, her hands holding the rope.

Olga climbed on behind Rian, arms tight around her waist. "Catherine the Great would have had you drawn and quartered."

"Catherine the Great would have listened to my plan first, then decided."

"Then I am a worthy descendant of my great-grandmother."

Rian woofed out a deep breath, equal measures because of the impending descent and how persuasive she would have to be over the next few minutes. Mikhail's friend gave them a vigorous shove that would have been worth a kopek. A second later, the descent forced all thoughts—her family and friends in jail, the precariousness of her life at the moment, the potential that she could soon be shot by a firing squad, doubts about whether the plan would even work—out of her mind. The sledge rapidly accelerated and the crowd below turned into a blur.

Two hours later, Rian returned to the Manege, then exercised and fed the horses. She ate some bread and smoked sausage that she had bought at the carnival. She crawled into the landau, wrapped herself in a horse blanket, and lapsed into a troubled sleep.

TUESDAY, FEBRUARY 27
(FEBRUARY 15 O.S.)

· RIAN ·

The next day, Olga and Konstantin appeared outside of Frank's stall in the Manege. Madame Parshakov stood a discreet distance behind them.

Rian couldn't keep a big smile off her face. "Olga, what are you doing here? I thought you were going to send Kostya."

"This is my declaration of independence."

Konstantin climbed onto the bottom board of the stall so he could peer over at Rian. "I told Gospodin Litke I wanted to skip morning class and have an adventure. He didn't even ask what the adventure was going to be."

"I was jealous," said Olga. "I told Madame Parshakov that I wanted to get my hands on the latest Charles Dickens installment."

Rian quickly glanced at Frank. The horse was preoccupied by the oats she had scooped into his feed box. She opened the stall door to let the royals in. "Yes, it's in here someplace." She groped around the cabinet that housed horse brushes, liniment, and other tinctures for the *Bentley's Miscellany*. Olga followed.

"Any luck?" Rian whispered.

"I snuck into Volkonsky's office last night," the grand duchess said, her voice barely audible. "It was very exciting. I slipped the memoirs into the bottom of the pile on the right front corner of his desk."

Bless you, Olga, thought Rian. She found the *Bentley's Miscellany* and handed the magazine to Olga.

The grand duke and Rian walked Wash and Frank down the long corridor together. Rian was about to mount Wash when Olga said, "No, I want to ride him."

Rian turned to Olga. "We don't have any sidesaddles here."

"I am not interested in riding sidesaddle anymore. I want to learn to ride like a man." She smiled at Rian. "Like you."

Rian considered this, then held the reins out to Olga. Olga accepted the reins, put her left foot in the stirrup, and deftly mounted Wash. Rian turned to see Madame Parshakov cross herself, but the guardian of Olga's virtue said nothing.

The horses properly exercised and brushed down, the royals and Rian walked to the Neva River with Madame Parshakov trailing behind. The twice-daily high tides had left thick chunks of ice on the river shoreline that gave just a hint of warming temperatures.

Rian inhaled the fresh, salty air of the sea. They walked through the nearly completed St. Isaac's Cathedral, its construction suspended and its craftsmen instead working to rebuild the Winter Palace. They watched hundreds of workers installing new floor joists on the first floor of the palace.

Olga turned to Rian. "It's time for us to get back to the Anichkov Palace." Konstantin joined them.

"I probably won't ever see you two again," said Rian. "It has been the most amazing adventure of my life."

"An interesting statement from a girl who ran away to Russia and fought the fire in the Winter Palace," said Olga, her eyes twinkling.

"And stabbed a man," added Konstantin. He hugged Rian, then turned and started walking back toward Nevsky Prospekt.

Olga stayed. "I know you won't betray us. You are a good . . . a good person. I am sorry we will never see each other again." She awkwardly moved in to hug Rian.

"*Nyet! Nyet! Nyet!*" screeched Madame Parshakov.

WEDNESDAY, FEBRUARY 28
(FEBRUARY 16 O.S.)

· RIAN ·

Rian wore Captain Stepanov's Imperial Guard greatcoat over her good suit.

A week ago, she had seen the man in the greatcoat entering a café on Nevsky Prospekt. She returned to the café in hopes that he was a creature of habit. Fortunately, he was eating alone at a table right by a window. He caught sight of her the same moment she spotted him.

Rian entered the café and walked to the man's table. "Do you remember me?"

The man finished cutting his pork chop. "That coat's a little big for you, isn't it?"

Rian shrugged. "I'll grow into it."

"I hear you're sleeping in the stable. That was smart, since you don't have the Tsar to protect you anymore. The Horse Guards won't let Volkonsky's men inside to slit your throat. Assuming he still gives a shit about you, that is. What do you want?"

"You saved my life."

The man shrugged.

"General Benckendorff owes me a favor. I would like to cash it in."

"How old are you?"

"Almost fourteen."

"You're pretty cheeky for an almost-fourteen-year-old."

Rian placed a rolled sheet of paper that was tied with a piece of twine onto the man's table. "I've heard that before. Please deliver this to the general. Tell him there are fifty more sheets like this. The reading gets even more interesting. If he wants to see me, you know where to find me."

THURSDAY, MARCH 1
(FEBRUARY 17 O.S.)

· RIAN ·

Rian, accompanied by the man in the greatcoat, entered the office of General Alexander Benckendorff, head of the Third Section.

Quid pro quo. Rian had learned that phrase long ago from her Latin teacher. *You give me something. I give you something in return. That's my goal for this meeting. General Benckendorff, I'm going to give you a chance to wound Prince Volkonsky. You're going to free my family and friends. If that doesn't work, then. . . .*

"Thank you, Kiserev. Please wait for my visitor outside." Benckendorff, who was gazing out an arched window, gestured to Rian to take a seat. "I understand you are living in a horse stall. A bit of a comedown from companion to a grand duke."

Don't screw this up, Eena. "Thank you for seeing me, Gospodin."

"What is the purpose of your visit?"

"You owe me a favor. I would like to cash it in."

Benckendorff seemed more interested in watching the birds outside his window than facing Rian. "Even an insolent American child like yourself couldn't assume that the loan of a few periodicals is enough to get your uncle and cousin out of Peter and Paul Fortress."

"No, but I come to you offering to do you an even bigger favor, so perhaps the release of my family and the count and colonel will balance the scales."

"You are a child pretending to bargain like an adult. I assure you; you have nothing I want. You have no power here."

"Did you know that my uncle and Count Sheremetev intended to offer you a share of the railroad?"

For the first time, Benckendorff turned from the window. His eyes bore into Rian.

Rian plowed ahead. "Prince Volkonsky didn't want that to happen. That's why he had everyone arrested. I guess you'll never get a chance to become a railroad man, but you might be able to get some payback. I know you don't like Volkonsky, and he doesn't like you."

"Enough banter. What is it that you are offering?"

Rian gestured to the fifty pages of Catherine the Great's memoir sitting in her lap. "A chance to diminish Prince Volkonsky's influence with the Tsar; maybe even get him out of your way."

Benckendorff folded his arms in front of him. "You have my attention."

No turning back now. Yana had said I'm going to leave Russia soon. She better be right, because otherwise I'm going to spend the rest of my life rotting away in the Peter and Paul Fortress because of what I'm about to do. She gripped the memoir to prevent her hands from shaking. "Prince Volkonsky is plotting something against Tsar Nicholas. In fact, he is a threat to the entire Romanov Dynasty."

"Your accusation is highly unlikely, but let us explore this a bit. I assume that this threat to the Tsar has something to do with that page that Kiserev brought to me."

Rian placed the memoir on Benckendorff's desk and withdrew her hand quickly for fear that Benckendorff would see her shaking. "Yes, and here is the rest of it. I stole this off Prince Volkonsky's desk the day he arrested my cousin."

Benckendorff idly leafed through the document. "And what do you think this is?"

Rian picked her words carefully. *Don't overplay your hand, Eena.* "It is the memoir of Catherine the Great. She describes an affair she had with an army officer named Saltykov. Saltykov is the real father of her son Paul, not Peter III. If there is no Romanov blood in Paul, then there isn't any in his son Nicholas. Tsar Nicholas is not a true Romanov."

"Who prompted you to say these words?"

"How could anyone have prompted me? Everyone I trust in Russia has been arrested."

"Where did this document come from?"

"I told you. I stole it off Prince Volkonsky's desk. I didn't know what it was at the time. I saw him cover it up when my cousin Seamus and I entered his office."

"And why was a child of thirteen at a meeting with the Minister of the Imperial Court?"

"The prince had arrested my uncle. My cousin scheduled an appointment to tell the prince that my uncle was innocent. He needed me to be his interpreter. Volkonsky didn't like it when Seamus protested, so he called the guards. He was distracted when Seamus struggled with his men. I snuck the file off his desk and tucked it into my coat."

"I don't believe you."

Rian shrugged. "How else could I have got it?"

Benckendorff charged at the sitting Rian and loomed over her. "You insolent little mosquito. I will squash you right now."

Rian stuffed down the urge to throw up. Rather than look up at the general and be even more intimidated, she shifted her gaze toward the window. "Well, I've been thinking about that. You could do that, but then you would miss out on an opportunity to get back at the prince."

"I can do that whenever I please. Kiserev!"

The man in the greatcoat reentered the office.

"Escort this little shit out of the building. No need to be gentle about it."

"I wrote out a copy!" Rian blurted out. She had only intended to divulge this gambit if all else failed. *Nice job, Eena. You haven't even been here three minutes and you're already down to your last resort.*

Benckendorff held up his hand to halt Kiserev. "You did what?"

"I copied the document. Fifty pages. Word for word. It's on its way to America."

"You have told nothing but lies since you entered my office."

"No, it's true. The only reason I've waited this long to meet with you is to make sure it is so far gone that even Volkonsky's fastest riders can't catch up to it. If my uncle, my cousin, Count Sheremetev, and Colonel Malkovich are not freed, if I don't arrive in Philadelphia by April 23, this entire document gets delivered to the *Philadelphia Independent*. It will be published the next day."

"April 23. Which calendar, Julian or Gregorian?"

Benckendorff's question immediately sowed a seed of doubt into Rian's soul. "Gregorian," she said, but her mind was already reeling.

"That is less than eight weeks from now. You are lying. You have condemned your companions to tortures you cannot possibly imagine."

Sour vomit snuck up into Rian's throat. She swallowed. Her whole body shook uncontrollably. "I'm telling the truth. I could have sent the package through Riga. It would have arrived in Riga days ago, but I didn't want to take the chance that Riga was still icebound, so I sent it all the way through Hamburg. It's already gone. It will arrive in Philadelphia by the middle of April."

"Kiserev, take this little turd to join his relatives."

Rian, on the verge of panic, forced herself to maintain her composure. "General, the Winter Palace burned down two months ago. The people of Russia consider that a bad omen, and that weakens the Tsar. The publication of Catherine the Great's memoir would be devastating in his weakened state.

What is he going to say when he learns that it could have been easily avoided by freeing some innocent men from prison?"

"Most likely, he'll say this is a forgery. An utter fabrication."

"There are fifty pages there, with lots of information. I bet a knowledgeable Russian historian will be able to verify that it's Catherine's memoir."

"Historians will never be allowed to read such a thing."

"They will when the Paris newspapers get hold of it. Or Hamburg. They will publish it for sure. One section at a time. Over weeks and weeks. You told me yourself that banned literature gets past your censors all the time. Do you want your Tsar to become the laughingstock of Europe? Or do you want to avoid it all when the solution is so easy?"

"No thirteen-year-old could concoct such a plan as this. Who is pulling your strings? Someone inside the palace? One of the Imperial Guards? I will squeeze this information out of you and find your puppet master. Then you and they will die. Possession of this document is a treasonous act."

"Maybe you're asking the wrong question. You've been trying to figure out who is behind me. You should really be asking, 'What was the document doing on Volkonsky's desk?'"

"Volkonsky will deny that he was ever in possession of that document. It will be your word against his, and I assure you, the prince is an infinitely more reliable source than you."

Rian rose and pointed to the document she had placed on Benckendorff's desk. "What if this document isn't Catherine's original memoir? It's a transcript, like the one I sent to America. What if the original, much more extensive than this, in Catherine's own hand, was still in Volkonsky's office?"

Benckendorff, who had been looming over Rian for minutes, finally turned away from her. "That would change things considerably. How could you possibly know this?"

Rian shrugged. "Do you want to punch the prince in the nose or not? Count Sheremetev was going to make you a rich man. Volkonsky has now made that impossible."

"I told you before, favors—not riches—are my currency."

Rian shrugged. "But I assume that favors *and* riches are even better."

"How much money does your puppet master want?"

"There is no one behind this scheme but me, and I don't want any money."

"So what are the terms of this blackmail scheme of yours?"

"I want you to arrange the release of my uncle, my cousin, Count Sheremetev, and Colonel Malkovich. I want the Tsar to know that Catherine's memoirs only fell into my hands because Prince Volkonsky was up to something. Please tell the Tsar that I bear him no ill will. I don't want the memoir to become public, but I am forced to do this to get innocent men out of prison."

"And if I agree?"

"As soon as the ice breaks and we can secure passage out of St. Petersburg, we will get out of your hair. We will have plenty of time to get to Philadelphia to head off the package. Catherine's memoir will never be published, and you will never hear from us again."

The general disdainfully poked at the memoir with his finger, fanning the pages slightly on his desk. "I suppose I must read this and come to my own conclusions about it. I'll make some inquiries about the prisoners. But I tell you, His Majesty will never believe your story about Volkonsky. The prince may give the Tsar bad advice occasionally, but he is not disloyal."

"Are you sure? It would look pretty bad for him if the Tsar found Catherine's memoir in his office."

Benckendorff smiled for the first time. "That alone would be worth quite a bit. This transcript. How many copies did you write out?"

Rian felt her shaking ease a bit. "Two. This one before you on your desk and the one that's on its way to America." She played her final card. "If I can guarantee that you will find the original in Volkonsky's office, will you grant me another favor in return?" *Come on, General, I know you don't believe my story, but don't you want to give Volkonsky a black eye?*

"It depends. Your favors don't seem to be small ones."

"The night that Mr. Kiserev here saved my life, your guys beat the stuffing out of a friend of mine. One of the Tsar's serfs named Lev."

"What about it?"

"I want him to come to America with me."

Benckendorff considered Rian's request. "The man you refer to has been relocated to the Tsar's estate at Tsarskoye Selo. I may be able to make this happen."

"In that case, when you inspect Volkonsky's office, pay special attention to the prince's desk . . . on the bottom of a huge stack of files at the right front corner. You might find something of interest there."

* * * * *

As Kiserev escorted Rian out of the Third Section, she felt lightheaded. She had confronted Benckendorff, a man who had the power to swat her like a mosquito. She was walking out of the meeting with his begrudging acquiescence to her blackmail scheme.

But during the meeting, she began to suspect that her scheme—a plan she had obsessed and machinated over, revised and refined a dozen times—might be flawed. When she planned their departure from St. Petersburg, she assumed the ice in the Baltic would break up sometime in the first week of March. Her calculations were based on an English almanac she had bought in a bookshop on Nevsky Prospekt.

She could picture the page in her mind's eye.

Navigation on the Baltic Sea
Break-up of Ice at Kronstadt

Light Winter	First week in March
Typical Winter	Mid- to late-March
Severe Winter	Early- to mid-April

All winter long, Russians had commented that this winter was a light one. Rian had used the almanac to plan her departure from St. Petersburg in early March. That would give Seamus, Adrian, and her eight weeks to sail to Philadelphia.

She ran back to the Manege and retrieved the almanac from the ledge in Franklin's stall. She opened the pamphlet to the title page, a page she had never bothered to read. There it was, evidence that threw her entire plan into doubt. Despite the fact that the almanac had been published in English, it had been printed in St. Petersburg. Rian felt the blood drain out of her head.

Sheremetev had explained it five months ago when they first arrived in St. Petersburg. *"Starting in the time of Julius Caesar, everyone used the Julian calendar. But the Romans didn't get the formula exactly right for keeping the equinoxes and solstices on track. By the 1500s, the calendar was off by ten days. To correct the problem, in 1582, the Roman Catholic Pope Gregory decreed that the month of October would only have twenty days. But change does not come easily in Russia, and we do not take orders from your Western Pope. We never adopted the new calendar, and since Pope Gregory's decree, we have fallen behind two more days."*

The dates this almanac referred to were from the Julian calendar. Twelve days of travel time evaporated in a heartbeat. Her plan had fallen apart before the prisoners were even sprung from jail.

* * * * *

· OTTO ·

Otto was drafting a new design for a passenger coach when Jules entered the office with the announcement, "Mail's here. There's a letter from Adrian."

Otto eagerly grabbed the letter and broke the wax seal. "Finally." He read the first line out loud. "'January 1, 1838.' My God, that was almost seven weeks ago."

"Skip the commentary, Otto, What does the letter say?"

Otto rose in excitement and read out loud as he paced.

Happy New Year, Brother!

I hope this note finds you well. I have just finished a letter to Mila and Jabez, and figured I should fill you in on the news directly. All the news is good, although you probably won't be pleased to hear some of it.

Four nights ago, there was a big fire in the Tsar's palace and the whole place burned down. We had been living there for a few weeks but got kicked out, so what we thought was a misfortune turned out to be lucky for us. Tell Jules his steam-driven fire pump performed admirably and was still chugging after thirty hours, long after most of the Tsar's equipment had broken down.

Meanwhile, speaking of performing admirably, Seamus, Rian, and I also helped to fight the fire. Seamus and Rian were part of a group that pulled the throne of Peter the Great out of the Great Hall before the roof collapsed. It turned out one of the other people was Tsar Nicholas! Anyway, the Tsar took note of our bravery and resourcefulness—not to mention our manufacturing proficiency thanks to Jules's fire pump—and finally granted us the contract to build a railroad from St. Petersburg to Moscow, plus set up factories to manufacture locomotives, rails, and rolling stock. Otto, in a few years we are all going to be millionaires!

This is where the news gets even more interesting. Like I said, Rian was involved at the fire as well. It was hard to keep track of your daughter when things were happening so fast, and she was fearless. The Tsar has taken a shine to her and has asked her (which means ordered, because a request from the Tsar of All the Russias is really a command) to become a companion to his ten-year-old son. This is a bit sticky, because the Tsar thinks that Rian is a boy.

Seamus and I have talked about this. Except for Ambassador Dallas, we are the only two who know Rian's secret. Even Sheremetev and Malkovich have no idea. We think Rian is a little too close to the fire and we should yank her out of St. Petersburg as soon as the ice breaks here, which, given that it has been a light winter, should be early- to mid-March. So, figure nine weeks or so for the return. By my estimate, you should see your daughter and Seamus somewhere around the middle of May.

Meanwhile, Rian says she's going to continue acting as our coachman, which means caring for two horses I bought when we first arrived. Their stable is the home for the Tsar's Imperial Horse Guards, which has an indoor practice ring that is larger than any building in Philadelphia. It's going to be hard to pry her out of here. She likes being a coachman and she thinks she's going to influence the future course of Russia by putting a good word in for the end of serfdom to the brother of the future Tsar of Russia.

Good luck when you get her back. You're going to have your hands full. Meanwhile, I promise to keep her out of trouble until we get out of here.

Your loving brother,
Adrian

SATURDAY, MARCH 3
(FEBRUARY 19 O.S.)

· RIAN ·

It had been two days since Rian met with Benckendorff. Rian hunkered down in the safety of the Manege, exercising Frank, Wash, and the horses of a handful of Imperial Guardsmen.

Kiserev, the man in the greatcoat, showed up at her stall late in the afternoon of the first day.

"Why are you here?" asked Rian.

"I'm what you get when you kick the hornets' nest," was Kiserev's only reply. Rian didn't know if he was her guard or her guardian.

Late that night, Kiserev was replaced by a man who yielded even less information. He sat in a chair in the dark all night long while Rian slept in the carriage. Another guard-or-guardian showed up shortly after she woke up. He watched her give Frank and Wash their morning exercise and feed. He walked behind her as she went out briefly for food.

Kiserev returned late in the afternoon and dismissed the other man. He settled onto the chair but offered no information and no conversation. Rian spent the afternoon feeding and exercising four horses that belonged to guardsmen. She gave Frank and Wash their afternoon laps around the Great Hall, always under the watchful eye of Kiserev. She was eating her dinner—bread and cheese, the same meal she had eaten for breakfast and lunch—when Prince Volkonsky arrived at the stall, illuminated by a whale oil lamp.

"*Ubiraysya* [Get out]," he said to Kiserev.

Kiserev rose from his chair but remained with his back to the wall. "My orders come directly from General Benckendorff. I'll stay, thank you."

Volkonsky set his lamp on a shelf and directed his attention to Rian. "It seems we shall be conducting this discussion in English. No matter."

Rian noted that he pulled a truncheon out of his coat pocket but held it at his side. The implied threat was unmistakable.

Rian laid her meal on an upside-down wooden box that she used as a table. She stood, planning which way she would dodge if Volkonsky charged her. She looked the Minister of the Imperial Court in the eye. "I expected you would be here sooner."

"You are an insolent little child."

"And somehow, you are forced to visit me in a stable."

"I could beat you senseless."

"Perhaps. Here I am."

"Do you think you have won? That you can defeat me?" Volkonsky touched his thumb to his forefinger. "Do you think you can drive even this much space between me and the Tsar?"

The wisdom of Sun Tzu came to mind: *If sovereign and subject are in accord, put division between them.* "So I guess they found Catherine's memoir on your desk, huh?"

Rian's danger-sense kicked in even before Volkonsky started striding toward her, raising his truncheon as he approached. At the same time, from behind her, a click; the unmistakable sound of a pistol being cocked. Kiserev now stood behind and to the right of her, his pistol barely visible in her side vision, and it was pointed at Volkonsky's heart. *Well, that answers one question: He's my guardian.*

The prince halted.

Rian never backed up. Not an inch. "You know, I really should thank you. I've learned a lot during my time here in Russia. But the most valuable thing I will take back home came from you."

Volkonsky lowered his arm. "And what is that?"

"An accusation doesn't have to be true. It has to maybe be true."

"*Yebat' tebya* [Fuck you]!"

"Yeah, well back at you. You killed Captain Stepanov. I saw you do it, and I know you did it on purpose. You deserve whatever damage I have done to you."

"I will kill you yet!"

Rian shrugged. "So when you come right down to it, I hurt you because I had the power to do it. Congratulations. You taught me that, too."

* * * *

· JULES ·

Jules noted the scowls on the painters' faces as he reached the top of the stairs and entered the Grand Saloon. *You men have been here for four days. You should be used to me meeting with your boss every morning.*

Jules approached the painting subcontractor, Erasmus Shetzline, a man who didn't seem to share the antipathy toward Negroes that some of his men so sullenly displayed.

"Any problems?"

"None at all. This job continues to be straightforward. I always appreciate following Rudolf Bartle's crew. They do their job and leave a clean worksite for me. I saved something for you though. One of the men was reading it. I figured you oughta know. I can translate it for you."

Shetzline handed Jules a copy of *Das Philadelphische Patriot*, the German-language newspaper that was anti-Black, anti-Irish, and anti-Catholic. *This isn't going to be good*, Jules thought as he accepted the paper. "No thanks. I can read it."

Shetzline pointed to an article entitled ***Schwarze nehmen weißen Handwerkern Arbeit weg*** [**Blacks Taking Work Away from White Craftsmen**]. Jules translated as he read silently. *The Panic of '37 has now stretched well into 1838 with no relief in sight. And now, skilled artisans are being fired in order to make way for cheap labor offered by Africans, Irish, and even women. The building projects at Pennsylvania Hall and the Shelter for Colored Orphans proceed with mostly African crews, including African bosses, and exclude honest Germans who want to put food on their families' tables. Meanwhile, escaped slaves flood the streets, job markets, and domiciles of Philadelphia, creating additional competition with honest citizens for scarce resources. Enough is enough!*

Jules quit reading. "This is all garbage. I haven't fired a single white. They quit because they didn't want to work for a Black man. I put the word out for more skilled craftsmen—or unskilled, for that matter. No white men showed up, and I was happy to hire my brethren. Or Irish. Or one young woman. I've got a job to do, and I've got a tight deadline. I can't do it with only the few whites who are willing to take direction from me. Damn these people!"

Shetzline gently took the paper out of Jules's hands. "I'm on your side, Jules. I wanted you to know what's out there. You should be careful until this project is finished."

"You think I don't know what I'm facing every single day?"

Shetzline raised his hand defensively. "Like I said, I'm on your side."

WEDNESDAY, MARCH 7
(FEBRUARY 23 O.S.)

· RIAN ·

Seamus, Sheremetev, and Malkovich were released from prison on March 4, the day after Volkonsky confronted Rian in the stall. Adrian wasn't that lucky.

"Your uncle will remain in the Peter and Paul Fortress to ensure that you return Catherine's memoir as promised," General Benckendorff told Rian.

Seamus, euphoric to be free, was more than ready to return to Philadelphia. "Let's just call it a learning experience with a happy ending," said Seamus, "that is, assuming we get to Philadelphia in time to grab the memoir."

When Count Sheremetev heard about Catherine the Great's memoir, he wished it could have been published in Paris and spread throughout Europe. "Alas, publication of the memoir would have changed Russia's future. Instead, it was used to save our sorry skins."

The ex-prisoners intended to sail from St. Petersburg as soon as the ice broke in the Baltic. "It's been a light winter," declared Sheremetev. "The ice should be gone from Kronstadt in a week or so."

Rian had told General Benckendorff that she had to be back in Philadelphia by April 23, but she hadn't revealed her plans beyond that. She had sent a copy of Catherine's memoir to Lucretia Mott, her next-door neighbor. *Dear Lucretia,* Rian's note said, *if I haven't returned to Philadelphia by April 23, 1838, please give this package to the reporter Harold Foote. Tell him to publish the manuscript immediately in the* Philadelphia Independent. *Tell him to send copies of the paper to newspapers of his choice in Paris and Hamburg.*

General Benckendorff assigned Kiserev, Rian's former guardian, to accompany Rian, Seamus, and Lev back to the United States. If they were able to depart in early March, the travelers would easily arrive in Philadelphia by April 23. Kiserev would return to Russia with the memoir. Adrian would be released.

Count Sheremetev and Colonel Malkovich were going to retire to the safety of Sheremetev's ancestral estate in Saxony, twelve hundred miles from the vindictive Volkonsky.

Most of Rian's travel cushion had already disappeared. The plan unraveled further when a late cold snap returned to Eastern Europe, followed by a massive blizzard that blanketed St. Petersburg with a foot of snow and drifts much higher. The Baltic ice stopped melting.

"What if we go by land?" asked Rian. "We could take a sleigh to Riga or even Hamburg."

"You are talking about a twenty-day trip if the weather were perfect," responded Sheremetev. "In these conditions, we are better off waiting for the weather to break."

"Gotta admit, Rian," Seamus commented. "Your scheme to spring us from jail was brilliant. But the clock's running. Ambassador Dallas said it took him five weeks to get here, but he had the prevailing wind at his back. We have to figure five to six weeks to get home, and that includes the shortest of layovers in London to find a ship to Philadelphia."

On March 7, General Benckendorff arrived at Count Sheremetev's mansion, their temporary quarters. "I have been watching the calendar. Had you left St. Petersburg a week ago, you would have had no trouble getting to America in time to reclaim the memoir. Now it is in doubt."

"What will happen to Uncle Adrian if Seamus and I don't get there in time?" asked Rian.

Benckendorff shrugged. "If the memoirs are published, Adrian Krieger will be put to death."

* * * * *

· JULES ·

"How many?" Jules asked, afraid to hear the answer. He and Marcus Edes were standing at the makeshift desk that was Jules's base of operations in Pennsylvania Hall's Grand Saloon.

"Three," said Edes.

Four weeks ago, Jules had said goodbye to Edes, nine white master carpenters, and three relatively unskilled helpers as Edes moved his crew to the Shelter for Colored Orphans. Jules had told Edes that he would find work for all of them at Pennsylvania Hall when they finished at the Shelter, even though the painters weren't going to be happy with a bunch of carpenters getting in their way. His hope was that Edes and his crew would return to Pennsylvania Hall accompanied by some of the skilled carpenters from the Shelter.

"Three of Hunnecher's men?" Jules stammered incredulously. "What about your guys?"

"One quit two weeks ago to go fight in Canada. So, I'm coming back to you with eight of my guys and three of Hunnecher's. That's two more master carpenters than we had before."

"And I was hoping for four more than that," said Jules.

"Jules, I tried. I talked to Hunnecher, and I talked to his men. Even though they're going to be laid off for more than a month, they don't want to work here for honest wages because . . . because . . . well, you know."

"Because they don't want to take orders from a Black man."

"You've treated me and my men fairly ever since you got here. Truth be told, things went a lot better here than they're going up at the Shelter. Randy Buck—remember him? The guy who can't work and talk at the same time?— He said he can't wait to get back here. The rest of my men feel the same way. We're glad you're running things here. They all know the painters are going to be irate when we come back early, so we're grateful. Grateful to have the work and grateful to work for a GC who knows what he's doing."

Jules perused the wall calendar he had brought from his kitchen to the worksite. He didn't like what he saw. The painting crew still had two weeks of work left. The interior of the Grand Saloon shone brightly with the first coat of white paint. The painters hadn't started on the street level yet. Even so, he wanted the carpenters back as soon as possible, especially now that he had lost a lot of manpower.

Jules had hoped to have fifteen master carpenters and the same number of helpers to back them up. The tasks ahead required the skills of trained craftsmen: baseboard trim, window trim, interior doors, interior shutters, the blasted sunflower on the ceiling, additional ventilators in the ceiling, finish work on the stage, removal of the mammoth scaffold in the middle of the Grand Saloon, oak flooring on all three floors, oak stair treads.

In his original projection, he had blocked out eight to twelve weeks for the finish carpenters to do their work. With reduced numbers of master carpenters, this could easily stretch out to four months and he would blow through whatever deadline the Board of Trustees had set for him. The meeting of the Philadelphia Female Anti-Slavery Society would take place in a worksite. *And everyone present will know that a Black man was in charge of the construction project. I—and my entire race—will be painted as incompetent.*

* * * * *

Jules and Maddie read the sixteen handwritten pages at their kitchen table while Robert Purvis and James Forten sat stolidly opposite them. Jules finished and looked at Purvis, then Maddie did the same.

"What do you think?" asked Purvis.

"I think it is brilliant," said Jules. "Reasoned. Methodical. Measured. Anyone who reads it cannot fail to see this argument from our side."[10]

"I wouldn't change a word," said Maddie. "What happens next?"

"We present this resolution to a meeting of the city's most prominent Black citizens at the Presbyterian Church on Seventh Street a week from today," said Purvis.

James Forten leaned forward, his elbows on the table. "They better ratify it without much discussion because Robert has researched every detail, agonized over every sentence."

Purvis smiled and put his hand over his father-in-law's. "I am confident it will survive relatively intact. I'll walk the resolution to Merrihew Andgunn's shop the next day, and he will print as many pamphlets as we can afford."

"And how will they be distributed?" asked Maddie. "I fear for the safety of anyone passing out such a pamphlet as this. I feel the antipathy on the streets every morning when I walk to the shop. The ill will has been quite palpable lately."

Jules stiffened. *Maddie has not mentioned this to me. But I feel it at work as well. Men less inclined to take direction from me. Another fight broke out between a Black carpenter and a white painter yesterday.*

"I admit it has been bad in Philadelphia lately," said Purvis. "Lucretia Mott said we can count on most of the Quaker congregations in the state to pass them out. If we are judicious, we can also work with other churches. Getting the pamphlets into the hinterlands will be vital. Voters throughout the Commonwealth will be voting on the new constitution, not just in the City of Brotherly Love. I hope the rest of Pennsylvania will counterbalance the animosity that we are experiencing here."

"And what if they don't?"

"Then it will be forty years before we have an opportunity to regain a privilege that should be ours by natural right. I shudder at the thought."

---

10. The *Appeal of Forty Thousand Citizens, Threatened with Disfranchisement, to the People of Pennsylvania* was drafted by Robert Purvis to counter the rising tide of anti-Black sentiment engendered by the protracted depression and the "white-only" clause that threatened to exclude Black male voters from future elections. The appeal started by thanking those members of the Constitutional Convention who had stalwartly defended the right of Black men to vote. It based the thesis in well-researched historical contexts: that in the colonial era, both white indentured servants and Black slaves were excluded from voting because they lacked status as freemen. That the state constitutions of 1776 and 1790 mentioned only freemen, making no reference of color, in determining voter eligibility. That there were proportionately fewer poor Black people than whites. That Blacks consumed fewer public services than their white counterparts.

Thursday, March 15
(March 3 O.S.)

· SEAMUS ·

Seamus awoke in the middle of the night to the sound of sobs coming from Rian's room. He knocked on her door.

"Go away."

Despite the admonition, he entered Rian's room and sat down on her bed.

"What is it, me darlin'? I've never heard you like this."

Rian lay with her face away from him. "It's all my fault."

"What's all your fault?"

"Uncle Adrian's going to die because of me."

"That's not so. You're the one who got us out of prison."

"But if I hadn't sent the copy of the memoir to Mrs. Mott, we wouldn't be in this fix. Ambassador Dallas said I should leave it to the adults. I should have listened to him."

"But if you hadn't done something, we'd all still be rotting in prison. We all agreed; you made the right decision. Philadelphia was the safest place to send the memoir. Don't worry, Rian, we'll find a way to get home in time."

"But we can't possibly do it. It takes at least a week to sail to London. Then another four weeks to cross the Atlantic. More likely, it'll take six weeks, or even seven. April 23! I shouldn't have put such a tight deadline on it. It's all my fault. What was I thinking?"

"There, there, me darlin'. It's gonna be all right." But Seamus didn't know if it was going to be all right. He had been watching the calendar, too, and yesterday was his private deadline for the last day to be able to make it in time, and that was if everything went perfectly. *Nothing ever goes perfectly.*

* * * * *

The next morning, Seamus and Rian walked to the docks at the mouth of the Neva River. Since before sunrise, thousands of serfs had been laboring to cut a twenty-mile channel in the ice from the docks to Kronstadt, St. Petersburg's deepwater port. An army of men were using long-bladed saws to cut the ice into blocks a foot wide and two feet long. Others were wielding long-handled pikes to push and pull the ice blocks to shore through smaller side channels, where they were hauled away by wagons and sleighs. The main channel was already ten feet wide and extended in a straight line for miles.

"See, me darlin'? The Russians know things are about to get busy in Kronstadt. We'll be using this channel to steam out of here before you know it."

"Quit referring to me as your darling. You only call me that when you're worried about me. I don't want to be worried about."

Seamus acknowledged to himself that she was right. "Fair enough. Anyway, the count says they do this every year when the ice in the Baltic is breaking up. In two more days there will be a channel a hundred feet wide from here to Kronstadt. A steamship will transport us to Kronstadt. We'll board a ship and be on our way."

MONDAY, MARCH 19

· LOGAN ·

Logan and Cee-Cee had been working at the Shelter for Colored Orphans for three weeks, and the end of the job was in sight. Charlie had given both of them a shot at applying some of the scratch coat and brown coat, and Logan enjoyed it and felt like he could be good at it. The first two coats were now complete and today the plasterers had started in on the finish coat. Charlie wouldn't let either one of them near the finish coat, however, so they were back full time to supplying water to all the plasterers and mixing plaster for Charlie.

As was now their long-established routine, Logan and Cee-Cee pulled up and down on the handles of the fire pump until they heard Charlie call "STOP!" from inside the Shelter. Except for their break for dinner at midday, they had little other time to talk. Charlie always kept them busy, and he didn't like it when they chatted on the job.

Since Cee-Cee weighed a lot less than Logan, she had to work harder than he did when they pumped. When it was her turn to push down, she put all her weight on the handle with her feet off the ground.

Logan pushed up on his handle as Cee-Cee temporarily disappeared from his sight on the other side. "Did you see your girlfriend yesterday?" His tone was a bit mocking, but in a big brother sort of way.

"Of course. We sang together in the choir."

"You're lucky. You get to see Grace twice each week. I only see Martha on Thursday nights."

Cee-Cee reappeared as she pulled up on her handle with a slight grunt. "Oh, I've got a message for you. Martha can't meet you on Thursday night. She's helping her grandfather out with a catering job."

Logan was crestfallen. His evenings with Martha, lit only by the glow of coals from the potbelly stove, were the moments by which he measured his week. *Three days until I see her. Two days. Tomorrow. Tonight.*

Cee-Cee again descended out of sight. "Gracie and I had an idea. You two could switch with us. You take our Tuesday and we'll take your Thursday."

"You would do that for me?"

Logan heard the slight Cee-Cee grunt as she started to lift the handle. Her head appeared on the other side of the pump. She smiled. "Sure. That's what friends do."

That means there's only one more day, Logan said to himself.

"STOP!" yelled Charlie from inside the Shelter.

* * * * *

It was the end of the workday. Most of the plasterers had left the Shelter. Logan and Cee-Cee walked around the building, marveling at how much brighter it was now that the lath was covered with plaster.

"I think I want to become a plasterer," said Logan.

"Not me," replied Cee-Cee. "I want to go back and bang nails."

"Look at this place. It's beautiful. And we had a hand in it."

"And in a few months, there will be forty orphans living here. I might even volunteer here. Teach kids to read and write."

"Gotta hand it to you, Cee-Cee, you're trying to make the world a better place."

"And the Shelter is going to be a part of that better world."

TUESDAY, MARCH 20
(MARCH 8 O.S.)

· SEAMUS ·

On March 18, the British steamship *George IV* was the first foreign vessel to tie up at Kronstadt. Seamus bought tickets to London. "Not entirely good news, Rian. It's a twelve-day trip. We stop in Helsinki, Stockholm, Copenhagen, Hamburg, and Amsterdam and arrive on March 31. If we're lucky, we'll hop on a ship to America right away. Even then, the deadline is going to be tight."

The morning they were to depart, Seamus sent their small amount of luggage to the docks. Then he and Rian returned to Peter and Paul Fortress to bid farewell to Adrian. He had been moved to a cell that was sunlit by two barred windows and big enough to hold a rickety but serviceable writing desk.

Adrian rose from a cot when he saw them. "Welcome to my humble abode." The guard opened the barred door and allowed Seamus and Rian to enter.

"It's been quite the adventure," Seamus said after numerous failed attempts to lighten the mood of the visit. "Thanks for dragging me to this iceberg. And don't worry. We'll head off the memoir somehow. You'll be back home before the end of the summer." His heart broke when Rian wordlessly hugged her uncle. She wiped tears from her eyes as they left the fortress.

They stepped out of the landau at the dock near the mouth of the Neva River. Numerous other hacks disgorged passengers in haphazard fashion with no deference to whoever had arrived at the dock first.

* * * * *

Ferrying from St. Petersburg to Kronstadt through the newly cut ice channel would take two hours. Because of the prison visit, Seamus, Rian, Sheremetev, Malkovich, Kiserev, and Lev boarded the steamship *Herman of Valaam* for its last trip to Kronstadt before the *George IV* sailed. Seamus suspected the *Herman* was fresh out of winter drydock. Its deck had been newly varnished, its paddlewheel painted. The steam engine idled, ready for departure.

Rather than go below to the warmth of the ship's passenger deck, the travelers remained topside to watch the crew release the lines. The deckhands prepared to pull up the gangplank but paused for a few moments to allow a woman wearing a full-length sable coat to stroll aboard. She seemed oblivious to the workers, who waited, admiring the sight of her, before they resumed their tasks. As she approached the top of the gangplank, her features came into focus.

Tall, blond, and beautiful, Seamus noted. *Older than me. Twenty-eight? Thirty?*

"Thank you," the woman said to a deckhand who extended his hand to her as she crossed the threshold onto the ship.

English? American? "This voyage just got a bit more interesting," Seamus uttered to himself.

Sheremetev put his hand on Seamus's shoulder. "That's Delilah Winter. Watch out for her."

"Why?"

"She mingles with Count Golitsyn's crowd."

"Volkonsky's brother-in-law?"

Sheremetev nodded. "They're all vipers." He squeezed Seamus's shoulder. "If you can't stay away, I suggest you keep your hand on your money clip."

After fifteen minutes observing the steamer's progress along the ice channel, Seamus went below to explore the *Herman of Valaam*. *And perhaps make the acquaintance of Delilah Winter.* He took a right at the bottom of the stairs and found a reading room that was occupied by a couple of men. He backed out, closed the door, and entered the only other room that accepted passengers, a saloon that could seat fifty or so but held only two: a bartender and Delilah Winter. She sat at a table for two with an empty glass, her sable coat draped over the back of the only other chair at the table. Now that she had shed the coat, Seamus noted that she was thin and shapely. *Just me type.*

Seamus ordered an Irish whiskey and turned to face Delilah, his back to the bar.

Delilah met his gaze. Without saying a word, she reached over, lifted her coat off the chair, and tossed it onto a nearby table.

Nice trick, thought Seamus. When he was eight, he used to pick up spare change by emptying chamber pots and sweeping up at a whorehouse in Moyamensing. He remembered a prostitute making room for a patron on a loveseat with much the same gesture, except that instead of a sable coat worth hundreds of dollars, the pro removed a smelly old blanket. Delilah Winter was no prostitute—she was far too classy for that—but she wasn't an innocent either.

"Can I buy you another drink?" he asked.

"That would be lovely. Irish whiskey, please. No ice necessary."

From her accent, Seamus guessed that the woman was from the United States. *Perhaps New York. But upper-class New York.* He placed the drinks on the table and sat in the chair formerly occupied by the coat. "Heading back to the States?"

"Yes. Are you heading back to Ireland?"

"Nope, Philadelphia. Me family moved to America when I was four."

"Where's the rest of your party? It seemed like there was a number of you when I boarded."

"They're still up on deck, watching the ice go by. How long have you been in Russia?"

"A year. It's time to go home. How about you?"

"Six months. Me uncle and I came here to build a railroad for the Tsar."

"So you're the ones. I've heard about the two of you. Plucked from Philadelphia by the good Count Sheremetev to circumvent all the state's bureaucracy. The darlings of the Tsar after the fire. Seems you ran into a bit of a hiccough with Prince Volkonsky recently."

Seamus took a sip of his drink, savored its richness after too many nights of vodka. "That's an acceptable version of the story. Seems we should have met before now." Seamus offered his hand to the lady. "Me name is Seamus Gallagher."

The woman warmly accepted his hand, even leaned in toward him a bit. "Delilah Winter. Unfortunately, most of my Russian friends favored Volkonsky's brother-in-law, Count Golitsyn, on your railroad project. You wouldn't have been invited to those parties. So, you're heading home?"

"Aye, it's time. I think I got in a bit over me head here."

"What are you going back to?"

"Me ma, two brothers, and three sisters. Probably a little firefighting. Some side projects." *Like pilfering whatever I can shake loose on the docks. Siobhan, unless she married Mikey McGuire.* "What about you?"

"I'm not sure. Perhaps New Orleans."

"Why New Orleans?"

Before Delilah could answer, Rian, Lev, Kiserev, Count Sheremetev, and Colonel Malkovich, all noisily babbling in Russian, entered the saloon from above deck. They shed their coats in the warmth of the large room. Sheremetev spotted Delilah and gave a polite, courtly bow but headed to the bar to order drinks. Lev, Rian, and Malkovich rearranged chairs around the largest table in the room. Kiserev pulled out a deck of cards. Sheremetev delivered drinks to the table.

"Interesting group," commented Delilah.

"We've been through a lot together."

"What game are they going to play?"

"It's daytime. Most likely durak."

"I see Count Sheremetev is with you. I heard he was leaving the country. Of course no one in my circle would lift a hand to help him when Volkonsky threw him in prison. Is he returning to America with you?"

"Nope, he and Colonel Malkovich will be getting off in Hamburg. They'll take a stage from there to Saxony."

Delilah sipped at her whiskey. "His exile won't be a hardship. His chateau in Leipzig dwarfs his home in St. Petersburg. I wonder which is better: being a minor noble in the Tsar's court or major noble in a minor German state?"

"Beats me. He made his attempt to modernize Russia, but now he's happy he got out with his skin intact."

Delilah returned her gaze to the card players. "And Colonel Malkovich is sticking with him?"

"For a while, I guess."

"Very loyal of him. Gossip in Golitsyn's crowd is that the count and the colonel are lovers."

Seamus was taken aback by this turn in the conversation. He had heard of men who loved men before but had never known such people. He couldn't tell by Delilah Winter's tone what she thought about it. "I have no reason to think so. They certainly enjoyed the ladies when we stopped over in London."

"But what if they were?"

Careful, Boyo. In two seconds, Seamus came to a conclusion that he knew would shock his friends at home. "Sheremetev and Malkovich are good fellows. I guess what they do in private is their own business."

"Good answer," said Delilah. "Who are the others at the table?"

It was obvious that Delilah Winter dealt in gossip. Seamus was willing to oblige—up to a point. "The big one is named Lev. A week ago he was a serf on the Tsar's estate in Tsarskoye Selo."

"He's dressed very well for a serf."

"He's wearing a suit that Sheremetev was going to throw away when he closed up his house. He's got two more in his suitcase. He's a good guy. Helps wherever he can. Plays the balalaika to entertain us. Practices his English. He's going to work in me uncle's factory when we get to Philadelphia."

"He is not hard on the eyes. Why is he with you?"

"He was freed as part of the deal that was struck with Volkonsky when we got sprung from prison." *The deal me cousin, who is masquerading as a boy, brokered by blackmailing the Tsar, who isn't really a Romanov.*

"And what was the deal?"

"I'm afraid I can't say."

"And who is that man?"

"His name is Kiserev. I don't even know his first name. He works for General Benckendorff."

"My, my, you have been swimming in the deep part of the pond. And what is Mr. Kiserev doing in your party?"

"He's running an errand for the general. Coming to Philadelphia with us, then returning to St. Petersburg."

"And of course you're not going to tell me what the errand is."

"Correct."

"The boy at the table. Who is he? He seems to fit right in with the rest of your motley herd."

"That's me cousin, Rian. Up until—"

A masculine presence loomed over their table. "Delilah, I thought you weren't coming."

Delilah and Seamus looked up to see a handsome, well-dressed man in his early thirties. His most distinguishing characteristic was a healthy mustache similar to those of many Russian cavalry officers.

"I changed my mind," said Delilah. "Seamus Gallagher, this is my husband, David Winter."

David Winter bowed politely to Seamus. "Thank you for keeping my wife occupied, Mr. Gallagher. Darling, I think we should talk."

Winter offered his hand to his wife, who accepted it. She picked up her coat from the adjoining table. "Nice to meet you, Seamus. See you on the *George IV*." Husband and wife departed the saloon arm-in-arm.

Seamus shook his head and smiled. *What just happened?*

Rather than join the card players, Seamus took the opportunity to watch his cousin from a short distance. It was almost fortunate that David Winter interrupted his conversation with Delilah, for what would he have told her?

He no longer knew who Rian was. She had witnessed the death of a dozen soldiers in the palace fire and the murder of a man she admired. Lev had been beaten because of his friendship with her. She brought to light a document of history-altering significance. And then, the arrests had left her on her own for sixteen days. She was forced to survive by using her wits, when one wrong move would have been disastrous. She had planned and schemed. She risked her own life to secure the freedom of her loved ones. She went eyeball-to-eyeball with two of the most powerful men in the world and had come out with at least a draw. And now, she was dealing with the fact that her Uncle Adrian might be put to death, and if it happened, it would be her fault.

It seemed like all of this had knocked the childhood right out of her. Previously, everything had been a game to her, every rule could be circumvented, every new person could be approached with a twinkle in her eye. That was all gone now. No coltish energy. No playfulness. No twinkle.

But right now, Rian was dealing a new hand of durak. She said something to Lev in Russian that Seamus didn't understand, but it got a chuckle out of the rest of the table. Seamus got up to join the others.

* * * * *

The *Herman of Valaam* passengers transferred to the *George IV* in Kronstadt. This much larger ship steamed west in the Gulf of Finland to Helsinki. Some passengers disembarked in Helsinki. As the crew would spend hours loading coal and provisions, those travelers who were continuing on to points west took the opportunity to see whatever sights the city had to offer.

Rian chafed at the delay in their journey, machinating at how to get to London faster. Seamus knew she regretted setting such a tight deadline for the publication of the memoir. *Well, Adrian's life is constantly on my mind as well, but Rian acts as if it's her responsibility and nobody else's.* They returned to the docks and joined a stream of new passengers who strode aboard, laden with all sorts of baggage and baubles.

During their days at sea, Seamus often found Rian on the deck of the *George IV*, wrapped in Captain Stepanov's voluminous Imperial Guardsman's coat. It was so long that it grazed the top of her shoes. Rian obviously treasured the coat and Seamus never commented on how ridiculous she looked.

And what's all this about playing poker? The evening poker games that she had rejoined while they were waiting for the Baltic ice to break had become an obsession to her. The interesting thing was, she was inevitably the best player in the game.

* * * * *

· RIAN ·

Rian had to admit that the only time she was able to forget about her Uncle Adrian was when she was concentrating on a poker game. Fortunately, on the first evening aboard the *George IV*, Sheremetev had organized a game and insisted that Rian be included.

Since Rian engineered Sheremetev's release from prison, the count had reverted to his former benevolent, paternal interactions with her. He even went along with her masquerading as a boy.

It's time to play poker, she thought to herself. *No worrying about Uncle Adrian dying by firing squad. Not the time to wonder about the count's change of heart.* Rian surveyed the table: Sheremetev, Seamus, Lev, Kiserev, David Winter, and his wife Delilah.

Rian had played with Sheremetev and Seamus often enough to know the strength of their hands by the ways their behaviors changed.

Lev was already a strong player. Russians seemed to thrive on betting, but he was shrewd and measured in his wagers. Kiserev often sat at the table but didn't play. He had said many times he was more motivated to learn English than to play poker. When he did play, he bet little and won little.

The most intriguing people at the table were the American portrait painter David Winter, and his wife Delilah. During their year in St. Petersburg, he had studied the many grand masters displayed in the Hermitage. Rian got the impression that the missus held the purse strings. Winter drank too much and his betting, sharp and measured in the beginning of the evenings, became imprudent later on. Delilah had a very different style. If her hand was weak, she dropped out early. She won some small pots and lost some small pots. She never bluffed.

On one memorable hand, most of the players had dropped out, leaving only Rian and Delilah with skin in the game. Rian sat on an ace-high nothing. Delilah asked for two cards and threw two rubles into the pot.

Rian saw the two and raised another five. *She rarely bets big. Let's see how much of a risk she is willing to take.*

Rian expected her to drop out but instead she saw the five rubles. Delilah fanned three queens on the table, and Rian was forced to lay down her ace-high nothing.

The table reacted with a mix of consternation and disappointment. Delilah raked the pot toward her and started stacking the rubles in front of her, a faint smile on her face.

Good, said Rian to herself. *Now they think I'll bluff with a crap hand. Sure, this hand cost me a bit, but the next time I won't be bluffing, and I'll win it all back and then some; if not tonight, then tomorrow night.*

* * * * *

· LOGAN ·

Logan and Martha were lying in each other's arms next to the potbelly stove when he heard a sound out in the Freeman Hydraulics shop. His first thought was that Grace and Cee-Cee had forgotten they had switched rendezvous nights with them. Then he heard the unmistakable baritone voice of Martha's father, and he didn't sound happy.

Having learned their lesson from the time they were discovered by Grace and Cee-Cee, the two lovers knew exactly where their clothes were. They dressed, but the sounds of a conversation—no, an argument—got no closer. Logan realized that the other participant in the argument was Martha's mother, Maddie.

Logan and Martha tiptoed to the door and listened.

Maddie: "*No, you can't have them. I need them here.*"

Jules: "*I need them more at Pennsylvania Hall than you need them here. They are skilled craftsmen and I am about to be down at least half a dozen men. If we don't have a finished showcase for the anti-slavery movement by May 14, I will be blamed, and my failure will be smeared over our entire race. I won't allow that to happen.*"

Maddie: "*Husband, I want you to evaluate the state of this carriage. The contract with the LaFayette Hose Company says we've got to deliver by April 2. Now you tell me, how can you take all the skilled craftsmen in this shop over to Pennsylvania Hall and expect us to deliver a fire pump to LaFayette in two weeks?*"

Light from a lantern shown faintly through the space between the door and the floor. Logan whispered into Martha's ear. "Your da's not thinking clearly. Freeman Hydraulics already has a fire pump. It's supposed to be delivered to Baltimore, but we've been using it to pump water for the plasterers up at the Shelter."

The sounds of Martha's parents' voices moved toward the office door.

Jules: "*Then we need to check the contract. There must be some way we can extend it.*"

Maddie: "*Of course we can extend it—if you're willing to pay a penalty for every day we are late.*" A hand turned the doorknob and the door opened a crack. "*That was the deal we cut when they said they would pay cash.*"

Logan stepped away from the door and braced himself to face the wrath of the towering man whom he admired and feared.

"*Hello?!*" A third voice came from the front of the shop.

The door opened no further but remained ajar.

Jules: "*Hello, yes, who is it?*"

The third voice: "*Mr. Freeman, is that you? It's Fred Hailer, the night watchman. I saw the light through the window. Just wanted to make sure you weren't being burgled.*"

Logan heard both Jules and Maddie moving toward the night watchman.

Jules: "*Fred, thank you for looking out for us. We appreciate it. All is well. We are working late.*"

Fred: "*Can't be too careful, Mr. Freeman. Your kind especially. The lower elements don't like it when a member of your race rises too high above his station. Of course, I don't feel that way. I'll take my leave now.*"

Logan heard the faint voice of Fred Hailer coming from the street. "*Eleven o'clock and all's well.*" By the time he repeated the call in German, his words were indistinct. Jules and Maddie's footsteps again approached the door.

Martha pressed something into Logan's hand, pulled the door open, entered the shop, and pulled the door closed behind her. "*Mother, Pop-Pop, I think I have a solution to your problem.*"

Maddie: "*Martha, what are you doing here? I thought you were in bed.*"

Martha: "*I couldn't sleep.*"

Jules: "*Are you working? On what?*"

Martha: "*Oh, you know . . . bookkeeping.*"

Jules: "*What bookkeeping do you have that is so pressing?*"

Martha: "*I'm helping Grandpa Hercules on Thursday, so I decided to come here and get some work done to make up for the time I'm missing. But I overheard you arguing. Mother, you are worried about not making the deadline for the Lafayette Hose Company. Pop-Pop, you need workers. Why don't you deliver the fire pump that's up at the Shelter for Colored Orphans to Lafayette? You've already told the Baltimore fire company they aren't going to get a pump until after the Hall is finished.*"

Jules: "*Hmm. It's the same design.*"

Martha: "*All we would have to do is paint a new name on the side.*"

Jules: "*Maddie, did I ever tell you how brilliant our daughter is? Come on, family, let's go home. No need to lose any more sleep than we already have.*"

Logan listened at the door as the footsteps receded toward the front of the shop. He felt the unmistakable weight and shape of Martha's key. He turned and shut the door to the potbelly stove, thus turning the office pitch black. He felt his way out of the office, through the length of the shop, unlocked the door from the inside and relocked it once he was out of the shop.

I'm in love with a girl who is fooking brilliant, he thought as he turned south. And then . . . *I can't keep doing this.*

FRIDAY, MARCH 23

• SEAMUS •

Seamus knew in his heart that his uncle was as good as dead. Today was March 23. If they were lucky, the earliest they could get to America was April 27. His job now was to relieve Rian of the guilt she would inevitably feel. *And how can she not feel guilty?*

During their layover in Stockholm, the voyagers visited the Swedish royal palace, an enormous building that should have amazed even the most jaded tourist. Seamus was taking in the view: a brisk early spring afternoon, a cloudless blue sky, and the spectacular baroque palace backed by a bustling harbor. The moment should have been perfect.

"I've lived in better," muttered Rian.

Seamus pivoted from the waterfront and again regarded the palace. "Well, I guess this palace is spectacular unless you've lived in its big brother in St. Petersburg."

"We're running behind," said Rian. "When we get to London, maybe there will be a ship that leaves for New York, not Philadelphia. We can take that and then hop the train to Philadelphia. That might even shave a day or two off our trip."

Seamus silently chastised himself for forgetting, even for a moment, that Rian had not yet given up hope. He did admit, though, that Rian's idea was better than anything he had come up with.

SUNDAY, MARCH 25

· SEAMUS ·

A British businessman named Dunworthy boarded the steamship in Stockholm and enthusiastically joined the poker game. He was rash and careless.

Seamus didn't like him and hoped to be lucky enough to clean him out before they arrived in London. He could detect the disdain in Dunworthy's voice as soon as he identified Seamus as Irish. He also spoke disparagingly about the work ethic of Russian iron miners.

"They are serfs," said Lev, his English getting better by the day. "They have no choice but to work in mines."

"Still," said the businessman. "They take no pride in their work. They live like filthy pigs."

Lev did not respond. Rian noted that he and Kiserev, the only Russians at the table, had made eye contact but could read nothing more into it. Dunworthy lost a pile of money but showed no inclination to stop playing a game he was clearly no good at.

The following afternoon, the *George IV* steamed into Copenhagen harbor. Tired of the ship, many of the voyagers decided to take rooms on shore for the evening. Seamus commented to the hotel owner that he was impressed by the freshness of the buildings. Their host told him that as most of Copenhagen had been burned during an English naval bombardment in 1807, the bulk of the buildings were only about thirty years old. Despite the modernity of the architecture, Seamus thought the city seemed rather crowded and narrow, pinched within the ramparts of a long-antiquated fort.

Seamus, Sheremetev, and Malkovich decided to go to a restaurant for dinner. Lev and Kiserev, on a more limited budget, tried their luck on the street. Rian buried her nose in a pile of English newspapers that had been left in the hotel's reading room by previous travelers. "I'm not hungry," she said. "I'm going to stay here and catch up on the news."

* * * * *

An hour later, Rian flew into the restaurant. "We can do it! It's a sure thing. It's all right here, in this newspaper." She thrust a newspaper in front of Seamus.

Steamships Race to be First to Cross the Atlantic

March 15, 1835. For months now, Isambard Kingdom Brunel, president of the Great Western Steamship Company, thought the race was already won because there were no competitors. His ship, the *Great Western*, the largest passenger vessel ever built, would be the first steam-driven ship ever to cross the Atlantic. But now, ladies and gentlemen, we have a horse race.

A late entry now jeopardizes Mr. Brunel's dreams, which have been years in the making. The rival British & American Steam Navigation Company, intent on spoiling Mr. Brunel's one-horse race, has chartered the *Sirius*, a sidewheel steamship built for voyages between Cork and London, to challenge the *Great Western*.

Skeptics claim that no steamship built for trips within the British Isles can possibly cross the Atlantic. Undeterred, the directors of British & American, willing to forego profit to beat Brunel, instructed their ship architects to tear out passenger berths to make room for additional coal bunkers. This guarantees that the *Sirius* will have more than enough fuel to steam the entire way.

When queried by this reporter, Mr. Brunel claimed that his ship will complete its sea trials on its voyage from London to Bristol and will depart for New York soon thereafter. "From Bristol," he said, "I predict that my ship will make the crossing in sixteen days or less. Even if the *Sirius* leaves ahead of us, we will surely pass her and be the first to New York City."

Sirius is scheduled to depart London on March 28, refuel in Cork, and make the dash to New York starting on April 4. *Great Western* is scheduled to depart from London on March 31 and Bristol on or about the same time as *Sirius*. The race is on!

Seamus read the story aloud to Sheremetev and Malkovich, then looked up at Rian, who had been hopping up and down from excitement. "Okay, Rian, you're a bit ahead of me. What's going through that brain of yours?"

"We arrive in London on the April 28. If we're lucky, we can catch the *Sirius*. Let's say the *Sirius* takes eighteen days to cross, that's still a lot faster than the four or five weeks it usually takes to cross westbound. That means we get to New York on April 22. That gives us time to hop a train to Philadelphia and get there on the twenty-third, one day ahead of the deadline. If we miss the *Sirius*, we can still get on the *Great Western*. We've got it!"

* * * * *

After dinner, the poker players convened in the hotel parlor. Rian dealt to the table: first to Seamus, then Sheremetev, Lev, the obnoxious British business-man Dunworthy, David Winter, Delilah, and finally herself. Malkovich merely sat and watched and drank.

Given the news about the steamship race across the Atlantic, Seamus noted that Sheremetev, Malkovich, and Rian were noticeably more lighthearted. The change in his cousin's demeanor was probably the most dramatic of all the voy-agers. For the first time since they left St. Petersburg, she believed they would make it to Philadelphia on time. *Maybe we're going to save Adrian after all.*

As the evening progressed, David Winter was losing money, and Dunwor-thy and Rian were winning. Everyone else was pretty much breaking even. On the last hand of the night, Rian lost a big pot to the businessman: her two pair to his three sevens. It was uncharacteristic of Rian to overbet a relatively weak hand like that.

"Sorry you lost that last hand to Dunworthy," Seamus said to Rian as they headed to their cabins. "I'd like to see that fool get a good comeuppance."

"Don't tell anyone, Cousin. I lost on purpose."

"Why?"

"We arrive in Hamburg in two days. That's where the count and the colonel get off. Ever since we left America, they've been the ones who have organized the card games. They always insist that I be allowed to play, and the count gets away with it because he's a count. If I had beaten Dunworthy tonight, he wouldn't have forgotten it. After the count and the colonel are out of the picture, Dunworthy would exclude me. But now, since he thinks he can beat me, it's more likely that he'll let me sit in."

Seamus shook his head. *She'll be fourteen tomorrow,* he said to himself. *What is she going to be like when she's my age?*

Thursday, March 29

· LOGAN ·

Martha shed her rain-soaked slicker, opened the door to the potbelly stove, stood to hug Logan, and turned her face up to kiss him. Logan didn't respond.

"What's the matter?" Martha asked.

"I can't do this anymore. Last week we almost got caught. We both know there's no place in Philadelphia for us, and I can't imagine you ever leaving your family. I'm doing us a favor. I hate what I'm doing, but I'm ending this. Ending our love because sooner or later one of us is going to get hurt. Your parents were right from the very beginning. I've got to go."

With that, Logan left the office of Freeman Hydraulics, felt his way through the pitch-dark shop, and walked out to the rainy night.

"*Ten o'clock and all's well,*" the night watchman yelled in the distance.

Liar, Logan responded silently.

MONDAY, APRIL 2

· SEAMUS ·

On March 26, Rian's fourteenth birthday, the *George IV* steamed out of Copenhagen as scheduled. As soon as they left the harbor, they encountered rough weather on the Kattegat Sea. Before the *George IV* had reached the northern tip of Denmark, huge waves washed over the ship's port quarter. Half an hour later, a monster wave tossed off the skiff that had been lashed to the stern. When much of the wooden cover protecting the portside paddlewheel was torn off, Seamus knew they were in trouble.

The captain appeared unperturbed. "I've seen much worse," he declared as he passed through the ship's dining area. "We've sustained some damage, but as long as the engines are running, we'll be fine."

Then the packing that surrounded the rudder post failed, thus allowing seawater to wash into the cabin-level with every large swell.

"We've changed course and we're heading for shelter," the captain told the passengers on his next walkthrough. "I'm afraid we'll be laid up for a bit."

Late in the morning of March 27, the *George IV* steamed up Winga Sound and laid anchor a few miles southwest of Gothenburg, Sweden. "We can do all the repairs ourselves," the captain informed them, "but it will take time."

"How much time are we going to lose?" asked Rian.

The captain shrugged. "Three days. We can make some time back up by shortening our stays in Hamburg and Amsterdam. Altogether, we'll probably arrive in London two days late."

Rian reverted to her previous somber demeanor. The only time Seamus saw a sign of life in her was when she was playing poker. Fortunately, there was plenty of time for that.

Wednesday, March 28: With repairs far from complete, Rian and Seamus joined a group that rented a skiff and sailed to Gothenburg. Seamus thought the houses were generous and smartly built. He enjoyed walking along the canals that laced through the city. Rian took no joy in the excursion.

Rian and Seamus had purchased bread and cheese for their afternoon meal and were sitting on a bench near a canal. "The *Sirius* leaves London for Cork today," Rian said, gripping the London newspaper that held the race article. She had brought it along on their expedition and read it a dozen times as if to squeeze more information, or better yet, different information, out of it.

George IV's guns sounded as they sailed back from Gothenburg: repairs were complete. Rian's mood darkened. "We're holding the ship up." In fact, they hadn't held the ship up at all. Half an hour after the sightseers returned to the *George IV*, the ship's steam engines engaged and she paddled down Winga Sound and shortly thereafter into the North Sea.

Thursday, March 29: Rian stood on the foredeck of the ship. "It's too late. We're going to miss both the *Sirius* and the *Great Western*."

Friday, March 30: The *George IV* steamed up the Elbe to Hamburg in the midmorning with the intention of leaving by midafternoon to make up time. Rian and Seamus bid farewell to Sheremetev and Malkovich on the wharf.

Sheremetev hugged Rian, then held her by the shoulders so he could gaze at her one last time. "I sorely misjudged you, dear Rian. When I learned you were a girl I dismissed you on many different levels. I was wrong. Of all my friends in St. Petersburg, you are the one who got us out of a rather nasty fix. No one else had the balls to do what you did. And I don't know which scares me more, the way you bested Volkonsky or your abilities at poker. Rest easy. Despite the storm, I know you will get to Philadelphia in time."

Although Seamus was a bit surprised at Sheremetev's breach of decorum with the "balls" statement, he couldn't argue with the count's assessment. He noticed that Rian skipped up the gangway when she returned to the ship.

Even before they left the mouth of the Elbe, Dunworthy appointed himself to organize the evening poker game and included Rian. By the end of the evening, David Winter was the big winner despite drinking heavily.

Late at night, Saturday, March 31: Seamus and Rian watched an Amsterdam harbor pilot climb aboard the ship to guide the ship to its berth. "The *Great Western* left London today," said Rian. "That was our last hope to get to New York on time."

April 1: The crew of *George IV* worked through the night to perform another quick turnaround in Amsterdam. The ship steamed out of port at ten o'clock in the morning. In the last poker game of the voyage, Rian, Lev, and Dunworthy were betting over a huge pot toward the end of the night. Dunworthy laid down a full house. "Queens full of sixes," Dunworthy declared proudly.

Lev had a better hand—kings full of threes.

Rian threw her cards face down on the table. "That beats what I've got."

Dunworthy had lost a fortune during the voyage, but this pot was the largest. He didn't take it well. Kiserev, who had dropped out of the hand early, glanced at Lev, nodded, and smiled.

"Rian," Seamus said after the game. "You didn't show your cards on that big hand with Dunworthy."

"Yeah, I know."

"So you could have taken the pot?"

Rian shrugged, neither confirming nor denying.

"Tell your Cousin Seamus."

"I've relieved Dunworthy of a lot of money during this voyage. Lev's going to be just starting out when we get to America. This way, he'll have a little bit of money to get himself going."

Seamus put his arm around Rian's shoulder. "You're a good person, Rian."

She didn't respond.

On April 2, the *George IV* sailed up the Thames to London. Rian was the first to disembark. She ran up and down the wharves, reading the schedules of each of the berthed ships. "Nothing at all is heading to Philadelphia or New York. Not even a cargo ship. No one's heading to the United States for days."

"Rian, this isn't the best way to figure out how to get ourselves home in time," said Seamus. "There's got to be a clearinghouse nearby. Some office where they can lay out our options."

Minutes later, with Rian in the lead, the voyagers, including David and Delilah Winter, entered an office of the British Steamship Authority. Rian approached a clerk standing behind a counter. "We understand that the steamship *Sirius* is leaving for New York City from Ireland the day after tomorrow. Is there any way we can get there in time?"

The clerk smiled indulgently. "I'm sorry, young man. The last packet for Cork left this morning. Besides, it would take you three days to get to Cork anyway."

"When does the next ship leave London for New York or Philadelphia?"

"Not for days. There's not a ship in port at the moment that makes any of those trips."

"What about out of Southampton? When does the next ship leave for America?"

The clerk consulted a ledger. "Let me see. The *Eagle* departs for New York City in the afternoon, day after tomorrow."

"When would it arrive in New York?"

"Well that depends on the weather, of course, but the average trip is thirty-two days. That would get you to New York on May 7."

Rian spun around a complete revolution in frustration. "What other ports do ships sail to America from?"

"Why, there's Bristol. That's on the west coast of England. Perhaps you could catch the *Great Western*."

"The *Great Western*? That was supposed to have left days ago."

"You must have just got off the boat, laddie. You haven't heard? There was a fire on board the *Great Western* even before she left the Thames. Mr. Brunel was injured. The ship has laid over in Bristol for repairs."

"When does she leave Bristol?"

"Why, as soon as the repairs are done, I suppose."

"How far is Bristol from here?"

"Oh, 130 miles or so."

"Can we buy train tickets to Bristol?"

The clerk laughed. "Why sure, if you wait until next year. They're laying the track as we speak."

"What about a ship to Bristol?"

"That would be the *Coastal Queen*. That will take you five days including a stop in Southampton."

"What about a stagecoach?"

"Well, you'll have to buy tickets next door, but stages leave London for Bristol twice a day."

"How long will it take to get to Bristol?"

"Three days, unless the rain slows you down."

"Do you think there will be any room aboard the *Great Western* if we get there on time?"

"Oh, of that I am certain. The fire spooked the passengers. The newspapers say they all asked for their money back except for one. I imagine the largest passenger ship in the world will be heading to America almost empty."

Rian led the way to the stagecoach ticket office.

SUNDAY, APRIL 8

· SEAMUS ·

Seamus hoped Rian would relax a bit with the near-certainty that they would be able to catch the *Great Western* before she sailed from Bristol. Such was not the case.

His cousin chafed at every delay on the 130-mile journey from London to Bristol—at each stop of the stagecoach to exchange horses, eat a meal, or take on passengers; at the inns both nights after grueling, bumpy, occasionally rain-soaked days. Even after they shared an evening meal with an eastbound traveler at the inn in Swindon, who told them that his friend James Hosken, captain of the *Great Western*, intended to sail on the afternoon of the seventh, and they had plenty of time to catch the ship.

They arrived in Bristol on April 7, only to learn that the *Great Western* wasn't in Bristol. She was docked at Avonmouth, a twelve-mile steamer ride away. When they boarded the *Dunnock*, a dinky little steamer that supplied all the great ships that called on Avonmouth, their passage aboard the *Great Western* was guaranteed, yet Rian never left her position at the bow. She groused that the *Dunnock* could barely best the incoming tide on the Avon River. During that three-hour journey to the giant Severn River, she ignored the stupendous granite cliffs, some easily three hundred feet tall, on either side of the river. She paid only passing attention to workmen who were building huge abutments on either side of the river, anchors for a suspension bridge that would take years to complete.

Another delay occurred when they finally arrived at the *Great Western*. The *Dunnock* idled within hailing distance of the magnificent ship while another steamer with a noisy crowd of well-wishers belatedly left the *Great Western*'s side.

Seamus took in the expanse of the ship from her port side. A deckhand, with little to do until the well-wishers' steamer cleared out, stood and admired the giant steamship. "There she be," he said to Seamus and Rian. "She's the biggest ship I've ever seen and I've worked this river for twenty years. She's

236 feet long, displaces 1,320 tons. She's got two engines that produce 700 horsepower each."

Seamus could tell by the deckhand's lilting brogue that he was a fellow Hibernian. "She's a steamship all right, and she certainly is grand, but she's got four masts. Seems to me the builders didn't have much confidence she'd stow enough coal to get her across the Atlantic if they needed masts."

"Not to worry, Bucko. Admittedly, the masts will provide the *Great Western* with a modest amount of push when the wind is right, but they're mostly there to stabilize her during rough weather. Mr. Brunel wanted to make sure that both the paddlewheels are in the water all the time."

The *Dunnock* finally started up again, and the little steamer closed in on the much larger *Great Western*.

"Okay, laddies, me break is over. Have a safe trip."

As the deckhands attended to their duties, Seamus examined the behemoth up close. She gleamed with new varnish and paint. The smell of tar hit him as the two ships were tying up together. "What do you think, Rian? Are we going to make history on that ship?"

"I don't care about history as long as we get to Philadelphia in time to catch the memoir."

Rian's focus on the deadline continued after they boarded the ship, when the breeze of the early afternoon became a gale, prompting Captain Hosken to declare it would be best to lie by until morning. "Damnit," said Rian.

Seamus awakened in his berth at 8:00 A.M. to the low roar of the ship's furnaces. *Maybe Rian will relax once we're underway.* By nine, the steam was up. At noon on Sunday, April 8, 1838, after more delays that drove Rian to distraction but seemed to perturb Captain Hosken not a bit, the *Great Western*, the largest passenger ship in the world, departed on her maiden voyage to New York. The ship, built to transport 128 passengers, all in first-class cabins, left Bristol with seven: Seamus, Rian, Lev, Kiserev, David and Delilah Winter, and Dewey Percell, a major stockholder in the Great Western Steamship Company.

By dark, they had cleared the mouth of the Bristol Channel and were making their way into a headwind on a surly Celtic Sea.

* * * * *

Rian and Seamus arrived in the Grand Saloon for dinner and found Delilah Winter standing near the bar with drink in hand. She was dressed in a long, midnight blue evening gown with scooped neck that revealed a hint of her generous bosom.

Seamus did his best not to stare. *Now that's something I'm going to miss about Russia. No fashion like that in Philadelphia.* He still hadn't figured Delilah out. She was always a bit warmer toward him than seemed typical of a married woman, but he took Sheremetev's cautionary comment seriously: the crowd she mingled with in St. Petersburg were all vipers. "Greetings," he said to Delilah. "I guess we don't need to worry about getting a seat for dinner. I counted twenty-five tables when I was exploring the ship this afternoon. Where do you want to sit?"

Delilah casually handed Seamus an envelope and nodded at a table at the near end of the saloon. "Apparently David and I are eating at the Captain's Table this evening. This was slipped under our door a couple of hours ago."

The envelope was addressed to Mr. and Mrs. Winter. Seamus pulled out a card that had an expensive feel to it. In flourishing calligraphy, the note said:

Captain James Hosken
Requests the pleasure of your company
At his dinner table this evening
7:00 p.m.
Formal dress.

Seamus showed the card to Rian. Rian left Seamus and Delilah and took a quick trip around the table. "There are place cards for Captain Hosken, Mr. Winter, Mrs. Winter, Mr. Kiserev, and Mr. Percell."

Seamus surveyed the saloon. "So that leaves Rian, Lev, and me. Where are we supposed to eat?"

"I can guess," said Delilah.

"And where is that?"

Delilah flicked her head toward the far end of the cavernous Grand Saloon, sixty feet away. "I've already taken a tour around the room. There are three places set at the table at the other end. No place cards, though."

"And why are we all the way over there?"

"Another guess? Rian, you're too young to be of interest to the captain. A few weeks ago, Lev was a serf bound to the Tsar's land. He's learning fast, but it doesn't take long to tell he's still illiterate. And you, dear Seamus? Your lilting Irish brogue apparently excludes you from membership in polite society."

Delilah's words stung Seamus. *There's the viper that Sheremetev was talking about.* "Well, that's something else I'll miss from Russia," said Seamus. "No one in St. Petersburg knew I wasn't polite."

As if on cue, the rest of the voyagers arrived in the saloon. Seamus filled them in.

Dewey Percell didn't seem to think there was much of a problem. "Don't worry, old chap. You'll be eating the same food as we do. The ship's staff will serve you, same as us. The captain told me it's only fitting. After all, you've paid for first class tickets, and it gives the maître d' the opportunity to train his people."

Kiserev, who had also arrived with his invitation, said not a word. Shortly thereafter, Seamus noticed him speaking to the maître d'. And moments later, a waiter moved Kiserev's entire place setting to the outcasts' table.

* * * * *

· RIAN ·

After dinner, Rian was pleased when, despite the rough weather, the group reconvened for poker. David Winter had been a bit too well attended by the ship's waiters. He was drunk when the game started.

Dewey Percell, who had never played poker, observed. "This is quite enjoyable. It seems that unlike the captain's dinner table, the poker table is blind to class distinctions."

Rian had vowed not to dip into her considerable winnings from the voyage from Kronstadt to London except for the small amount she started the game with. She won early and mentally put her nest egg away.

In what became the biggest hand of the evening, David Winter dealt her a pair of kings, an ace, a seven of spades, and a five of clubs. She tossed the two junk cards. Winter dealt her replacements. She opened her new hand to find three kings and two aces—"kings full of aces"—a full house that would be hard to beat, especially since she had noted another ace on the bottom of the deck when David Winter was dealing the hand.

Winter drew two cards for himself. Delilah Winter dropped out. Lev threw two kopeks into the pot; a pittance that kept him in the game. Rian saw the two kopeks and raised them with a Swedish krona. Kiserev saw and raised with a few English pounds. Seamus dropped out. Winter matched the betting so far and raised five pounds. Lev dropped out. Rian saw the five pounds, then threw in all her winnings for the evening, including the starter pot that she had vowed not to touch. Kiserev dropped out.

Winter addressed his wife. "Delilah, my dear, my friend Rian seems very confident about his hand. I could use a temporary loan."

Delilah smiled at her husband but shook her head. "You are on your own, my love."

"Okay, Rian, you have me at a bit of a disadvantage. I would like to call your bet, but I don't have the money with me right now. If I lose this hand, how about I paint a portrait of you during the voyage?"

Rian smiled wryly at Winter. "It depends. Are you any good?"

Delilah rose from the table to refill her glass with water. "Of that, I can assure you. In St. Petersburg, David's portraits sold for much more than is in the pot right now. If you win, you will get a bargain and possess a family heirloom."

"Then I accept," said Rian. She fanned her kings full of aces onto the table.

Winter hesitated, then threw down his cards so hard that the entire hand flipped over, exposing jacks full of aces. A chorus of oohs and oofs arose from the other players. Winter regained his composure. "Well, I guess that concludes my play for the evening. Rian, if the weather is calm tomorrow, we shall start your portrait." He rose from the table and took the stairs to the main deck.

Dewey Percell moved into Winter's seat. "Well, I think I have a grasp of the fundamentals. How hard can it be? Apparently the most important things are to chest your cards and watch out for Master Krieger here."

Percell struck Rian as the kind of person who was used to being the center of attention. She noticed that the more he talked about himself, the more the poker players' demeanor changed toward him.

"I am on the board of both the Great Western Railway Company and the Great Western Steamship Company. I was at the directors meeting of the Railway Company when Isambard Brunel first put forth his vision—that a traveler be able to buy one ticket in London, take a train to Bristol, board this ship, and disembark in New York City all in a mere sixteen days. We are about to prove the seafaring part of that in this voyage."

Delilah Winter seemed most attentive. Seamus winked at Rian as Percell held forth, which Rian took to mean *let the man have his fun but don't take him too seriously*. Rian saw Lev and Kiserev make eye contact, not unusual for the two Russians, who had developed a bit of an alliance. She interpreted their nonverbal exchange as an assessment of Dewey Percell: He's a blowhard.

Rian dealt a new hand. "Were you on board the ship when the fire happened?"

"I was. A number of us were on board. Brunel and his wife, some other stockholders, a few dignitaries."

"Why was the *Great Western* in London if it's going to operate out of Bristol?"

"She was built in Bristol but sailed to London a year ago to be outfitted with two side-lever steam engines by Maudsley. The return trip to Bristol was supposed to act as her sea trials. The fire broke out in the engine room. Brunel feared his darling creation was going to be destroyed before she even cleared the Thames. He got careless. Fell twenty feet off a scaffold in the engine room. We put him and his wife ashore on Convey Island. The rest of the folks—twenty or so—disembarked in Southampton. The list of passengers who were waiting for us in Bristol evaporated. Thus, it seems the seven of us are the only people destined to make history when we pull up dockside in New York."

"Is Mr. Brunel okay?"

"Oh, he'll recover fully, I'm sure. Very disappointed not to be making this trip. He was relieved when I didn't turn in my ticket."

Rian fanned her cards. Her hand wasn't promising. "And besides being a participant in history, Mr. Percell, why are you going to New York?"

"History is more than enough. But I have business interests in both New York and your Philadelphia. I suspect I'll be in the United States long enough to catch the *Great Western* when she returns to Bristol in early May."

* * * * *

· SEAMUS ·

Seamus answered the knock on his stateroom door to find his cousin.

Rian shouldered past him before he could invite her in. "Shut the door," she said.

"Good time tonight. You were the big winner."

Rian sat down heavily on Seamus's bed. "I think David Winter was cheating."

Seamus crossed his arms and leaned his back into the cabin door. "If he was cheating, he didn't do a very good job of it. What did you see?"

"He's careless. The way he deals, about half the time you can see the card on the bottom of the deck. On that big pot, the one I won from him, there was an ace on the bottom."

"So?"

"So I had kings full of aces. His cards flipped over when he threw them on the table. He had jacks full of aces. Counting the one on the bottom, that makes five aces."

"Pretty sloppy of him. That man drinks too much. What do you want to do about it?"

"I've got a plan."

MONDAY, APRIL 9

· LOGAN ·

Carpenters and journeymen had reconverged back at Pennsylvania Hall even before the painters had wrapped up. The gang of twenty-five workers included Marcus Edes's crew, a handful of white guys who had been at the Shelter for Colored Orphans and willing to work with Negroes, the men whom Jules had hired since he started running the job, and the entire production crew from Freeman Hydraulics.

Logan was a bit taken aback to realize that, with the addition of the craftsmen from Freeman Hydraulics, there were now more Black workers than white.

Although racial tension hadn't diminished, there was now a growing sense that the construction of Pennsylvania Hall would be finished on time, perhaps even ahead of schedule.

As the carpenters made their final sprint to finish Pennsylvania Hall, Logan rarely picked up a hammer or a saw. More often, he hauled trim boards up from the ground floor, held boards securely while a carpenter sawed, ran for more nails, or cleaned up when no one had a job for him.

Cee-Cee, on the other hand, had made herself far more useful. Where sawing a perfect ninety-degree angle continued to elude Logan, Cee-Cee practiced, practiced, practiced until the finish carpenters trusted her to make the cut while they attended to the next task.

Everyone in the city seemed aware of the increasing tension between the races. Papers like *Das Philadelphische Patriot* continued to publish incendiary articles. The *Appeal of Forty Thousand Citizens, Threatened with Disfranchisement, to the People of Pennsylvania*, which Logan had laboriously waded through in its entirety, had backfired. Somehow the whites of the city were incensed that the Blacks were protesting their proposed fate.

At the Hall, Black workers mostly stuck with their kind, and so did the whites. Jules had invited Pepper Pot Penny to cart her stew up to the Hall one Friday, but the mixing of Black and white during the dinner break never repeated itself.

There were a few exceptions to the lack of Black/white fraternizing. Jules and Marcus Edes worked well together. Homer Good and Emil Harberger continued to fabricate Doric columns, although they always seemed to bicker with each other about the best way to do things. And lastly, although they were too far down the ladder for anyone to give a shyte, there were himself and Cee-Cee. On this occasion, they had combined forces to haul ten trim boards at a time upstairs.

"Homer told me that he thought we were going to finish ahead of schedule," Cee-Cee said from behind him as they maneuvered the boards around the landing of the stairway.

"Homer and Emil better finish the columns. They haven't installed a single one yet."

"He's not worried about that. . . . Logan, I've got a message from Martha. She wants to talk to you. It's important."

Logan kept trudging up the second set of stairs. "We broke up," he whispered. "If I see her again, I'm afraid we'll start right back up where we left off. That can't happen."

"She knows that. She doesn't want to meet at the potbelly stove. She says she'll meet you back at the rock."

THURSDAY, APRIL 12

· RIAN ·

On Monday, April 9, the passengers awoke to glassy seas and a light breeze from the northwest. Good to his word, David Winter corralled Rian after breakfast to start painting her portrait. They settled in the middle of the Grand Saloon, where crew members on deck had removed a hatch to admit sunlight during the benign weather. "The way the light streams down through the hatch will be fun to play with," Winter commented.

The artist experimented with Rian's two hats—her coachman's top hat and the mink-lined ushanka that she had purchased after she first experienced the bitter cold of St. Petersburg. He played with her costume and finally decided on her "Imperial Family" suit covered by Captain Stepanov's greatcoat.

Chatting as he worked, Winter sat Rian in a chair and draped her arm over the back of another chair. He told Rian he had studied the masters in both the Louvre in Paris and the Hermitage in St. Petersburg. He was most particularly influenced by the works of Jacques-Louis David, and planned to paint Rian in that neoclassical style. Rian had never heard of David, and she didn't know what the neoclassical style was. She had a difficult time sitting still as Winter painted, but the thought of returning home with a portrait motivated her.

As Winter worked away on his canvas, he chatted amiably. "I had a great idea, a way I was going to make my fortune by creating a cyclorama of the Winter Palace from the interior courtyard. I was going to create a painting that was 25 feet high and 350 feet around."

"What happened?"

"I created one panel and a number of illustrative sketches. I peddled them all over St. Petersburg, trying to sign up investors."

"And . . . ?"

"None of the potential investors thought having a painting you could walk into was a very good idea when you could walk through the courtyard for free."

"Do you still have the sketches?"

"I do. I even brought the panel with me. Before I left I tried to sell it for a song, but still no bites. So it's down in the hold of the *Great Western*. I'll have to find a place to store it when we land."

As the morning progressed, Rian had a hard time reconciling the talkative, engaging painter with the cheating poker player. She started to doubt her suspicions.

At noon, the *Great Western* came to a halt leeward of the American ship *Neponset*, four days out of Liverpool and bound for Charleston, South Carolina. The delay irked Rian.

That night, with dirty seas returned, the poker players reconvened. David Winter dealt three hands over the course of the evening. Rian detected no cheating.

On Tuesday, the rough seas continued, so Winter canceled the portraiture for the day. The captain stopped the *Great Western*'s engines twice to greet other ships: the *South America* seven days out of Liverpool, and the *Atlantic* out of Southampton and heading for New Orleans. That established the pattern for the rest of the voyage: stop engines; "Hail!" "Where from?" "How long out?" No significant information was ever transferred. Each stop irritated Rian.

The seas remained rough into the evening. At the poker table, David Winter drank heavily. He dealt three times. One time Rian saw the king of diamonds on the bottom of the deck. During the bidding, she arose from her chair, walked to a table that held a water pitcher, and penciled *KD* on a sheet of paper she had placed on the table earlier. She gave Seamus a quick nod as she returned to the table. Winter folded before the betting finished, so Rian didn't know if the king ended up in his hand or not.

On Wednesday, David and Rian resumed their portrait sessions. Dewey Percell watched David paint for a while. "Mr. Winter, you are quite accomplished. I may commission you to paint my portrait when you are done with young Master Krieger here."

They broke when the engines stopped so the *Great Western* could hail a French ship heading east. This time, the two ships exchanged mail. They did the same for an American ship heading to London. Neither ship offered significant news from America.

Rian thought Winter played on the up-and-up at the poker table after dinner. She was the big winner that evening.

On Thursday, Winter finished the portrait. "I would have taken much longer with a client in St. Petersburg, but I think this portrait satisfies my debt. Come. See for yourself."

What Rian saw took her breath away. Staring back at her from the canvas was a young man with sparkling green eyes, high cheekbones, and slightly olive skin. His unruly light brown hair peaked out from beneath a top hat cocked at a jaunty angle. This young man was determined, calculating, and intelligent. He leaned back confidently in his chair, his arm draped over the back of a second chair. Given the posture, you would assume this young man didn't have a care in the world until you noticed his left hand. Instead of relaxed, his hand was balled into a fist, as if he were ready to lash out at any moment. You really couldn't tell if the boy was fourteen or four years older, because the artist had given him a strong jaw and the bulk of his Russian greatcoat implied that he was solidly built. The young man's lips were parted slightly, as if he were about to reveal a secret that would be amusing both to him and to his confidante. You could see a generous gap between his two front teeth, but this gap would not cause the subject of the portrait embarrassment. Oh, no. This young man was proud of that gap. He undoubtedly could use it to project a stream of water a bet-winning distance.

Behind the boy appeared the faint outline of the Winter Palace. The palace was obviously on fire, not because you could see the flames, but because they were reflected in the clouds above.

Rian's knees went a little weak. "This is who I want to be."

Winter leaned back in mock indignation. "This, Young Rian, is who you are. I believe I have captured your soul."

Rian was not inclined to disagree.

* * * * *

Winter celebrated the completion of the painting by starting his drinking long before dinner. He was particularly noisy at the Captain's Table that evening.

The first time Winter dealt that night, Rian couldn't see the card on the bottom of the deck. He won the pot with three queens. He rose, held his glass aloft, and made eye contact with the bartender—the signal for another whiskey. The second time he dealt, Rian saw a king of hearts on the bottom of the deck. She rose from the table, filled her water glass, and surreptitiously wrote *KH* on the pad of paper. Winter folded before any significant betting. The third time Winter dealt, Rian clearly made out the king of spades. She wrote *KS* on the paper when she refreshed her water.

Please, please, please, be wrong, Eena. Don't let David be a cheater.

Rian held two pair—jacks over tens—enough to keep her in the bidding before the second round of cards was dealt. She threw away a useless five of diamonds but received a six in return. Betting was light by the time it got to her. She threw in a couple of kopeks to stay in the hand.

Kiserev and Seamus folded. Winter drained his glass, took one card, and matched Rian's kopeks. Mrs. Winter dropped out. Dewey Percell drew two cards and raised the stakes considerably.

Rian dropped out. David Winter saw and raised, also by a lot. Dewey Percell saw and raised; another big bump. David Winter called. There was a lot of money in the pot; probably the biggest pot in the trip so far. Percell laid down aces full of threes, a hand that would have won almost every pot that evening, but not tonight. Winter fanned four kings and started raking the pot toward him.

Rian felt the blood drain out of her body. When she made eye contact with Seamus, he questioned her with his eyes. Rian nodded.

Seamus put his hand on Winter's arm. "One moment, David," he said. "You may have noticed my cousin went to that table over there and filled his water glass. There's also a pad of paper there. If Rian ever sees the card on the bottom of the deck when you are dealing, he goes to refresh his glass and makes a note of the card. If the bottom notation on that paper is a king, that means you are a cheater."

David Winter froze, the rake only half-completed, his boozy gaze focused on the pot. He seemed unsure of what he should do next.

Delilah rose from her chair. "Seamus, this is absurd. What have you two been cooking up?"

Rian stayed in her seat but stared down at the table. "I've suspected for a couple of nights now that Mr. Winter is dealing from the bottom of the deck. This time I saw the king of spades at the bottom when he was dealing."

"My husband's reputation is at stake here. Where is your proof?"

Seamus kept his hand on Winter's arm. "Like I said, the proof sits right over there on the table with the water jug."

Dewey Percell rose from his seat and retrieved the paper. "The bottom entry says *KS*; King of Spades. Winter, I believe these two. You are a cheater. I don't know much about this game, but I assume that means you forfeit this pot. I would also vote to banish you from poker games for the rest of the voyage."

Winter unsteadily rose from his seat and took the stairs to the main deck. Delilah followed him.

Percell sat and contemplated the pot. "Rian, I believe I owe you a big debt. To me, the amount of money sitting in that pot is not particularly substantial, but no man likes being made a fool of. I would like you to take the money in appreciation."

Rian was still devastated that she had exposed the man who had that very day completed a portrait that was already her most prized possession. She stared at the pot for a long moment. "When I was in Russia, I had some dealings with the head of the Third Section, the Russian Secret Police. He told me he wasn't very interested in money. He collected favors instead because they were more valuable to him. I think you should keep that pot but owe me a favor. I'll still do my best to take your money from you but by playing fair and square."

"And what is the favor you would like me to grant you?"

"Oh, I have no idea, but I'm sure something will come up. If not tomorrow, then next week. If not next week, then next year."

"May our lives be long enough that I will be able to grant you the favor. Gentlemen, I believe it is time for us to have a drink."

* * * * *

· LOGAN ·

The night was balmy, giving a hint that spring was here to stay.

Logan leaned into the rock, the blanket draped over his shoulders as if it were the middle of winter. He welcomed its warmth. He was nervous. He was pretty sure why Martha had asked him to meet her.

He heard Martha's footsteps coming and lifted the blanket to accommodate her next to him. Instead, she stood facing him in the darkness. "I've missed two monthlies," she said.

"What does that mean?" Logan responded with growing dread.

"I'm pregnant."

FRIDAY, APRIL 13

· RIAN ·

The next day, Delilah Winter moved into one of the many vacant staterooms on the *Great Western*.

That evening, David Winter joined the outcasts at their table for dinner. He had been drinking all afternoon. "Percell better watch himself," he muttered, his boozy gaze focused on the Captain's Table sixty feet away. The stockholder had just said something that made Delilah laugh. "She'll clean him out as soon as she gets a chance."

After dinner, Delilah and Percell joined Rian, Kiserev, Seamus, and Lev for poker.

"Mr. Percell," said Delilah after a few hands. "What was the captain saying about squares and cubes? I was embarrassed to admit that I didn't understand it all."

"Well, it is quite a handful, and I wouldn't expect a woman to understand it." Percell nodded toward Rian. "Or a child as precocious as Master Krieger here. But essentially, Isambard Brunel came to understand a principle that will affect marine architecture for generations."

"And what is that?" asked Rian, piqued that Percell assumed she couldn't grasp a concept because of her age. *Not to mention my sex, you horse's ass. I should have let Mr. Winter cheat you last night.*

"Brunel claims that the carrying capacity of a vessel such as the *Great Western* increases in proportion to the cube of its dimensions, but the resistance it encounters from the water only increases in proportion to the square of its dimensions. I agree with you, Mrs. Winter, it is a difficult concept to grasp."

"No it isn't," said Rian. "It means that the larger the steamship, the more fuel-efficient it is going to be. I imagine that Mr. Brunel spent a lot of time calculating how big the *Great Western* had to be to carry enough coal to get across the Atlantic."

"Why yes, I believe you are right, although many knowledgeable people do not agree with him."

"My family encounters similar issues because we're building larger locomotives than we used to, except we also had to factor in the capacity of the track to carry heavier loads. We'll find out if Mr. Brunel is right by the end of this voyage," Rian said. "And if he is, I bet people will start building larger ships."

Delilah brightened. "Why, that's what the captain was saying."

"Indeed," said Percell, trying to reestablish the superiority of his understanding of maritime innovation. "Currently a ship of sail might make the crossing in four weeks, but depending upon the weather, it could just as easily be five. Think what it will be like a few years from now. Steamships will adhere to regular schedules, maybe doing a complete round trip in the time it previously took to go one way. They'll depart on the same date every month. Passengers won't tarry at port for days, waiting for their ship to arrive."

"Like railroad schedules have become," said Rian.

"Yes," responded Percell, not particularly happy to give Rian the last word. Percell bet heavily and won big over the course of the evening. Delilah was the big loser.

* * * * *

Delilah continued to shower Dewey Percell with flattery and attention. Yet a day later, it was obvious that something had occurred between her and the businessman. It was made all the more apparent when Delilah chose to take her meal at the outcast table.

"What happened?" asked David Winter. "Couldn't catch Percell in your spiderweb?"

"Shut up, David," Delilah retorted. "Go get another drink."

By the next day, Delilah Winter had shifted her focus and taken an interest in Lev's education. As the days progressed, Rian and Delilah spent increasing time conversing with Lev in English. "The more English you know by the time you arrive in America, the easier you're going to have it," Delilah told Lev.

* * * * *

· SEAMUS ·

Although the travelers played poker only at night, betting was an all-day activity. Anything and everything was fodder for wagers.

What is the exact length of the Grand Saloon?

Which of the waiters would enter the saloon from the galley next?

Will the entrée be beef, pork, chicken, or fish?

How many porpoises will we see from the deck in the next half hour?
How many tons of coal will be left in the bunkers when we arrive in New York?
How many revolutions will the engines have made when we dock in New York?

And then there was the biggest bet of all: *What day and time will we arrive in New York City?*

Rian optimistically bet that the steamship would arrive in New York City by noon on April 22, which would give them a day to take the train to Philadelphia and head off the memoir.

* * * * *

As had been her habit of late, Delilah sat next to Lev at the dinner table. She took it upon herself to broaden his education to every aspect of comporting himself well in polite company. In this case, at the dinner table it included which fork to use when, posture, wines, interactions with the waiters, and the art of conversation. Seamus, still stinging from Delilah's comment about polite company, paid attention.

Lev addressed the table. "What exact time will Captain Hosken check in with us outcasts after his dinner?"

David Winter placed his pocket watch on the table. "I say he will utter his first word to us at 9:30."

The betting was on.

* * * * *

The poker game ended late. Dewey Percell was the big loser, his money spread around the table in relatively equal measure. Like the Englishman Dunworthy before him, his losses throughout the voyage had been disbursed among all of the poker players. *But,* Seamus noted, *Rian's amassing a hefty share of the money that's been floating around.*

After this evening's game broke up, Seamus, Lev, and Delilah remained at the table, determined to finish off the last two inches of a bottle of Jameson whiskey. They idly played "high card wins" with kopeks that had populated their poker pots since Russia.

Seamus splashed whiskey into his glass and made eye contact with Delilah. She gave him a quick nod and a smile, pushed her glass toward him. Lev waved him off.

The saloon's steward approached the table. "Excuse me, lady and gentlemen, will you be wanting anything else from the bar? Otherwise, I'm going to lock up for the evening."

Seamus tapped the Jameson bottle with his fingernail. "I think we're good here. Thank you." He returned his attention to Delilah. "So, does your husband mind that you stay up late, drinking with the boys?"

Delilah laid the deck on the table and cut the cards, exposing a queen of diamonds. "David has no say in what I do."

"So it's over between you two?"

"He knew our time was coming to an end. We actually broke up in Russia, but I decided to give it one more try at the last minute. I almost didn't make it to the *Herman of Valaam* in time."

"So you're separating? How will you get a divorce?"

"That won't be hard. David isn't really my husband."

Seamus tried to hide his surprise. He cut the cards to a jack of diamonds and returned his gaze to Delilah.

"We met in Paris. I was the guest of a baron. David was painting a portrait of the baron's wife. The baron caught the two of them in bed together. He told David he would make sure David never painted another portrait in Paris."

Lev cut the cards, turning up an ace of spades. "That is it for me. I go to bed now. Good evening to you both." He rose unsteadily from his chair, raked three kopeks into his palm, and walked toward the staterooms.

Seamus was surprised that Lev left. The conversation was just getting interesting. He idly mixed the cards. "So then what happened?"

Delilah shrugged. "I'd tired of the baron, or maybe he'd tired of me. St. Petersburg seemed like an interesting place to visit. I thought David could probably find commissions there pretty easily. Traveling is easier for a woman if the world thinks she is married."

"What did you do while you were in St. Petersburg?"

"David painted—very successfully, until too many husbands got wind that he was getting to know his subjects a bit too well. I fell in with Count Golitsyn's crowd. We played vingt-et-un at night. Eventually I tired of that as well."

"So now what?"

"I don't know. It depends on the next couple of days." Delilah sighed. "It's time for me to retire to my cabin. Goodnight, Seamus." She rose, stooped as if on impulse, and gave Seamus a soft kiss on his cheek. "Thanks for listening. You are a good man."

Seamus shook his head in admiration as he watched the alluring woman exit the saloon. He had scruples about bedding another man's wife, but with the knowledge that David Winter had no claim to Delilah's affections, he saw a new future for the remaining days of the voyage.

He eyed the cabinet doors that guarded the liquor bottles behind the bar, secured by a single padlock. *Not much of an impediment for a man who used to make a living by breaking and entering.*

Ten minutes later, Seamus stood at the door of Delilah's cabin with a fresh bottle of whiskey and two glasses. He knocked softly. No answer. He knocked a little harder. Still nothing. *Well, bucko, it appears you misjudged your situation. Either she doesn't want to see you or she's already asleep.*

As he walked by Lev's stateroom, he heard the unmistakable lilt of a female voice and Lev's raspy Russian-accented English. *Didn't even consider a third option. Guess I've misjudged things a wee bit.*

* * * * *

· SEAMUS ·

As Seamus waited for his bacon and eggs to arrive, he mused about the doings of the previous night. He didn't know which surprised him more: that Lev, who was a charming but illiterate peasant, had the good fortune to entertain Delilah in his bed, or that a cultured woman like Delilah Winter would go to him. *And what really hurts is that she picked him over me for a shipboard romance.*

Lev strode into the room with a skip in his step, sat down opposite him, and placed his napkin in his lap. "Good morning, Seamus. Short night last night."

Their waiter approached, and Lev ordered ham and eggs.

"Shorter for you than me, I suspect. Have a good time with Mrs. Winter last night?"

Lev smiled sheepishly. "She told me she told you Winter is not her husband."

Seamus gave Lev a conspiratorial smile. "You should keep the noise down in your cabin. Otherwise the whole ship is going to know about you two."

"Watch out for her."

"Why should I worry about Delilah?" Seamus asked. "She kicked her husband—her pretend husband—out for cheating at cards."

"She did not kick him out for cheating. She kick him out for getting caught. Well, that and he drink too much when he play poker game."

TUESDAY, APRIL 17

· RIAN ·

The voyagers gathered on deck in midmorning to view Labrador in the distance to the starboard. They had crossed the Atlantic in nine days. It felt like they were almost home.

"Don't be fooled, lad," one of the deckhands said. "It always seems that way, but we're still a long way from New York. But I admit, it is sweet to spot land every once in a while."

The ship stopped engines to perform scheduled maintenance. Rian chafed at the delay.

On the twentieth, they passed within sight of Nova Scotia.

Rian came out on deck before sunrise on the twenty-first as they passed the single beam of the lighthouse on the island of Nantucket. Her stomach started to knot. They had to get to Philadelphia in time to intercept the memoir before Lucretia delivered it to Harold Foote on April 23. To do that, they had to arrive in New York City on the twenty-second. They were going to be one day late.

Rian became aware of a presence by her side. Seamus had also risen early. "You too?" she asked him.

"Yeah, now that we're getting close, I'm having a hard time sleeping. What are you thinking about? Anything besides the obvious?"

"Isaac Newton, I guess."

"I don't know much about Isaac Newton."

"Konstantin's tutor told us about him a few months ago. Newton formulated a law. *For every action, there is an equal and opposite reaction.*"

"So why is Mr. Newton on your mind at five in the morning?"

"Remember Rose, the slave we helped escape from the Tucker family?"

"Of course."

"No one should be a slave, so when we had the opportunity to spring her, we did. So that was a good thing, right?"

"I think so."

"But when the slave catchers turned Moyamensing upside down searching for her, they broke into the houses of some of the Black families. Roughed them up. Destroyed their furniture. Do you think those Black people were happy that we helped Rose escape?"

"They suffered to help a Black woman get free. I hope they were able to put it into perspective."

"I used Catherine's memoir as a bargaining chip in order to get you free. The Tsar's reputation was weakened by the palace fire. It will be weakened more if Catherine the Great's memoirs are published. Count Sheremetev said it might weaken him so much that he has to make compromises, like forming a constitutional government, maybe even freeing his serfs. Was freeing you worth *not* freeing twenty million serfs?"

"Hmm, a couple of thoughts there. There's no guarantee that publishing the memoirs will lead to freeing the serfs. And Sheremetev would be the first to acknowledge that the Tsar would likely clamp down harder before he gave up power. For me? I'm grateful you made the decision you made."

"David Winter is a brilliant artist. That painting he made of me belongs in a museum someplace. Yet five days ago, we ruined his reputation by exposing his cheating. Is that fair?"

"Hey, David Winter made his own bed. All we did was call other peoples' attention to his cheating. Rian, you're doing a lot of heavy thinking here. I don't have answers to your questions, but yes, I guess that Mr. Newton got it right. Every time you try to change something, somebody or something else is going to push back. But you can't let that stop you from doing what is right."

"Then I should have gotten you and Uncle Adrian and Sheremetev and Malkovich out of prison another way. Or done nothing at all and let Ambassador Dallas handle it."

"Let's say for the moment that Dallas could have sprung Adrian and me from jail some months from now. By his own admission, he couldn't have helped the count and the colonel. They probably would have rotted in jail for years."

"But was their freedom—the freedom of all four of you—worth the price? Catherine's memoir should be published. The Tsar should be weakened. He should be forced to free the serfs and form a constitutional government."

"The only way that's going to happen is if we don't get back to Philadelphia on time. Nope, we're going to save Adrian, and the memoir goes back to St. Petersburg with Kiserev."

"God, I hope I made the right decision."

SUNDAY, APRIL 22

• SEAMUS •

The *Great Western* had been steaming for two weeks. Seamus kept an eye on the calendar, the same as Rian. Throughout the voyage, he felt that somehow they were going to arrive in Philadelphia in time to save Adrian. As they got closer to New York, his spirits started to sink.

Rian was still the focused, determined, driven Rian—always planning five steps ahead, always with a plan and another plan if the original went off the rails, never giving up on her goal, no matter how desperate things seemed.

As usual, Captain Hosken and Dewey Percell finished their dinner and ambled to the six passengers eating at the outcast table at the other end of the passenger saloon.

"I have a bit of news that might be of interest to you all," Captain Hoskin announced.

"Nine thirty-seven," David Winter muttered, precipitating a small shower of coins to be tossed to Rian's place at the table. "Hard to find news aboard this ship after two weeks, Captain. We're all ears."

"I did a reckoning of our position before dinner. We have been steaming at the record-breaking rate of 8.6 knots since we left Bristol."

"Excuse me, Captain Hosken," asked Lev, "how much is that in versts?" Seamus noticed Delilah nudge Lev. "Uh, in miles?"

The captain smiled at Lev, undoubtedly noting his improved English as well as the formality of his words. "That is approximately ten miles per hour. At this rate we should arrive in New York City by midday tomorrow, April 23."

Rian got up from the table and climbed the stairs to the main deck.

Winter took a piece of paper from his pocket and quickly scanned it. "That means that Delilah, Mr. Percell, and I are still in the running."

"Well, I'll leave you all to your betting," said the captain.

"One more thing, Captain," said Lev. "We also have wagered money on which of the steamships will reach New York City first, the *Great Western* or the *Sirius*. Do you have any news of the other ship?"

"That is my only disappointment so far during this entire voyage. We haven't spotted the *Sirius*. Now mind you, our lookouts are very vigilant at night, but we may have missed her in the dark. Honestly, I fear she will arrive in New York before us. Even though she had a four-day head start, I was confident we would catch her before now. I wanted to be the first to cross the Atlantic under steam."

Seamus followed Rian out onto the main deck. He knew what she was thinking. They were going to sail into New York on the day they needed to arrive in Philadelphia. Now only a miracle is going to save Adrian.

"Rian, we're not out of options yet. We can head straight to the office of the *Independent* when we get to Philadelphia. There's fifty pages in that document. It'll take them forever to typeset the thing. They'll never publish it all in one day. We'll surely get there before they get to the juicy parts."

Rian, her elbows on the rail, stared into the darkness. "You know as well as I do that once Harold Foote gets his hands on the memoir, he'll never let it go."

"Darlin', after all we've gone through to get home on time, now's not the time to lose heart. We'll tell Harold that Adrian's life is on the line. He'll definitely give the manuscript back to us."

"Harold is an abolitionist and a newspaperman. He wants to have an influence on history. If he can't help end slavery in America, at least he'd be helping to free the serfs in Russia."

"We don't know that. If he won't give us the memoir, then we talk to me boys at No Name. They love Adrian. If it hadn't been for him, we would never have had our first steam pumper. They'll be happy to rough Harold up if it means saving Adrian's life. Don't give up now, Rian. Adrian's still breathing."

* * * * *

· RIAN ·

As she had done every night since the voyage began, Rian surveyed the table. Everyone's habits were well known to her by now—Seamus, Lev, Kiserev, Delilah, and Dewey Percell. Percell had lost a ton of money over the course of the voyage. He bet heavily and bluffed often. Big pots had become the norm.

Even Delilah became more aggressive in her bidding. "If I don't bet, I'm never going to get a chance to play a hand."

Rian noted Delilah close her hand, place it on the table, shift uneasily in her seat, then bet heavily. When Lev called Delilah's bet, it turned out that she had bet heavily on three sixes; not a particularly strong hand. Lev won the pot.

Two other times that evening, Rian noted Delilah close her cards and place them on the table. Both times she held a middling hand. One time she won. One time she lost. *This game is so easy when you pay attention to the other people at the table*, she said to herself.

As the evening progressed, Rian and Delilah were the big winners, but everyone was playing with Dewey Percell's money. "This voyage has proved to be a lot more expensive than I anticipated," he groused.

On the last hand of the night, Rian and Delilah were the only two still betting. Rian remembered David Winter's comment about his pretend wife cleaning Dewey Percell out of his money. Seamus had told Rian about Delilah and Lev. Rian fanned her hand again. She had been dealt three fours and two trash cards. She threw her money in the pot—now a stew of Russian, Swedish, Finish, Danish, German, and British coins and notes—and asked for two cards. She made a point of not reacting when Kiserev dealt her two aces. "Check," she said, hoping that her lack of a bet would beef up Delilah's confidence in her own hand.

Delilah asked for one card. Kiserev slid it to her. She closed her hand and placed it on the table. She pushed a pile of rubles into the pot. "This should be worth what you've got sitting in front of you, Rian. In or out?"

Delilah was probably dealt three of a kind and a high card, Rian thought to herself. *Probably an ace or a king. She took one card, hoping for a full house or four of a kind. I don't think she got it.*

Rian pushed everything she had won since London into the middle of the table. "Let's see what you've got."

The table erupted when Delilah fanned out four sevens. Just like that, Rian was cleaned out of her first fortune.

* * * * *

Rian stood at the bow of the *Great Western*, stinging from the loss. The headwind had a good bite, but Rian leaned into it. The rush of the wind drowned out the rhythmic splashes from the two paddlewheels at midship and the faint thrum of the steam engines two decks below.

Delilah appeared beside her and rested her elbows on the railing. "You okay?"

"I'll live. Did you cheat?"

"Didn't need to."

"How did you know you had the better hand?"

"I didn't for sure. I knew you were sitting on something pretty strong because you went all stony. I've been working toward this evening since Helsinki. I know you watch the other players. There's a name for what they do. They're called *tells*. Players have no idea that their behavior changes depending upon how strong or weak their hand is. I set you up by signaling a false tell to you."

"How did you know that I look for tells?"

"I've known you were the best player at the table ever since we were on the *George IV.* I watched you watch the others. One of the advantages of playing with David at the table was that he was the one who attracted all the attention. It allowed me to sit in the bushes. Win some small pots. Make like I was lucky when I took a big pot. Sad part about David is that he drinks too much and loses toward the end of the evening."

"And cheats."

"Yes, he cheats when he's drunk. As you know, he's not very good at it."

"So you've been setting me up ever since Helsinki?"

"Take it as a compliment. Rian—you are a helluva player. Consider this an expensive lesson."

"What is it that I should be learning from this expensive lesson?"

"Take your pick. You might not be the smartest person in the room. Luck isn't always on your side. Never bet everything you own. I guess the most important thing is that you'll bounce back from this."

Rian turned and leaned into the railing, facing the door to below deck. "What are you going to do now?"

"Head back to New Orleans. That's where I learned to play poker."

"New Orleans? I thought you were from New York."

Delilah turned her back to the headwind, leaning her elbows on the ship's railing. "I'm not from New York. Nor is David. I assume you know we aren't married."

"Well, I know he's a portrait painter."

"Oh yes, and a very good one. But from the very beginning, all his painting ever did was give us access to people who had money. It didn't matter what the card game was as long as there was betting involved."

"And you two have split up for good?"

"Definitely. It's time for us to go our separate ways. But I've got some news for you. I think Lev is going to stick with me when we get off the ship tomorrow."

"Lev? Lev's going to Philadelphia with us. He'll work in my father's factory."

"You should ask him, but I imagine he thinks it would be more fun to be a Russian count on a Mississippi riverboat than a woodworker at Krieger Coach."

"Lev is a serf. He can't read or write. No one will ever believe he's a Russian count."

"For a while, maybe, but he's a fast learner. Look at me. I passed as a lady in the fanciest drawing rooms of St. Petersburg. When I was your age, I was a mill girl in Lowell, Massachusetts. To my credit, I dreamed of a different life. Fifteen years later, here I am."

Agitated, Rian walked to the foremast, spun around, and returned to Delilah. "No one will believe Lev is a Russian count."

"No one who's been to Russia maybe. Or speaks Russian like an aristocrat. But how many of those people are going to be on the Mississippi?"

"But it's a lie."

"Really? That's your problem? Because it's a lie? That surprises me coming from you."

Rian froze, but not from the biting headwind. "What do you mean?"

"I mean you are a girl pretending to be a boy."

"How do you know that?"

"Like I said, I study people when they think I'm not watching. Don't worry. I don't judge. And look at you. You have been more than holding your own at the poker table with a bunch of adults for five weeks. That's all Lev and I will be trying to do on the Mississippi—gain access to people who wouldn't give us the time of day if they knew our real backgrounds."

"Maybe that should be my real lesson. I can become anything I want to be."

"Having watched you since St. Petersburg, I couldn't agree more. Rian, you are going to go far in life."

* * * * *

· SEAMUS ·

Seamus found Delilah leaning against the foremast, facing into the wind, faintly illuminated by the lanterns at the bow.

"Rian told me you know she's a girl."

"Her secret's safe with me."

"And you've been gunning for her since Helsinki."

"I told her she should consider it a compliment."

"And you're taking Lev off to New Orleans, and he's going to pretend to be a Russian count."

"He still needs a bit of spiffing up, but there's a lot of men on the Mississippi who'll want to play poker with a Russian noble."

"So, does that mean you're going to be a countess?"

Delilah shook her head. "That's not really my style. I like to have the man be the peacock, attract all the attention."

"So David isn't your first partner?"

"Not at all, and I doubt Lev will be my last."

Seamus shook his head. *In admiration? Wonderment? Lust?* "Delilah, I've gotta ask. How come you didn't pick me?"

Delilah reached out and touched Seamus's cheek. "I considered it. It would have been fun. But I'm a gambler. That's how I make my living. I had to think about my future. Seamus, you are a fine man. But you're an Irishman. Irishmen are a dime a dozen. Your accent alone will prevent you from being admitted to some of the places where I intend to make a fortune."

MONDAY, APRIL 23

• RIAN •

True to Captain Hosken's prediction, the *Great Western* arrived at the mouth of New York Harbor on the morning of April 23, the Union Jack flying from the foremast, the Stars and Stripes flying aft from the jiggermast. The ship entered the harbor under steam, with all sails furled.

Six of the *Great Western*'s passengers had gone to their staterooms to change clothing from their shipboard garb to what would be more appropriate for land travel. Too disconsolate to go below, Rian stood at the bow and let the cold wind bite into her. The voyagers had traveled from St. Petersburg to New York City in thirty-four days. Despite many frustrating delays, they had lopped almost two weeks off their travel time, only to arrive in New York one day late. At five o'clock today, Lucretia Mott would follow instructions and deliver Catherine the Great's memoir to Harold Foote.

A crewmember joined Rian briefly at the railing near the bow of the ship. "It's 42 degrees out here, Master Krieger, much colder than yesterday. You might consider going below to get a coat."

Rian shook her head. As the *Great Western* passed through the narrows between Staten Island and Brooklyn, a cannon announced their arrival with a booming salute. Rian took in the first tentative greens of springtime that were barely evident on both shores. She gazed aloft, eyeing the furled sails.

Dewey Percell appeared at her side, stared momentarily at the Brooklyn hillside, then followed Rian's gaze up to the rigging. "Smart. Captain Hosken wants everyone in New York to know there's still plenty of coal left in the bunkers."

Rian didn't respond.

Shortly thereafter, the harbor pilot's boat, a graceful little schooner, approached the *Great Western* before a fine breeze. Captain Hosken ordered the steamship's paddlewheels halted. The schooner hauled to windward.

Rian and Percell leaned on the railing and watched the pilot's men row him to the *Great Western*. "The pilot boat got to us pretty quick," Rian noted.

Percell pointed to a tower on Staten Island, now behind and to port. "See that stone optical telegraph tower back there?"

Rian looked behind her. "That's a semaphore tower? I didn't know New York Harbor has them."

"Oh, yes, for quite some time now. We find that even a few hours advance notice of arrivals gives us a significant business advantage."

"Us?"

"I'm part of a business consortium that owns the towers. It's six miles from Staten Island to Manhattan Island. You can't see it from the water, but there's another semaphore station on the roof of the Merchants' Exchange Building on Wall Street."

Rian turned her attention to the north. Lower Manhattan Island was barely visible, more a collection of masts and spires than distinct buildings. A score of ships-of-sail and steamships filling the harbor provided a better indication of the activity that they were soon to encounter.

Dewey Percell continued. "I imagine everyone in New York already knows we have arrived. I expect there will be quite a crowd at the docks to greet us. And in fifteen minutes or so, my associates in Philadelphia will also know we've arrived."

"What do you mean?"

"My consortium owns more than the two stations in New York Harbor. We own a string of towers that allow us to communicate business news all the way to Philadelphia."

Rian's attention pivoted. "There's a station on top of the Philadelphia Merchants' Exchange on Dock Street in Philadelphia. You own that?"

"Well, myself and a few other businessmen. There's a movement afoot to install towers up and down your Atlantic Coast. All the way to New Orleans, actually. New Orleans money would like to know what our stock market is doing. We would benefit by knowing what the current cotton prices on the docks in New Orleans are. I'd like my consortium to be a part of it. That's one of the reasons I'm here. Amos Kendall, your Postmaster General, has already endorsed the project."

"What sort of information do you send to Philadelphia and back?"

"Stock market information, mostly. But any news that will affect stock or commodity prices."

"And news of the *Great Western*'s arrival will be one of today's messages?"

"To be sure. Today we have proved that steam travel across the Atlantic is viable. I suspect that within a matter of days, there will be numerous meetings as a result. Financiers will suddenly become interested in building steamships to compete with the *Great Western*."

"Could I send a message on this system?"

"I'm afraid not. Only members of the consortium can send messages. That's how we maintain our business advantage."

"But you can send a message?"

"Of course."

"And you owe me a favor."

Percell turned toward Rian as if she had his full attention for the first time. "I do."

"In that case. I'd like to cash in my favor."

"What do you have in mind, Master Rian?"

"I need to get a message to Lucretia Mott at 136 North Ninth Street in Philadelphia before five o'clock today. Can that happen?"

Percell smiled and consulted his pocket watch. "It is technically possible, although I cannot guarantee it. If you can compose a short message, I will try to get it into the queue as soon as I get to Wall Street."

* * * * *

The harbor pilot came with the news that the *Sirius* had arrived the day before, and the information spread quickly around the ship. With the harbor pilot now in control, the *Great Western*'s paddlewheels again propelled the ship forward. When they passed the *Sirius,* which was lying at anchor at the southern tip of Manhattan, her decks were lined with spectators, all cheering the *Great Western* as she steamed by.

"Seems the semaphores have conjured up a crowd for us, Master Rian," said Percell. "We're making history today."

* * * * *

The *Great Western* tied up at the dock at New York City before noon on Monday, April 23, less than a day behind the steamship *Sirius*. Her crossing had taken a mere fifteen days and five hours. Captain Hosken reported she still had two hundred tons of coal in her bunkers. Although the *Sirius* had crossed the Atlantic in the shortest time ever, her speed record stood for less than twenty hours. The arrival of both ships caused such local fanfare that crowds of well-wishers thronged the docks.

Rian came closest in their bet on how many revolutions the engines would make during the crossing, which clocked in at 287,324. She split the pot with two others who predicted the *Sirius* would arrive first. Those winnings plus what she had won between Helsinki and London soothed the pain of losing so much money the previous evening.

Rian, Seamus, and Kiserev chose not to spend much time basking in the accolades of the throng at the dock. As the *Great Western* held only seven passengers, they breezed through customs and bid adieu to Lev and Delilah.

"Thank you, Rian, for all you have done for me," said Lev. "I hope we meet each other again."

"It's not too late to change your mind. You can still come to Philadelphia with us."

Lev smiled and shook his head. "Ever since we board *George IV*, even though I was serf previous day, staff on ship served me dinner. Served me, Lev of Tsarskoye Selo. I never dreamed could ever happen. Now, here I am in America, a place I had never heard of until I meet you. Delilah say I can be anything I want in America. Can I make people think I'm count? Probably not. But, this trip is only dream anyway."

Delilah stepped forward and hooked her arm around Lev's elbow. "Maybe you should join us, Rian. There's more money on Mississippi riverboats than you can imagine. Everyone plays poker, but the three of us are better than ninety-five percent of the gamblers you'll ever meet. We can work our way up and down the river. They'll never know what hit 'em."

Rian smiled and shook Delilah's hand. "That's an exciting offer, but I think my future is tied to railroads. Who knows, maybe someday the railroads will get as far west as the Mississippi. Then I'll come find you."

"I'm telling you. We'd be unstoppable."

"I won't forget, but I'll also be planning to get some of my money back."

Delilah threw her head back and laughed. "I can't believe you're only fourteen. And I look forward to giving you that opportunity. So until then, we bid you adieu."

Rian caught sight of David Winter, who had found two laborers to lug his giant painting of the Winter Palace courtyard, now folded into a canvas sack, to a place unknown. She was about to catch him and apologize for exposing him as a cheater, but Dewey Percell grabbed her and shook her hand. "Fear not, Master Rian. It will be my highest priority to assure that your message gets to Mrs. Mott on time. I am happy to have my debt to you cleaned up so soon."

Rian hugged Percell a second time. Rian, Seamus, and Kiserev made their way to the ferry that would take them to Amboy, New Jersey, and on to Philadelphia via the *Camden & Amboy Railroad*.

* * * * *

· SEAMUS ·

The three travelers enjoyed having the passenger compartment to themselves as the locomotive *John Bull* chooshed rhythmically five cars ahead. Seamus and Rian faced forward, sitting opposite Kiserev. With Adrian's freedom virtually guaranteed, Seamus hoped that Rian's mood would lift a bit. Such was not the case.

"Why so glum, darlin'? We'll be home in a couple of hours. You've saved Uncle Adrian's skin. Kiserev's going to take the memoir back to Russia. What's got you worried now?"

"First of all, we don't know for sure that Mr. Percells's message got to Philadelphia. But there's one more thing that I haven't had room to worry about until now."

Poor kid. She's about to face her father. She's going to have to start wearing a dress again after seven months without ever having to think about it. "Don't worry about your da'. I'll be with you when you see him for the first time. I'll make sure he hears from me that you saved our lives."

Rian snorted and gazed out the window at the New Jersey countryside. "More like almost got Uncle Adrian killed. But that's not what I'm worrying about." She turned to Kiserev, whose English had become quite passable since they left St. Petersburg. "Are you planning to kill all of us once you reclaim Catherine's memoir?"

Seamus froze and eyed Kiserev. Kiserev stared at Rian without responding for so long that Seamus thought that he might not have understood her question.

Finally, Kiserev cracked the slightest of smiles. "You ask question—you already know answer."

Rian nodded. "The answer is no. Because you suspect I made a third copy to guarantee our continued safety."

Kiserev returned the nod. "General Benckendorff and I discussed cleaning up all loose ends: you two, Adrian, Count Sheremetev, Colonel Malkovich. We decide it not be wise."

"And why is that?"

"You thought scheme out so completely when you were living in stable, it would have been . . ."—Kiserev hesitated as he searched for the right word—". . . inconsistent for you not to have done this. Our assumption is second copy will also be returned to General Benckendorff after a while, once Tsar has normalized his situation back home and revelation can no longer destabilize empire."

Rian nodded. "Ten years."

Kiserev shifted in his seat but never took his eyes off Rian. "Ten years. That is very long time. We will all probably have died of natural causes before second copy returns to Russia."

Seamus, who had been merely a witness to the conversation to this point, stifled his shock that his cousin had been yet again one step ahead of him. "Oh, I think we've all got a lot more years than that. But only time will tell, Kiserev. Only time will tell. Meanwhile, switch places with me and enjoy our beautiful American countryside as it passes by."

* * * * *

LUCRETIA

Lucretia Mott put down her book and rose from the parlor chair as soon as she heard footsteps on her porch. She snatched up the whale oil lamp and opened the front door before the knock came.

Rian Krieger stood before her, buried in a navy blue military greatcoat whose previous owner had likely been a much larger man. The fourteen-year-old had grown some in eight months and now towered over her, and that perception was exaggerated by her coachman's top hat. Rian's cousin Seamus Gallagher stood behind her, and behind him stood an individual Lucretia didn't know.

Lucretia set the lamp on the porch table and pulled Rian into an embrace that knocked the top hat off her head. "Rian, dear, I didn't know if thee would arrive tonight or tomorrow morning. Hello, Seamus, welcome home." The third person—a man, she concluded—remained standing, barely visible in the faint island of light cast by the lamp.

Rian pulled away. "You got the message? You didn't send the manuscript to the newspaper?"

Lucretia eyed Rian without her hat. Her hair had darkened during the winter. It was cut short, like a boy's. "Rian, what happened to thy hair?"

"I cut it off on the way to Russia."

"Why would thee do such a thing?"

"So people would think I was a boy. The manuscript. Is it still here?"

"Yes, dear, I have thy package right here." Lucretia gave Rian another appraisal, then retreated into the parlor to retrieve the packet. "I was going to take it to the newspaper office this afternoon, but thy message headed me off. I daresay it was a novelty to receive an important communication from the Merchants' Exchange Building. Conor said it came all the way from New York City in a matter of minutes." She handed the package to Rian. "We do live in modern times, don't we?" she added, as if she were commenting about the weather.

"Conor delivered the message?"

"Yes, he is very excited to have his friend back."

Rian inspected the parcel, which was wrapped in brown paper and secured with twine. "Thank you for holding onto this. I guess now I have to go next door and face *Vater*. Does he know I'm home?"

"Yes, Conor and I ran to the factory to tell him. That was hours ago, of course."

"How is he?"

"I think thee should find that out for thyself, dear."

"Is he going to kill me?"

Lucretia smiled. "Probably not tonight."

Seamus picked up Rian's hat, then tugged at her sleeve. "The wagon driver's waiting . . ."

"Rian, is thee all right, dear?" asked Lucretia.

Rian held up the package. "Better now that I've got my hands on this, but it's been a long day." Rian started to descend from the porch, then stopped and turned back toward Lucretia. "There are more streetlamps than when we left."

"Yes, I imagine there are. The ditchdiggers quit when the ground froze, but they've been back at it for a few weeks now, and the pipefitters are right behind them. I think thee will find that other things have changed a bit in eight months."

"Good or bad?"

"A little bit of both. I'm glad thee is home, Rian. Good luck with thy father." Lucretia picked up the lamp and watched the trio walk toward the Krieger house next door. Before they all disappeared into the darkness, she saw Rian hand the package to the stranger.

* * * * *

· RIAN ·

Rian, Seamus, and Kiserev walked across the front lawn to Rian's house. Despite the greatcoat's warmth, Rian was shaking.

"Nervous?" asked Seamus.

"Even more scared than when Volkonsky said he was going to kill me." In the faint light of the crescent moon, Rian nodded to the wagon driver, who took that as a signal to start unloading Rian's baggage.

Seamus pointed to the items: four in all, including the portrait. "Do you want us to grab some of your stuff while we're heading in?"

"No, let the driver do it. I need you with me."

"Your da's not going to kill you, darlin'. He's going to be so relieved to see you he'll forget that he's angry. No matter what, I'll stay by your side until he's done storming."

"Good. After you leave, Kiserev will make sure he doesn't kill me."

Kiserev, now a step behind them, chuckled. "Only for tonight," he said in his heavily accented English. "I have manuscript now. Leave tomorrow. Go back to Russia. Suggest you make peace with father before that."

Rian climbed the five steps to her front porch. No lamp was visible within the house. *Maybe* Vater*'s gone to bed.* For days, she had been dreading the confrontation with her father when she arrived home. *Maybe there won't be a fight at all tonight.*

Rian opened the front door and entered the unlit parlor. Seamus followed, then Kiserev. No one spoke in the darkness. Rian was about to fumble her way to the mantel to find a candle when she heard the handle of the Franklin stove creak. An unseen hand opened the cast iron door. In the light of a recently tended fire, she saw a figure seated in a wingback chair next to the stove.

"*Vater?*" Rian ventured.

"*Ich habe mir Sorgen um Dich gemacht* [I worried about you]."

"*Vater, es tut mir leid* [Father, I am sorry]."

"*Ich glaube dir nicht* [I do not believe you]."

The silence stretched until it became excruciating. "*Vater,* I—"

"Good evening, Seamus. Will you be staying with us for the night?"

"No, Uncle Otto, I'll be heading to me mum's as soon as . . . as soon as we get Rian straightened away here."

"*Und wer ist das* [And who is this]?"

Rian turned. "This is Kiserev. I don't even know his first name. He works for General Alexander von Benckendorff, head of the Tsar's Secret Police."

"The Secret Police. Is he staying the night?"

"Yes."

"I am sure you are all weary from your travels. Have you eaten?"

"The schnitzel man was still on the path down from the train to the ferry. We cleaned him out."

"Then please take Mr. Kiserev to Conor's room. We will talk in the morning."

"Is Conor here?"

"He has been staying with me on and off since you left. I asked him to return to his brothers until you and I had a chance to talk."

"Can we talk after I show Kiserev to his room?"

"Tomorrow will do. It is late."

"But *Vater*—"

"I assure you, Rian, this will go better if we speak in the morning. Good evening, Seamus. Thank you for ensuring that Rian got home safely." With that, Otto Krieger rose from his chair, walked past his daughter, and strode toward the stairs. He took the first two steps and turned. "Your hat and coat make you look ridiculous."

TUESDAY, APRIL 24

· RIAN ·

Rian descended the kitchen stairs to the smell of cooking bacon. She was wearing an old set of shop clothes, although the pants were now a bit short. Her father stood at the stove, wearing an apron. He didn't turn around to greet her. *You knew this wasn't going to be easy.* She walked to the kitchen table and held onto the back of the chair for support. "You haven't left for work yet."

"I told you we would have a talk in the morning."

"Where's Kiserev? The door to his room is open, and his bed is made."

"In the privy. He said he was going to go for a walk after. He wants to explore the city before he leaves. We did talk a bit. He confirmed my suspicions about his boss. General Benckendorff fought against my father in the Battle of Leipzig. My father described him as a vicious foe. Is this who you choose to ally yourself with?"

Well, he came out swinging, just as I feared. "I am not friends with General Benckendorff, but our needs temporarily aligned. *Amicus meus, inimicus inimici mei* [My friend, the enemy of my enemy]."

Otto cracked four eggs into the cast-iron frying pan. "I assume you haven't lost your taste for fried eggs since you have been gone. Kiserev wouldn't tell me what he is doing here."

"He is taking a package back to the Tsar. We picked it up at Lucretia's last night."

"How did this package find its way to Lucretia's house?"

"I sent it to her from Russia." *He hasn't turned around yet to look me in the eye.*

Otto pulled two plates from the cupboard and placed them next to the stove. "And what is it?"

"I'm not allowed to say. It's information that Tsar Nicholas didn't want to have made public. *Vater, turn around and look at me!*

Otto forked bacon onto the plates and continued to poke at the edges of the eggs with a spatula. "General Benckendorff blackmailed the Tsar of Russia?"

"No, I did. A man named Volkonsky, the Tsar's Minister of the Imperial Court, threw Uncle Adrian and Seamus and Sheremetev and Malkovich into prison. I used the information in the package to get them out."

"Why were they thrown into prison?"

"Volkonsky accused them of bribing an official, but it wasn't true."

Her father dished the eggs onto the plates and turned toward Rian for the first time but still didn't look at her. "Who took care of you when they were all in prison? Sit."

Rian sat opposite her father at the kitchen table. "I took care of myself. I lived in the Manege, a stable of the Tsar's Imperial Horse Guards. I had been friends with one of them, but then he died. He was killed by Prince Volkonsky. I slept in the landau that we brought with us. I was safe there." *Well, somewhat safe.*

"And who told you this information that the Tsar did not want to be made public?"

"It came to me from a member of the Tsar's family. This person didn't know how important it was until a little later."

Otto took a bite of egg. "And all that time, the Tsar and his family never suspected you are a girl?"

"Grand Duchess Olga Nikolaevna figured it out. Then she told Grand Duke Konstantin. They never told anyone."

Otto sat back in his chair. He looked at Rian for the first time. "Adrian went straight home to Mila and Jabez last night?"

"No, he's still in prison in St. Petersburg. When Kiserev gets home with the package, he'll be let out."

Her father's fork clattered on his plate. "How do you know that this Volkonsky won't just leave him in prison?"

"Because I made another copy of what's in the package."

"And where is that?"

"I sent it to someone else. A person in Massachusetts."

"Who?"

"I would prefer not to tell. I don't know him very well."

"So nothing has changed. You had secrets before you left. You still have secrets. You defied me. You ran halfway around the world for reasons I cannot understand. You have cut your hair. You come home looking like a court fool in a top hat and a winter coat that is far too big for you. You continue to defy me by wearing boys' clothing on the first morning of your return. Why did you even bother to come home? You seem to have been doing quite well."

Rian momentarily considered grabbing her coat and fleeing to . . . someplace, any place. "There was a part of me that didn't want to come home, although we wouldn't have been welcome in Russia anymore. I liked it when people thought I was a boy. I could do things that girls couldn't."

"Why did you run away from me?"

"I didn't want to go to that school in Switzerland. I would have had to wear dresses all the time."

"Dresses? That's what this is about? Dresses? You ran halfway around the world in order to avoid wearing dresses?"

"Well, I thought Adrian and Seamus were going to be setting up a locomotive factory in St. Petersburg, and I would be able to help them the way I helped when you opened the new factories here. They never got that far because of Volkonsky. Then the fire happened. Then I became Grand Duke Konstantin's companion. Then they all got thrown into prison. We had to come home."

"I recommend that you not get too settled in. I intend to send you to that finishing school in Switzerland. Part of a school year will be better than none."

Rian tried to take a first bite of egg but, with no appetite, put her fork down. "*Vater*, I want to live here with you and work in the factories, but if you make me go to that school, I'll run away again."

"And they will catch you and bring you back. You will have no friends or family to help you this time, no money to pay for food or transport or lodging."

Rian rose from the table. "I need to show you something." She ran into the parlor and up the stairs. Moments later she returned to the kitchen and threw a cigar box on the table.

"*Was ist das* [What is this]?"

"That is money that I made in twelve days aboard a ship between St. Petersburg and London. There are bills and coins from five different countries there, but I figure it's all worth about a thousand dollars."

Otto lifted the lid of the cigar box, briefly peered inside, and let the lid drop. "How did you make this money?"

"I played a card game called poker, but it wouldn't have mattered if it had been whist or vingt-et-un or faro or betting on which waiter came out of the galley next. I would have won. I lost more than five times this much on our last night before the *Great Western* arrived in New York. That will never happen to me again."

"I doubt that school girls in Switzerland gamble. You would never have the opportunity to amass the kind of money that you would need to survive all alone in Europe."

"In St. Petersburg, I made money loaning installments of *The Pickwick Papers* and *Oliver Twist* to people in the Anichkov Palace. When I was living on my own in the Manege, I made money exercising the horses for the Tsar's Imperial Guardsmen. Then I froze my rear end off, launching sleds off an ice mountain during a winter fair. I did what I had to. No one knew I was a girl. I could do that sort of thing all over again if I needed to. I just don't want to. *Vater*, please don't make me do this. I want to work in the factories. I want to go back to keeping the books."

Otto pushed his plate toward the middle of the table. "If I allowed you to return, it would be just to keep the books. There will be no need for you to wear shop clothes because you will never labor in the factories."

"But people treat me differently when I'm wearing a dress. Even when they know I'm a girl, if I'm wearing boys' clothes, there's something different about how they talk to me, look at me. I love the bookkeeping, but that is only half of what I love. I want to be out in the shop."

"We don't have enough work for you to be out in the shop. I can't afford to pay you."

"Pay me for the bookkeeping. I'll work in the shop for free."

"Dresses. The misery I have felt for the past eight months has been over dresses?"

"Yes."

"If I relent on this, will you promise not to run away again?"

"Yes."

"When we get home at the end of the workday, you will change into a dress for dinner."

"Why?"

"Because if you do not spend some significant amount of time acting like a girl, you will never learn to become a young woman. You will never attract a suitable man. Rian, you have incredible intellect. Krieger Coach is leading Philadelphia out of this depression. In a few years we will have the social standing for you to marry a man of substance. You will be his helpmate. A very capable helpmate. The two of you will rule Philadelphia society. You will travel the world."

Even though her father had already made significant concessions, Rian again fought off the urge to flee. She took a deep breath. "*Vater*, perhaps we can strike a compromise. I don't want to wear dresses because people treat me differently. You want me to wear dresses so that I can someday marry someone important."

"And what is the compromise?"

"I wear shop clothes to work and at home. For special occasions, I'll wear a dress."

"Special occasions. When we travel. When we go to Lucretia's house for dinner. When we go to mass."

"We never go to mass."

"Maybe we will start going."

"I won't wear a dress when I'm with my friends."

Her father stared at her for what seemed an eternity. "This isn't an open-ended agreement. We will have this same discussion in the fall. I still reserve the right to send you to that school."

"Then you are on notice. If you do that, I will run away again."

Otto leaned forward and again opened the lid of the cigar box. "What I should do is confiscate this money."

"If you do, I will find a way to make more."

"You think making money is that easy?"

"It's not easy, but I'm fourteen years old, and I've been able to do it so far. I think like a businessman. I learned that from you."

Her father smiled for the first time. "I think the proper term in your case would be businesswoman." He poked at the mound of bills and coins in Rian's cigar box. "What do you intend to do with this . . . this collection of rubles and riksdalers and pounds?"

"I guess I should invest it. Do you need it?"

"Not right now. Maybe when we choose to expand when the depression ends. A lot of my money is invested in railroad stock. I would not recommend following my example at the moment."

"Then I shall find some other promising business."

"Good. You do that. Make it something that you can't pull out of at the drop of a hat. It will make it more difficult for you to run away again."

It took Rian a few moments to realize her father was making a joke.

* * * * *

· JULES ·

Spring had finally arrived in Philadelphia. Puffy white clouds drifted lazily toward the Delaware. Blue wild indigo, cranesbill, tulips, and daffodils competed with one another to see which could bring the most color to streetside gardens. Zinnias seemingly appeared overnight and dominated window boxes.

Jules held the front door of Pennsylvania Hall open for four men who were carrying the first of three hundred pews into the building. At this rate, the deliveries alone would take the rest of the week.

"If you're holding doors for deliveries, I guess you're not feeling the pressure anymore," came a voice from the sidewalk. Jules turned. It was Fred Hinton, the barber who chaired the Pennsylvania Hall Association's Construction Committee. He held a weighty, flat object that was wrapped in brown paper.

Jules smiled. "I believe you are correct. The carpenters finished yesterday. The pipefitters are inside installing gas fixtures. Don't touch anything that is light gray because it hasn't dried yet and still needs another coat. As you can see, furniture has started to arrive, but it'll take all week to get it installed. But Fred, I believe by May 1 this building will be ready to host a convention, two weeks ahead of schedule."

Hinton unwrapped his package to reveal a brass plaque. "In that spirit, I thought you should be among the first to see this."

Pennsylvania Hall
The Pennsylvania Hall Association's
Temple of Freedom
Dedicated May 14, 1838

Board of Managers
Daniel Neall - President
Samuel Webb - Treasurer
William Dorsey - Secretary

Construction Committee
Frederick A. Hinton - Chairman

Architect
Thomas Stewart

General Contractors
Mason Edes (dec'd.)
Jules Freeman

Jules scanned the plaque and noted both Hinton's name and his own. "Well, this is gratifying. Two Black men immortalized in brass. Did you know about this?"

"It was the board's decision. Jules, your stock could not be higher right now. When we made the decision to ask you to replace Edes, half the men on the committee thought you would fail because we had lost so much time. Despite their desire to see an end of slavery, many of the whites thought you would fail because you are Black. And now, here we are, two weeks ahead of schedule. Clearly, you were the right man for the job."

* * * * *

Jules and Maddie Freeman and James and Lucretia Mott sat in a walnut and cherry pew that had been delivered by a crew of men two hours ago. The workers had hauled it up to the Gallery and placed it opposite the stage. The long light of the setting sun streamed through the windows to their left, and they had a commanding view of the Grand Saloon below. The huge scaffold was long gone. The golden sunflower in the middle of the ceiling somehow managed to pick up reflected rays and did indeed sparkle. The recently laid and oiled oak flooring, soon to be filled with pews like the one they sat in, was currently an unbroken expanse. Homer and Emil's beautifully simple Doric columns supported the Gallery, their alignment perfect to the eye. The stage—also finished—was flanked by two Ionic columns that supported an arch. Homer had engraved the words VIRTUE, LIBERTY, and INDEPENDENCE into a walnut board that was easily two feet wide and eight feet long. His lettering had been gold-leafed by the gilder Peter Jeffries.

The Freemans and Motts had relished the moment, each voicing his or her own sense of pride, optimism, and, yes, even victory.

After a protracted, comfortable silence, Jules said, "Have you seen her?"

Lucretia stirred slightly. "Rian? Yes, she arrived at my house late last night. She was with Seamus Gallagher and someone I didn't know. I gave them the package that Rian seemed to be so concerned about."

"How did she seem to you?"

"Tired. Focused. Her hair is cut short. Different. Certainly not the twinkly elf who left here eight months ago. She was wearing a coat that was too big for her."

"I'm not sure she was ever a twinkly elf," Jules responded. After another silence, he added, "Well, things are different here, too. Eight months seems like forever. I'm back to my old schedule now, dividing my time between Freeman Hydraulics and Krieger Coach. Hopefully I can check in with her in the next couple of days."

Maddie stirred in her seat. "Back up a bit, Husband. That is not what we discussed. You aren't going back to your old schedule. You admitted that I did a fine job running Freeman Hydraulics while you were so busy. Your new schedule is going to be one-quarter Freeman Hydraulics and three-quarters Krieger Coach."

Jules chuckled. "My apologies, my dear. James and Lucretia, please shake hands with the newly appointed co-president of Freeman Hydraulics: the lovely, capable, talented Madeline Freeman."

FRIDAY, APRIL 27

· RIAN ·

It had been three days since Rian and Seamus had returned to Philadelphia. Rian closed her ledger and rose from her desk. Her father looked up from the morning mail but didn't say anything. Rian could tell he wasn't yet used to having her back in the office. *Easy, Eena,* Rian said to herself. *He's probably fretting that you're going to run away again.*

"I'm going to find Jules and see what he wants me to do for the afternoon." She walked out into the din of the factory in time to see the new guy, whose name she hadn't even learned yet, throw a punch at Jules.

Jules adeptly dodged the man's fist, swung him around, pushed him into a wall, twisted his arm high behind his back, and said, "One last time, Ethan. Help out in the steam room or you're fired."

A knot of workers watched the altercation.

"Fook you," muttered Ethan.

Jules twisted Ethan's arm a little higher to set him on his way. "Okay, that's the answer I was hoping for." Rian followed as Jules hustled Ethan the length of the factory, past workers at their machines, some so absorbed in their work they didn't notice the brouhaha.

"Someone open the door!" Jules yelled above the factory din. Rian scooted ahead and slid the big slider open enough to allow Jules to propel Ethan into the street, where he collapsed in a heap. Rian slid the door back after Jules reentered.

"Thank you, Rian . . . Show's over, gentlemen!" yelled Jules to those men who had taken an interest. "Get back to work." Rian had a hard time gauging if folks had sided with Jules or with Ethan.

* * * * *

Half an hour later, hot condensed steam trickled out of the drain hole of the wooden steam box that was more than twelve feet long and a foot square. Rian, wearing a leather mitt, unlatched the door at the end of the box. Jules handed her six oaken slats that she inserted into the steam box, making sure they rested on a series of dowels two inches above the bottom of the box. She jockeyed the slats around so that there was plenty of space for the steam to get to each of them. Jules handed her another six slats that she inserted into the "upper level"—another set of dowels above the first.

All of this was accomplished without a word between the two. Rian closed and latched the steam chamber's door.

Once the slats had properly steamed, they would be pliable for a short period—five minutes tops—before they returned to their natural rigidity. Rian would bend each slat around its own jig, a form that was specially made to the dimensions of a hoopstick, a bent wooden strip that supported the soft collapsible top of a landau.

"How long do you want me to steam them?" Rian knew the answer to the question, but she wanted to get Jules talking. She could tell that he was still agitated by his altercation with Ethan.

"One hour ought to do it. I should go check on the men."

"What was the big deal with that guy? It's fun to steam wood."

"He claimed it was too hot to work in the steam room, but his real problem was taking orders from a Black man."

"When's the last time you had to solve a problem that way?"

"Years. But it's getting worse. The depression hasn't helped. And then there's the new Pennsylvania Constitution."

"Before I ran away, you were confident that the 'white-only' amendment wouldn't have enough votes. The delegates wouldn't pass it."

"Well, that changed. The last week in December, a judge in Bucks County handed down a decision that really set us back. He cited documents as far back as William Penn's charter. Since Blacks were never mentioned as having the right to vote, that meant that we didn't have that right. So just like that, as far as he was concerned, we were disfranchised, and the election in Bucks County that was so close was overturned."

"In other words, the judge doesn't like Negroes."

"That's how I see it. So then in January the Pennsylvania Constitutional Convention voted in the 'white-only' clause. That's when Robert Purvis wrote the *Appeal of Forty Thousand Citizens*."

"What's that?"

Jules reached into his back pocket, pulled out a pamphlet, and handed it to Rian. "Here, read it when you get a chance. It's a beautiful piece of work. It also kicked up a ruckus."

Rian fanned her way through the pamphlet. "So the new proposed constitution takes away your right to vote, Robert writes a sixteen-page protest, and white people are angry about the protest?"

"That about sums it up. Well, that and Pennsylvania Hall."

"I hear it's all finished. Lucretia said it wouldn't have been finished if it weren't for you."

"My name's on the plaque. The Philadelphia Female Anti-Slavery Society is going to be the first group to hold a convention in it in a couple of weeks."

"So white people are also angry that there's a building in town that's dedicated to the abolition of slavery."

"Well, technically, it's dedicated to the discussion of all sorts of issues—temperance, Indian removal, prison reform, support for the poor. But that's just window dressing. Its real mission is bringing an end to slavery. Anti-Negro sentiment has always been ugly in this town, but lately it's been more out in the open."

"How are you doing?"

"Oh, I'm fighting. Fighting with my wife because she's assuming more responsibility at work, and I'm not used to it yet. I'm fighting with Robert Purvis because he's fighting so hard. Rian, I'm even fighting with myself—my old self—because that man used to think that if the Black man got too far ahead—got too big for his britches—he would be sure to get smacked down. And here I am, the man who pulled a rabbit out of his hat and got Pennsylvania Hall built on time. My old self thinks that shit's going to soon rain down on our heads, and my new self isn't sure he's wrong."

"Jaysus, Jules, this sounds really bad."

"There's a new word that's being thrown in the papers a lot: *mobocracy*."

"Rule by the mob?"

Jules nodded. "The pro-slavery press says that a threat to slavery is a threat to the U.S. Constitution. They're making up stuff like the anti-slavery folks are British agents paid to stir up trouble. They say that if the Black man has the right to vote, it will lead to amalgamation."

"What's amalgamation?"

"Uh, that's a bit of a moving target. Some people think things as innocent as white people fraternizing with Black people."

"So the Kriegers are amalgamators because we've had you and Maddie over for dinner?"

"Absolutely, and that offends a lot of people. So does Maddie and Lucretia Mott working together on a committee or walking down the street together.

But, what really gets the crowd riled up is that all this leads to a Black person having sex with a white person."

"And that's a bad thing?"

"I don't think our two races should be mixing in that way, but what those people are really saying is that Black men will start violating white women."

"So where does mobocracy come into this?"

"The press says that when things get too far out of kilter, then the people should resort to direct action and set things straight. They think Negroes already are getting too big a piece of the pie. They're whipping up hatred and encouraging exactly the kind of thing that you just saw."

"What are you going to do?"

"My old self wants to keep his head down. My current self is determined to forge ahead. But I'm scared, Rian. Scared for me, for Maddie, and for the kids."

* * * * *

Rian and Jules had finished bending the last of the oaken slats into the shape of a hoopstick. They carried the hoopstick, still constrained in its jig, and leaned it up against its mates along the wall.

Jules returned to the long steam chamber and unscrewed the drain cock so that it was wide open. The trickle of hot water became more of a stream that emptied onto the floor. "Are you okay to take the hoops out of the jigs tomorrow?"

"Yeah, I'll do it after I finish catching up on the books. I'll hang them next to the Finish Room."

Jules bent and turned off the gas to the steam generator. "It's good to have you back, Rian."

"It's good to be back, mostly."

"Now that I've fired that guy, Krieger Coach has to hire someone. Do you think Conor would be interested in coming back?"

"Maybe for the mornings. He's making pretty good money delivering messages from the telegraph towers in the afternoon. I'll ask him tonight. He's moved back in with *Vater* and me."

* * * * *

· OTTO ·

Otto was working at his desk when Seamus Gallagher entered after a polite knock. He put down his quill and rose to greet his nephew. "Seamus, come in. How are you settling back into Philadelphia life?"

"Oh, you know, Uncle, still navigating me way a bit. I'm here to check in on Rian; see how she's doing."

"She's in the steam room with Jules. He fired one of the men and he's a bit shorthanded. You wouldn't be interested in coming back to work for us, would you?"

"Afraid not, Otto, but thanks. How's she doing?"

"Well, I guess we are still navigating our way, as you would say. We talked the morning after you all arrived. It seems the sole reason for her running off to Russia was that she did not want to wear dresses, which would have been mandatory at the finishing school in Switzerland. I gave in to her wearing shop clothes, for the most part, figuring that sooner or later she will grow out of this stage."

Seamus shrugged. "Suppose so. She did a crackerjack job of letting people think she was a boy in Russia. I recommend you choose your battles with this one. I found she was usually about three steps ahead of me anyway."

"Seamus, I'm afraid I've lost what little control I had over her. Or thought I had. Apparently, she acquitted herself quite well when she was in Russia. If I try putting the screws to her, she will run away again, except she would not have you and Adrian watching out for her."

"More like she was watching out for us. But I don't think she's going to run away any time soon. She's pretty committed to someday running Krieger Locomotive. She wants to learn everything she can about the business. In the office and on the factory floor."

"Rian is a young woman, not a businessman. She will marry a suitable man and be a helpmate to his career. Nothing more."

"That's one of the battles you should think long and hard about, Uncle Otto."

"Thankfully, we are years away from that battle."

"Uncle, did Rian tell you about the fire at the Tsar's palace?"

"She said that you and Adrian and she helped to fight the fire for well over a day, and that Jules's fire pump performed admirably."

"Did she tell you she saw men die that night, including a man she had become close to?"

"No."

"Captain Stepanov, head of the Imperial Horse Guards. That was his coat that you told her is so ridiculous, by the way. The Horse Guards gave it to her in honor of her friendship with their fallen leader."

Otto sat heavily in his chair. "Oh, no. I had no idea."

"That coat means more to her than you could possibly imagine. Did she tell you that after Adrian and I were arrested, she lived on her own for sixteen days, abandoned, sleeping in a carriage, all the time plotting how she was going to spring us?"

"Well, yes, but she described it as if it were an adventure."

"Uncle, Rian lived on her own, not knowing a soul, for all that time. She rejected the support of Ambassador Dallas because he couldn't help us fast enough. She blackmailed the Tsar of Russia. Went toe-to-toe with his most powerful ministers. Set the two of them against each other. One tried to have her killed."

Otto leaned back in his chair and crossed his arms. "She never described it like that."

"Otto, I'm telling you all this to let you know that your daughter isn't the same little girl who left Philadelphia last September. She is like those bulldogs that I saw in England. She goes after something like it is a bone, and she doesn't quit—doesn't let up until the bone splinters."

"Her time alone—in the stable. Was she harmed?"

"Naw, nothing like that. But I think it knocked some of the childhood out of her. She always used to have a bit of a twinkle in her eye. She got around you or me or Jules by being so goddamn charming. I think she's lost the twinkle."

"Now that I think about it, that's something that has been absent. I knew something was amiss, but I assumed it was that she had not settled in yet."

"Rian is not going to be content to be some slick's helpmate. She is a force of nature. If she took on the Tsar of Russia and came out on top, I'm afraid you don't have a chance."

"Then what am I to do?"

"Don't be too sure about the path that you have laid out for her. Think creatively. Don't box her in. Listen to her."

"That's a tall order, Seamus. I'm afraid I will need help."

* * * * *

· OTTO ·

The afternoon mail included a letter from Otto's half-sister Hilda. He had seen Hilda and Maria only once since he and his brothers and sister emigrated to America in 1820. Four years ago, he had returned to Stuttgart after his stepmother died. Otto barely recognized much of the city. New palaces and a new university had disrupted much of his old neighborhood. The streets were still little more than what Philadelphians would call alleys, and they twisted and turned, reflecting their medieval origins. *Hmm, Hilda is twenty-one, Maria nineteen. They will soon be spinsters.*

The letter was written in German.

19 March 1838

Dear Brother Otto,

I hope all is well with you. I have heard nothing from Rian in St. Petersburg, not that I would expect my niece to write to me. It is hard to believe that she is closer to me here in Wurttemberg than she is to you. In any case, I am sure she is safe. I heard that the Tsar's gigantic palace in St. Petersburg burned to the ground. I wonder if she was affected by the conflagration.

I have big news. Both Maria and I are getting married . . . in America! The two of us have been corresponding with reputable young men from our village whom you probably don't remember. My Oskar—his uncle is Rudolf Becker—left for America ten years ago, and we have been writing ever since. I haven't seen him since he was fourteen. He lives in a village in your Pennsylvania called Newport. Oskar tells me it is a day's travel from Newport to Philadelphia.

Maria's Klaus Ritner—a cordwainer like his father—also lives in Pennsylvania, in the village of Chambersburg.

Maria and I are desperately in love with our two men despite the impediments of time and distance. We want to marry as soon as we arrive in America, then travel with our new husbands to their homes. As you are the eldest Krieger male and nominal head of our family, I would very much like to have your blessing, but please know that I will marry him if that is not forthcoming. We are intent on this plan no matter what.

If we have your blessing, we would like to be married in Philadelphia as soon as we arrive. We have booked passage aboard the *King of Hanover* from Hamburg to New York. Oskar and Klaus will meet us and we will all come to Philadelphia by train to be married. I am so excited. I will set my feet in America, hug my future husband for the first time in ten years, ride a train, and see you all in one day. If all goes well, we should arrive in Philadelphia by May 21, so we could be married on Wednesday, May 23.

By the time you get this letter, we should already be on the high seas. I am sorry that both Rian and our brother Adrian will not be able to attend the wedding, but I hope that brother Kurt will be there. Please gather others of your friends and relations to celebrate our joy with us.

Your sister,

Hilda

Otto had encouraged his two half-sisters to come to America during his visit four years ago, but this letter brought complications. *I'm just getting used to having Rian back in the house.* He perused his wall calendar. *I told Lucretia I would put up one or two women from out of town who are attending the anti-slavery convention. Hopefully, they'll be gone by that time.*

He was pleased for his sisters. *Not everyone marries for love, even a love that bloomed "over time and distance."* But something about Hilda's letter struck him as odd. Why was she fearful that he wouldn't give the marriages his blessing?

He remembered a bakery owned by a man named Becker, and a shoemaker named Ritner, but they both lived in a Protestant neighborhood not far from his stepmother's inn.

My God, my Catholic sisters are planning to marry Protestants.

* * * * *

· RIAN ·

Rian climbed through the hatch in the roof of Sparks Shot Tower,[11] eager to once again see the city from this great height. She stood and waited for Conor McGuire and her cousin Jabez Howes to join her.

The city of Philadelphia spread out below them. Directly north lay miles of wharves along the Delaware, many occupied by ships with sails furled. Most of the waterfront's work was done for the day. Rian could see the length of Front Street all the way to Northern Liberties, where the Delaware bent to the right. Given the hour, wagon traffic was light, though sailors and stevedores hunting diversions now filled the street and sidewalks. They flowed around the few remaining delivery carts like a slow stream around rocks.

To the northwest, the city had settled down for the night. The sun, now approaching the horizon, turned the tentative greens of early spring to gold. Church spires and factory smokestacks cast long shadows across shorter dwellings and places of business. Rian further oriented herself by finding the open spaces of Washington and Franklin Squares. To the west ran the lazy Schuylkill River with its coal wharves. To the south, South Philadelphia transitioned to countryside.

As Rian completed her circumnavigation of the tower, directly to the east flowed the wide Delaware River and beyond that Camden, New Jersey. Steam ferries squeezed in one last trip before sunset. Fishermen and farmers sailed

---

11. The 142-foot-tall Sparks Shot Tower was built in 1808 to manufacture spherical bullets by dropping molten lead from a great height. In 1838 it was the tallest structure in Philadelphia.

back to New Jersey after a day of hawking their goods on Market Street. A tugboat with ten oarsmen pushed a large ship-of-sail to its berth somewhere up near Chestnut Street.

Rian's attention was drawn to activity half a mile upriver. "Conor, what's going on over at Windmill Island? There are still men working there."

"Day workers. They're digging a channel right through the island—130 feet wide. One crew digs from the east, another from the west. Every day but Sunday. I suspect two of me brothers are out there; that is if they got picked for the day. They won't knock off until candlelight."

"What's the channel for?"

"The ferrymen are tired of having to steam around the island to get to Camden. They figure it'll be easier to go straight through it. Should be done by the end of the summer."

"Welcome back to America," Rian said wryly. "I go away for seven months, and stuff changes. It seems busier than when I left. Is the Panic over?"

"It's better," said Conor, "but still not good. Your father told me he hired a new guy last week. I'm not sure he's going to work out, but he needed somebody because a couple of guys quit."

"That guy's already gone. Jules fired him this afternoon." Rian shifted her attention to her cousin. Jabez was two weeks older than Rian and the resemblance between the two was remarkable, right down to the wide gap between their two front teeth. "Did you get in trouble for ducking out on the trip to Russia?"

"Yeah, but it was no big deal. I'm always in trouble."

"I hear you've been skipping school."

Jabez sat down at the railing, faced toward the west, and took out a whiskey flask. He dangled his legs over the edge of the platform and took a sip from his flask. "School's not for me."

Jabez offered the flask to both Rian and Conor. They both declined the whiskey.

* * * * *

An hour later, Rian had told the story of her Russian adventure to Conor and Jabez. The sun had long since set. They leaned into the crossbar that would have been at knee height had they been standing.

"I don't get it," said Conor, who was only interested in the soothsayer predictions. "Are you going to run Krieger Locomotive, or not?"

"Well, I admit that part's a bit confusing. First I'm not going to take it over, then I am."

"Sounds like a pretty stupid prediction to me."

"Well, I figure I'm going to have to wait. Maybe until I'm twenty-one or something. But until that time I intend to learn as much about the business as I can."

"How are you gonna do that? Harry's the foreman at Krieger Locomotive. He hated having you in the shop before you ran away, but back then your Uncle Adrian thought it was funny when the men let you help them. Now he's not going to be around to protect you from Harry."

"I don't know. I'll figure something out." The conversation paused as the trio watched the sun slip beneath the horizon. "Yana said I am filled with fire. That fire's going to be a part of my life forever. Some fire will be like the Winter Palace fire. But there's some other kind of fire: fire I think I am in control of, but I'm really not."

Conor snorted. "What the heck is that supposed to mean?"

Jabez took another slug of whiskey from his flask. "I don't think it's fair that Uncle Otto doesn't pay you when you work in the shop in the afternoons."

"Oh, I don't know," responded Rian. "What do I need the money for? I lost more than I would make in three years at the poker table the night before we got to New York."

"You're that good a poker player?" asked Conor.

"Apparently not good enough."

"Well, it sounds to me like your trip to Russia was a success," said Conor. "You won. Your da's not planning to send you off to Switzerland, at least for a while."

"Doesn't sound like a win to me," commented Jabez. "Bookkeeping? Working in the shop for no pay? Those are jobs your father tried to train me to do. I hated them. He and Aunt Mila gave up and enrolled me in school."

"Which you hate and don't go to."

"Hate less than working."

* * * * *

Rian, Conor, and Jabez descended the steps of Sparks Tower to walk home. Front Street's evening persona was now in full force. Sailors, released from their ship duties, idled with ladies of the evening. Taverns rollicked with the sounds of laughter, sea shanties, and occasionally a squeezebox. The aromas of unfamiliar spices and men freshly washed—or at least perfumed—in anticipation of the pleasures of shore leave, mingled with the pungent smells of the wharves.

Jabez parted from Rian and Conor at Walnut Street to return to his Aunt Mila's house. When Rian and Conor crossed Chestnut, the arrhythmic sound of metal striking metal emanated from the steamboat landing and caught her attention.

Rian checked her pocket watch. "It's 7:30. Most work at the docks should have wound down by now. Let's go see what all that noise is about." She and Conor changed course and walked toward the racket. The midship of the steam ferry *Falcon* was dimly lit by a whale oil lantern. Rian stepped aboard and walked toward the light. Captain Ames, who had ferried Krieger coaches to the *Camden & Amboy Railroad* for years, straddled a bar lying on the ferry deck and was whaling the tar out of it.

"Hi, Captain Ames. What happened here?"

Ames looked up from his task. "Rian, Conor. Hello. The water was a bit rough in the middle of the river this morning. Some arsehole didn't keep control of his horses. The horses spooked when the *Falcon* listed a bit more than they were comfortable with, and the cargo in his wagon shifted and fell into this support rod. Bent it all to thunder. Threw the reach rod out of line. Slowed me down a bit for the rest of the day."

"Need any help?"

"Well, yeah, I could use a couple extra hands. I think I've got this back into shape. Time to bolt it back in place. I'm a little bushed. Rian, you feel like climbing the ladder?"

Rian accepted two nuts and bolts and climbed a wooden ladder that leaned precariously against a vertical steel beam. Conor held the support rod toward her. She inserted the bolts through the rod and into a flange connected to the vertical beam. "Do you do all your own repair work on the boat?"

"Gotta. Can't afford to pay someone to do it for me. Can't afford to stay docked up while I wait for them to show up. Problem is, Old Bessie is getting kind of old."

Rian quickly assessed Old Bessie, the *Falcon*'s steam engine. "I believe it. This is a Cornish boiler system. No one's made them for years."

"My daddy had it built for the first *Falcon* in 1816. I bet I've replaced every part on this engine since then."

"The Lancashire systems that we're manufacturing at Krieger Locomotive are a lot more efficient."

"Two problems with that. Number 1, I can't afford a new engine. Second, a Lancashire system would be too big for this boat."

"Oh, I don't know. We're making a locomotive for a sugar plantation in Cuba right now. It's not very big. The engine's done already and would fit in here easy."

"I'll tell you one person who would be thankful if I had a new engine. My wife. She thinks Old Bessie here is on borrowed time. Sooner or later she's going to blow up on me."

"Well, we can't have that."

TUESDAY, MAY 1

· SEAMUS ·

It was 2:00 in the afternoon. Seamus, Braden McSweeney's only customer, sat at the bar of McSweeney's Saloon. Seamus's hands were wrapped around an almost empty glass, his elbows on the bar.

"What'd you expect, Seamus? That Dylan would just roll over? Welcome you back with open arms? I'll tell you, Boyo, he likes being the fire brigade's president. It makes him somebody."

"But I started the No Name. That should count for something."

"You abandoned them. You went gallivanting off to Russia to seek your fortune. Your boys didn't know if you were ever coming back. They moved on without you, and they're doing pretty well, by the way."

Seamus looked up from his drink. "Fighting fires?"

"Well, sure. Even in Black houses, just like you planned when you started No Name. But they've also kept the truce with Hugh. Nobody's stealing each other's fire pumps. And now that trade is picking up a bit, they've been able to lift a good bit from the docks."

"I need to get back into all that. I missed it while I was gone."

Braden picked up a bar rag and wiped some rings that didn't need wiping. "You sure about that?"

"What do you mean?"

"Seamus, you came home with more money in your pocket than your boys'll ever make in a year. You tell stories about living in a palace. You discussed the differences between slavery and serfdom with the future Tsar of Russia. Are you going to be content swiping carpets off the docks for the rest of your life?"

"I'm good at it."

Braden took a sip of his drink, savored it, then . . . "You're good at a lot of things. You're still wearing the fancy suit you bought in London. And now you've moved your ma and sisters and brothers out of that rattrap and into a better part of town."

"I'm taking care of my family, is all."

"Seamus, listen to yourself. You don't even speak like a good Irish lad anymore."

Seamus emptied his glass and shoved it across the bar for a refill. "Okay, you got me there. A beautiful woman recently told me that my Irish brogue limits my options. I'm trying to speak a little bit more like the richies and a little less like my boys."

Braden drained the last drops out of a whiskey bottle, uncorked a new one, and poured three fingers into Seamus's glass. "What about Siobhan, was she happy to see you?"

"Oh, you know, typical Siobhan stuff. Happy, mad, surly."

"She never married Mikey McGuire," Braden noted as he poured himself a glass.

"Nope. Turns out Mr. McGuire's got a taste for opium. Siobhan saw where that was going."

"Think you'll get back together with her?"

"I'm not sure. She asked me if I figured out who I was while I was gone."

Braden took a sip from his whiskey glass and winced. "What'd you tell her?"

"I told her I'd get back to her on that." Seamus took his first sip from the new bottle. It tasted like swill. "Jaysus, Braden, what the hell is this?"

"Yeah, I noticed that meself. This is shyte."

"Where'd it come from?"

"Same guy who's been supplying me for years. Same box of bottles as the one we just finished. Should be from the same batch of corn whiskey, but it's obviously not."

"What are you going to do with the rest of the bottle? It's not fit for pigs."

"This one's particularly bad. I'll save it for a night when everyone's so far gone they won't notice a bad batch."

"How often do you get a bad bottle?"

"Oh, sometimes an entire shipment. That doesn't please the customers."

"I could make better whiskey than this."

"Have you ever distilled whiskey?"

"Nope, but how hard can it be? That could be my new great idea."

Seamus's brother Logan appeared from the darkness at the rear of the saloon. "Seamus, I've got to talk to you."

"Why're you sneaking in the back way, Logan? You're old enough to come in through the front."

"Seamus, could you please come out the back with me? It's important."

Seamus slid his glass across the bar at McSweeney. "Might as well throw the rest of that away, Braden. It's not worth drinking."

Seamus followed his brother out the back of the saloon and was assaulted by the smell of urine. So many of Braden's customers relieved themselves out here that the alley always smelled like piss. "What's so important that you take me out of a business meeting, Logan?"

A Black girl that Seamus vaguely recognized stepped out from behind an oaken barrel.

"Who's this?" asked Seamus. "What's going on here, Logan?"

"This is Martha Freeman. She's Jules and Maddie's daughter."

A spasm of dread rippled through Seamus's body. "What have you done, Logan?"

Logan hung his head for a few seconds, then looked Seamus in the eye. "Martha's pregnant."

* * * * *

· RIAN ·

Conor found Rian standing at a bench at the far end of the Krieger Locomotive factory, illuminated in the glow of a single gas lamp. "There you are. Jaysus, Rian, now that you've decided you're essential in two factories, it's getting harder to find you. C'mon, it's well past candlelight. Time to go home."

"Not until I file the burrs out of the inside of this cylinder."

"What's the problem?"

Rian rolled a 6-inch diameter piston across the workbench toward Conor. "Here, you tell me."

"Where'd you get this?"

Rian jerked her head over her shoulder. "From that loco over there. It's supposed to be shipped to Montevideo on Thursday."

"This is pretty scarred up. How old is it?"

"It was installed today. Some idiot didn't bother to clean out the burrs on the inside of this cylinder. The burrs bitched up the piston after the engine ran for about two minutes. Harry was willing to send it off to Uruguay like that. It probably would have been the last locomotive we ever sold to them."

"Harry, the foreman Harry?"

"Yeah, him."

"He probably had his reasons. Why don't you just let it go?"

"Because my name's on the side of the loco."

"Well, technically, it's your uncle's name."

"Yeah, but Uncle Adrian's still in prison in Russia, and *Vater* is too busy running his side of the alley to get over here much. And apparently Harry isn't up to the job."

"Who is? You?"

"That's my plan."

"Rian, you're fourteen years old. There's no way you're going to run Krieger Locomotive."

"Eventually I will. Meanwhile, I'm going to learn everything I can, do everything I can, to make sure Krieger Locomotive is still running when I'm old enough to take it over."

"Jaysus, Rian. You've changed."

"I'll take that as a compliment."

"I'm not so sure. You used to not take things so seriously."

"Well, back then I didn't know what I wanted. Now I do. Thanks, by the way."

"For what?"

"For not saying that I'll never get to run Krieger Locomotive because I'm a girl."

Conor shrugged. "It crossed my mind, but I know what you're like when you get up a head of steam. 'You can't do this because you're a girl.' Are you hearing that from people?"

"More like feeling it. The guys on the floor don't treat me the way they used to before I ran away to Russia. If they're talking when I walk by, they stop. If I'm working on something, they ignore me. If I ask them to help me with a job, they tell me they're too busy."

"Maybe they are too busy."

"Conor, you've started working here again. Do you think the men are too busy? The factories aren't running full-throttle the way they used to be before the Panic, and don't forget: We shipped half our machine tools to Russia last year."

"I mostly work across the alley. I don't get over here that much, but I'll take your word for it. But my best guess is that you're different, too."

"What do you mean?"

"First of all, you grew about three inches when you were in Russia. You're not a little kid anymore. You're taller than some of the men. Before you were like their little pet. You ran errands for them. You helped them out. You said yourself that now you ask them to help you out. That's not the way it used to be."

"But there are jobs to be done, and they're just standing around."

"But it's Harry's job to keep them busy, not yours."

"Well, Harry's not doing his job."

"And there we are, back to Harry. Rian, if running Krieger Locomotive is what you want to do, that's what I want, too. But can we still have a little fun along the way?"

"Sure, as soon as I reinstall this piston inside the cylinder."

"Are you getting paid for this?"

"Of course not."

"So that means if I help you, I won't get paid either."

"Correct."

Conor started rolling up his sleeves. "Okay, but then we go home and eat. Your da says Alice is cooking shepherd's pie, and I'm already hungry."

* * * * *

· MADDIE ·

Maddie was still getting used to strolling home with Jules at the end of their work day. His new habit was to close up at Krieger Coach, walk to Freeman Hydraulics, and pry Maddie away from whatever tasks anchored her to her desk. The ten minutes it took to get home allowed enough time to cover the headlines of their days but few of the details.

For Jules, today's headline was that Samuel Webb, treasurer of the Pennsylvania Hall Association's Board of Directors, had stopped by to pay Jules proceeds from rentals for their shares in Pennsylvania Hall. "The place hasn't officially opened yet, and we're already renting space. Maddie, I took the job to prove that I could do it, but it has also turned out to be a good financial decision. Our shares will be producing additional income every month for the rest of our lives."

Maddie's headline was equally optimistic. "We received three new orders today in the afternoon mail: one from New York City, one from Northern Liberties, and one from Lancaster. It is so odd: The city—the whole country—is still in the midst of a depression, and we get three orders in a day."

Their strides already in lockstep, Jules wrapped his arm around Maddie's shoulder and pulled her in tight. "This has all occurred while you were tending the store, dear wife. All evidence indicates we should have declared you co-president from the beginning. Were the children pleased when they heard about the new orders?"

"Gracie and Rufus certainly were. The littles are barely aware. Martha doesn't know yet. She left to run errands right after dinner and was gone all afternoon. Jules, she has been in a mood for weeks. What do you think is up with that girl?"

As if to answer Maddie's question, as they approached their home they found Martha standing with Seamus and Logan Gallagher on the front porch.

"Mr. and Mrs. Freeman," said Logan, "Martha and I have something to tell you."

* * * * *

· RIAN ·

Rian walked into her bedroom after playing the violin with her father for the first time since before she fled to Russia.

Conor was sitting on her bed, staring at her portrait, which he had propped up on her washstand. "You two sounded pretty good down there. I imagine your da is happy to have you back. He tried to teach me how to play while you were gone, but I don't think the violin will ever be me chosen instrument."

"Funny thing is, I'm a better violinist than my father now. I guess all that practice with the grand duke's tutor helped. What are you doing on my bed?"

"Perusing your portrait. I think it's pretty good."

As she had done every morning since she returned to Philadelphia a week ago, and every evening before she turned down her oil lamp's wick and blew out the flame, she gazed fondly at the portrait. "David Winter said he captured my soul. It's my favorite possession."

"Did he know you are a girl?"

"Nope. That's one of the things I love about it."

Winter's image of Rian stared back at her from the canvas. *This is who I want to be . . . who I want to become.*

"Why haven't you hung it up?"

"*Vater* won't let me hang it downstairs."

"Then let's hang it up here. If you get a hammer and nail, we can do it right now. I think it would look great over on that wall."

"That's an offer I can't refuse. Let's get to it quick before *Vater* goes to bed."

WEDNESDAY, MAY 2

· JULES ·

Jules and Maddie sat in their parlor. Jules was bent forward in his chair, his elbows on his knees, his head in his hands. "All this time, I've maintained that white Philadelphians have no reason to fear amalgamation. It's a bogeyman that those who hate us have manufactured to stir up the rabble. And now, here it is, right in my own household."

Maddie wiped her eyes. "What are we going to do?"

Jules straightened. "I'm at a loss. Maybe claim Martha had a dalliance with a light-skinned Negro who was passing through, then we help Martha raise the child. Which of course will confirm everything they say about our people, raising another baby born to a husbandless mother."

"Jules, there are more fatherless white children running around Moyamensin than colored ones."

"Yes, I know that, but when the stories of moral laxity appear in the pennies, our beloved press seems to neglect that fact."

Maddie rose, paced up and back in the parlor. "They claim they love each other."

"Pshaw. She's eighteen years old. He's seventeen for Chrissakes. What do they know about love?"

"They say they want to live together."

"How?" asked Jules. "In this day and age? People will hate them for what they have done. The two of them will confirm every prejudice, every hateful thought that they have about miscegenation. And you know what really gets me huffed? For two centuries, Black women like my mother have been raped by their white enslavers. Now, our Martha could have had her pick of the brightest young Negroes in our community, and who did she pick? A barely educated Irish boy."

"And I thought she was going to marry Thomas Forten."

"That would have been such a good match. She would have been at the top of Black society in Philadelphia. And she threw it all away. Fell in love, she says. For an Irish nobody. I'm going to wring Seamus's scrawny white neck. He should never have gone to Russia. He wasn't taking care of his family."

"Jules, there's plenty of blame to go around. If the two of them are determined to stay together, they have to go away."

"Where to? Where can a white man and a Black woman live together in peace?"

* * * * *

· RIAN ·

Lucretia Mott's son Tom greeted Rian with a smile as she walked up to the freight wagon in front of Benjamin Lundy's[12] house. "Benjamin, this is my next-door neighbor, Rian Krieger," he said. "She has volunteered to help us tonight."

Rian tried to ignore a flicker of disappointment that Tom had let the cat out of the bag by referring to her as "she." *Watch. It'll start right away.*

Rian's hair was still short from her time in Russia. *And now Mr. Lundy is going to react to me totally differently than he would have if he thought I was a boy.*

Lundy straightened from his position atop the wagon, which was partially filled with wooden boxes and furniture. He lifted a lantern so he could see Rian. "I thank thee for volunteering to help me this evening, Rian Krieger, but I'm sure we can manage without thee."

Two weeks back from Russia, Rian was still refamiliarizing herself with the patterns of Quaker interactions. *Quakers call you by your first and last names until they are comfortable with you.* "You can call me by my first name, Mr. Lundy. We've met before. At Lucretia's house three years ago, the night you brought President Adams to a gathering there."

"Ah, I remember now. Thee was covered in tallow after working on a steam engine. I still believe we can get along without thee."

Rian shook her head. *And there it is. He doesn't want me to help him because I'm a girl.* She looked at Tom Mott for a little assistance. *C'mon, Tom, you're the one who recruited me for this job.*

Tom put his arm around Rian in a supportive gesture. "She can do the job, Benjamin."

---

12. Benjamin Lundy was an ardent abolitionist who had moved frequently to publish anti-slavery newspapers, often amidst hostile audiences. In Baltimore, he had been severely beaten by a slave trader who objected to criticisms that appeared in Lundy's paper. The slave trader was fined only a dollar for his actions because the judge determined that Lundy had provoked the attack with his criticism of a lawful occupation.

And children address adults by their first names. I guess I should start doing that.

"She's as strong as I am," Tom continued. "Tell Benjamin what you did today, Rian."

"I helped assemble a drive wheel to the axle of a steam locomotive. Every part we were wrestling with weighs over a hundred pounds."

"Thee lifted a hundred-pound wheel?"

"Not by myself, but I carried my share of the weight."

* * * * *

An hour later, Rian was helping Lundy carry a wooden box of books and papers into a storeroom on the first level of Pennsylvania Hall. The hallway was lit by gas wall sconces and smelled of newly applied paint and varnish.

"Rian, I thank thee for helping me this evening. I believe I underestimated thee. It sounds like thee has already put in a long day at thy father's factory. I am sure thee has other things thee would rather be doing."

"Truly, I'm happy to help. There's no one at home anyway. My father is at a dinner at the United States Hotel."

"And thy mother?"

"She died when I was eight. Why are we moving your personal possessions into Pennsylvania Hall?"

"Poor timing, I suppose. I'm moving to Illinois next week. I delayed my departure because I want to attend the opening of Pennsylvania Hall and the ladies' convention. Those two wagons outside hold all my worldly possessions. Since I have already sold my house, all this has to go somewhere. The board of Pennsylvania Hall graciously allowed me to move my things into the hall for the week."

"Everything you own?"

"Yes, everything. As thee can see, it is mostly books and papers. My anti-slavery activities have generated a great deal of documentation. Many articles. Correspondence." Rian and Lundy placed the box on top of another box and straightened up. "Lucretia said that thee became a companion to the Tsar's son while thee was in Russia. What did thee learn while living there?"

"A lot of things. Mostly about power—and riches, I suppose. If you are powerful enough or rich enough, you can do anything you want."

"That is a heady concept for one as young as thee. And what is it that thee want to be powerful enough to do?"

"I want to run Krieger Locomotive someday."

"So thee think that a woman can summon up enough power to run a large manufacturing company?"

Rian tried to shrug off the implied judgment, but . . . *Damnit, it's never far below the surface.* "I know I can," she responded to Lundy. *Eventually. A soothsayer in Russia told me that first I wouldn't, then I would. I don't know what that means, but I can feel it in my bones. Someday I will run Uncle Adrian's business.*

Lundy glanced around the storeroom. "Rian, I'm going to tidy up some of this. Thee can go back to the wagon and come back with the next box." He smiled. "Something not so heavy that it takes two people to carry it."

Rian was walking back down the hallway when a clatter and a muttered "Tarnation!" emanated from the office of *The Pennsylvania Freeman.* She went to the door to find a man in his late twenties picking himself up from the floor after what had been a nasty fall. He was thin, with close-cropped hair and dark, piercing eyes. Hundreds of pieces of lead type were scattered on the floor.

Rian helped the man up. "Are you okay? What happened?"

"Oh, it's my own fault. I'm still settling in here. I was moving a drawer of type and tripped over a box. I'm afraid I've scattered the letters all over the floor."

"Yeah, you made a mess. I can help you out. I'm Rian Krieger."

"Rian Krieger, the young woman who just returned from Russia?"

Does everyone know my business here? "Yup, that's me."

"I am John Greenleaf Whittier. I'm the new editor of *The Pennsylvania Freeman.* Perhaps I should interview thee. I understand thee assisted in the freeing of a serf from the Tsar's estate while thee was in Russia."

"Yes, I did." *Although I wasn't assisting anyone. Everyone I trusted was in prison.*

"That was very good of thee. Slavery is slavery, no matter what it is called. Would thee be interested in sitting for an interview about the serf?"

"No thank you. Lev was supposed to come to Philadelphia with my cousin and me, but he changed his plans when we landed in New York." *Right now he's probably on a ship to New Orleans with Delilah Winter. Playing poker for a living.* "It wouldn't be much of a story."

"Why is thee here in Pennsylvania Hall, Rian? Thee should be home eating supper."

"I'm with James Mott and his son Tom. We're helping Mr. Lundy move his belongings in. Is *The Pennsylvania Freeman* a new paper? I've never heard of it before."

"Yes and no. The paper belongs to the Pennsylvania Anti-Slavery Society. Up until last week, it was called *The National Inquirer*. Benjamin, who thee is assisting, used to publish the paper out of an office downtown. When he decided to move to Illinois, PASS asked me to become the new editor. We renamed it *The Pennsylvania Freeman* and moved the office into Pennsylvania Hall."

"Do you like your new office?"

"I will eventually, I'm sure. But right now, I must get things a bit more organized."

Tom Mott appeared at the door. "Rian, we need thy help."

An hour later, the moving was done. James Mott turned to Rian and his son Tom. "Do thee want to see the rest of Pennsylvania Hall?"

James guided Tom and Rian through the "Free Produce" store that shared the street level of the building with conference rooms and *The Pennsylvania Freeman*. It was chock-a-block filled with goods untainted by the scourge of slavery. The free cotton had been cultivated and picked in the South by paid labor, not by slaves. The clothing had been made in the North using free cotton. Similarly rice, sugar, shoes, soaps, dry goods, and even candy—all deemed produce—had been shipped from the South after being made by free Blacks. James was unapologetic about the higher prices in the store, stating it was worth it to pay a little more if it meant bringing an end to slavery.

James escorted them upstairs to the Grand Saloon. "This is the most modern facility in Pennsylvania, perhaps in all of America. The Pennsylvania Anti-Slavery Society will use Pennsylvania Hall as its headquarters in the fight against slavery. I am confident that our Temple of Freedom will help us bring that fight to a successful conclusion."

They climbed another set of stairs to the Gallery. Rian put her hand on the balcony's half-wall, peered down into the Grand Saloon, and imagined thousands of people chanting and praying and organizing for an end to slavery. "How long do you think it will take, James?"

"How long? Between thirty and fifty years."

THURSDAY, MAY 3

· JULES ·

Jules entered the office of Krieger Coach to find Otto engrossed in a task at his desk.

"Otto, I've got a problem. I need your advice."

"And I have something that I need to tell you."

"Then why don't you go first."

"My two half-sisters are arriving in America in a few weeks. They intend to marry two men who live in the hinterlands of Pennsylvania. They have asked me to bless the unions and arrange the weddings."

"I am happy for all of you. Is that what you needed to tell me?"

"Not entirely. Jules, you are my closest friend, but I can't invite you to the wedding. The way the city is lately, it wouldn't work."

Jules stiffened. "You mean George Shippen wouldn't be happy to drink a toast while standing next to a Black man."

"You are right about Shippen, but I do not intend to invite him. However, my late wife's Irish relatives will have the same sentiments."

"If you thought I would be hurt by this, you are right, but I've got bigger fish to fry. Otto, Martha's pregnant. And the father of her child is Logan Gallagher, your Irish nephew. What are Dierdre's brothers and sisters going to say about that?"

WEDNESDAY, MAY 9

· JULES ·

It had been almost a week since Otto told Jules he was not invited to Hilda and Maria's weddings and interactions between them were still frosty. As had often been the case lately, Jules entered the Krieger Coach office to find Otto reading a penny paper with his feet up on his desk.

"Otto, I won't be in to work for the rest of the week. I leave tomorrow to deliver a pump to Baltimore that I have been putting off far too long. Then I'm taking the whole of next week off to attend the anti-slavery convention."

Otto sat up and tossed the paper on his desk. "Jules, you cannot choose to skip work arbitrarily. We have just started the passenger car for the *Philadelphia & Columbia*."

"Otto, I told you about this months ago when I made the sale. Steam fire pumps are more complicated than hand pumpers. The only way I could close the deal was if I delivered the pump in person and gave the hose company a lesson. I delayed delivery until after I wrapped up at Pennsylvania Hall."

"Have you prepared Ernst to run the shop while you're gone?"

Jules nodded. "I've got all the ducks lined up. Ernst knows what to do."

"We've got twenty railroad cars to build for the *Philadelphia & Columbia*."

Jules stuffed down his irritation. *Which has been delayed because Harry took so long to deliver the first sets of wheels and axles.* "And now that Krieger Locomotive has delivered the wheels to us, we have started production. We can only build four cars at a time. As soon as one is done, we will deliver it and make room for the next one in the queue. That won't happen 'til long after I get back. You can handle anything that comes up while I'm at the convention."

Otto took off his reading glasses and ran his hand through his hair. "My hands are full at the moment."

"Doing what? When I came in here you were reading the paper."

"It's nothing to do with work."

"What is it, then?"

Otto idly rearranged a few items on his desk. "I'm having difficulty finding a priest to marry my sisters. There are eight Catholic churches in this city, and no priest will perform the ceremony unless the men convert to Catholicism."

Jules stifled a retort: *I guess you'll have to solve that problem on your own.* Instead, he said, "Try finding someone to marry a Black girl and a son of Hibernia."

"So, they are going to go through with it? Getting married?"

"They are resolute. Martha wore Maddie down. The two of them wore me down. My minister at Bethel AME flatly refused. I have been a member there for eighteen years, Maddie for longer than that. Seamus has run into the same problem at St. Philip Neri. Martha has no desire to become a Catholic."

Otto smiled for the first time since Jules entered the office; not a friendly smile, more a brotherly *so-I-guess-we're-in-this-together* smile. "I'm thinking of asking an alderman to do it. A civil ceremony may be the only way to go. Maybe you should consider the same thing."

Jules shook his head. "There's no way I can chance that. There's not an alderman in the city who favors the Negro in Philadelphia. Worse yet, any one of them would probably blab it all around the city. Martha and Logan would be greeted by a mob when they left the courthouse."

Otto idly picked up the penny paper, then let it waft back onto his desk. "Let me ask you a question. This fire company in Baltimore. Do they know you are Black? That Freeman Hydraulics is owned by a Negro?"

"Of course not. Do you think I would have been able to make the sale if they had?"

"No, I do not. But what about this demonstration? What if they don't want to receive instruction from a Black man?"

"That's a worry. If that happens, I'll have to bring the pump back with me."

"When was the last time you set foot in Maryland, a slave state?"

"Since I self-emancipated. Eighteen years."

"Would it help if you had a white friend to back you up?"

"Who've you got in mind?"

"Me. I successfully delivered that pump to New York City four months ago. No reason I can't do the same in Baltimore."

MONDAY, MAY 14

· JULES ·

Still weary from the successful but grueling trip to Baltimore, Jules started Dedication Day by walking to Pennsylvania Hall and assuring himself that all was shipshape. Then he backtracked to Freeman Hydraulics to escort Maddie to the Hall for opening ceremonies.

When he entered the office, he found Hugh Callaghan sitting in the chair in front of his desk. "What are you doing here?" he asked Hugh in an unfriendly tone and knowing immediately he'd shown too much of his emotions. *Careful, Jules. Keep your ire stuffed down tight.*

"Just talking to your lovely wife."

Jules glanced at Maddie. She gave a slight shrug of her shoulders and a wide-eyed look to indicate *I have no idea what the man is doing here.*

"Seems to me," continued Hugh, "that you've got quite the successful enterprise going on here. I wonder if you would be interested in a little business proposition. Actually, three propositions."

Jules walked behind his desk, feeling not particularly threatened but somewhat comforted by the presence of the pistol in his upper left-hand drawer. "I doubt it, but I'm willing to listen."

Hugh put up a cautionary hand. "Hear me out. First, I'd like to order another fire pump."

"We just sold one to you four months ago. You already want another one?"

"Yes, we do. The city's growing. We're serving a lot more people than we used to."

And likely increasing the territory of the Ratters—Hugh's Moya boys without their fire hats. "I'm happy to talk to you about that."

"Good. See, we're already making progress. Second, since you are going to continue to make fire pumps for us, I'd like you two to be the first to know that the Moyamensing Hose Company will break precedent and extend its fire protection to Freeman Hydraulics."

"That is welcome news. What has changed? We've had fire insurance since we set up this shop. You have always made a point of ignoring fires in Black homes and businesses whether they were insured or not."

"Well, what has changed is that you and I would come to a special arrangement. I would expect a monthly fee."

"I pay a fee or you don't respond to a fire?"

"That's about the size of it."

"I believe that's called extortion."

"It's only extortion if I threaten to start the fire if you don't pay me. I have no intention of doing that. Before I go on to my third proposition, I want you to consider two things. First, tension between Black and white is at an all-time high. This city is about to blow."

"It's been bad before. The Flying Horse Riots[13] were only four years ago."

"Ah, but your situation is different than it was then. Now you own this fine business and employ only your fellow Negroes. And for the past four months, you've been running mixed crews at that cursed Temple of Freedom. With all that notoriety, I figure it's only a matter of time before someone—not me or any of my lads, of course—decides you've gotten too big for your britches."

The implied threat sent a spasm of adrenaline throughout Jules's body and called to mind his mother's old Ashanti proverb: When you are hiding, don't light a fire. *But that was the old me. Maddie and I decided two years ago that we were going to light that fire to demonstrate to our children that they can do anything in life. And now, here we are, too big for our britches.* Jules did his best to keep his face an unperturbed mask. "The answer is no."

Hugh frowned. "A pity. Then third, I heard you and Herr Krieger made a delivery to Baltimore. How did it go?"

Jules made eye contact with Maddie. She shook her head: *I didn't tell him anything.*

"It went well."

"I'm happy for you, Jules. Must have been gratifying, selling a fine piece of fire apparatus to an outfit in a slave state. How would you like to make more sales south of the Mason-Dixon Line?"

"I'll sell to any fire brigade, no matter where they are. Why? What's your point?"

"Because I would be happy to take over making deliveries for you."

---

13. In August 1834, a dispute between the Irish and Blacks over a place in line at a carousel sparked three evenings of rioting in Moyamensing. The predominantly Irish mobs destroyed Black homes, a church, and a grog shop that catered to both Blacks and whites.

"For a fee?"

"Of course, certainly not out of the goodness of my heart."

"My answer is yes to number one, assuming we can agree on a price, and no to number two and number three. Now, if you will excuse us, we have to attend the opening ceremonies at our Temple of Freedom."

* * * * *

· LUCRETIA ·

Second Day—what non-Quakers call Monday—Fifth Month 14: The day of Pennsylvania Hall's dedication.

This day should be joyous, Lucretia said to herself. *Instead, my heart hangs heavy with sadness for my own shortcomings.*

The past few days had been a whirlwind.

On Seventh Day—Saturday—female delegates from all over the country started to arrive in Philadelphia for the Anti-Slavery Convention of American Women. Lucretia felt honored that the managing board of the Hall chose the women's convention to be the first gathering in the newly constructed Temple of Freedom.

Prominent male abolitionists had also traveled here to honor the women's convention, participate in the dedication of Pennsylvania Hall, and attend the wedding of Theodore Weld and Angelina Grimké,[14] the darling couple of the abolitionist movement.

Always empathetic to those who were on a tight budget, Lucretia opened her home to out-of-towners, both Black and white. When a contingent from the Boston Female Anti-Slavery Society arrived, her daughter Anne opened her home next door to the overflow. Otto Krieger, on the other side of her home, offered up one room to guests. Lucretia didn't know where Rian or Conor would sleep, but knew young people were much more resilient than adults.

---

14. Angelina Grimké (b. 1805) and her sister Sarah (b. 1792), were the daughters of a wealthy South Carolina plantation owner, but they grew up with a congenital hatred of slavery. When Angelina accompanied her father to Philadelphia, she became enamored with Quakerism because of its relative egalitarianism between the sexes and its anti-slavery history. As an adult she moved to Philadelphia, joined a Quaker church, and jumped wholeheartedly into the abolitionist movement.

Theodore Weld (b. 1803) was a noted abolitionist and leader in the "immediatist" faction; those who believed that slavery should be ended immediately, without compensation to the slaveholders.

Grimké and Weld met when she attended a training session for abolitionist agents in New York City and he was an instructor. After a two-year courtship, they had planned their wedding to coincide with the dedication of Pennsylvania Hall so members of the country's abolitionist elite could attend.

After their congregation's meeting—what those outside her faith would call church—on First Day, Lucretia and James took a contingent of out-of-towners on a sightseeing tour of Philadelphia, including the famous waterworks at Fairmount Park and the Philadelphia Museum with its displays of animals and birds preserved through taxidermy.

She had arranged to have a tour of the State House so her guests could see the place where the Founding Fathers had signed the Declaration of Independence. Some folks were disappointed that they couldn't climb the steeple to see the State House Bell because the steeple was in such poor repair. In recent publications, the New York Anti-Slavery Society had adopted the cracked bell as a symbol and dubbed it the "Liberty Bell." As other anti-slavery organizations had followed suit, it seemed the bell was becoming a bit of a celebrity in its own right.

On Dedication Day, Lucretia and James walked with their visitors the four blocks to the radiant new Pennsylvania Hall. Lucretia confessed to her guests that she was a little miffed at the twenty-five-dollar fee the managing board of the Hall was charging the Philadelphia Female Anti-Slavery Society for the use of the hall for the week.

During the dedication ceremony, Lucretia was happy to see both Otto and Rian Krieger playing their violins in the small orchestra of musicians. *Such a pleasure to see Rian in a dress,* she thought to herself. Although music would not have been appropriate during a Quaker meeting, she welcomed its inclusion in the dedication ceremony. Men read letters of congratulations and encouragement from former President John Quincy Adams, short homilies by various dignitaries, and a poem by Mr. Whittier.

The keynote speaker for the dedication ceremony was David Paul Brown, who had worked tirelessly alongside James in the abolition movement both locally and nationally. With the long-awaited dedication complete, a handful of dignitaries left the Hall to attend the Grimké-Weld wedding.

As her husband James, who was on the Hall's board of directors, had an emergency meeting, Lucretia was free of obligations and houseguests for the afternoon.

Otto and Rian Krieger, both carrying their violin cases, approached as Lucretia watched the wedding-goers board carriages.

"Care to walk home with us, Lucretia?" said Otto.

Lucretia smiled at her next-door neighbor. "I would be delighted. How good to see thee wearing a dress for a change, Rian."

The trio walked for a block or so before Otto spoke. "What did you think of Mr. Brown's keynote speech, Lucretia?"

"Truth be told, I was disappointed. Mr. Brown declared himself to be an 'immediatist'—an advocate of an immediate end to slavery—but when he delved down into what that meant, it didn't seem immediate at all. For instance, he called for slave owners to immediately start giving slaves free time to become educated and work on their own projects to amass savings. I know Mr. Garrison was not pleased, and I fear that if he is called upon to speak tomorrow, he will give a passionate rebuttal. I spoke to him before he left for Angelina's wedding."

"I'm surprised you are not attending the Grimké-Weld wedding. I know you are close to the bride."

"Oh, Otto, I am so torn and so disappointed in myself. Theodore Weld is not a Quaker. We Quakers are forbidden to marry people outside our faith. The elders leaned hard on Angelina, forbidding her to marry him. She persisted. I fear they will excommunicate her from the faith."

"The response of the elders does not strike me as much of a surprise, Lucretia. I told you a couple of weeks ago that my half-sisters are coming to America to marry young men. What I didn't tell you is that both of them are Protestants. I am having difficulty finding a priest to marry them."

Lucretia gathered her thoughts as she waited until a freight wagon rumbled by on the cobblestone street. "I am bereft that marrying outside one's faith is so frequently frowned upon."

"My understanding is that Miss Grimké has already frustrated the elders. She is much more outspoken in her sentiments about slavery than they are comfortable with. I'm afraid there are limits even amongst your Quaker brethren as to what a woman is allowed to do. This may be the last straw."

"I suspect it will be. And I know excommunication will cause her anguish. She is a headstrong woman. But that is not what troubles me."

"Then what is it?"

Lucretia hooked her arm into Otto's. "The elders have also stated that they will excommunicate any Quaker who attends the wedding. James and I have both knuckled under. We won't attend the wedding this afternoon, even though we admire both of them."

"I'm sure they will understand."

"I have already spoken to Angelina. She was very gracious. John Whittier is Theodore Weld's best friend. He is in a similar circumstance, although I know he presented them with a poem in honor of their nuptials this morning."

Rian stopped briefly to read a broadside that had been tacked on a tree. She tore it off and caught up to her father and Lucretia. "Have you seen this? Somebody's putting them up all over town."

ACTION!

A CONVENTION FOR THE AVOWED PURPOSE
OF BRINGING ABOUT THE IMMEDIATE ABOLITION
OF SLAVERY IN THE UNION
IS NOW IN SESSION IN THIS CITY.

ALL CITIZENS WHO ENTERTAIN A PROPER RESPECT
FOR THE RIGHT OF PROPERTY
AND THE PRESERVATION OF THE CONSTITUTION
OF THE UNITED STATES
ARE CALLED UPON TO MEET
AT THE INTERSECTION OF SIXTH AND HAINES STREETS
AT 11:00 AM WEDNESDAY, MAY 16
TO INTERFERE, FORCIBLY IF IT IS NECESSARY,
TO PREVENT THE VIOLATION OF SACRED
CONSTITUTIONAL RIGHTS.

PATRIOTS UNITE!

Lucretia read the broadside and handed it to Otto. "This document advocates for the preservation of the constitutional right to own another human being. Those people are so misguided."

"Lucretia," said Otto as he read. "I fear you have missed the most important point of this handbill. It is a call for people to use force to prevent the convention from meeting."

"Oh, Otto, I expected there would be some noise, but do thee really think this will descend to violence?" He and Maddie were guests in the home of Anna Frost, the widowed sister of Angelina Grimké, who had offered up her home as the venue for Angelina's wedding and reception.

* * * * *

· JULES ·

Is this a hint of a bright future or a spark to a fiery present? Jules asked himself as he eyed the gathering.

They had been surprised and flattered when they were invited to the Grimké-Weld wedding, even though Angelina Grimké and Maddie had worked together often at the Philadelphia Female Anti-Slavery Society.

The event was unusual—perhaps even unprecedented—on many levels. The bride and groom were both white, but Mr. Weld was not a Quaker. Two ministers officiated; one Black, one white. Of the thirty or so wedding guests, perhaps a third were Black, including Jules and Maddie's friends James and Charlotte Forten and Robert and Harriet Purvis, plus two women formerly enslaved by Grimké's father. The white guests included the publisher of *The Liberator*, William Lloyd Garrison, and Lewis Tappan of New York, who financed numerous abolitionist initiatives around the country.

Jules and Maddie had eaten dinner at Otto Krieger's house many times, but the meals were always private family affairs. *Public socializing between the races like this wedding isn't done*, Jules said to himself. *Like Otto demonstrated to me two weeks ago when he told me we weren't invited to his half-sisters' weddings. Yet, here we are . . . Blacks and whites attending a wedding together, sharing food, talking. Maybe there is hope for the future.*

Even if he ignored race, the wedding would have been controversial. The bride pointedly did not include the word *obey* in her wedding vows. In his vows, the groom denounced *feme covert*, the principle behind the construct of laws in which wives gave up all power of ownership of previously held real estate and fortune to their husbands.

Maddie and Jules found themselves both observing the two ministers, their official duties completed, standing and talking together, eating cake made with slave-free sugar. Jules placed his dish down on a side table. "Do you think I should . . ."

"Yes," said Maddie. "This may be the answer to our prayers."

Jules walked over to the two officiants. "Gentlemen, I want to thank you for conducting this service today. I have recently found my family in a bit of an awkward situation. My daughter has fallen in love with an Irish boy. My wife and I aren't very enthusiastic about the union but are not willing to forbid it. My minister at Bethel AME will not conduct the wedding, nor will any Catholic priest. I wonder if either of you would consent to do it. We would like it to occur a week from Wednesday."

The Black man was the first to speak. "I would be willing to do it but have to return to New York when the convention ends on Friday."

The white man put out his hand. "My name is William Henry Furness. I am the minister at the First Unitarian Church of Philadelphia. Not only would I be willing to conduct the service, but I would be happy to make the church available as a venue."

Jules shook Furness's hand and made an appointment to bring the bride and groom to meet with him on Friday.

Taking heart from Furness's response and the two races mingling amiably around the room, Jules walked back to Maddie with a smile on his face. "We've got both a minister and a church to hold the wedding." *And, given what I see in this room at this hour, maybe—just maybe—someday the Marthas and Logans of the world will go out into a kinder city in which race plays a less important role. Damn, wouldn't that be sweet.*

TUESDAY, MAY 15

· RIAN ·

Rian was milling a piston down to size for Locomotive Number 14, third in line in production. As three-quarters of the machines in the shop were currently engaged, the din was significant. *Music to my ears*, she thought. *It's good to even have a locomotive third in line. Before I ran away to Russia, there was no line at all.*

A tap on her shoulder. Rian turned.

Harry the foreman yelled, "Rian, what are you doing?!"

"Milling a piston for Number 14!"

Harry signaled her to disengage the continuous belt and move away so they could talk without yelling. She pushed the lever, which moved the rapidly spinning belt to the idler pulley on the machine. Ever so slowly, the lathe started to decelerate. Rian followed Harry to a relatively quiet spot away from the machines.

"Why are you milling a piston? I didn't tell you to do that!"

"No one is working on the pistons for Number 14. The lathe was free. I checked. There aren't any pistons made yet. The raw stock is here. I figured I would get us ahead of schedule."

"I want Georg to do that."

"Georg is busy. I'm a better lathe worker than he is anyway."

"You do not belong in this shop. If I need you to do a task, I'll send someone over to Coach to find you. Until then, stay on the other side of the alley."

"But there's nothing pressing over there. That's why I came over here."

Harry shook his head and briefly surveyed the shop. "Okay, here's what I want you to do. The Harbor List says that the *Regal* docked at the Willing & Francis Pier. I want you to go over there and see if the shaper we ordered from Liverpool is aboard."

Harry's trying to get rid of me. "Willing & Francis? The *Regal* doesn't usually tie up that far south."

"Yeah, I know. Nose around a bit. See what you can find out . . . And Rian, if the shaper is there, don't come back here without it."

* * * * *

· JULES ·

After attending the morning session at Pennsylvania Hall, Jules and Maddie accepted Robert and Harriet Purvis's invitation to dine with them on their front porch at Ninth and Lombard.

Harriet poured coffee from a sterling silver pot into Jules's cup. "I understand you made a business trip to Baltimore last week."

"Yes, my first sale south of the Mason-Dixon Line. Frankly, I think I was a bit too filled with myself. I had intended to make the delivery on my own, but Otto Krieger volunteered to go with me, and I'm glad he did."

Robert held his cup for Harriet to freshen. "I imagine returning to your birth state with forged papers caused some anxiety. Did you feel at risk?"

"Not threatened for my freedom. My forged emancipation papers have passed the test a hundred times. Otto and I gave the appearance of two workers delivering a new piece of equipment. No one questioned our mission, but, I'll tell you, traveling with a steam-powered fire pump, which no one has ever seen before, attracted a lot of attention."

"Positive attention, I assume," said Robert.

"Yes, for a while. Remember that each of the pumps we have manufactured so far . . . all six of them," Jules said with a smile, "have gone out the door with an oval brass plaque that says *Freeman Hydraulics, Philadelphia U.S.A.* prominently displayed on the side. Aboard the freight boat on the Chesapeake and Delaware Canal, a young white gentleman took a particular interest in the machine. I spent half an hour talking with him. I imagine he assumed I was just the delivery man. Then I identified myself as the *Freeman* named on the plaque. He immediately turned quite frosty."

"Of course he did," interjected Purvis. "Your position, your aspirations, your success upset the order of things."

"That's the conclusion Otto and I came to. For the rest of the trip, Otto became the representative of Freeman Hydraulics, delivering a steam-powered fire pump to a fire brigade in Baltimore. Me? I was introduced as Jules. I still answered a lot of peoples' questions. They still listened."

"Jules, that must have been so humiliating," said Harriet

Jules leaned back in his chair. "By the time the fool has learned the game, the players have dispersed."

Harriet passed the plate of sandwiches around again. "An apt aphorism, but I don't understand the reference."

"It's an Ashanti proverb. Before I was sold away from my first enslaver, my mother told me hundreds of stories and proverbs from the land of her birth. This one came to mind when Otto and I were still on the canal. If the men who I was about to meet objected to a Black man owning Freeman Hydraulics, they were fools. I didn't mind using their foolishness against them. Otto and I were in and out before they knew there was a game being played. Their fire brigade got a beautiful machine, I walked away with a healthy profit. Everyone benefited from the transaction, despite their ignorance."

"Sad," said Robert. "An opportunity lost. It would have been gratifying to educate them."

"There will come a time when white people think nothing of dealing with a Black-owned business. This wasn't the time or the place. I am content."

"A wise perspective. How did you find conditions for our brethren in Baltimore?"

"There is a sizable population of free Negroes in Baltimore, though not as many as here in Philadelphia. By appearance, they seem to be less well-off as we are. But, there is a calmness between the races in the city. As you said, the order of things is firmly established there. The white man runs things, and the Black man knows his place. As long as I kept my place, I was treated more kindly in Baltimore than I often experience here in the City of Brotherly Love."

"Thank you for your measured words," said Harriet. "Well, I for one am happy that you have returned home safely. I will make a point of thanking Mr. Krieger for his kindness when I see him next."

The luncheon completed, the foursome boarded Purvis's landau to return to Pennsylvania Hall for the afternoon session.

"Up or down?" Purvis asked Jules.

"Pardon me?"

"Do you want to travel with the canopy up or down?"

"Given current tensions, I guess I'd prefer it to be up."

The Freemans and the Purvises boarded the landau. "Had we not been with you, Robert, would you have preferred to have had the canopy down?"

Purvis smiled. "Oh, I don't think your instincts are unfounded. If I were traveling alone on a warm sunny day like this, I would be happy to travel with the top down. But then I acknowledge that my skin is so light, people who don't know me think I'm white. I have the prerogative of being seated at a table at any restaurant in the city, riding on an omnibus or a train, sitting in the white section of any theater. Riding down a city street in this fine carriage—built by the finest carriage-maker in the country—people assume I am a businessman going about his day. In those instances, I suppose your mother's Ashanti proverb applies to my circumstance as well. Those passersby and me? Our interactions are fleeting. They have no idea a game is being played. They have no idea that I am legally Black in most states, nor that I consider myself a Black man. I make no attempts to hide that fact. What people *assume* is their problem, not mine.

"You said that if you were traveling alone you would travel with the top down. What about if you were traveling with Harriet?"

"Now that is a different story. Having a wife who is quite obviously a Negro makes us stand out as a couple. On a few occasions, that has become problematic."

* * * * *

· RIAN ·

Rian walked around a sail—or it could have been two or three sails—that was ill-folded into a pile at the foot of Willing & Francis Pier, and walked unchallenged up the *Regal*'s gangway. It took a while, but she finally found the first mate in the hold of the ship. The hold was dank and lit by two whale oil lamps. It smelled of bilge, tar, and mildewed canvas. Crates and barrels were lined up and stacked cheek-to-jowl the length of the hold, with gaps barely wide enough for a man to pass through if he walked sideways.

The first mate was telling a strawboss the order he wanted cargo unloaded. Rian stood on the periphery for minutes until he dismissed the man and turned to her. "Who might you be? State your business."

"Good morning, sir. Harry from Krieger Locomotive wants to know if you have a shaper for us."

The first mate leafed through a stack of papers. "Krieger Locomotive? Yeah, it's here. It's a heavy son of a bitch. We'll probably have it out this afternoon. If you're in a hurry, you can pick it up sometime after 3:00. Otherwise, you'll have to find it all over again in the warehouse off Lombard Alley."

Rian did her calculations. *Half an hour to walk to Kent's Livery. Half an hour to pick up the horses and a wagon. Half an hour to get back here. I've got a lot of time to kill.* "I imagine I'll be picking it up today. Looks like you had some trouble."

The first mate turned away from Rian and started climbing the ladder that led back to the deck. As Rian followed at his heels, he said, "Bit of a blow off Labrador. Nothing we couldn't handle, but a healthy gust caught us by surprise. We lost three sails off our foremast. A shame, since we re-outfitted the whole ship six months ago. Had to finish the trip with old canvas. Docked here to see if Forten's outfit can get us out of port on time."

Rian thanked the first mate, who left her without saying another word. As her eyes adjusted to the bright sunlight, she surveyed her surroundings from the height of the ship's deck. A forest of masts and cranes stretched out to the north and the south. A quarter mile to the east, she could make out hoards of day workers digging the cut through Windmill Island with picks and shovels. The island blocked the mile-wide expanse of the Delaware beyond, and then Camden, New Jersey. In the opposite direction, the three-story bulk of James Forten's sail loft bustled with activity.

As Rian walked down the gangplank to the dock, she spied Mikey Mc-Guire, one of Conor's three older brothers, standing in a knot of other day laborers. These were men who reported to the docks before sunrise every morning, hoping to get picked to load or unload ships for the day.

Rian didn't much like Mikey, mostly because he hated anyone who wasn't 100 percent Irish, but especially Negroes. She knew that her 50 percent Irish blood wasn't good enough for him either. Also, he was a braggart and talked like he knew things that he really didn't know. She was surprised when Mikey broke away from the others and walked over to her.

"Conor told me you were back. What are you doing down here, Ispini?"

Ispini. Irish for sausage. "I'm checking on some cargo. I see you got picked today."

Mikey spat some tobacco juice at Rian's feet. "It's been regular lately. I've got some advice for you. Stay away from that new African freedom hall. It's not going to be there for long. Be a shame if you were in it when we burn it down."

"Who's we?"

"Everyone in Philadelphia but you and your smoky friends."

Rian turned to walk north along the docks toward Pine. "Thanks for the warning, Mikey. I guess I'll see you there," she said over her shoulder.

"Don't say I didn't warn you!"

Before Rian reached Pine Street, a two-wheeled cabriolet with driver standing on a platform high in back came to a halt beside her. James Forten leaned forward from the passenger seat. "You are Rian Krieger, are you not?"

Rian had never met Forten but knew him by sight. He was Robert Purvis's father-in-law, the owner of the sail-making business that drew the *Regal* to the Willing & Francis Pier, and reputed to be the richest Black man in North America. She assumed he was a good guy. He had loaned money to Jules to get him started with Freeman Hydraulics. "Yes, I am, Mr. Forten."

"Are you heading north? If so, hop in. I would like to hear about your time living with the Tsar."

Rian boarded the carriage and sat next to Forten. "I never actually lived with the Tsar. His palace was much too big for that, but after it burned down, he asked me to be his son's companion. We were tutored together for a couple of months before I had to leave. How did you know about me and Russia?"

"Oh, I check in with your friend Jules regularly to stay current with his business. He said that one of his fire pumps performed admirably during the fire at the Tsar's palace. But I also know that before you went to Russia you were supportive of our cause and actively assisted him in his evening activities."

"Yes, sir. I used to, but my father found out about it and made me quit. Mr. Forten, you should know that Jules has told me not to talk about that." *Rule Number 1 in the Underground Railroad business: If someone doesn't have to know about something, you don't tell them.*

"Ah, yes, Rule Number 1. I understand. So Russia. . . ."

"I'll make you a deal. I'll tell you about Russia if you tell me about fighting in the Revolution."

"Well, it is very flattering that you would be interested in an old man's reminiscence. Truth be told, my time fighting for American independence was very brief. I signed on as a powder-boy on the privateer *Royal Louis* when I was fourteen. How old are you now?"

"I turned fourteen in March."

"Well, as I think about this, you and I may have something in common. On our first cruise out of Philadelphia, we were extremely successful. We captured four vessels. But our second foray was in support of Washington's siege of the British at Yorktown. October 1781. We encountered the British ship-of-the-line *Amphion* as we left Delaware Bay. We turned tail, they gave chase. Our entire crew was captured.

"Half our crew was sent aboard another ship for transport back to a prison ship in New York. My half of the crew remained aboard the *Amphion*. We were mostly kept below decks, but occasionally brought on deck to perform tasks. Because I was so young I was given a bit more freedom and came to the attention of the captain, I suppose like you came to the attention of the Tsar. The captain's two sons were with him aboard the *Amphion*. The elder was already working his way toward midshipman. The younger was only twelve and prone to get into mischief. The captain asked me to become his companion and keep him out of trouble."

"Were you successful?"

"Apparently. The ship saw a great deal of action before we finally made our way back to New York. Captain Bazely gave me a choice. I could join the rest of my former crew in a prison ship, or I could accompany his son to England and attend school with him."

"What did you do?"

"I chose the prison ship. I told Captain Bazely that I would never become a traitor to my country's interests."

"How long were you on the prison ship?"

"Seven months. When I was released, I had no food, no shoes. I had to walk back to Philadelphia. I got as far as Trenton before someone gave me an old pair of shoes. And of course, when the good people of Philadelphia celebrate America's victory in the War of Independence, somehow the contribution of the Black man gets ignored."

As the carriage crossed Mulberry Street, the white marble walls of Pennsylvania Hall a block away became clearly visible. Rian chose to change the subject. "Mr. Forten, I'm afraid that the good people of Philadelphia are going to try to burn down Pennsylvania Hall."

"Rian, I think your fears are well founded. My sources tell me the same thing. I haven't seen racial tensions this fraught since the Flying Horse Riots." Forten paused to turn his attention north on Sixth Street. "It seems that a crowd has gathered outside our Temple of Freedom. I can't tell from here if they are friend or foe. I fear that some among them might object to the two of us sharing a moment together. Rather than take any chances, how about if my driver lets you off here and you walk the last two blocks?"

* * * * *

As Rian approached Pennsylvania Hall, she estimated that a couple of hundred people were congregated near the intersection of Sixth and Haines Streets; likely an equal number of conventioneers and those who came to gape at them. It wasn't difficult to figure out that not all the observers were friendly. As she picked her way through the spectators, she heard muttering from more than a dozen people; some dressed like what Seamus would call "the impatient class," others obviously less privileged.

Rian ducked around a final knot of bystanders to establish a good observation post on Sixth Street. Pennsylvania Hall was a glorious structure. *Dang, Jules has every right to be proud of this building. It's beautiful.* Conventioneers were returning to the Hall for the afternoon sessions. Pedestrians, both men and women, entered the Hall through the generous front doors. Carriages lined up to unload their occupants, then move on.

"Hi, Barn Door."

Rian looked to her left to see Wilhelm "Billy" Schiffler, the son of the president of the Bank of Industry. Billy called her "Barn Door" because of the gap between her two front teeth. It was a name she resented, but it no longer hurt her the way it used to. She ignored him. Rian didn't like Billy and generally tried to avoid him. He was a nasty kid who loved to bully those who were less powerful than him. He took special joy in tormenting Irish and Negroes, and even more so if they were girls. Sadly, he was bigger than most of the kids his age, and he had grown even more than she had since she saw him last.

Billy didn't take well to being ignored. "I thought you ran away to Russia."

Rian was surprised Billy even wanted to talk to her. They were eleven the last time she spent much time with him. Rian continued to ignore him.

The driver of a cabriolet similar to Forten's brought his carriage to a halt, and two passengers stepped down to the street. Rian recognized the abolitionist newspaperman William Lloyd Garrison and John Greenleaf Whittier, the new editor of *The Pennsylvania Freeman*.

"Did you hear?" asked Billy.

Billy's third attempt at a conversation was hard to disregard. "Hear what?"

"There was a wedding yesterday. An African married a white woman down on Spruce Street."

"That's not true. That wedding was between two white people, Miss Grimké and Mr. Weld."

"That's not the way I heard it. There were Africans there and everything. They're amalgamators."

As soon as she heard the word, Rian thought about Logan and Martha. "Where did you hear that? It's not true."

"My dad was talking about it at dinner last night. He thinks something should be done about it."

Before Rian could respond, a landau stopped almost in front of them to let off its passengers. Rian knew the carriage. Krieger Coach had built it three years ago for James Forten's son-in-law, Robert Purvis. The first person out of the carriage was Jules, dressed in his Sunday best. Jules turned and extended his hand to Maddie to help her step out of the carriage. Next came light-skinned Robert Purvis. Robert turned and offered his hand to assist his wife Harriet.

Billy elbowed Rian in the side. "See, they're all amalgamators. I'm going to tell my dad." Before Rian could respond, Billy was gone. Rian considered following him to tell him that Robert and Harriet Purvis were not amalgamators because they were both Black when she noticed others in the crowd watching Purvis and his wife walk into Pennsylvania Hall. They had obviously come to the same conclusion as Billy.

Rian turned to walk the eleven blocks to Krieger Coach. *This is awful. Half the people in that crowd are there only to stir up trouble. I know how this is going to end. James Forten knows it. Can't anyone stop this? I guess my only question is, when is it going to happen?*

* * * * *

· JULES ·

I knew we shouldn't have come tonight, Jules thought to himself.

So many out-of-towners had traveled to Philadelphia to attend the Anti-Slavery Convention of American Women that local abolitionists had opened their homes to accommodate them. Otto Krieger had graciously offered one of his bedrooms to Lucretia's overflow, a twenty-two-year-old woman from New York City named Juliana Tappan.

In honor of Miss Tappan's presence, Otto had invited Jules and Maddie Freeman to join them for dinner. Conversation had been awkward from the moment they arrived. It didn't take long for Jules to suspect that they were socializing with an abolitionist who didn't want anything to do with Negroes.

As the diners were taking their last bites of salmon, a knock on the door signaled the arrival of additional visitors: publisher William Lloyd Garrison and Lewis Tappan, Juliana's father. "We've been house-hopping all evening," announced Garrison as he settled into a chair next to Jules. "It is positively balmy outside. The neighborhood is crawling with convention-goers visiting one another."

Miss Tappan became more animated once the visitors joined the table. "Mr. Garrison, what has been the reaction of people to your rebuttal of Mr. Brown's keynote address? Your disdain for his definition of immediacy was quite evident."

Garrison nodded to Miss Tappan in appreciation of her question. "Oh, I think most people were supportive. Poor Brown. He tried to offend no one, and he ended up disappointing everyone. He claimed he was for the immediate abolition of slavery, then he humiliated himself and the movement by defining *immediate* in wishy-washy terms. *Immediate* to him meant demanding that slaveholders immediately start giving their chattel time to learn to read and earn money. It meant that babies born right now become free when they reach a certain age. That isn't immediate. It's not a solution. I hope a chorus of white voices, both male and female, join me and more stridently demand an immediate end to slavery—a real immediate end, not Browns's namby-pamby end."

Garrison noted that Jules stirred uneasily next to him. "Does what I say make you uncomfortable, Mr. Freeman?"

Jules silently chastised himself for allowing his emotions to be so evident, even in such benign company. "I am resolute as we all work hard to bring an end to slavery, but I know there will be repercussions. There is a history in our city . . . When the successes of the free Black community in Philadelphia become too prominent, someone is sure to declare that we are getting too big a slice of the pie. That gives free rein to a lurking, malicious element that is all too happy to smack us down. So, my suspicion is this: When white folks with good intentions—and that includes all of you at this table—advocate for the freedom of my brethren who remain in chains, the people who pay the penalty will be the free Negroes of Philadelphia."

"Do you feel vulnerable, Mr. Freeman?"

"Of course. My name appears in anti-Negro newspapers every once in a while."

"For what?"

"Well, until recently, my greatest notoriety had been that I was a Black foreman in charge of whites at Krieger Coach, Otto's factory. Then in '36, I started my own business, Freeman Hydraulics. We make fire pumps."

"My friend Jules is being far too modest," Otto interjected. "Freeman Hydraulics makes the first steam-powered fire pumps that we know of. In the world, that is. In fact, one of them was used to fight the fire at Nicholas I's palace in St. Petersburg. It was still running after thirty hours. Then this winter, the Board of the Pennsylvania Hall Association asked him to take over the construction of the Hall. His crews finished three weeks ahead of schedule. And, by the way, while he was occupied running both my factory and the Hall construction, Maddie took over the running of Freeman Hydraulics."

Garrison bowed forward in his chair in acknowledgment of the accomplishments. "Very impressive, Mr. and Mrs. Freeman. But besides setting an entrepreneurial example for the Black community, do you engage in no other activities to advance the cause of your race?"

Even amongst these dinner guests—all abolitionists—Jules silently invoked Rule Number 1: *They don't need to know. I don't tell them.* "No, Mr. Garrison, I resigned my committee positions to devote time to the Pennsylvania Hall project. My days have been filled."

"I must confess, I am a bit disappointed. You are in a position to do so much more," said Garrison.

The unfairness of Garrison's words stung, but Jules didn't rise to the bait. "My plate has been full enough, sir."

"Well, perhaps someday you will find time to start lecturing."

Jules placed his hand on Maddie's. "Oh, I think one speaker in the family is enough."

Garrison turned to Maddie. "Oh-ho! Mrs. Freeman, are the convention-goers going to hear from you this week?"

"I am on the schedule for Thursday afternoon, when PFASS meets without men present. I must confess, I am a little nervous about speaking to such a large audience. I am glad it won't be a promiscuous[15] one."

"And what is going to be your topic, Mrs. Freeman?"

"I have been asked to speak on the topic of amalgamation. I am going to point out that the amalgamation so prevalent in this country has occurred through the violation of Black women by their white male enslavers. It seems rather ironic that those who object so vociferously to amalgamation seem to minimize that point. However, I am going to stress that equality and fraternization between the races does not mean that they will inevitably intermarry."

Jules inwardly winced at the thought of Maddie's upcoming speech. At this moment, it seemed rather hypocritical, given that Martha was pregnant with an Irish boy's baby.

Garrison pulled a piece of paper out of his breast pocket, unfolded it, and handed it to Maddie. "I tore this off a tree near Pennsylvania Hall. I believe that your speech may be received like Mr. Brown's. You may end up pleasing no one."

Jules and Maddie read it together.

PENNSYLVANIA HALL—A TEMPLE OF AMALGAMATION!

---

15. In this era, an audience was considered "promiscuous" if it included both men and women. Most people of both sexes considered it unseemly for women to address a promiscuous gathering.

CITIZENS OF PHILADELPHIA
THE EVIDENCE IS THERE FOR YOU TO BEHOLD YOURSELVES.

WHITES AND AFRICANS
PARADING ARM-IN-ARM DOWN THE FASHIONABLE
PROMENADES OF OUR CITY.

SITTING TOGETHER AS IF THEY ARE EQUALS.

ORATING FOR AN END TO THE CONSTITUTIONAL RIGHTS
OF HONEST CITIZENS.

THESE AMALGAMATORS MUST BE STOPPED!

VOICE YOUR DISPLEASURE
AT THE INTERSECTION OF SIXTH AND HAINES STREETS
AT 11:00 AM WEDNESDAY, MAY 16
INTERFERE, FORCIBLY IF IT IS NECESSARY.

Maddie passed the broadside around the table. "I doubt that I will be speaking to the people that this document is intended for, Mr. Garrison. Hopefully, the women in Pennsylvania Hall on Thursday will be a little more receptive."

Lewis Tappan, who had been silent up to this point, straightened in his chair, then leaned forward and put his elbows on the table. "I'm afraid that my friend Mr. Garrison is trying to goad me into stating my true beliefs, which in the spirit of open discussion at this table, I will now lay out." Tappan took a sip of his brandy and then a deep breath. "Mrs. Freeman, I stand in opposition to your basic premise."

Maddie smiled at Tappan. "You think fraternization will lead to amalgamation?"

"I believe that amalgamation is in fact the only solution to the problem of race in our country. In contrast to the equal but separate future that you envision, Mrs. Freeman, I dream of an America populated by copper-skinned citizens. That is the only way that race will no longer be used to define who we are."

Jules was shocked. "Do you mean that you are in favor of amalgamation, or you see it as inevitable?"

"It is what I would like to see in America. I believe that as long as there are black skins and white skins in this country, Blacks will suffer. The social stigma against marriage between Black and white must be removed. Of course it may take many generations for us to get there. I acknowledge that these sentiments are extreme. Even in my own family."

Juliana shifted uncomfortably in her chair. She looked down at the table. "My father and I do not see eye-to-eye on many topics, including my own judgment. I am a member of the Ladies' New York City Anti-Slavery Society. Father does not approve of that organization because it doesn't allow Black women to become members."

"What my daughter is saying is that although she works passionately for an end to slavery, she has no interest in advocating for social equality between the races. In fact, I would wager a hundred dollars that this evening is the first time that Juliana has ever broken bread with a Negro."

Juliana threw her napkin on the table and rose from her chair. "Papa, you are insufferable! You had no right to say that." She strode to the front door and stormed out of the house, slamming the door behind her.

Tappan also rose from his chair. "Ladies and gentlemen, please excuse me. Sometimes I can't resist pointing out to my daughter some of the contradictions in her life. Now I must follow her and see if I can hammer home the lessons of this evening's discussion."

Garrison smiled after Tappan closed the front door behind him. "Poor Tappan. He and Juliana have scrapped ever since she was a little girl. The sad thing is, he doesn't recognize his own hypocrisies."

Jules was still reeling from the thought of a copper-skinned America. "His vision of America's future is the most optimistic one that I have ever heard. What hypocrisy could there be in that?"

"Tappan wants to see equality between the races but sees no need for it between the sexes. For instance, if men were allowed to attend your speech on Thursday, Mrs. Freeman, I doubt he would honor you with his presence. He has no interest in hearing what women have to say in public, nor would he ever work with a woman on a committee. He criticizes Juliana's activity with the Ladies' New York City Anti-Slavery Society because it won't admit Black women, but he would be apoplectic if it were an organization that also admitted men."

Maddie stood to clear some of the plates from the table. "And you don't share his sentiments, Mr. Garrison?"

"Not at all. And I witness hypocrisies amongst our fellow conventioneers that make it difficult to bite my tongue."

"Such as?"

"We all patted ourselves on the back for sitting with our Black brethren in the audience the past two days, yet not a single Black man—a Black woman would have been far too much to ask—was asked to speak at the dedication.

We would have been far better off hearing from James Forten, Robert Purvis, or even yourselves, Mr. and Mrs. Freeman."

Jules gave a brief nod of gratification to Garrison's sentiments but said nothing.

Garrison was just getting started. "Women such as Mrs. Mott have put a tremendous amount of effort into the free produce movement, yet I know in my heart the movement is doomed. Those very people who decry the sin of slavery are only too happy to purchase cheap cotton goods created by slave labor. In our alleged Temple of Freedom, only passing mention has been made of the plight of the American Indian. At this very moment, General Scott is evicting the last of the Cherokee from their ancestral homeland in Georgia. The United States Army is attacking the Seminoles in the Florida Territory for their twin sins of refusing to bow to the will of the American government and harboring fugitive slaves. To me, it makes no difference if a man's skin is black or red. It is a crime if he is being oppressed. Not all my friends share my opinion."

Otto stirred uneasily at the head of the table. "Mr. Garrison, you have deepened the level of discourse at my table this evening, and in honor of your candor, I offer this confession. My factory is days away from completing a narrow-gauge locomotive that will shortly be shipped to a sugar plantation in Cuba. I conjecture that, in your opinion, that sale makes me as guilty as the people who purchase slave-tainted cotton goods."

Garrison regarded Otto for a few heartbeats. "Otto, I believe that each of us is responsible for judging our own level of culpability in this sinful system. I certainly have my own opinion, but it is not my responsibility to share it with you. I will ask you this question, however: Do you think your actions help to perpetuate the sin of slavery?"

Otto stared at the table. He fingered his dessert fork. He looked up, not at Garrison, but at Jules and Maddie. "Yes, I do."

The table fell silent. No one seemed willing to either pursue this thread or change the subject. Jules raised his glass to Garrison. "You have great clarity in your sentiments, sir. Perhaps you have helped us all to see the ramifications of our actions."

Garrison raised his own glass. "I would say my sentiments put me at the extreme end of this discussion. Shared guilt for the sin of slavery. Equality among the races. Equality between the sexes. I have made more enemies than friends for my beliefs. Including, I might add, amongst the fairer sex."

"I understand there is a price on your head," said Jules.

Garrison nodded. "The Georgia legislature has honored me by offering a $5,000 reward to anyone who can kidnap me and transport me to Atlanta for trial."

"And what was your crime?"

"Oh, take your pick. Sending seditious material through the mail. Inciting slave rebellion. Disrespect of the Constitution."

Otto raised a teapot, a silent query if anyone wanted more tea.

Jules passed his cup to Otto. "You don't fear kidnapping here in Philadelphia? It would be quite easy for those who wish you ill to make it happen. We are only miles away from two slave states."

"I was almost tarred and feathered in Boston a few years ago. I was arrested to save me from the mob's wrath. I have faith in the justice of my cause and the beneficence of our Maker."

"I'm sure Elijah Lovejoy[16] felt the same way," said Jules. "The mob in St. Louis disagreed. He is now a martyr to the cause."

"And perhaps I shall become a martyr as well."

The broadside had now been passed around the table, giving Jules the opportunity to read it again. "I saw a sheet yesterday that was similar to this one. It seems to me that someone is intent on stirring up trouble. The way this reads, though, the trouble is going to start in the northern part of the city. Pennsylvania Hall is only four blocks from here. My home, and much of Philadelphia's Black population, is in Moyamensing, well over a mile to the south. If my theory is correct, even if it starts up here, the trouble will surely migrate to my neighborhood."

Garrison wiped his mouth with his napkin, then tossed the napkin onto the table. "I never underestimate my fellow man's propensity for evil. But in this case, I believe Pennsylvania Hall is safe. My understanding is that your Mayor Swift is not inclined to allow a bunch of hooligans to rule the streets. Especially—and it pains me to say this—in the more prosperous sections of the city."

* * * * *

· SEAMUS ·

Seamus sat at a table near the back of McSweeney's Saloon with three members of the United No Name Fire Brigade when Braden McSweeney approached them. "Seamus, there's a guy at the bar I think you ought to meet."

---

16. Elijah Lovejoy was an abolitionist newspaper editor who died defending his printing press from a mob on November 6, 1837. His assailants were tried starting in January 1838. The jury foreman was suspected of having been a member of the mob. All assailants were declared not guilty.

Seamus excused himself from the No Names and walked to the bar to find a man who could have been forty or could have been sixty. His hair was thick, without any gray, but his face was lined, and he stood with a distinct stoop. He was shorter than Seamus, with a tentative smile and a well-worn suit that smelled like it had gone too many days in a row without a good cleaning.

"Seamus," said Braden, "this is Mr. Ruben Hasselbach. He has brought in some whiskey for me to sample. I think you should take a sip."

"I hope it's better than that shyte you were serving us the other day, Braden. Me boys are talking about setting up shop someplace else if you don't find a new supplier."

Braden poured a splash into a glass and pushed it toward Seamus. "Quit your yammering and take a sip of this."

Seamus sniffed at his glass; raised his eyebrows and returned Hasselbach's gaze with approval. He took a sip. Seamus always expected the first sip of a new glass to have a bit of a bite. Every case that Braden brought up from the basement seemed to have a new taste; some pretty reasonable, some downright awful, none wonderful. His first sip of Hasselbach's whiskey was smooth, rich, with the faint taste of roasted barley. "I think that this whiskey would generate more than a bit of loyalty, Braden. You definitely should start serving it and get rid of that other stuff."

Hasselbach lifted the bottle and poured more of the brown liquid into Seamus's glass. "That's the thing. I only brought a couple of cases with me from western Pennsylvania. That's where I started my life in the distilling business."

"That's a long way to ship a cask of whiskey, but I suppose Braden could make a profit by selling this for a bit more than we're used to paying."

Braden poured himself three fingers. "Mr. Hasselbach isn't interested in shipping whiskey from western Pennsylvania. He's interested in making it here in Philadelphia."

Hasselbach bowed slightly to Braden, then turned to Seamus. "I'm interested in exploring the possibility. I've had some health issues recently. My daughter and her husband have volunteered to take care of me, so I've moved in with them here in Moyamensing. I only know one trade: distilling whiskey; as you can taste, it's very fine whiskey. I want to start a distilling business here in Philadelphia. But I have no money."

Seamus raised his glass in salute. "Well, Mr. Hasselbach, I think you walked into the right saloon."

* * * * *

· OTTO ·

Otto escorted the last of the house-hoppers out of his home. As his next-door neighbor Lucretia was doing the same thing, he walked across the grass to her brick walkway. "Good evening, Lucretia. It's late. You must be exhausted."

"Exhausted, elated, worried."

"I think I understand all those things. How were your evening conversations?"

"Oh, we talked mostly about the free produce movement. Everyone is extremely excited about it but, I must confess, a bit pessimistic about its long-term success."

"James no longer trades in slave-tainted goods. Has that affected your family's circumstances?"

"A combination of the Panic and the higher price of our slave-free goods, but yes. We are tight to the line but determined to weather it out. Could I ever convince thee to join us?"

Otto smiled down at his much shorter neighbor. "As a result of your influence, I have already cut back quite a bit on cotton goods, sugar, molasses, and rice. William Garrison and Lewis Tappan stopped by for dessert. They both had a great deal to say. Until this evening, I was not rigid about purchasing slave-tainted goods, but given Mr. Garrison's persuasive argument, I believe that is about to change."

"I am gratified by that, but I was thinking of a more significant commitment."

"And what is that?"

Lucretia hesitated a moment, as if she were considering betraying a confidence. "Rian told me that Krieger Locomotive is building a machine to haul sugar cane on a plantation in Cuba."

"Yes, that is true. It will be the second one I have shipped there."

"Otto, there is not a grain of sugar that is produced on Cuba without slave labor. By selling to those slaveholders, thee is only one step removed from perpetuating this system."

Otto turned his eyes to the night sky. "If I didn't know better, I would think you and Garrison are colluding. His statements have started me questioning my own actions. But the Krieger companies are barely hanging on as it is. This depression has already put three Philadelphia locomotive manufacturers out of business. I have my livelihood to think of. My daughter. My employees."

"And that is the response of every cotton mill owner in Lawrence, Massachusetts. Every shipbuilder up and down the coast who builds the ships that haul the sugar. Every rum distiller within two miles from here. The manufacturing economy of the North is inextricably tied to the slave economy of the South. Those few of us who object to the institution of slavery make a great show of objecting to the abomination of it all, but state more strongly in our actions—our everyday actions in our personal and our business lives—that our beliefs are shallow. When we help these plantation owners to prosper, we say we are willing to perpetuate slavery because it makes our lives easier."

"Lucretia, it is not that it makes my life easier. It is essential in order to keep my factories afloat."

"Dear Otto, I know that I am asking a lot of thee. But I will leave thee with this thought. Thy daughter became a conductor for Jules and Maddie at age twelve. She ran away to Russia at age thirteen. I suspect that in the next few years, her willfulness will become even more pronounced. When she starts to make the connections that we adults are capable of making, how do thee want her to view the decisions that thee has made in thy life?"

"Well, I assume Rian will absorb the wisdom of the man she marries."

Lucretia stepped back a bit. "Otto, I do not in the least bit criticize thy decisions as a parent. In fact, I applaud them. But what evidence does thee cite that Rian will ever knuckle under to the will of a husband? Did thee hear about the Grimké-Weld wedding?"

"I heard that there were both Black and white in attendance and it all went peacefully."

"But I am referring to the fact that Angelina pointedly omitted the words *to obey* from her wedding vows. If Rian becomes the young woman I expect she will become, I see her making a similar omission."

"Have you been talking to Jules? He frequently cautions me to let Rian set her own course. My nephew Seamus takes a similar view. And this evening at dinner, Mr. Garrison spouted all sorts of nonsense about women becoming the equal of men. I have problems with that."

"Thee may have problems with it, but I suspect thee will have bigger problems if thee doesn't listen to thy daughter over the next few years. She is a force."

The conversation made Otto uncomfortable. He decided to end it as diplomatically as he could. "Well, Lucretia, we have strayed from your original question. I promise to examine my business practices as well as my household decisions in light of their connection to slavery."

"And that, Beloved Neighbor, is no small task. I have confidence that thee will make a well-reasoned decision."

WEDNESDAY, MAY 16

· OTTO ·

Rian entered the Krieger Coach office. "*Vater*, I found Harry and told him you wanted to speak to him. He had some things to finish, but he said he'd be over directly."

As she had done since she returned from Russia three weeks ago, she buried herself in the accounting of the three Krieger factories. Five minutes later, Harry Vogel, foreman of Krieger Locomotive, entered without knocking.

"*Sie wollten mich sehen, Herr Krieger* [You asked to see me, Mr. Krieger]?"

"Thank you for coming over," Otto said without getting up from his desk. "Number 14, the locomotive that we are building for the plantation in Cuba, I would like you to stop production on it. I have written them today and canceled the contract. Bump the next one up in line. Where is that one going?"

"Why, that one's going to the *Camden & Amboy*, but they don't expect delivery for a couple of months."

"Then they will be pleased when we deliver early."

"Sir, I can't stop production on an engine. I have no place to store it. It's going to be in the way. It will take days to put everything right again."

"And it will be your job to figure that out."

"May I ask why you have canceled the contract?"

"Yes, you may. I have decided that the three Krieger factories will no longer sell to slaveholders."

"You are going to turn down business because these customers own slaves?"

"Yes, and feel free to tell the men my reason."

Harry turned on his heel and slammed the door on the way out. Otto heard a loud bang seconds later that he assumed was an ash can kicked hard.

Rian put down her steel-tipped pen and looked at Otto. "*Harry ist verärgert* [Harry is upset]."

"Harry has a right to be. I have interfered with his schedule."

Rian ran her finger down one page of her ledger. "*Vater*, are you really going to go through with this?"

"Yes, I made the decision this morning as I walked to work. Garrison and Lucretia have convinced me that by trading with these people, I am helping to perpetuate the slave system."

Rian paged further back through her ledger. "We sold one locomotive to Puerto Rico and another to Louisiana while I was gone. That's a third of our business."

"Then I guess you should take that as an indication of how strongly I believe in the decision."

Rian paged back and forth in the ledger for another minute, as if to glean every ort of information she could out of the numbers. Finally, she looked up at Otto. "*Vater*, I'm proud of you."

"Thank you, *Leibling*, that means a lot to me. I made this decision because of you."

"Me? I never . . ."

Otto put up his hand. "No, we have never talked about this. But if you haven't already, you will soon become aware of the connection between Northern businesses and the plight of millions of people held in bondage. I don't want the Krieger companies and myself to be judged harshly by that young woman."

"*Vater*, thank you for telling me this. I will remember this day as long as I live."

Otto got up from his desk. "And now I must go drum up some more business to make up for my crazed moral decisions and see if I can figure out how to get that Cuba engine out of Harry's way."

* * * * *

· MADDIE ·

Maddie, sitting in the third row on the main floor of the Grand Saloon in Pennsylvania Hall, started at the sound of shattering glass. A stone thrown from Haines Street crashed through a window thirty feet to Maddie's right, hit the louvered interior shutter, and clattered down to the sill. *The first but I fear not the last*, Maddie thought. *They grow bolder in the darkness.* The hate-filled jeers of a crowd that was becoming a mob snaked through the broken pane and the shutter and competed with Mr. Garrison speaking at the dais.

Maddie paid little attention to Garrison. All day, she had listened to men debate in the small meeting rooms and Grand Saloon. Some discussions centered on the evils of slavery. Other topics included Cherokee removal, the plight of the Seminoles, the role of armed self-defense in the movement in light of the death of Elijah Lovejoy, the morality of women speaking to a promiscuous audience, and the contradictions between the Declaration of Independence and the very existence of slavery.

During an intermission, Maddie stepped outside for a breath of fresh air. She noted that the crowd in front of the Hall had grown in the hour since the last break. *Mostly curiosity seekers*, she judged. *People who heard that Blacks and whites were meeting as equals in a public space and wanted to see it with their own eyes.* When she made eye contact with someone, she would give a nod. Sometimes they smiled and nodded back. Mostly, though, they looked away.

At the end of the afternoon sessions, conventioneers dispersed to cafés, hotels, or private homes. When Maddie arrived for the evening session, she feared the broadsides that had been prominently posted around the city had done their wicked work. The crowd outside Pennsylvania Hall had swollen into a sullen cesspool. Men carried shillelaghs,[17] pitchforks, and torches.

Many of Maddie's friends and acquaintances, both Black and white, had chosen to stay away from the evening session. Those who returned passed along rumors of impending violence. As Maddie took her seat between Lucretia Mott and Angelina Grimké, she surveyed the Grand Saloon and estimated that a thousand female conventioneers and a hundred men had ignored the ominous rumors to listen to Garrison and witness women speaking to both men and women. *There were three thousand people in the Grand Saloon this afternoon. The mob has already bullied us.*

Mr. Garrison railed on, seemingly unintimidated by the mob outside. Maddie surreptitiously peered at Lucretia to her left and Angelina to her right. Both seemed enrapt by Mr. Garrison's oration. *Much as I appreciate sitting with these two fine women, I would feel much safer if Jules were here holding my hand.* The thought of her beloved Jules caused her to reflexively glance to the rear of the Saloon. Jules, Otto Krieger, and a mixed group of Black and white men were standing guard at the doors. *Please keep us and yourself safe, dear husband.*

Outside, a mob grew more raucous. They yelled and chanted. Somehow, they knew that it was the hated Garrison who was speaking.

Not long ago, when I thought about this week, my biggest apprehension was speaking about amalgamation in front of a large audience.

The stone thrower who shattered the window moments ago inspired others. A shower of rocks pelted the side of the building. Some broke windows, but they could not penetrate the shutters.

---

17. A shillelagh is an Irish walking stick stout enough to be used as a club.

Then Martha tells us she is pregnant with the child of an Irish boy, making my speech about the bogeyman of amalgamation seem quite hollow.

"Amalgamation abomination! Amalgamation abomination! Amalgamation abomination!" chanted the crowd outside.

The mob's threshold for what constitutes amalgamation is pretty low. By sitting next to two white women, that makes us all amalgamators.

A group of ruffians forced their way into the hall but were pummeled and shoved back by the guards.

Maddie turned at the commotion. *Not low-class ruffians. These men were well dressed. Does everyone hate us?*

Mr. Garrison finished his hour-long speech and announced Angelina Grimké Weld as the next speaker. The mob outside raged.

They hate her most of all. She is a Southerner, the daughter of slave owners. A traitor to her race, made more odious by the horrifying and untrue rumors that she married a Black man on Monday. The mob feeds on lies and hate.

Grimké Weld spoke for almost an hour, heroically yelling over the mob outside.

She was unwilling to be cowed by their threats.

They were unwilling to allow her to speak unchallenged.

A smattering of agitators who had entered the building masquerading as abolitionists rose to yell obscenities at Grimké Weld. Maddie turned at the ruckus and saw Jules and Otto manhandle one of the troublemakers out of the saloon.

"I will not be silenced as I exercise my constitutional right to free speech," announced Grimké as the men barred the doors. She received a thunder of applause from the audience and increased howls from outside.

Juliana Tappan and one other female speaker followed. At the end of the evening's orations, Lucretia rose from her seat and climbed the three steps to the platform. "I would like to remind the audience that not all in attendance this evening agreed about the propriety of women speaking to a promiscuous audience. Therefore, this assemblage was not an official meeting of the Anti-Slavery Convention of American Women. I hope that such notions of delicacy and propriety will not live much longer in this enlightened country."

At least that's one thing that isn't causing me distress at the moment. I believe that any woman should have the right to speak to a mixed-gender group. I am thankful that my husband fully supports me in this.

Lucretia gave the dais one sharp rap of her gavel. "It is 10:00 P.M. I now declare this meeting to be adjourned. We hope to see you all at our sessions tomorrow. In the morning we will discuss the free produce movement. In the afternoon, numerous speakers will orate on topics such as amalgamation, violence in other parts of our country against both Negroes and Indians, and the creation of new anti-slavery newspapers."

Maddie stood and quickly assessed the demeanor of the convention-goers. *After a normal meeting, or in church, people typically smile greetings to one another. They socialize. They rise or sit, talk with friends or scurry out. Maybe they congratulate the speaker and move gradually toward the doorway.* On this night, everyone in the audience rose in unison, thankful to finally be released from their seats. But then, in anticipation of the threat that waited for them outside, a thousand faces looked around expectantly, unable or unwilling to take the next step. *Oh my goodness, how frightened we all are.*

Lucretia descended from the dais and found Maddie. "Link arms, dear Maddie. We sisters shall leave the building together." The two of them strode up the aisle.

"Join arms with your sisters," both Lucretia and Maddie exhorted the women as they passed. "Join arms with your sisters. They won't harm us if we pair up Black and white together."

Can Lucretia really be so intrepid? thought Maddie. *Or is she like me—making a show of confidence for the rest of the women here?*

Maddie and Lucretia, still arm-in-arm, were the first to leave the Hall. Maddie was astounded at the size of the mob. *I figured it was probably three thousand people when we arrived. It must be twice that now.* These people were no longer sullen. Their torch-lit faces were belligerent, whipped to a fever by hate, alcohol, and numbers.

Oh Lord, please part this sea of evil and keep my sisters safe.

Maddie and Lucretia waded into the raging mob. Miraculously, the hostile sea opened before them, but the narrow corridor became a gauntlet of taunts and threats. Female delegates to the Anti-Slavery Convention of American Women followed behind, also marching two-by-two.

How many are there? Four thousand? Six thousand? Maddie had no way to judge. It all occurred in a blur. Men and boys shouting bile-filled words. Torches. Spittle. Distorted faces. Clubs, axes, shillelaghs, sledgehammers; all wielded overhead. Maddie feared that at any moment a first blow would be struck and would start a bloody slaughter.

Mercifully, the blows didn't descend.

Thursday, May 17

· JULES ·

The next morning, Jules and Homer Good walked to Pennsylvania Hall at dawn to start cleaning up debris in and around the building. Glaziers arrived midmorning to replace the fifty or so broken window panes. Three sets of interior shutters were beyond repair and would have to wait to be replaced until after the convention ended.

"Could have been worse," Jules muttered.

A crowd that Jules judged to be more curious than hostile churned across the street. Men and women, young and old, "respectable" and scruffy, filtered in, conversed with those who had preceded them and again with those who followed, then walked away. *And not a Black face among them. Our brethren are staying away.*

Over time, gawkers were replaced by those of a more menacing demeanor. The hostility became more palpable.

An emergency session of the Pennsylvania Hall Association Board ended and Jules's friend, the barber Fred Hinton, found him.

"How did it go?" asked Jules.

"Not good," said Hinton. "A delegation met with Mayor Swift to ask him for protection tonight. He was more interested in determining if the city will be responsible for any damages as a result of mob action." Hinton pulled a paper out of his pocket. "Daniel Neall wrote down his exact words. 'There are always two sides to a question—it is public opinion makes mobs—and 99 out of 100 of those with whom I converse are against you.' Neall got the impression that Swift won't be calling the militia to protect us tonight."

Jules stared at the crowd across the street, now well into the hundreds. "So it's up to us."

"No, it gets worse. Our legal eagles have weighed in. They claim that if we take any action to resist the rioters, it could be deemed a provocation. That will jeopardize any future demand on our part for damage compensation under the riot law."

"So by protecting Pennsylvania Hall, we will be provoking the rioters."

"That's about the size of it. And Jules, the board is encouraging us to stay away tonight."

"By *us*, I assume you don't mean convention goers."

"Right. *Us* means Negroes, both men and women. Our presence would also be a provocation." Hinton was so frustrated, his eyes began to water. "Jules, I suggest that you go inside and say goodbye to the building you've put your heart and soul into for the last four months. I don't think it's going to be here tomorrow."

* * * * *

· SEAMUS ·

Seamus left the restless crowd in front of Pennsylvania Hall to do a complete circumnavigation of the building. He didn't like what he saw. Clots of people loitered on the sidewalks and streets. Some groups seemed merely curious. Others were more purposeful, searching by the light of day for weaknesses in the new building's architecture.

He eyed Jules Freeman talking to someone in front of the Hall, but rather than approach his friend, he parked himself on the corner of Haines and Sixth Streets to watch the crowd watch Jules.

"I heard you came back from Russia with your tail between your legs. How long you been back, kid?"

Seamus turned to see his old nemesis, Hugh Callaghan, standing next to him with his hands in his pockets. Like Seamus, Hugh's attention was focused on the crowd.

"Three weeks."

"I also heard that weasel Dylan wasn't interested in moving over and handing back the presidency of No Name Fire Brigade. Don't mind telling you, Seamus, that's what you get for deserting them."

"Ah, you're making too big of a deal of it, Hugh. I didn't push too hard. I'm happy to keep my hand in if I'm needed, but it's good that Dylan keeps the lead. After what I saw in Russia, no fire in Philadelphia's going to impress me much."

"So what're you doing here then?"

Seamus shrugged. "I figured I should survey the place by the light of day. If the rumors are true, I figure this might be one of the occasions I'd be useful."

"Don't you love democracy?"

Hugh's out-of-the-blue comment took Seamus aback. He turned his attention away from Pennsylvania Hall. "What do you mean?"

"Majority rule. One of the fundamental tenets of our Constitution. Here's how I see it. These abolitionists have gone too far. When folks get too far away from what the bulk of the people think is appropriate, then it's the responsibility of the people to put them back in their place."

"And how's that supposed to happen?"

"Oh, I suspect that before too long, they'll start by burning this place down. I'm surprised they didn't do it last night, so I'm betting it'll be tonight. If not, then some other night. Soon though."

"So you condone a mob torching this place? Last I heard, arson is against the law."

"What you don't understand, kid, is that it's about community standards."

"What do you mean, 'community standards'?"

"It's the sensibilities of the body politic. You can pass all the fancy laws you want. Try to legislate fairness into your precious system. But ultimately, it's the community that decides what is appropriate and what has just plain gone too far."

"And by the community, you mean a mob."

"If that's what it takes, yeah. But it's not really a mob; it's citizens exercising their rights. I consider it the purest form of democracy. Direct action."

"Every self-appointed committee at the edge of town with tar and feathers or a noose. Is that direct action?"

"In my opinion, yes."

"And what part of this process is democratic?"

Hugh chuckled, obviously pleased that Seamus had taken his bait. "Ah, Seamus, sometimes democracy needs a little nudge."

"A little nudge. Is that what you think mobocracy is? I think you better be careful what you wish for, Hugh. The problem with mobs is that once their blood is up, there's no controlling them."

"Let me give you a piece of advice, Seamus. When and if this place starts to burn, don't try to put it out."

"If that's what you want, what are you doing here?"

"Just because Pennsylvania Hall should be destroyed, these other buildings don't need to suffer. I'm planning where to position me boys to hose down the neighbors so they don't burn as well."

"So if the fire bell goes off, you won't try to put it out?"

"Not a chance. And if your little outfit tries to do it, you're sure to take a licking. If not from Moya, then any other fire brigade that answers the call. You got no friends in this fight, kid."

"We'll have to see how it goes, Hugh. Seems we've all got our roles to play. Speaking of rumors, I heard Siobhan broke it off with Mikey McGuire."

"Yeah, my daughter and I had a little heart-to-heart about that. Turns out Mr. McGuire has a taste for opium. I don't think she wanted to spend the rest of her life wiping Mikey's arse."

"Nine months ago, I said I wanted to marry her, and you told me that you would end the truce between Moya and No Name if I did. Is that still the deal?"

"Well, I'll tell you, Seamus, I admit that Mikey was a bit of a disappointment, and there's no one in the neighborhood who has the balls to keep Siobhan in line. So that puts you back in contention. You went off to Russia to make your fortune. You came back nine months later with a pretty suit and what seems to be a little bit less of that beautiful Irish brogue of yours. You've lost an interest in firefighting. I haven't heard any rumors that you're back to lifting anything big from the piers. I'll make you a deal. You show me that you're making something of yourself in the next couple of months, I'll reconsider. Until then, you keep your distance from my daughter."

Despite the fact that Hugh had pretty much guaranteed that Pennsylvania Hall was as good as burned down, and if Seamus tried to prevent it, he would get a thrashing, he left his encounter with Hugh quite elated.

Because I've got an idea how I'm going to make me fortune—I mean my fortune—and that means I've still got a chance to marry Siobhan.

* * * * *

11:45 A.M.

· JULES ·

Jules and Homer sat in the front pew of the Grand Saloon for half an hour.

Jules was angry and agitated. He had worked for four months for virtually no wages in order to gain shares of Pennsylvania Hall. His dreams of sharing in the profit from rent of the Hall's ground floor operations and stream of conventions were disintegrating. *All this time, I've been silently critical of Otto Krieger for accepting payment in the form of railroad stock. I thought I was the smart one. Now, maybe he's been the smart one after all. Or perhaps both of us have made unwise decisions.*

All his life, Jules had tamped down his resentments and chosen instead to concentrate on the many blessings in his life. This felt like it might be the last straw. His anger was a hairbreadth away from boiling over. But there was something else gnawing at him. He was surprisingly wistful. "No one is ever going to know that this beautiful building was built by crews of Black and white men," he muttered to himself.

"And one Black girl," Homer added, which surprised Jules that he had spoken loud enough to be heard. "The people who matter will remember. They'll know you were the man that made it happen. It couldn't have been done without you."

"I suppose it was too much to ask."

The sound of three sharp blows coming from the front of the building drew Jules's attention and he left his words unexplained to Homer. "The crowd is getting restless. C'mon, let's get out of here." *Maybe I should take down the plaque and save it as a memento. If my role in this project is going to be erased from history, at least it can become part of my family's story.*

As Jules and Homer left the building, they faced a more hostile crowd across Sixth Street than when they had gone in. Jules turned to lock the door, only to notice Hugh Callaghan reading the brass plaque. "Hugh, what are you doing here?"

"I was talking to Seamus Gallagher. It's good to have the kid back in town. Now I'll have someone else besides you to kick around. Jules, there's a lot of people watching us right now, so play your part."

"What's that supposed to mean?"

Hugh wagged his finger in Jules's face. "I'm going to give you some information, but I sure don't want those bully boys across the street to know it, so listen up. You know this building is as good as gone, right?"

Jules felt no need to respond.

Callaghan put his hands on his hips and leaned toward Jules. "This isn't going to be a one-night affair," he continued, "If they don't burn Pennsylvania Hall tonight, they'll be back tomorrow night."

"Thanks for the information," Jules said sarcastically.

Callaghan put his hands to his head, as if vehemently disagreeing with something Jules had just said. "And Jules, watch out. Our old friend is back in town."

"Who?"

"Austin T. Slatter. And here's a bit of news for you. He's brought his little brother with him."

"Why should that concern me? He doesn't know I burned his slave ship."

"You think Slatter needs an excuse to hurt you? Austin Slatter and Jules Freeman have a long history. Believe me, he's got it in for you."

"How do you know that?"

"Read the plaque. Slatter was here three minutes ago. He took a paving stone to it."

Jules turned to the plaque. He scanned all the way down to read the last lines, which had been defaced by three violent blows.

General Contractors

M on Edes (dec'd.)

Jul Fre n

* * * * *

7:00 P.M.

· RIAN ·

Rian, still easily passing as a boy with her short hair and dressed in her shop clothes, stood on Sixth Street at the front of the crowd that numbered well into the thousands. Philadelphia's mayor John Swift faced the mob from the shallow portico of Pennsylvania Hall. "This better be good," she said to Conor McGuire. "Otherwise they're going to burn the whole place down."

The mayor spun his watchman's rattle[18] around and around over his head so many times that the irritating, almost ear-splitting sound finally quieted those in the front of the mob a bit, but certainly not enough for him to be heard above the taunting and jeering in the back.

The mayor held up his other hand as well, as if the mob was obeying him and the gesture would get them to quiet further. It didn't. "Pennsylvania Hall is now officially closed, and there will be no more meetings this evening! I must hope that nothing will be transacted contrary to order and peace! Our city has long held the enviable position of a peaceful city, a city of order!"

"Jaysus, who is he kidding?" said Conor. "I guess he doesn't know what it's like to be Irish in Moyamensing."

---

18. A watchman's rattle was a gadget that contained a ratchet and vibrating tongue. It made a loud clacking noise when spun, and thus was used by watchmen to warn of danger.

"Or Black," added Rian. The thought prompted her to scan the crowd to see if there were any Negroes nearby. There were none. *This would not be a good night for any Black person to be out on the street.* She observed a man attempting to dislodge a paving stone with the heel of his boot.

"I truly hope that no one will do anything of a disorderly nature!" continued the mayor. "The managers of Pennsylvania Hall have a right to hold their abolitionist meetings here, but as good citizens they have, at my request, suspended their meeting for this evening!"

The mob burst into cheers and applause. They raised sticks, pitchforks, pickaxes, and shillelaghs in victory.

"No more meetings tonight," said Conor. "Do you think that's enough to satisfy this mob?"

"Not a chance," said Rian. "There's got to be ten thousand people here. Their blood is up. They'll not settle down until they've burned something to the ground. If not Pennsylvania Hall, then something else."

"I ask that you good citizens of Philadelphia return to your homes!" The mayor pointed to a knot of bully boys in the front that had temporarily quieted. "You! You men over there! Yes, you ten men!"

Rian looked toward where the mayor was pointing. She counted two shillelaghs, three pitchforks, and four torches among the ten men. She recognized the slave catcher Austin T. Slatter and his employee Hans Schmidt.

"I deputize you ten men to keep order in this group and assure that this gathering abides by the law."

A cheer went up from the crowd.

"That's it, then," said Conor. "The foxes are guarding the henhouse."

Mayor Swift stepped away from the front door of Pennsylvania Hall and waded through the crowd. People cheered as he strode by, shook his hand, and clapped him on the back.

Rian elbowed Conor and jutted her chin toward the front door of the Hall. Two of Conor's older brothers and a half dozen other rowdies had somehow manhandled a huge wooden beam—an ideal battering ram—from the waterfront. Newly deputized Hans Schmidt was urging them along. "I know that man. He used to work for my father. He's German and hates the Irish. What's he doing consorting with your brothers?"

Conor shrugged. "Rian, you weren't gone that long. Philadelphia hasn't changed, except maybe it's worse. Yeah, the Germans hate us Irish, but we both hate the Negroes—or at least we're supposed to. Whatever happens tonight, the krautbreaths and the Hibernians'll be back to fighting each other tomorrow."

A man with a pickaxe strode forward from the crowd and struck at the gas pipe that fed the gas lights that illuminated the portico.

Rian shook her head. "That's it. They're going to torch the building." Her thoughts flashed back to Yana the soothsayer's words three months ago in Russia.

"Still so hot. No less than the last time. You still have much fire left in you."

"What kind of fire? Fire like when the Tsar's palace burned down?"

"All kinds of fire. Fires that are out of control. Many of them. Fires that you think you control, but you don't."

Rian stared at Pennsylvania Hall. *Well, there is no way I'm going to be able to control this fire. What do I do now?*

The battering ram crew muscled the beam up the three steps to Pennsylvania Hall's portico. Rian tugged on Conor's sleeve. "We've got to do something."

The crowd cheered when the vandals smashed their battering ram into the Hall's pristine front door. They cheered louder with the second hit.

"Rian, are you fooking crazy? If the mayor couldn't rein this crowd in, we sure can't."

"I know that, stupid. But everything Benjamin Lundy owns is in the building. Mr. Whittier's newspaper office is there."

Conor watched his brothers for a moment longer, then turned away. "Too bad for them."

"I'm going to go in and see if I can save some of their things."

Conor pivoted to Rian. "That is a terrible idea. This mob is going to burn the Hall down. If the fire doesn't kill you, me brothers will."

With the third hit, the front doors of Pennsylvania Hall splintered and separated from their hinges. The crowd whooped and roared. Each member of the battering ram crew momentarily stumbled over the debris as they stepped through the threshold, then the vandals disappeared into the building to wreak more havoc.

Rian surveyed the crowd and concluded that no one would stop them if she sprinted across the street and into the building. "Your brothers are pretty busy."

"Rian, you think because some old hag in Russia told you that fire is your friend, you can go in there and save a couple of papers?"

"I've been in a fire that's a lot bigger than this is ever going to be. I'll know when it's time to get out. I'm not asking you to go in."

Conor shook his head. "One time. We go in, save what we can carry out in one trip, then we go to the Motts' and report in."

Men and boys started to peel off from the crowd and enter through shattered doors. Rian and Conor followed them. They stepped around debris in

Pennsylvania Hall's foyer to find chaos; books and shattered furniture in a pile. A bully boy with a crowbar hammered at a gas pipe until it separated from its sconce. He bent the pipe so it aimed directly at the pile.

"We better hurry, Conor. If they're using coal gas to get this fire going, it'll be raging in a couple of minutes."

* * * * *

"Destruction by fire of Pennsylvania Hall, the new building of the Abolition Society, on the night of the 17th May" by John T. Bowen. (Courtesy of the Library of Congress)

9:30 P.M.

· SEAMUS ·

Seamus stood at the bar opposite Braden McSweeney. "I'm telling you, Braden, Ruben Hasselbach and I can make better whiskey than this."

"Seamus, you don't know the first thing about distilling."

"Yeah, but I'm a quick study. Hasselbach said he'll teach me everything he knows. I learned how to set up the Kriegers' new factories fast enough."

"Then you got fired."

"And I did pretty well in Russia."

"Until you got thrown into prison."

"Me point is . . . my point is . . . I can learn the whiskey-making business. And I doubt anyone got poor selling liquor to Irishmen."

The State House bell sounded the alarm: one *clong* for north, three *clongs* for east. *Northeast. That's most likely Pennsylvania Hall.* Seamus checked his pocket watch. *Right on schedule.* He turned to two tables of No Names. "That's it, boyos. Put your hats on. Time to go save the world."

It became evident within three blocks that *the world* wasn't interested in saving Pennsylvania Hall.

Seamus and Dylan ran between the traces of the steam-powered fire pump, heading north on Sixth Street. A dozen other No Name members trotted alongside to relieve them when they flagged.

"Take your African friends back to Africa, you filthy traitors!" yelled a well-dressed woman standing on the second-floor balcony of her stately home. She wasn't alone in her sentiments. Blocks away from the fire, other people on balconies pelted them with food and chanted, "Go back home! Go back home!"

At Market, they could see the blaze reflected in the clouds in the night sky. At Mulberry, the crowd of gawkers was so thick it filled the street, and the brigade was forced to halt. Kevin Fitzpatrick grabbed the captain's speaking trumpet from its hook and yelled for the crowd to clear a path. He was pelted with stones and horse dung.

"Come on, Dylan. Ram our way through," Seamus said. "Kevin, you're going to take your licks, but keep yelling through the fooking trumpet!" They started hauling again and gained enough momentum to demonstrate that they meant business. Angry onlookers pulled their friends out of the way of the onrushing fire pump.

"Jaysus," said Dylan as they finally arrived at the blaze. "I've never seen a fire this big. How about if you take over?"

Seamus wasn't surprised by Dylan's request. *My boyo knows his limitations.* "Kevin, unwrap the intake hose and screw it into the fire hydrant over there. Jameson, hook your hose up. When we get a stream going, train it on that lower window there."

When the crowd realized the No Names were there to put out the fire, not douse nearby buildings, a rain of stones descended upon them. The fire pump generated a healthy stream of water for about thirty seconds. Then someone unscrewed the hose from the hydrant. Seamus told the Fitzpatrick brothers to reconnect the hose and guard it. A man wielding a shillelagh threatened Silken McDonald, who was waiting for the stream to revive so he could train it on the fire. Seamus tackled the assailant, ripped the club from his hands, and took a defensive posture near the hose team.

Five men drove the Fitzpatrick brothers from the hydrant. So many rocks were lofted at the hose team that they had to turn their backs to protect themselves. Silken McDonald took a shot to the head and fell down.

"All right, now, they've had enough!"

The crowd parted and the massive bulk of Hugh Callaghan strode through the gap. He held his hand up and the rain of rocks ceased. Hugh walked up to Seamus. "I told you, kid. Democracy in action. Look at this crowd. Rich, poor, Irish, German, men, women, young, and old. You couldn't have a more representative cross-section of America. No one here wants an end to slavery. You're beat."

Seamus surveyed the situation. He knew that any thought of saving Pennsylvania Hall was hopeless. *No sense putting the boys in any more danger.* He helped Silken regain his feet and wiped some blood from his friend's forehead, then turned to Hugh. "Beat for now, Hugh. Beat for now."

"If you still want to use that toy of yours, we need help dousing the other buildings. But if you train your stream even once on Pennsylvania Hall, the crowd'll turn on you again, and I won't lift a finger to save you."

Seamus wiped Silken's blood on his trousers. "We can do that. And Hugh?"

"What?"

"Thanks for saving our hides."

* * * * *

10:30 P.M.

· RIAN ·

Rian and Conor, indistinguishable from the looters exiting the burning hall, had saved one small trunk of Benjamin Lundy's papers and carried it four blocks to the Mott house. Twenty people—men and women, Black and white, many in Quaker garb—were gathered in the Motts' front yard, horrified but mesmerized by the glow of the conflagration reflected in the night sky and the sounds of the riot four blocks away. Some men and women were crying.

They found Lundy standing with William Lloyd Garrison and set the chest down. "This is all we could save, Mr. Lundy."

"Thee went into Pennsylvania Hall to rescue my papers? Thee shouldn't have risked thy lives for them, but I thank thee. We heard a cheer about half an hour ago. What was that?"

"That was when the roof caved in. I imagine there's ten thousand people there. Not many abolitionists in the crowd. I saw a few Quakers getting beat up. No Negroes, though. They were all smart enough to stay home."

"Well, I'm not dressed like a Quaker," announced Garrison. "I'm going to let those people know that we will not be intimidated by mobocracy, and we are not defeated."

Rian turned her attention to the newspaper publisher. "I don't think that's a good idea, Mr. Garrison. Their blood is up. You have a price on your head. If anyone recognizes you, you'll be carted off to Georgia before you know it."

"As I told your father, Rian, I will not be intimidated by a few low-class rowdies." Garrison squared his shoulders and marched north on Ninth Street.

Conor watched Garrison disappear into the darkness. "We should go after him. That crowd will tear him apart."

"I want to check in with *Vater* first. I thought he'd be here." Rian walked to a group of people that included Mrs. Mott. "Lucretia, have you seen my father?"

"He was worried about thee, Dear. He is out searching for thee. He said that if thee returned here that thee were to go to thy house and stay there."

Rian nudged Conor. "Come on, let's go."

"I take it we're not going to your house."

"Not for a while yet."

* * * * *

· OTTO ·

Desperate to find Rian, Otto circulated through the mob. For the most part, he found the people at the edge of the rioters to be in a jovial mood. *They've won. The mob has imposed its hateful will over the abolitionists.* The roof of Pennsylvania Hall collapsed with a roar and the throng screamed with glee.

Oh Jules, I am so sorry for you.

The fire was so hot that the mob had backed up at least a hundred feet all the way around the building. As Otto strode between the crowd and the fire, the people's faces were lit as if it were daylight. He expected the rioters would be made up mostly of Irish, those who were fighting tooth and nail with the Negroes for whatever scraps the limping Philadelphia economy deigned to throw to them. That wasn't how he would characterize this mob. Sure, he could tell the lower elements were here, judging by dress alone, but by far the majority of the crowd were the type of people with whom he interacted every day. *How naive of me.* He saw George Shippen, chairman of the Board of the Bank of Industry, standing next to Edward Schiffler, the bank president. They both had their hands in their pockets and appeared to be in fine fettle.

"George, have you seen Rian? I'm afraid she's around here someplace."

"This is no place for a girl, Krieger. Honestly, I figured you would have reigned her in after her Russia fiasco."

Otto didn't bother to respond. He continued his search.

A man yelled a profanity-laced diatribe at some Quaker men who were obviously distressed over the fire. Three boys about Rian's age ran by, one of whom was carrying a bolt of cloth. *Likely free produce looted from the Hall.* Belatedly, Otto realized that the boy with the cloth was Billy Schiffler, son of the bank president.

"Billy! Have you seen Rian?"

Billy glanced over his shoulder as he continued to run, but never responded. *I guess I'm not the only one who isn't reining in his child.*

He found Seamus Gallagher training a fire hose on a house across Haines Street from the burning Pennsylvania Hall.

"Seamus, have you seen Rian?"

"I've had me hands full here, Uncle, but I haven't seen her. She would have checked in if she'd seen me, though. Have you tried Jules's house?"

"Why there? That's ten blocks from here."

Seamus shrugged and returned his attention to his hose. "Just a thought. I wouldn't worry about her, though. She's got a good head on her shoulders."

And a knack for finding trouble, Otto said to himself as he continued his search. *Trouble I hoped that was behind her after she came home from Russia.*

* * * * *

11:30 P.M.

· RIAN ·

Rian and Conor found Garrison at the back of the crowd at the intersection of Cherry and Sixth. He was engaged in a heated debate with a well-dressed gentleman and a more shabbily clad Irishman who carried a shillelagh.

Rian tugged on Garrison's sleeve. "Sir, we should go."

At that moment, another man walked up to the group. His face, illuminated by the burning Pennsylvania Hall, was flushed with the unsated desire to bully any abolitionists who had unwisely come to witness the arson. He pointed at Garrison but spoke to the others. "Hey, I think this is that newspaper guy who spoke inside the building last night. Yeah, that's you, isn't it? What's your name, fella?"

"Sir, we should go," Rian repeated.

The man with the shillelagh raised it up to rest on his shoulder; not yet an overt threat, but menacing nonetheless. "Yeah, tell us your name."

Then, to Rian's horror, the slave catcher Austin T. Slatter shouldered his way out of the crowd and into their midst. "Excuse me, I'll handle this," he said to the group. Then he turned his attention to Garrison. "I've been deputized by Mayor Swift to maintain order here. I'm arresting you as a disturber of the peace."

"Me?!" protested Garrison. He swept his arm toward the mob. "These people are burning down a Temple of Freedom and you want to arrest me?"

Rian's thoughts raced. *Slatter knows there's a $5,000 reward waiting for him in Georgia if he can deliver Garrison hog-tied to Atlanta. He's definitely not interested in sharing.* She gave Conor a wide-eyed look. *Do something. Anything.*

Conor gave Rian a slight nod in the firelight, then rushed the man with the shillelagh, ripped the purse off his belt, and ran into the crowd.

Shillelagh-man and one other ran after Conor, yelling, "Come back here! Thief! Thief! Stop him!"

For three seconds, Slatter and the other guy took their eyes off Garrison to see if their allies had caught Conor.

Rian knew that a mere tug on Garrison's sleeve was no longer enough. She shoved him into the crowd, away from the direction Conor had run. After a few paces, she grabbed him by the elbow. "Walk faster! Your life is in danger if you stay here."

Garrison stole a look over his shoulder. "I think your instincts are prudent, Rian. We should return to the Motts'."

"No, not there. Your presence would put them in jeopardy, and they are Quakers. They will do nothing to defend themselves."

"Then we should return to the Needles' house. I've been staying with them."

Rian shouldered into Garrison, forcing him to double back through the crowd. "Stop for a minute." She spotted Slatter on the far corner of Cherry and Sixth, eyeballing anyone who was leaving the crowd to the south and the west. His acolyte Hans Schmidt stood next to him, also surveying the crowd. Slatter pointed in their general direction and gave Schmidt a shove. Still sweeping his eyes around the crowd, Schmidt walked toward Rian.

Rian pulled Garrison by the elbow. "No, we can't go this way." They started walking away from Schmidt. "The Needles are Quakers too, aren't they?"

"Of course," said Garrison.

"Then we can't go there either." She grabbed Garrison by the elbow. "I have a better idea. Keep up."

As they weaved their way back through the mob, Rian heard snatches of conversations. The rumor of Garrison's presence was spreading explosively.

". . . Garrison . . ."

". . . five thousand dollars . . ."

". . . string him up . . ."

". . . amalgamator . . ."

Rian's danger sense told her that Schmidt was somewhere behind them. She tightened her grip on Garrison's arm. "Don't turn around. Keep on walking."

A man who was tall and thin like Garrison ran past them with two others chasing him a few yards behind. One of the pursuers lost his beaver hat as he brushed by Rian. She stooped to pick it up and handed it to Garrison. "Here, put this on."

* * * * *

Rian found the key to Kent's Livery in its hiding place under the rock. With a sliver of moonlight to guide her, she unlocked the door and entered the complete darkness of the stable. She took in the smells she loved: fresh hay, sawdust, and even the manure, all of which had a comforting familiarity.

Garrison, virtually blind in the darkness and unfamiliar with his surroundings, kept his hand on her shoulder. "Are we hiding here?" he whispered.

Rian felt her way through the darkness and located the whale oil lamp on its usual hook. She found the loco-focos in their niche and scraped one on its sandpaper strip. It lit with a brief spasm of fire.

Rian handed the lit lantern to Garrison. "Hold this."

As the lantern's light filled the stable, Garrison surveyed his surroundings. Rian grabbed a harness off the wall and entered Walker's stall.

"Are we stealing horses?"

Rian draped the harness over Walker's back. "Follow me around. Hold the lantern higher so I can see what I'm doing."

"Why a harness? I don't see a carriage here. Why not saddle the horses and we can ride out of town?"

"Everybody and his brother is sure to be dogging you all night long. You'll be better off in an enclosed carriage."

"But where is the carriage?"

"Across the street."

"Are we going to steal that, too?"

Rian threw a scoop of oats into Walker's box. *You'll need the extra energy before this night is over.* "Follow me," she said to Garrison. "We've got one more horse to harness."

* * * * *

Rian and Garrison led Walker and Red across Broad Street toward Krieger Coach. "Rian, I have put myself in your hands, and I appreciate your obviously intimate knowledge of the neighborhood. But apparently we are engaging in horse thieving and other crimes, and I believe I deserve at least an outline of your plan."

"Rule Number 1 in the Underground Railroad is that if someone doesn't need to know something, you don't tell them."

"Are you involved with the Underground Railroad?"

"Used to be. Guess for tonight I am again."

Garrison was silent for a bit as he took in this information. "Then don't you think you can waive Rule Number 1 in this instance? It seems that all will soon be revealed anyway, that is unless you intend to put a feedbag over my head for the rest of the night."

Rian assumed Garrison was making a joke, but his plea for more information made sense. "Krieger Coach rents horses from Kent's Livery to deliver carriages and rolling stock to its customers. It turns out Mr. Kent shares our sympathies. Before I ran away to Russia, Jules and I had a need for horses at odd hours to get self-emancipators out of town. Mr. Kent showed us where the key was so we didn't have to wake him up in the middle of the night."

"Jules. Jules Freeman, the Black man whom I met at your father's house the other night?"

"Yes."

"He claimed he was not a part of the Underground Railroad."

"He lied."

"Because of Rule Number 1? He must know that our sympathies are aligned."

"What if you had been captured back there at the fire. Slatter, the man who tried to arrest you? He would have beaten you until you told him everything you knew about the Underground Railroad."

"I did not consider that. You assist Jules?"

"I used to. Then my father found out about it when I got pistol-whipped by Slatter."

"You've had dealings with him before?"

Rian unlocked the factory door and slid it open. "I've got the scar on my back to prove it."

Garrison peered into the cavernous darkness of the building. "This is your father's factory?"

"Yes."

"I take it he doesn't approve of Jules's activity."

"He didn't approve of Jules getting me involved, even though I really got myself involved. I think his sentiments are changing. He canceled a locomotive order to Cuba because he doesn't want to sell to slave owners anymore."

"He mentioned he was about to sell that locomotive to Cuba at the dinner at your house. He must have . . ."

A whispered voice came out of the darkness down the street. "Rian, is that you?" Conor was striding toward them, silhouetted by the light of a distant streetlamp.

"Conor, did you lose the guy with the shillelagh?"

"Yeah, it was easy. I let him chase me for about twenty seconds, then I tossed his purse up in the air. He was more interested in getting his money back than catching me. I figured you would come here. Where are we going to take Mr. Garrison?"

"To Jules's house. This is going to be a long night."

* * * * *

· OTTO ·

Otto knocked on Jules's front door. He heard heavy footsteps approaching and the door opened to reveal Jules with a pistol in his right hand.

Jules pulled Otto inside and shut the door. "Is it gone?"

"The roof to Pennsylvania Hall caved in around ten o'clock. I'm afraid it has been totally destroyed, my friend. I am so sorry."

Jules looked down for a moment, as if saying a silent prayer, then returned his attention to Otto. "How bad is it out there?"

Otto preceded Jules down the hallway to the kitchen. "It is quiet enough in Moya. You can tell which homes are Black and which are Irish. The Negroes are hunkered down. The Irish are buzzing back and forth with news from the mob."

When he arrived at the kitchen, Maddie rose from the table and greeted Otto warmly. "Pennsylvania Hall is gone," Otto said. "I am so sorry. You two worked so hard to bring it into being."

Jules showed no emotion. "What brings you here, Otto?"

"I am looking for Rian. Seamus suggested that she might have come here."

Jules pulled a chair to the table and bade Otto to sit, then sat down next to Maddie, placing the pistol before him on the table. "No, we haven't seen her. I'm sorry you had to come all the way down here for nothing."

"I was hoping that with my daughter's return from Russia, her penchant for finding trouble was behind her."

Rap. Rap. Rap. A knock on the kitchen door. Jules reflexively reached for the pistol on the kitchen table, then put it back down and muttered to no one in particular, "I suppose rioters are not going to knock."

Maddie rose and opened the kitchen door wide. Rian, Conor, and William Lloyd Garrison entered, Garrison much more agitated than the youngsters.

Garrison put out his hand to Jules. "Mr. Freeman, it seems I owe you an apology. At dinner the other night I belittled your commitment to the cause of freeing your brethren. I have since learned about Rule Number 1, and I understand why you chose not to reveal yourself. Now I find that I must put my safety in your hands and request that you spirit me out of town."

Otto pulled Rian into a hug. "*Liebling*, I was worried about you. Were you in danger?"

"Nothing we couldn't handle."

Garrison surveyed the kitchen, then turned to Otto. "Your daughter and her friend demonstrate the proclivities of a Charles Dickens street urchin. I say this with admiration, not criticism. They were very resourceful. Herr Krieger, Rian did not mention that you are part of Mr. Freeman's Underground Railroad. Or does Rule Number 1 apply here as well?"

"I believe you are in the circle of trust at this point, Mr. Garrison. I haven't been a conductor yet, but that may be about to change."

Rian sidled over to Conor. "Conor and I can take Mr. Garrison to the next station, *Vater*. We've got horses and your landau out back and ready to go."

"No, my attitude about your involvement in the Underground Railroad has not changed at all, but I think it is time that I joined in the struggle. Jules, how would you feel if I were the one who drove Mr. Garrison out of town?"

Jules made a slight bow of acknowledgment. "We would be pleased to have you join the cause, Otto."

Otto turned to Rian. "I have no idea if the burning of Pennsylvania Hall will satisfy the mob. The turmoil has not yet settled down. If I go away for a few days, you must promise me to stay out of trouble. No more hunting for wayward adults who were foolish enough to find themselves in the wrong place at the wrong time."

FRIDAY, MAY 18

• RIAN •

Conor and Rian remained at the Freeman's house until Otto and Garrison left for Robert Purvis's estate. Purvis's farm was twenty miles away, near Bristol, Pennsylvania, so Otto would be gone through the next day. Rian and Conor walked back to Lucretia's house, where they learned that the rioting had died down. They entered Rian's home, went to bed, and slept soundly until noon.

That afternoon, they walked to the burned-out hulk of Pennsylvania Hall. Its marble walls still stood, but its interior was nothing but smoldering timbers. Hundreds of people had also returned to see the wreckage, a few moving freely about, but most clotted together by their sentiments, either pro- or anti-slavery. Constables cautioned everyone to keep their distance, because the walls could collapse at any moment, but made no attempt to evict souvenir hunters who picked through the wreckage.

Rian and Conor watched two boys younger than them working at something in the portico. "Seems like there are three kinds of people here," Rian said to Conor. "Curiosity seekers, abolitionists, and folks who were part of the mob last night."

The two boys finished their task and walked across the street with what Rian realized was a broken part of the brass plaque commemorating the builders of Pennsylvania Hall.

"Hey, kid," she called to one of the boys. "What are you going to do with that?"

The kid stopped, looking quite guilty and almost about to run. "Dunno. Sell it."

"Let me see it."

The kid walked the rest of the way across the street and held it up toward Rian but distrustfully kept his distance.

Rian fished through her pocket. "I'll buy it for a quarter dollar."

The kid readily agreed.

The transaction complete, the two boys walked away and Rian and Conor watched the curiosity seekers for a few more minutes.

"Hi, Barn Door. Hi, Conor. Did you hear?"

Rian turned to see Billy Schiffler. "Hear what?"

"They almost caught Garrison last night, but he got away."

"Nope, didn't hear that."

"The abolitionists had a meeting this morning. Right inside the front door of the building. Some of us were hoping the wall would fall down on top of them. I saw one guy crying."

Rian wanted Billy to go away, so she decided not to take his bait.

"They're not done, you know," Billy continued.

This comment was harder to ignore. "Who's not done?"

"The pro-Constitution men. As soon as it gets dark, they're coming back."

"What are they going to do?"

"Hard to say. Maybe burn down that Quaker lady's house."

"Which Quaker lady?"

"You know. Tom's mother. Mrs. Mott."

* * * * *

· LUCRETIA ·

When Rian and Conor reported to Lucretia that the mob wasn't yet done with their hateful mischief and the new target was her house, she dismissed it as unlikely.

"I daresay burning our Temple of Freedom has satiated the mob," she said to her husband, James. "They will be idle tonight."

However, as other allies reported the same rumor, Lucretia and James began to think differently.

They found other accommodations for their houseguests and moved her mother and her youngest daughters to daughter Maria's home next door to the north. Rian and Conor helped James and Lucretia's son Tom move some furniture and clothing to the Krieger house next door to the south.

Then Lucretia started cooking.

"Why are you making all this food, Lucretia?" Rian asked her.

Lucretia continued her kneading. "Rian, there is always another way to respond to hate. My beliefs don't allow me to use violence to defend myself, even if it means the mob burns down my home. Perhaps if I lay out a banquet for them, it will moderate their temper."

"You didn't see them last night. These people weren't interested in moderation."

* * * * *

· JULES ·

Jules, Maddie, and Martha arrived at the First Parish Unitarian Church at the same time as Seamus and Logan.

"Jules," Seamus said with an unenthusiastic greeting. "Maddie."

"Seamus," responded Jules with an equal lack of warmth. "We better go in. The less we're seen in public together, the better."

A woman who sniffed her disapproval of the group of five ushered them into the anteroom outside of Reverend Furness's office. The windowless room was furnished with an old church pew that had been cut in half. One half-pew, with one end supported by an old apple crate, was placed along a wall, with the other half facing it from the opposite side. Jules and Maddie sat on one half-pew. Seamus took a seat on the other and indicated to Logan to join him. Instead, his brother put his arm around Martha, and the two of them remained standing. Everyone could hear arguing on the other side of the office door, but the voices were indistinct.

Jules took in a whiff of smoke, and scrutinized Seamus more closely. *His clothing was smudged with soot. He probably was fighting the fire all night.* Jules's ire at Seamus for sailing off to Russia when he should have been keeping Logan away from Martha softened a bit.

Five minutes later, the door opened. Two men exited, followed by Reverend Furness. "I appreciate your advice, gentlemen. I'll see you Sunday." The two men noted the presence of the visitors waiting in the anteroom but acknowledged none of them.

Furness greeted his visitors with a calmness that seemed contrary to the confrontational words that had seeped through his office door. "Welcome. Please come in."

After introductions, Furness bade his visitors to sit, but rather than take a chair of his own, he half-sat on the edge of his desk. "Well, Logan, Martha, you certainly have chosen to start your journey together in perilous times. I committed to marry the two of you next Wednesday here at First Parish, but sadly, the events of the past twenty-four hours have made that impossible. The church elders have forbidden me to hold the ceremony here for fear that our church will suffer the same fate as Pennsylvania Hall."

Jules harrumphed in frustration. "So you aren't going to perform the marriage?"

"On the contrary, I am still willing to perform the ceremony, but I am sorry to say you must find some other venue for it to take place. The stories that I hear about the violence last night indicate that the crowd was most incensed by their hatred of amalgamation. Black and white sitting together as equals was bad enough. Rumors that Angelina Grimké had married a Black man, which you, Mr. and Mrs. Freeman, can personally attest were false, heightened their indignation exponentially. The problem with our event here is that accusations of amalgamation will be fact, not fiction."

"So, my Black daughter can marry an Irish boy, but just not here."

"That is about the size of it. And your problem of finding another place to hold the wedding is significant. I fear that in the current climate, any building, whether it be a church, a courthouse, a private home, a tavern, or a store is likely to be burned down by a mob as soon as people hear what is happening there."

* * * * *

· RIAN ·

Rian and Conor watched the Mott family prepare a banquet for the mob from the Krieger front porch. "Fire will follow you," Rian said.

"What's that supposed to mean?"

"That's what Yana told me. 'Fire will follow you. All kinds of fire. Fires that are out of control. Many of them. Fires that you think you control, but you don't.'"

"You really do believe that, don't you. Jaysus. And I thought the Irish were superstitious. Rian, you didn't start the Tsar's fire, did you?"

"No, of course not."

"And you sure as hell didn't start the fire last night."

"No, but I was there."

"So you're telling me that you think the mob is coming back tonight, they're going to torch Lucretia's house, and it's going to be your fault."

"Kind of, yeah."

"Well, that's stupid. But if that's what you think, then there's only one way to disprove it."

"What's that?"

"Make sure it doesn't happen."

"How are we going to do that?"

"Beats me. You're the one who always comes up with the bright ideas. Start thinking."

* * * * *

· LUCRETIA ·

The Motts' house was only four blocks from Pennsylvania Hall. The night sky was dull, overcast; the mild springtime breeze carried the odor of charred wood in their direction. It also brought sounds of angry voices gathering.

Lucretia, James, Tom, Conor McGuire, and a few fellow Quakers stood in front of her house. Before them was arrayed the entire contents of Lucretia's larder, prepared as a feast to mollify the mob, which by this time everyone was certain was coming.

For no reason but to keep her hands busy, Lucretia started slicing a loaf of bread. "Conor, this isn't thy fight. Thee should retire to Rian's home. You can watch whatever happens from her front porch."

"I think I'm going to stay here, Lucretia," said Conor. "Rian has a plan."

"And where is she now?"

"Right now? Right now I suspect she's leading the mob."

As Conor spoke these words, the angry chanting in the distance started to move. Moments later, it was evident that the mob was making its inexorable way toward them on Sassafras Street.

* * * * *

· RIAN ·

Rian stood on the periphery of the crowd, which roiled near the remains of Pennsylvania Hall. She judged this group to be a tenth of the size of last night's mob; perhaps a thousand people or so. But these folks also struck her as people who hated abolition and abolitionists so much that last night's destruction wasn't enough.

Before she arrived, Rian did her best to disguise herself by donning boots that raised her height by an inch, an old frock coat of her father's that was too big for her, and a beaver hat that her father never wore. As it turned dark, the crowd became more restless. They lit torches. They shook pitchforks and shillelaghs overhead.

Last night, there were numerous individuals who initiated the destruction of the Temple of Freedom. This evening, the crowd seemed to be waiting for a spark, someone to spur it into action. "Come on, lads, it's time. On to the Motts'!" someone yelled, and the group slowly shifted to march west on Sassafras Street.

Rian joined the march, taking pains to not make eye contact with anyone. Someone began yelling, "Burn them down! Burn them down!" and the mob picked up the chant as they got closer to Ninth Street.

Okay, Eena, make this good. Now's the time to prove to yourself that fire isn't going to follow you wherever you go.

Rian hurried her pace and made her way to the head of the crowd as it arrived at the corner of Sassafras and Ninth. "This way! This way, everyone! No, this way! To the north! On to the Motts'! On to the Motts'!" With broad sweeping gestures, she willed the crowd to turn right on Ninth Street, away from the Mott house. "Come on, everyone! This way!" she repeated, gesturing and leaping.

The vanguard followed her and the rest of the mob followed the vanguard. Rian continued to dance ahead, gradually increasing the distance between herself and the rest of the mob. Then she started running north so fast that when there was a block between her and the nearest rioter, she took a left on Vine Street, ran to Tenth Street, took a left, and continued to sprint south. *Now if we're lucky, the mob will be totally turned around and not know where they're supposed to be. They'll never find the Motts'.*

* * * * *

Rian walked into the Motts' front yard to the tables that were arrayed with food. Conor saw her before she saw him. "Rian, I can tell they're still moving away from us. I think you did it."

"Yes, I believe I did. I proved that Yana was wrong. I actually prevented a fire. I feel like I just lifted a thousand-pound weight off my shoulders."

Lucretia saw Rian and walked over to her. "Was that thee who led the crowd away from our home, Rian?"

"Yes, it was." Rian turned to listen toward the north. "By the sounds of it they're milling about up there somewhere. Hopefully, they'll run out of energy and go home."

"Rian, this was a brave plan on thy part. May I suggest that we don't make thy role in this evening's events public? We have no way of knowing who might take offense at thy clever ruse."

"I think that is a good idea, Lucretia. I'm content with that."

Despite Lucretia's note of caution, word of Rian's accomplishment spread around the Motts' front yard and into the house. Numerous people approached her and clapped her on the back.

* * * * *

Two hours later, word made its way back to the Mott house: Having been lured in the wrong direction, the mob demonstrated no desire to turn around, find the Motts' home, and burn it to the ground. Instead, they turned left on Ridge Road. Rian had unwittingly aimed the mob in the direction of the newly constructed but not yet occupied Shelter for Colored Orphans. Angry at being tricked once, they turned their wrath on something that seemed almost as good. The orphanage was put to the torch. Rian had saved the Motts from disaster but diverted the destruction to affect another set of innocents.

* * * * *

Conor put his arm around Rian. "You did the best you could. It wasn't your fault."

"Then whose fault was it?"

"The mob's, of course."

"No, it was me. I have too much fire in me. Yana said it was going to follow me wherever I go."

"So what are you going to do? Never make a decision again for fear something else is going to burn down?"

"I don't know. Maybe. It seems like every time I make a decision, something pushes back at it. Between Yana and Isaac Newton, I can't catch a break."

"Who's Isaac Newton?" Conor asked.

SATURDAY, MAY 19

· JULES ·

"This isn't going to be a one-night affair."

Jules couldn't get Hugh Callaghan's words out of his mind.

Well, you bastards got two nights. First Pennsylvania Hall, then the Shelter for Colored Orphans. Are you done? What other evil do you need to do before you are satiated? Jules's one consolation was that the rioting in the previous two nights had occurred north of Mulberry, at least twelve blocks from his home in Moyamensing.

Grace, dressed in a light coat, headed for the front door.

"Where are you going?"

"Choir practice."

Grace always had choir practice on Saturday night. The choir at Bethel AME Church had been strong for decades.

Jules was proud that Grace was a part of it. "We don't know if things have settled down uptown. If you even get a whiff of trouble, you come home right away."

"Pop-Pop, you've been out in the neighborhood all day. Moyamensing is quiet. The trouble is probably over, and if it isn't, it will be a long way away from here."

Jules looked at Maddie. Maddie gave him a subtle nod. "Okay, but come home right after, do you hear?"

* * * * *

Bang! Bang! Bang!

Jules answered the front door to find Pepper Pot Penny Porter on his porch.

"Sorry to bother you, Mr. Freeman. Is Cee-Cee here?"

"No, this is choir practice night. I imagine she's there, same as Grace."

"Choir practice was canceled. There are rumors flying all over Moyamensing. The troubles are coming down to us tonight."

"Where have you heard this?"

"It's been spreading like a wildfire since suppertime. Minister's mustered a bunch of parishioners to help defend the church. He said you shouldn't come to church, though, 'cause you've got your own things to worry about."

For a moment, Jules thought the minister meant the fact that his daughter was pregnant by an Irish boy, but that didn't quite make sense. "What else do I have to worry about?"

"The rumors. There's bully boys going after the church. There's somebody else who's got you in his sights. He's intending to burn down Freeman Hydraulics."

"Who is it?"

"A slave catcher named Slatter. I've never had any doings with him, but I know he's a mean one, and story is he rolled back into town a couple of days ago."

*****

Jules grabbed his flintlock pistol and kit and headed for the door.

"Husband, no! You promised me there would be no more violence!"

"This isn't me burning an evil man's slave ship. This is violence coming to us."

"Freeman Hydraulics is not worth you becoming a martyr. Please . . ."

Homer grabbed his coat off the rack. "Jules, I'm coming with you."

Jules thought about it. He handed his pistol and kit to Homer. "Do you know how to fire a pistol?"

"Of course I do."

"Then you stay here and protect our families. I have another pistol in my desk at the shop."

"Jules, no!" Maddie yelled as he left his porch. He didn't stop.

"Jules, what about Gracie?" Maddie yelled.

Jules stopped, turned. "I'm sure Gracie's fine. There's no signs of trouble yet, just rumors. You stay inside."

As he hurried toward the shop, he realized that he had been in such a hurry that he never stopped to tell Maddie he loved her. *Never, ever, allow that to happen again.*

*****

Jules approached Fred Hailer, the night watchman, who was halfway up a ladder and lighting a streetlamp on the corner of Locust and Twelfth. "Fred, have you been by my shop in the last little bit?"

Fred glanced over his shoulder. "Good evening, Mr. Freeman. I was just by there. All's well at the moment. I've heard the rumors, though, so I'll be sure to pay special attention all night long."

As Jules continued the half block to his shop, he heard Fred Hailer far behind him. "Nine o'clock! Trouble's brewing! Mayor Swift says stay inside tonight!"

* * * * *

· OTTO ·

Otto drove his carriage—William Lloyd Garrison riding in the back—through the night. They stopped at Byberry, Robert Purvis's farm, to exchange horses and wolf down a meal, then proceeded to Trenton, thirty miles from Philadelphia. Garrison boarded a train to New York City, saying, "Thank you, Otto. I am pleased that you have joined the cause."

Otto drove back to Philadelphia via Byberry—an all-day affair—dropped the landau at Krieger Coach, led the horses across the street to Kent's Livery, and walked home.

He mounted the steps of his front porch exhausted. He hoped to spend some time with Rian and catch up on their separate adventures. Instead, he found Rian sitting at the dining room table with Conor McGuire, Jabez Howes, and their next-door neighbor Tom Mott.

"*Guten Abend, Kinder* [Good evening, children]," he said. "*Was geht hier vor sich* [What is going on here]?"

Rian rose and hugged him long and hard, then pulled back to look at him. "We had more trouble last night. We're killing time until Lucretia's confident that the mob isn't going to come to her house. I'm teaching my friends to play poker. It would be more fun if we had five players. Would you care to join us?"

* * * * *

· RIAN ·

Rian checked her pocket watch as Conor dealt a new hand. "It's 9:00," she said. "Maybe the bully boys aren't going to cause any trouble tonight."

"I think we should play until 10:00," said Otto. "If a mob has not formed outside Tom's house by then, I would say we can safely send him home and go to bed. Besides, I am enjoying learning to play poker with all you young people. Thank you for allowing me to sit in."

Jabez consulted the paper that Rian had written up when they started playing. It contained the list of hands: High Card / One Pair / Two Pair / Three-of-a-Kind / Straight / Flush / Full House / Four-of-a-Kind / Straight Flush / Royal Flush. "Aunt Mila said I should be home by 10:00, so I'm fine to keep playing."

Rian was happy to play poker for the first time since returning to Philadelphia almost a month ago. *Even though all of you are just learning the game. Even though we're only playing with matchsticks and toothpicks because Tom isn't allowed to gamble because he's a Quaker.* She suspected that, despite the fact that no money was changing hands, Lucretia would still be appalled that Tom had spent the evening playing cards. *But Lucretia has bigger things to worry about at the moment.*

Rian could already tell Jabez liked the prospects of his new hand. *He only checks the list when he's holding something interesting.* Jabez was probably a little miffed that Otto had joined them. He had previously been sipping out of a small whiskey bottle, but he hadn't taken any sips since Otto had arrived.

Rian surveyed the table. She had by far the biggest pile of "picks and sticks." Everyone else had lost a bit from their original allotment, except for Jabez, who bluffed often and bet foolishly. His pile was almost gone.

Bang! Bang! Bang! An insistent rap from the front door.

Otto leapt from his chair and grabbed his stout lumber measuring rule as he left the room. The rest of the card players threw down their hands and followed him into the parlor.

Bang! Bang! Bang!

Otto opened the door and Seamus Gallagher entered. "Uncle Otto, I think we could use you."

"At Lucretia's?"

"No, tonight the trouble's brewing in Moyamensing. Slatter's going after Jules."

* * * * *

Rian, Jabez, Conor, and Tom watched Seamus and Otto disappear into the darkness from the porch.

"Well?" asked Conor. "Are we going to follow them?"

"*Vater* told us to stay here."

"Since when has that ever stopped you?"

"The last two nights, I've been followed by fire. I don't want a third and I don't want it to happen to Jules."

"So that's it? You're gonna give up? You're gonna let doing nothing be your decision? To never help someone because it might get a little fiery?"

"Yes, I guess I am."

"Well, I'm going," said Conor. He stepped down off the porch and started walking.

"So am I," said Jabez, who followed Conor.

"I can't go," said Tom. "I wouldn't be any help. I couldn't lift a finger, even to defend myself."

"Sorry, Tom," said Rian. "I have to go. My friends need me."

* * * * *

· JULES ·

Jules entered Freeman Hydraulics and locked the door behind him. He lit the lantern that hung by the door, walked purposefully through the shop, opened the door at the far end, and entered his office. A scurry of activity came from his right. The door to the potbelly stove, which had been open, was slammed shut, casting the room back into partial darkness.

Jules rushed to his desk, opened the drawer, and grabbed his flintlock. He wheeled toward the intruder and cocked the pistol.

"Don't shoot, Pop-Pop. It's me," said a voice from the darkness.

Jules raised his lantern, extending the faint light farther into the room. "Gracie? What are you doing here? Choir was canceled."

"Pop-Pop, I'm not alone."

"Who are you with?"

A second figure stepped into the lantern light. "It's me, Mr. Freeman. Cee-Cee."

* * * * *

Jules was reeling. He grabbed the flintlock's kit out of the drawer, extinguished the lantern, and headed back into the darkness of the shop. "Gracie, I don't have time to deal with this now. There's rumors flying around that Slatter plans to burn the factory down tonight."

He left his daughter and her—*What? Girlfriend? Lover?*—back in the darkened office, worked his way through the shop in the dark, and peered out the front window. *Nothing.*

Five minutes later, Grace and Cee-Cee appeared at his side. Cee-Cee unlocked the door and left without a word. Jules watched her walking north until she disappeared in the darkness.

"What's going on between you two?" he asked.

"We love each other."

"Gracie, Logan Gallagher has got your sister pregnant. Two nights ago, a mob burned down a building that I dedicated the last four months of my life to. I thought 'Builder of Pennsylvania Hall' would most likely be the thing that would go on my gravestone. Now tonight we're hearing rumors that a mob is going after our church, and Austin Slatter wants to burn down this building. I can't worry about you two right now."

* * * * *

An hour later, there was still no threatening activity outside. The night watchman Fred Hailer walked by frequently, one time yelling, "Ten o'clock! Trouble's brewing! Mayor Swift says stay inside tonight!"

"Gracie, I have no idea if it's safer for you to be here or heading home by yourself. Perhaps you should go."

"I'm staying with you, Pop-Pop."

Despite the support implied in Gracie's statement, Jules's confusion about his daughter competed with his need to focus on the street. *Maddie. Maddie will know what to do. Lord, please let me get through this night. Maddie, tell me what to feel about this.* For the hundredth time, he peered out the window but saw nothing moving. "You know I'm going to have to tell your mother about you and Cee-Cee."

"Mother already knows."

* * * * *

At eleven o'clock, Jules spotted activity across the street, then four torches burst into life. "This is it, Gracie. You stay here." He double-checked the gunpowder in the pan and snapped the frizzen back into place.

He was about to reach for the door, then stopped. *No. This may be the last time you see her. You don't need Maddie to tell you. You already know how you feel.* He turned back to his daughter. "Gracie, I don't understand this thing between you and Cee-Cee, and I certainly don't approve of it. But this doesn't change anything between us. I still love you. Make sure you tell that to Martha and your mother if I . . . if I can't do it myself." Jules opened the door and left the building.

The four torches started to move across the street, shortly revealing six men. Jules recognized Austin T. Slatter; his right-hand man, Hans Schmidt; Ethan, the former Krieger Coach employee who refused to work in the steam room; and three men he had never seen before.

"I heard you were back in town, Slatter. How come you're not in the clink?"

"I went to the right magistrate. Magistrate Bowman thought his colleague had treated me rather unfairly, so we came to an accommodation. I sweep up as many fugitive slaves off the streets of Philadelphia as I can find, and he won't get in my way."

"So, what are you doing here?"

"I figured I'd torch your place. Flush out any African rats that are hiding here. Given that you burned my ship, I figure that might balance the ledger a bit."

"I didn't burn your ship, Slatter." *Although that's just a technicality. Jabez Howes beat me to it.* "I suggest you stop right there. I've got a pistol."

"A pistol only stops one of us. Get out of our way. If no one's in there, nobody gets hurt."

A voice came from the shadows to Jules's left. "Go home, Slatter. You aren't welcome here."

Hugh Callaghan sauntered into the light and took a position next to Jules. "And if this place ever gets burned down—ever!—I'm going to make it my mission in life to make you regret it."

"My, my, this is like a dream come true," responded Slatter. "Six against two. Even with that pistol, I think we've got you beat."

"Better count again, Slatter," said Hugh. With that, fifteen members of the Moyamensing Hose Company, a gang that took great delight in tormenting the Black families in the district, encircled Austin T. Slatter and his group. They went after Slatter and his men with shillelaghs and axe handles.

The melee didn't last long. Slatter and his confederates broke through the ring of Moya boys and retreated, bloodied and limping, to the north.

Jules watched the ruckus until the men disappeared in the distance. "What's going on, Hugh? Why are your boys here?"

Hugh put his hands in his pockets and stared up Twelfth Street. "Seamus got wind of Slatter's intentions. He came and got me. I gotta tell you, Jules, I had to ponder it all for a while before I made my decision. Turns out, I figured it was good business to protect my investment."

"What investment? I turned you down."

"Care to change your decision? Of course your monthly fee just went up."

"You never told me what the fee would have been."

Hugh ignored Jules's comment. "Actually, Seamus did you an even bigger favor. Of course, he didn't know about my previous proposition at your office the other day, so he felt obliged to do some fast talking. He told me with great conviction that if Slatter burned your factory down, that would be the end of our sweet little steam-powered fire engines. I think he made pretty good sense. Better yet, he convinced a couple of my lads."

"That's why you're here? To save my factory?"

"That's why I'm here as far as my boys are concerned. As for me? This balances things a bit for saving my life when we burned the ship. Besides, I figured you'd had enough heartache in the last few days. Even I have a modicum of compassion."

"I thank you . . ."

"Don't get used to it. I don't want my men thinking I've gone all soft on your race."

A few of the Moya boys who had chased Slatter and his men back uptown returned to Freeman Hydraulics. "We nicked 'em up pretty good," one of them reported. "They won't be back."

"If Seamus came and got you, how come he's not here?"

"I thought you knew. He went to your place. Slatter's brother is supposed to burn your home tonight."

The blood drained down to Jules's toes.

"Go," said Hugh. "We'll stay here for a little bit."

* * * * *

Jules ran down Twelfth Street with Gracie trailing behind him. *Please, Seamus, get there in time.* They crossed Pine Street. *No signs of activity in the distance.* Lombard. *Still nothing.* At Cedar Street, he heard yelling. He could make out activity in the distant darkness, and it was coming in their direction. He stopped in mid-block, alarmed at the activity but grateful to stop running, at least for the moment.

Four figures were being chased by a larger group. He didn't know who was friend and who was foe. "Get behind me, Gracie." He cocked and raised his pistol, aiming slightly above both the men in flight and their pursuers.

The first man passed through the aura of the gas lantern at the corner of Shippen and Twelfth. Jules didn't recognize the stranger and aimed his pistol at him. He continued to run toward Jules and Grace. *He doesn't see us in the darkness.*

With thirty feet to go, the man saw Jules, saw the pistol, veered to the other side of the street, and kept running. His footsteps sounded funny, like he was sloshing through a puddle. Two more men sloshed by moments later. As the fourth man passed them, Jules pivoted, always keeping his pistol aimed at the man.

"Don't shoot, Pop-Pop," Grace said from behind him.

Jules pointed his pistol straight up and released the cock with his thumb.

Most of the pursuers slowed, then quit running altogether, but one figure ran full speed through the aura of light. *Weepy-eyed Emil Harberger. What the hell . . . ?*

Emil spotted Jules and Grace and finally slowed down. "Evening, Jules. Everything okay down at your shop?" Emil put his hands on his hips to catch his breath.

"Yes it is. How's my family?"

Emil nodded and took a few more deep breaths. "Everybody's fine. Your house is fine."

"What are you doing here?"

"Homer came and got me. I live a couple of blocks from here."

Jules started walking toward the house, prompting Grace and Emil to do the same. "There were some others chasing those gumps."

Emil, despite being out of breath, quickened his pace to catch up with Jules. "Yeah, the rumors were flying all over Moyamensing. Your house, your factory, and the church: Those folks were intent on burning all of them. I'd say every Black carpenter you hired showed up to defend your place. Bunch of whites, too. Randy Buck is there. So is Bartle, the plaster subcontractor. Marcus Edes came with a couple boys from his crew and Jonas Longstreth, the lumberyard owner. That little girl Cee-Cee showed up, then she left and came back with Charlie the plasterer. Your friend Seamus came with his boys. Seems to me there's quite a few people who were sick and tired of those bastards burning stuff that shouldn't be burnt, and they damn well didn't want it to happen to you. Hell, Pepper Pot Penny is even there."

"How did the church make out?"

"A lot of your brethren were there to defend the church. Seems Mayor Swift finally got tired of all the destruction. He mustered a slew of deputies to ring the church. The mob was pretty sizable. Charged the church and got beat back. A bunch of folks who showed up to watch the altercation decided they'd had enough as well. I guess they had to decide which side they were on, and they chose to stand up against the mob. The mob charged a bunch more times but always got thrown back. Some of them got arrested."

It was 11:30 by the time Jules arrived at his home. He found Penny Porter and Maddie ladling out pepper pot stew to more than twenty people in front of the house.

Seamus was the first to greet him. "The shop okay?"

"Yeah, Hugh saved my ass. Thank you for talking him into it. And thanks for coming here."

"Ah, it was fun. We even brought a fire pump just in case. Turns out it wasn't necessary, but it worked real good on those four gumps. Our numbers and a torrent from the fire hose cooled their enthusiasm. Then we started them running."

"I owe you."

"You don't owe anyone here a thing. There's not a person here who you haven't stuck your neck out for at one time or another. This balances the ledgers a bit. And Jules, Logan's here. He was shoulder-to-shoulder with us until the men started running. Now he's inside with Martha."

Jules was overwhelmed by the number of people who came to defend his home, and who those people were: faces both Black and white. Otto Krieger, with his stout lumber estimating rule resting on his shoulder, was talking with sawmaker William Rowland. Rian Krieger huddled with Conor McGuire and Jabez Howes. Jules was surprised that Otto had allowed Rian to come, but more likely he ordered her not to come but she came anyway.

Jules wasn't sure how much he had stuck his neck out for each of these people, but he had tried to treat them all with dignity and kindness.

He walked over to Maddie. She put down her ladle and turned to him. He pulled her into him and sobbed.

* * * * *

· RIAN ·

It was 1:00 in the morning. The crowd protecting Jules and Maddie's home had heard enough stories coming from Bethel AME church to confirm that Moyamensing had settled down for the night. The group gradually dispersed.

"Remember Halley's Comet?" asked Conor as he and Rian walked north on Ninth Street.

"Of course I do. Why?"

"People said it was an omen that something bad was going to happen when it returned two years ago, then nothing bad happened."

"Well, there was that earthquake in Galilee."

"Yeah, but nothing bad happened here. You told me at the time that you didn't think that a stupid comet could predict the future."

"Yes, I did. So what?"

"But you think that some old hag in Russia can predict the future? We proved her wrong tonight. Nothing got burned up and it sure as hell could have."

Rian pondered Conor's words for half a block. "Maybe my fire has burned out for a while."

"Maybe, but that's not me point. You know the difference between right and wrong, probably better than any person I know. The difference between you and a lot of people is that you act. You do something about it. Now I'm afraid you are going to see something wrong, and you aren't going to do what needs to be done because you are afraid of making it worse. You can't let fear— your fear of the fire—keep you from doing what you know is right."

Rian pondered Conor's words for a minute. "You're right."

"Thank you," he said.

Still, her conversation with Yana remained vivid in her mind.

"Fire will follow you."

"What kind of fire? Fire like the Winter Palace?"

"All kinds of fire. Fires that are out of control. Many of them. Fires that you think you control, but you don't."

· RIAN ·

Two days after the mobs failed in their attempts at further arson, Rian and Jules sat atop the mammoth transport wagon as six Krieger Coach workers walked beside and behind, making sure that oncoming traffic didn't hit their wide load. They were delivering a new passenger coach across the river to the *Camden & Amboy Railroad*.

"*Vater* hasn't had any luck finding a priest to marry my aunts."

"Well, I'm only a little bit ahead of him. I found the preacher, but I haven't found a place the bully boys can't burn down when they hear about my amalgamating daughter. At least the city's finally settled down after Saturday."

"Settled down for how long?" asked Rian. "Are you talking days, months, or years?"

"It depends upon if we can avoid confirming the anti-amalgamators' worst fears, and that means not letting word of Martha and Logan's wedding leak out."

"Three people can keep a secret if two of them are dead," Rian said.

"Hopefully, Franklin's wisdom won't apply here. I hope we'll have a couple more people at the ceremony than that."

Rian sensed that something was wrong a block before they arrived at the ferry pier at the end of Chestnut. A fully loaded wagon with a painted side that said *Spring Garden Tube Works* passed them going the other way. *That wagon should be heading home empty, not loaded.* A block ahead of them, two other wagons turned around and headed back toward them. When they passed by, Rian noted they were similarly laden with goods.

Jules spotted a man from his church who was walking in their direction. "Jupe, what's going on at the pier?"

"Might as well turn around, Jules. That ferry won't be running today, or anytime soon, the way it sounds."

"What's the matter?"

"The *Falcon*'s engine up and died. Captain Ames told me if I have to get to New Jersey, I need to catch the *Dolly Mae* down at the Almond Street Landing."

"Shit," Jules muttered to Rian. "That's going to add miles to our trip on the Jersey side. We won't be able to get back to Philadelphia before the ferries stop running for the night." He climbed down from the wagon. "You men stay with the wagon. I'm going to talk to Ames."

Rian didn't hear herself included in Jules's order, so she reined the horses to the side of the street, set the brake, hopped down, and followed him.

Captain Ames was finishing up a heated discussion with the harbormaster, a man with the unfortunate name of Dicky Pricker. Rian saw Ames throw up his hands and turn away from Dicky and reboard the *Falcon*. He picked up a wrench as if he were going to work on the boat's steam engine, then sat down on a bench and put his head in his hands.

Jules walked to the side of the boat. "Done for the day, Captain?"

"Done for the rest of my life, apparently. Dicky's telling me I've got three days to get the *Falcon* fixed or towed out of the slip. My father started running a boat out of here twenty years ago, regular as clockwork. I haven't missed a day in a decade. Old Bessie shit the bed and I can't afford a new engine."

Rian stepped aboard the *Falcon*, ran her hand over Bessie's boiler, and turned to Captain Ames. "What if you could get a new engine?"

"I tied all my money up when I had the new *Falcon* built. I couldn't afford a new boat and a new engine, so we moved Bessie over from the old boat."

"But what if you could get a new engine at an affordable price? Maybe one that you could pay for over time? What if you could get it today? Would you be willing to grant me a favor?"

"Rian, you're talking crazy talk, but if that were possible, you could pretty much name whatever favor you wanted from me."

"Are you willing to stay with your boat for a few more hours? I promise to get back to you one way or another by six o'clock."

* * * * *

· OTTO ·

Otto looked up from his desk when Rian and Jules entered, both chattering about something. "What are you two doing back here so soon? Why aren't you delivering the passenger coach?"

Rian nudged Jules, which Otto interpreted as a prod for him to do the talking. Instead, Jules nudged her back. "No, you tell him," he said to Rian.

Rian squared her shoulders and faced Otto. "The *Falcon* broke down. We had to either turn around or go all the way down to Almond Street to catch the *Dolly Mae*. We got such a late start we would have had to spend the night in New Jersey."

"Then that is what you should have done. The *Camden & Amboy* needs that car."

Jules jumped in. "I sent two of the men down to talk to the captain of the *Dolly Mae* to see if he can take us first thing tomorrow morning. The delay won't inconvenience the *C&A* all that much. Otto, Rian has an idea . . ."

Otto sat back in his chair, crossed his arms, and stared at his daughter. He had heard from Lucretia about Rian's adventures—and misadventures—three nights ago with the Shelter for Colored Orphans while he was spiriting Garrison out of town. "And what is this idea?"

"Captain Ames needs a new engine for the *Falcon*. Otherwise, he's out of business for good."

"This is unfortunate. Ames is a good man."

"*Vater*, last week you decided not to send that little locomotive to Cuba because it would support slavery. Have you figured out what to do with it yet?"

"No, no one around here is interested in anything that small. I have yet to hear back from some of the mines in the coal region, but right now it is gathering dust. Harry is still upset with me because it is in his way."

"So, we solve part of Harry's problem by taking the engine and the boiler off the Cuba loco and selling it to Captain Ames. We offer him a payment plan at a reasonable interest so that he can afford it."

"I like this idea. We solve a problem and do a good man a favor. *Liebling*, this is brilliant."

Jules couldn't contain himself. "Wait 'til you hear, Otto. It gets better. We add one extra condition to the sale: transportation to a place where Logan and Martha can get married without fear of the bully boys burning things down."

"I'm not sure there is such a place these days."

"But there is," Jules continued. "Windmill Island. A quarter mile out in the Delaware. Otto, there's almost nothing there to burn. It's a big, long, deserted island with a canal dug halfway through it. We can hold three weddings there and no one will ever know they took place."

"Three weddings?"

"Sure," said Jules. "No priests will marry your Catholic half-sisters to two protestant men, but maybe Reverend Furness, who's going to marry Logan and Martha anyway, will also marry Hilda to Oskar Becker and Maria to Klaus Ritner."

Otto looked at Jules. "This was not your idea?"

Jules put his arm around Rian. "Otto, this is 100 percent Rian's idea. The only change I see is that we delay the weddings to Sunday so that there's no one working on the canal. Otto, I think this can work, but Harry's guys need to start disassembling that locomotive right away."

SUNDAY, MAY 27

· RIAN ·

Rian stood with Conor at the Walnut Street Wharf, observing the queue of five wagons and coaches and thirty-four people.

Conor knelt down, picked a dandelion that had somehow found a foothold in the gravel, and handed it to Rian. "You look funny in a dress."

"I feel stupid in a dress. I can't believe *Vater* made me wear it."

"That was your deal, right? Special occasions. If this isn't a special occasion, I don't know what is."

Rian returned her attention to the queue. "What if we go to all this trouble and fire keeps following me around?"

Conor shrugged. "Here's how I see it. You make a decision, it's a decision. You don't make a decision, it's still a decision not to make it. You can't go through your life afraid to make decisions."

"Well, I made a big decision with this wedding scheme."

"Actually, that wasn't your decision at all. Yeah, it was your idea, but all the adults jumped on it. I think you're safe."

Rian surveyed the wagons again. No one had disembarked. Occasional puffs of tobacco smoke rose from drivers' benches. Horses stood stolidly, tails swatting at the occasional fly. "Everybody's playing their part so far. They're all pretending like they don't know each other." On the *Falcon*'s previous run to Camden, Otto let two wagons that were in line behind him cut ahead. Now their five vehicles were first in line, and they would be the only ones loaded onto the *Falcon*'s next trip out. "I guess the rest of it depends on Captain Ames."

Rian turned to the north and saw the *Falcon* rounding the northern tip of Windmill Island. "Well, we're about to find out. My my, his new steam engine sounds like it's running like a Swiss watch."

"Yeah, well, too bad it's going to break down in about twenty minutes."

* * * * *

The *Falcon* docked at the Walnut Street jetty with barely a nudge. Rian's Uncle Kurt and Logan Gallagher stepped from the ferry onto the jetty and secured the bow and the stern.

"Wow," said Conor. "They look like they've done that for years."

"Well, Uncle Kurt probably has. I don't think a ship's carpenter sits around much when his boat enters port. But Logan had to learn on the fly."

Captain Ames didn't want any of his regular crew to witness the day's events, so he gave them the day off and told Otto he needed to supply two trusted crew members for the day. Fortunately, Kurt's layover in Philadelphia coincided with the weddings, so he volunteered. Logan figured it was a good way to spend the day since he wasn't supposed to see the bride beforehand.

The two newly minted crew members winched three heavy planks from the deck of the *Falcon* to the wharf. A freight wagon loaded with boxes and furniture tentatively inched down the planks. Once safely on the dock, the wagon driver flicked the reins and the horses picked up speed.

Conor gave a casual wave to the wagon driver as he passed the queue of surreptitious wedding-goers. "Only three wagons coming from Camden. Not much traffic on Sundays, I guess."

"That was one of the reasons why we delayed 'til today. That and we didn't want a bunch of canal diggers snooping around Windmill Island."

With the Philadelphia-bound wagons and pedestrians now offloaded, Captain Ames signaled for the queued vehicles to roll aboard. First came Jules and his son Rufus, driving a brand-new Krieger-built landau scheduled to be delivered to a customer in Berks County next week. With the landau's top up, no one could see the carriage's occupants: Maddie, Martha the bride, and the four other Freeman children. The bridegrooms Oskar Becker and Klaus Ritner, dressed like laborers, followed in a farm wagon rented from Kent's Livery. The minister William Henry Furness, acknowledging no one, drove his cabriolet aboard. Otto followed with a team pulling his landau. Inside were the newly immigrated brides, Otto's half-sisters Hilda and Maria Krieger as well as Maddie's parents.

Rian and Conor climbed to the driver's seat of the last vehicle in line, a small omnibus that Robert Purvis had purchased from a wildcat[19] who had bought a larger rig. Purvis intended to operate the omnibus on Broad Street, catering to Negroes denied access to most of the omnibuses in the city. But today, as Rian and Conor had worked their way south along a roundabout route, wedding guests climbed aboard in a festive mood. Lucretia and James Mott described themselves as friends of both the bride and the groom. Rian's aunt Mila Krieger and her nephew Jabez Howes each carried a picnic basket

---

19. Wildcats were independent omnibus owners who kept regular routes in Philadelphia but set hours to suit themselves.

aboard. The Gallagher family—Logan's brother Seamus, his mother, his three little sisters, and little brother—stepped in all noisy and aflutter. Homer, Coffey, and their baby, still living at the Freeman house, were the eleventh, twelfth, and thirteenth passengers to board.

Two additions were a bit of a mystery to Rian. One was a man named Hasselbach, a new acquaintance of Seamus, who joined them carrying a box of whiskey bottles. The other was a girl named Cee-Cee, whom Rian had seen at Jules and Maddie's house the night that Slatter's brother tried to burn it.

A man driving a buckboard inched forward with the intention of squeezing onto the ferry. Captain Ames put his hand up. "I'm sorry, but I can't let you aboard. I've just installed a new steam engine. It's much heavier than Old Bessie, and I don't yet trust how much weight I can load up. It's a bit choppy out there today."

"Oh, come on!" protested the buckboard driver.

"Sorry, you'll have to wait for the next trip."

Kurt and Logan cemented Captain Ames's declaration by winching up the planks. Ames entered his pilothouse and gave a blast of the *Falcon*'s whistle. Kurt and Logan untied the lines from their cleats, gave the ferry a good shove away from the jetty, and stepped aboard as if they were seasoned crewmembers.

Rian stood up from her perch on the omnibus driver's seat and looked back at the man who didn't make it aboard. She could still hear him swearing a blue streak from the dock, even over the *choosh! choosh!* of the new steam engine. The man threw a rock at the *Falcon*'s pilothouse. The rock found its target but ricocheted off the corner and plopped into the Delaware. "He's going to have a long wait," she said to Conor.

* * * * *

· OTTO ·

As the *Falcon* rounded the northern tip of Windmill Island, Otto could make out the outline of Camden, New Jersey, half a mile away. Safely out of sight of prying eyes, passengers descended from their vehicles and awkwardly greeted one another. At the appropriate moment, Captain Ames assessed the tide, current, and wind and disengaged the steam engine. The side paddle wheel stopped turning. The *Falcon* started to slowly drift south.

Ames descended the three steps from his pilothouse and found Otto. "Are you sure you want this to be the story? Your reputation's going to be mud.

Tomorrow this will be what everyone's talking about up and down the water-front: 'Krieger Locomotive engine fails in first week'."

Otto laughed. "A small price to pay, especially if it hides the real story. Besides, I will be able to tell things a bit differently. We worked through two straight nights to install a locomotive engine that was supposed to go to Cuba into your ferry. There were bound to be some problems."

The *Falcon* continued drifting south in the sedate Delaware current, pass-ing by Windmill Island to the west. Four minutes after Captain Ames cut the engine, Otto spotted the 130-foot-wide cut into the island that was their des-tination. From dawn to dusk, six days a week, legions of day laborers dug a passageway through Windmill Island with picks and shovels. But not today; today was Sunday.

Ames pointed to the sailboat *Isabella*, which was tied up to a few feet north of the cut. James Forten stood on the dock, holding a coiled rope in his right hand. "Is that man part of this plot too, Otto?"

Otto nodded. "I'm surprised you don't know him. That's James Forten. He owns the largest sailmaking shop on Delaware Bay."

"Heard of him. Never had the need to socialize."

Otto assumed that Ames, who was white, was referring to Forten's skin color. "Well, hang on to your hat, Captain Ames—you're going to get an eyeful today."

"Oh, no, it's nothing like that. I've got no beef meeting with Negroes. Doubt I would have agreed to this deal if I did. Men of sail and us steamboaters don't have much opportunity to socialize. I imagine sooner or later we'll muscle them all right out of the bay, then after that the high seas."

Forten skillfully tossed the line to Kurt Krieger and started to pull the steamboat toward the cut. "Keep pulling until we bottom out," Captain Ames said to Forten when they were within conversing distance. "High tide isn't for another three hours yet."

Forten waved, indicating he knew full well when high tide was, pulled the *Falcon* into the cut about fifty feet, and tied the line to a sapling. Robert Purvis appeared with a second line, which he handed to Logan. With the *Falcon* prop-erly moored, the new deckhands winched one of the planks to the shore, and the passengers disembarked carrying tables, chairs, linens, changes of clothes for the grooms, utensils, food, and spirits that had been stowed aboard the farm wagon and the omnibus.

* * * * *

· SEAMUS ·

Reverend Furness married Oskar Becker to Hilda and Klaus Ritner to Maria in a double wedding, then married Logan to Martha. After the ceremonies, the conglomeration of guests mingled with grace.

Ruben Hasselbach and Seamus stood behind the drink table, serving lemonade, a beverage new to most of the wedding guests, plus Ruben's whiskey to anyone who expressed interest.

Seamus surveyed the crowd. "I think folks are getting along pretty well, considering. And I think your whiskey's a big success."

"Whiskey's a fine addition to any celebration. This seems like a worthy occasion." Hasselbach scanned the small crowd with a smile. "I've been watching your cousin Rian. She navigates each of these groups without an awkward step."

"That is something very special about her. She finds the good in everybody. Well, almost everybody." Seamus took another sip of whiskey and savored its smoothness. "So, are we going to do this? Become business partners?"

"We would have to surmount some problems. We need a good source of clean water. We can't draw water from the Schuylkill or the Delaware since everyone upstream uses them as sewers. We would have to bring clean water in from some spring nearby. Second, we need to find some farmer who's willing to raise rye and barley for us."

"Not corn?"

"There'll be no corn in my whiskey, you can rest assured of that."

"I don't think we would have to travel too far out into the hinterland to find all the rye and barley we want. Probably could have it shipped in on the *Philadelphia & Columbia.*"

"Good. The cost of transportation for our raw materials is going to make our whiskey more expensive than that of our competitors. They distill right on the spot using local corn and water and then ship the whiskey to Philadelphia. Less weight, less shipping cost."

"So if our whiskey is going to cost more to produce, we'll have to charge more. It better be exceptional."

"It will be exceptional, although there are opportunities to save some money by setting up business in Philadelphia. First, rather than throwing a still together using our unskilled labor, we can contract with some of your fine mechanics in the city to do it. That will be a savings in the long run."

"I think I know just the outfit for that job."

"And then because of all of the coal that's coming down on the Lehigh Canal, we'll have all the heat we need."

"How much heat do you need to make a batch of whiskey?"

"Oh, not much at all, that's the easy part. But my whiskey's going to be aged for over a year, and it's got to be kept above seventy degrees during all that time, summer and winter. No one else is going to be doing that."

"You mean we won't be selling our whiskey for a year?"

"Longer than that. First we have to find the farmers and make sure they'll sell to us this season. Barley should ripen up next month, so we mustn't tarry. Next: Find a place to house our operation. It should be near the Schuylkill for access to the coal. Then we build the stills. I have all the plans in my head. We have our work cut out for us."

Seamus recalibrated his dreams of getting rich quick. *Guess I better not cut my ties with the No Names, and I should rekindle me evening operations on the docks.* "Seems like your plans for spending my money are well along. I think we should have a drink."

Hasselbach raised his glass.

"*Sláinte* [Health]," declared Seamus.

* * * * *

· OTTO ·

Otto stood with two of the bridegrooms, Logan and Oskar, and observed the socializing. "I think everyone's on their best behavior."

Logan chuckled. "This is how I used to feel at mass when me ma smacked Seamus and me on the back of our heads and told us we had to behave ourselves."

"It gives me hope for the future," commented Otto. "Especially after all that happened in the past two weeks."

Oskar turned to Logan. "What about you? How are you going to proceed, an Irishman married to a Negro?"

"Don't know, for sure. Live in Moyamensing. Be an outcast in me own neighborhood because me countrymen hate me for what I've done. I don't know if the boys in No Name will accept me. My wife and I will never be seen in public together. Martha and I are in love. I don't want to live without her, but I know how hard our lives are going to be. Then our lives will change again when the baby arrives."

"I have a suggestion, if you're interested," said Oskar. "I'm not saying there aren't harsh feelings toward Negroes or Irish in my neck of the woods, but there's so few of either of them where I live that I suspect you could go about your business and you would get a lot more fresh air than you could in Philadelphia. Why don't you bring your new wife to Newport. It's two days' travel from here—still in Pennsylvania, but it's like another world. You could work for me at the tannery until you get established. It's hard work, but it's honest labor. You might even find some work in the plastering trade if you are as good as that little girl Cee-Cee says you are."

"Now that is an interesting invitation. Let me talk to my new wife, and we'll get back to you."

* * * * *

· JULES ·

Jules and Maddie watched Grace and Cee-Cee from a distance. The two girls had returned to the *Falcon*, climbed atop Robert Purvis's omnibus, and were sitting on the roof facing toward Camden. Their shoulders touched. Their conversation—unintelligible from this distance—was animated. There appeared to be giggling involved.

"What are we going to do with those two?" asked Jules, but he and Maddie both knew the answer.

"Love them," said Maddie.

Jule pondered Maddie's statement for a minute. "If it hadn't been for the events of the other night, I probably would have spent months kicking and screaming before I came around to that."

"What happened?"

"I was about to leave the shop and face Slatter with my pistol. There was a good chance that I was going to die in the next few minutes. A few hours before, I had left you and never said 'I love you,' something we do most every morning when we leave for work. I didn't want to die and have Gracie wonder if I really loved her—all of her."

"That evening was so hateful, yet you concentrate on the good. That is the reason I fell in love with you eighteen years ago. We are very lucky, Husband.

Jules pulled Maddie in close and let her words wash over him, their attention still focused on Gracie and Cee-Cee. "You know it's going to be rough for them."

"Which part? Being Black, female, or sapphist?"

"Sapphist? There's a name for what they do?"

"What they do. What they feel. Who they are. Yes, Husband, there's a name for it."

"Do we know any other of these . . . sapphists?"

"Oh, I suspect a number of them, but one in particular."

"Who?"

Maddie shifted her gaze through the trees toward the dock to which James Forten's sailboat was moored. Rian, still looking awkward in her dress, Conor, and Jabez were standing on the dock and skipping stones into the Delaware. "Our favorite little ragamuffin."

Jules turned toward his wife. "Really?"

Maddie scrunched her face up as if that were the most obvious conclusion in the world.

"Hmm. Well, if that is true, Otto's going to have his hands full. But I'll tell you one thing, if it's the world against Rian Krieger, my money's on Rian."

"Well, I agree with you. But fortunately, it won't be the world. Same us, she has allies."

SUNDAY, JULY 1

· OTTO ·

Otto had been eagerly anticipating the gathering at the Freeman house since Jules invited Rian, Conor, and him a few days ago.

Six weeks had passed since the wedding. Jules and Maddie were hosting a farewell party for Logan, Martha, Homer, and Coffey, all of whom were leaving for Newport, Pennsylvania, the next day. No small part of the party's allure: Maddie's father Hercules, the finest caterer in Philadelphia, was providing the main course.

The sounds of activity drew the visitors to the backyard. Jules and Rufus had set a door atop two sawhorses. Homer and Logan marched behind them with a second door, and Grace and Cee-Cee were lugging a third door out of the house. Set end-to-end, there would be ample seating for a lot of diners.

Otto addressed Jules as his host turned to greet him. "I bet your father-in-law owns about twenty tables. I'm sure you could have borrowed a couple."

Jules shook Otto's hand and smiled. "Consider this my one act of defiance. He offered, but he's already supplying most of the dinner. Besides, if I'm setting up out here, I stay out of trouble."

"Where's Maddie?"

"In the kitchen, arguing with her father about who's in charge."

Otto smiled at Jules's quip, then turned toward his daughter. "Rian and Conor have something for you, but we thought they should give it to you out here because we didn't know what you would think of it."

Rian held out an oddly shaped object that was wrapped in heavy brown paper. "Conor and I bought it from a kid who was looting Pennsylvania Hall the day after the fire."

Jules unwrapped the paper, which contained the lower half of the plaque that for four days had commemorated the building of Pennsylvania Hall. It was broken at an odd angle. Although scarred, it had been cleaned up and polished.

Constructi
Frederick A. Hinton - Chairm

Architect
Thomas Stewart

General Contractors
M on Edes (dec'd.)
Jul Fre n

Jules looked at Rian. "This is very thoughtful of you, Rian. You need not have worried. My whole family will treasure this. I'll figure out a way to hang it in our parlor. It will forever be a reminder of this family's accomplishments, as fleeting as they may be."

"Phew," said Rian. "We didn't know how you were going to react. There was so much hatred that night. . . ."

"Yes," Otto interrupted. "Hatred that seems inescapable in our City of Brotherly Love." He surveyed the backyard, which was quite visible from Fitzwater Street. "In fact, I expected we'd be eating inside despite this perfect weather."

"Hang on to that thought. We can talk about it over supper."

* * * * *

The makeshift tables were littered with debris from a meal of soft-shell crabs, green peas, and boiled potatoes. Some folks were making first attempts to organize the kitchen for clean-up. Hercules Angell and the two youngest Freeman kids were churning ice cream. A dozen kids and adults were playing rounders in the adjacent lot. That left Otto and Jules alone at one end of the long set of tables.

Otto gazed for a while at the rounders game—Black and white, young and old, male and female—all playing noisily together in good-natured competition. "This was a big gathering of the two races, eating together outside for all to see."

"Hercules and I talked about it," said Jules. "We both agreed: The city has calmed down. The atmosphere on the streets has softened since the mob burned Pennsylvania Hall. Mobocracy had its way, well at least much of its way. But it's as if the rage of those three nights has somehow exhausted the mob's hatefulness."

"So you do not fear passersby taking issue with us eating together?"

"Not at the moment, no. Maybe I will sometime in the future. But I think things have changed. When they burned down Pennsylvania Hall, I thought it was one of the worst nights of my life."

"And that has changed?"

Jules nodded thoughtfully. "Now, I think it actually helped the cause of abolition."

"You can't be serious."

"But I am serious. When Homer first arrived here, I described the people of Philadelphia as five percent abolitionist, eighty percent apathetic, and fifteen percent hateful. I think those numbers have changed since the fire. My guess is that as a result of the destruction, a number from the apathetic group has come over to our side."

"How big a number?"

"Oh Otto, I don't know. A lot of people showed up to defend the church. People came here to save our house. My guess? Ten percent have changed their views."

"So that makes it fifteen percent who are with us, and perhaps seventy percent who don't bother to think much about the plight of the Negro in America. What about the remaining fifteen percent?"

"I believe they are still as hateful as ever. But I choose to be heartened by our growing fifteen percent. I feel it, Otto. Things have changed. If sacrificing a building was what it took to bring about a change this monumental, it was worth it."

"You are a more forgiving man than I am, Jules."

Jules reached over and picked up the remains of the plaque that had been passed around during dinner. He ran his finger over the lines that said

General Contractors
M on Edes (dec'd.)
Jul Fre   n

"Hmm," he grunted thoughtfully. "Forgiving. Yeah, forgiving on my good days . . . But never forgetting."

MONDAY, JULY 2

5:50 A.M.

· JULES ·

The next morning, Jules and his family, Maddie's parents, Seamus and his family, and Otto, Rian, and Conor gathered at the Vine Street Station to bid farewell to the travelers. The idling locomotive *chooshed* in anticipation of the train's departure promptly at 6:00.

Logan stood next to his bride of five weeks and shook Jules's hand. "Thank you, Jules. For everything."

"Are you sure you want to do this? Newport is a long ways away."

"We'll still be in Pennsylvania—not even two days of travel. Hilda and Oskar will be there." Logan gestured toward Homer and Coffey. "The Goods are coming with us. We'll be fine."

"Board!" yelled the conductor from the first passenger car.

"Got your bags loaded?"

"Yup, and two boxes on the flat car. Martha will write when we get settled."

"And make sure we hear as soon as she has her baby. Maddie will want to come to help out for a while."

"She might be fighting me ma for that privilege. Gotta go, Jules."

Even though there was space available in the passenger coach, Jules's pregnant daughter wasn't allowed inside. Martha hugged her mother, climbed to the roof of the passenger car, and sat on a bench. She waved down to the well-wishers and smiled. Logan, who could have taken a seat inside the passenger compartment, climbed to the roof and sat beside his wife. Homer and Coffey followed with their baby.

"You're lucky. It's a good day to travel," Jules spoke up to them above the occasional *choosh* of the locomotive.

"Your daughter married an Irishman. We're always lucky."

"Your lips to God's ears, Logan. Your lips to God's ears."

*****

· RIAN ·

Rian elbowed Conor. The two of them broke away from the group and worked their way up the platform—past the two other passenger cars; past the flat car loaded with boxes, mail bags, and other freight; past the tender that held water and firewood; and reached the locomotive. The engine idled patiently, only occasionally issuing a throaty *choosh*.

"Whataya know," said Rian. "It's one of ours. Hello, *Number 4*."

"*Number 4?*" responded Conor. "It says *City of Lancaster*."

"It was the fourth locomotive that we built. This was Uncle Adrian's first sale to the *Philadelphia & Columbia Railroad*."

The locomotive was a "hopper," a boxy machine with two pistons that extended out at an ungainly angle, giving the machine the appearance—and the nickname—of a grasshopper.

"Kind of ugly, isn't it?" observed Conor.

Rian laughed. "That's what *Vater* used to say. We only made three hoppers. Then better designs came along. But here it is, still running. Ugly but reliable."

"Kind of like you," Conor said.

Rian slugged her best friend on the arm.

Conor turned to Rian while rubbing his tricep. "You know you said '*we*' when you were talking about Krieger Locomotive. You're going to try to do it, aren't you?"

"Do what?"

"Run Krieger Locomotive."

"Well, a couple of things. First, Yana said that at first I wouldn't run it, then I would."

"You don't really believe that prediction, do you?"

Rian shrugged. "Maybe. But second, Uncle Adrian's going to get sprung from prison as soon as Kiserev gets back to St. Petersburg. When he gets home, he's going to take back his old position as president. That's okay. There's plenty I can learn from him."

The engineer, standing aboard the hopper, gave two short blasts of the whistle that were so loud that Rian and Conor covered their ears.

The *City of Lancaster* lurched forward. Rian waved to the engine driver, then watched the cars go by as the train picked up speed. First the tender, then the flat car, then the three passenger cars. Martha, Logan, Homer, and Coffey, seated on benches on the roof of the last passenger car, smiled and waved at them as they passed by.

Rian and Conor waved to the travelers and watched the train until it turned toward the west and *chooshed* out of sight.

EPILOGUE

THURSDAY, AUGUST 9

· OTTO ·

Rian rushed into the Krieger Coach office. "*Vater*, the mail's here. There's a letter from Uncle Adrian. It's addressed to you. It came from Saxony."

"Hurrah!" yelled Otto. "Finally!" He gratefully accepted the mail, unsealed the letter, and started reading aloud to Rian.

June 22, 1838

Dear Otto, Rian, and Seamus,

Well, since you have received this letter, you know that I am alive and well, and in Saxony, no less. My time in prison was not onerous. My accommodations were more like that third-rate hotel we stayed in before we got our bearings in London. Even the food wasn't that bad. I suspect General Benckendorff was looking out for me, just to further irritate Volkonsky. (Otto, I apologize if these names don't mean anything to you. Your daughter will fill you in.)

Kiserev arrived in St. Petersburg on June 10 with Catherine's memoir in hand. Apparently even though there was such fanfare surrounding the Great Western's fifteen-day crossing, there was still plenty of room available on the return voyage. (He says to tell you a man named Percell was on the ship as well, and the GW made the trip back to Bristol in fourteen days.)

Benckendorff personally sprung me from jail and took me out to dinner that evening. He was quite filled with himself, as he had successfully laid the loss of the memoir at Volkonsky's doorstep, and now he, Benckendorff, played the role of savior. Although he doesn't think he has fatally damaged Volkonsky's influence with the Tsar, the general has enjoyed watching him squirm.

Benckendorff was irritated—but not surprised—that Rian had made a third copy of the memoir. He assumes that Rian will keep her word and return it in ten years as promised. He did tell me to caution you, Rian, not to take chances with your life like you did during the palace fire. He doesn't want you to die and have the manuscript floating around somewhere, and he implied that the consequences of not returning the manuscript would be dire.

So here's an interesting little tidbit: Benckendorff knows Rian was lying and didn't steal the memoir off Volkonsky's desk. He assumes someone swiped the memoir in the confusion after the Winter Palace fire but can't figure out who. As I have no idea, it is a mystery to me as well. I look forward to someday learning the secret.

According to the general, Tsar Nicholas is taking the tale at face value and assumes Volkonsky had the memoir on his desk and was careless. The Tsar berated V. in front of the general, which got General B. laughing when he told me about it. V. had to find somebody to kick, so he summoned Ambassador Dallas to the Anichkov Palace and chewed him a new you-know-what. Dallas has no idea what is going on but assumes the Krieger clan is at the bottom of it. I'm afraid we have made an enemy there. Hope that doesn't haunt us in the future.

Benckendorff is a strange man. We enjoyed another excellent meal together before I left on the twelfth, yet I am sure that, had your mission to reclaim the memoir failed, he would have had me shot without a second thought.

Thank you for writing the letter from Copenhagen. Knowing that you were likely to catch either the Sirius *or the* Great Western *heartened me and made my prison cell much less dreary.*

Now that I am ensconced in Saxony at Count Sheremetev's estate, I realize how happy I am to be out from under the oppression that seemed so pervasive in Russia. Fear of informers, gray skies, cold; they're all behind me now. I feel much lighter already.

Count Sheremetev has lately met with a group of investors who are in the midst of building a railroad from Leipzig to Dresden and in need of more capital. It turns out they need a railroad man who can complete the project, and he has recommended me. I am tempted, but this time I plan to nose around a bit before I commit. I have written to Mila and Jabez to tell them that Leipzig is no St. Petersburg, but they would probably be happier here. I may not make any decision about stay or not stay for a few months.

In closing, I thank you, Seamus and Rian, for saving my life, and you, Otto, for supporting me and watching out for Mila and Jabez. It has been quite an adventure. May our adventures continue.

Adrian

P.S. Count Sheremetev found no need to ask for his money back, even though our mission was unsuccessful. There is still more than $10,000 in our account. So as the Russian chapter of this adventure draws to a close, we are still far richer than we were the day that Sheremetev and Malkovich walked into the office of Krieger Locomotive. I will get half the money to you via our bank in London.

P.P.S. Rian, I saw Frank and Wash being ridden by two Imperial Guardsmen the day before I left. The guardsmen both said they were very happy with their purchases, and they asked me to send their best wishes to you.

To read a transcript of a 1915 recording

of ninety-one-year-old Rian Krieger

reminiscing about the era,

contact me at

rogerasmith.com

and ask for Book 3 bonus material.

I promise: no spoilers (but I might tease you a bit).

Bonus materials are available

for each book of *Rian Krieger's Journey.*

Author's Notes

My wife jokes about both my writing and my woodworking projects: *Why make something incredibly difficult when you can make it merely difficult?* My answer: *Because it's fun.*

I take special pleasure in weaving real historical characters and venues into my stories. I want these figures to espouse opinions that they really held at a time and place where they really were. I want the venues—some of which still exist, some that have long ago disappeared—to come alive to the reader.

The problem is that research like this takes a ton of time. I buy a book or go online, follow reference after reference, three hours fly by, and all my new knowledge is distilled down to one or two (hopefully accurate) sentences.

In St. Petersburg, Russia

- Catherine the Great's memoir, with all its details and implications, did exist. It was kept under lock and key by successive Tsars: Catherine's (perhaps bastard) son Paul I, and his sons Alexander I and Nicholas I. Each new Tsar read the memoirs and understood their implications: that no Tsar after Peter III had a drop of Romanov blood in their veins. For a variety of reasons, copies of the memoir were penned but not made public, although rumors of their existence circulated among the Russian nobility and intelligentsia. In 1859, the exiled Russian radical Alexander Herzen, living in London, published the memoirs in six languages and caused a firestorm. Various historians have made the case that the publication of the memoir led directly to the freeing of the Russian serfs in 1861.

- The Manege, which was the stable and riding hall for the Tsar's Imperial Horse Guards, still exists, reconfigured as St. Petersburg's premier exhibition hall.

- After fire destroyed the Tsar's Winter Palace in December 1837, the Tsar moved his family to the Anichkov Palace.

- Lest you think it was a bit of a stretch for Tsar Nicholas to bring Rian into his home as a companion to his son, he did bring in a companion for his older son, Alexander, when he was in his early teens.

- Most historians consider the reign of Nicholas I a failure. The Decembrist Revolt during Nicholas I's first days as Tsar shaped the rest of his reign. He became a strict authoritarian, trusting only a small circle of advisors. He brutally put down a rebellion in Poland and was a noted anti-Semite. He was, however, a devoted family man, demonstrably loving to his wife and all his children.

  When the Winter Palace burned, Nicholas decreed that the symbol of his power would be rebuilt within a year. Although many experts believed that ten years was more likely, the Imperial Family moved back into the rebuilt palace by Easter of 1839, sixteen months after the fire. Contemporary accounts claimed that six thousand workmen died to make that possible. If true, that translates to fifteen men per day.

  Always fascinated by his army, Nicholas equated its million-man size with power. The Crimean War, which started in 1853, demonstrated otherwise. Modern militaries had become increasingly reliant on logistics, technology, and training, none of which was prevalent in the Russian Army. The Russians were beaten in a savage, butcherous war that exposed all these weaknesses. Nicholas died in the Winter Palace in 1855, before the war was concluded.

- If the Decembrist Revolt shaped the reign of Nicholas I, the defeat in the Crimean War shaped the reign of Alexander II. Having seen firsthand the ineffectiveness of poorly trained troops equipped with obsolete weapons, he vowed to change the face of Russia. His crowning achievement was freeing Russian serfs in 1861.

- Grand Duchess Olga Nikolaevna grew up to be a desirable potential consort for the princes of Europe. She married Charles, Crown Prince of Wurttemberg, at age twenty-four. Unfortunately, the union was not a happy one. Charles was homosexual. They had no children. Olga concentrated on social causes in Wurttemberg, most notably the education of young women.

- Grand Duke Konstantin Nikolaevich served his brother loyally after Alexander II succeeded their father. Trained to become a navy man from childhood, he spearheaded the modernization of the Russian Navy. He also ran roughshod over a recalcitrant committee assigned to formulate a plan for the emancipation of the serfs, which Alexander II signed into law in 1861. When Alexander II was assassinated in 1881, Konstantin's instincts were determined to be too progressive by Alexander's reactionary son, Alexander III. Konstantin was soon dismissed.

- George M. Dallas, the gift that keeps on giving, will make appearances in future books in Rian Krieger's Journey. After resigning his post as Ambassador to Russia, he returned to Philadelphia in 1839 and set up a law practice. He became vice president of the United States under James K. Polk. During America's war with Mexico, he was an outspoken advocate of annexing all of that country into the United States.

- General Alexander von Benckendorff, creator of the Third Section, increased the power of the Secret Police and its web of informants until his death in 1844. His monster's power became so pervasive that, without the Tsar's knowledge, agents of the Third Section even detailed agents to spy on Grand Duke Konstantin when he was head of the Russian Naval Department.

- Prince Pyotr Volkonsky, Minister of the Imperial Court, loyally served Tsar Nicholas I until his death in 1852. Although his reputation was diminished in the aftermath of the Winter Palace fire, Nicholas returned his minister's loyalty. They remained steadfast allies until Volkonsky's death.

- The story of Lev the serf's desire to flee from the Tsar's land is far from fanciful. Much as enslaved Americans risked punishment to be free, it wasn't unusual for Russian serfs to flee to neighboring provinces or countries. One of the reasons Catherine the Great pushed for the domination, then partition, of Poland was because so many serfs were fleeing to that country.

- Superstition was woven throughout the fabric of Russia during this era.

On the Atlantic

- Above all, I love finding those moments in history that are the unknowns; the gray areas that I can slip my characters and storylines through. It gave me great pleasure to populate the maiden voyage of the *Great Western*, which did indeed cross the Atlantic with a mere seven passengers, with my own set of characters. The *Great Western* arrived in New York City in the record time of fifteen days and five hours, one day behind the steamship *Sirius*, which had started its journey four days beforehand. The *Great Western* made forty-five successful Atlantic crossings before it was sold for service to the West Indies in 1847. In 1856 it ferried British troops to Crimea.

- Isambard Kingdom Brunel, the designer of the *Great Western*, recovered from his injuries and continued his career to become one of the most prolific engineers of the nineteenth century. His projects, often grandiose, included dockyards, railroads, bridges, and tunnels. His SS *Great Britain* was the largest passenger ship afloat from 1845 to 1854, and the first trans-ocean ship to combine an iron hull and screw propeller.

- James Hosken, captain of the *Great Western*, joined the Royal Navy when he was nine years old and worked his way up the ranks to command two packet ships before he left the Navy at age thirty-five. He ably captained the *Great Western* many times across the Atlantic. In 1846, he was appointed captain of the SS *Great Britain*. Unfortunately, on its fifth Atlantic crossing, the *Great Britain* ran aground off the coast of Ireland, thus diminishing Hosken's reputation. He continued to serve on the high seas through the Crimean War.

In Pennsylvania

- Lucretia Mott lived at 136 North Ninth St. in Philadelphia, next door to the fictional Otto and Rian Krieger. Lucretia is one of my heroes. I am convinced that her sensibilities and eloquence would enable her to fit seamlessly into the conversation at a dinner party today. Lucretia started the Philadelphia Female Anti-Slavery Society (PFASS) along with numerous other white and Black women, a fact that made PFASS quite controversial. In an era when the races were discouraged in a thousand ways from mixing, Lucretia persisted in inviting Black women into her home, visiting them in their homes, and working with them on committees.

- Robert Purvis was born in Charleston, South Carolina. His father was an English immigrant who had prospered in America. His mother was known as "mixed-race" in the South because her father was Jewish and her mother was a Moor from North Africa who had lived ten years as a slave in the New World. In the eyes of South Carolina law, Robert Purvis was Black. Purvis's father moved the family to Philadelphia, where they could lead a better life. Robert attended Amherst Academy and returned to Philadelphia. Light-skinned and able to pass as white, he chose to identify with the Black quarter of his heritage. When his father died, he became one of the largest property owners in Philadelphia.

- Purvis wrote the eighteen-page *Appeal of the Forty Thousand Citizens, Threatened with Disfranchisement, to the People of Pennsylvania* in the hopes of persuading (male) voters to reject the Pennsylvania Constitution of 1838 because it revoked the right of Black males to vote. It is a powerful, reasoned, respectful document. Sadly, it further inflamed racial tensions during this era.

- James Forten, Robert Purvis's father-in-law, owned a sail business housed off the Willing & Francis Pier on the Delaware. A true hero of the American Revolution at age fourteen, he apprenticed himself to a white sailmaker, became foreman of that mixed-race shop, and eventually bought the sail loft. He continued to innovate in his business, which made him by all accounts the wealthiest Black man in North America and one of the richest men in Philadelphia. He invested in Philadelphia real estate, loaned money to both Blacks and whites, formed and served on numerous groups to improve the lot of his fellow African Americans, and contributed to William Lloyd Garrison's *The Liberator* both financially and as a reporter.

- The Panic of 1837, belatedly precipitated by Andrew Jackson's Specie Circular, occurred as described. The resulting economic depression was long and hard, lasting more than six years and at times putting a huge percentage of America's workforce out of work.

- I was unaware of the Patriot War when I taught high school history. From December 1837 to December 1838, rebels seeking independence for Upper Canada clashed with British soldiers in numerous engagements along the American/Canadian border. Handfuls of men from the American Northeast responded to the siren song of adventure to fight for independence. The rebellion failed and became an almost forgotten footnote in Canadian-American history.

- Built in 1834, a chain of optical telegraph towers extended from the Merchants' Exchange Building in downtown Philadelphia to its opposite number on Wall Street in New York City. Even in this era, businessmen were hungry for whatever advantage a bit of information could give them over their competitors. This competitive advantage lasted until Samuel F. B. Morse's electric telegraph made semaphore towers obsolete in the mid-1840s. Although a string of semaphore towers from New York City to New Orleans was contemplated and endorsed by the U.S. Postmaster General, the project was never started.

- I now indulge in another one of those bits of historical trivia that has no relevance to this story. An optical telegraph system was completed from St. Petersburg, Russia, to Warsaw, Poland, in 1839, a year after Rian's fictional departure. A short message could be sent between the two cities, a distance of 750 miles, in fifteen minutes.

- The Sparks Shot Tower on Carpenter Street was built in 1808 and produced lead shot until 1913. It still stands, is not open to the public, and is currently surrounded by a public playground.

- A channel was dug through Windmill Island in the Delaware River in 1838 so that ferries had a more direct route to Camden, New Jersey. The northern island became known as Smith Island and had a brief moment of notoriety in the 1870s and 1880s as a summer destination for families, including a hotel, roller-skating rink, and separate baths for men and women. Frequent fights and charges of prostitution eventually tarnished the resort's image. Smith and Windmill Islands were dredged out of existence in the 1890s.

- The Pennsylvania Constitution of 1838, including the "white-only" clause, was voted on by the male citizens of Pennsylvania in October 1838. Delegates to the Pennsylvania Constitutional Convention played the roles as described. We will learn the result of the vote in *The Fiddler*, Book 4 of Rian Krieger's Journey.

- Pennsylvania Hall was financed and built as described, although the story of Jules's role as general contractor is a product of my imagination. I could find no mention of any African American artisans involved in its construction. Pennsylvania Hall's life, from dedication to destruction, lasted four days.

- Lewis Tappan was one of the foremost abolitionists of his day. He knew intimately the power of the mob. In 1834 in New York City, rioters, reacting to accounts of amalgamation in the local press, ransacked his house and destroyed other buildings associated with the anti-slavery movement, as well as private homes and businesses owned by African Americans. He frequently voiced sentiments that any future for racial harmony in the United States depended on a "copper-skinned America." Given his eldest daughter Juliana's membership in the Ladies New York City Anti-Slavery Society, which did not admit Black members nor advocate for racial equality, I assume she did not share Tappan's sentiments.

- On May 15, 1838, light-skinned Robert Purvis arrived at Pennsylvania Hall in his carriage and extended his hand to his dark-skinned wife, Harriet. That event added fuel to the flames of those outraged by stories of amalgamation.

- Angelina Grimké married Theodore Weld in the noteworthy ceremony described. She spoke passionately to a promiscuous audience on May 17. After the burning of Pennsylvania Hall, it was thirty years before she would speak publicly again.

- I have borrowed heavily from the book *Pennsylvania Hall* by Beverly C. Tomek to formulate Mayor Swift's words to the mob and Lucretia Mott's declaration to the assembly within the hall. In addition, I followed Ms. Tomek's timeline for the events before and after the burning of Pennsylvania Hall, occasionally taking license to insert my characters into scenes previously occupied by unknown individuals.

- In another one of those gray areas that I can slip my story through, William Lloyd Garrison, obviously in jeopardy on the night of the conflagration at Pennsylvania Hall, was escorted to safety by youngsters who were about Rian and Conor's age at the time. One credible account has him taken to Robert Purvis's farm in Bucks County.

- Similarly, the day after Pennsylvania Hall burned, a mob bent on destruction headed for Lucretia Mott's house, only to be led the wrong way on Ninth Street by an unidentified "quick-witted friend." I couldn't resist putting Rian in the middle of this action.

- The rioting that consumed Pennsylvania Hall on May 17, and heavily damaged the Shelter for Colored Orphans on May 18, moved south to threaten the Bethel AME Church and other buildings on May 19.

I am sure that this book includes numerous historical inaccuracies. I apologize in advance, and would appreciate hearing others' feedback on this. Please contact me through my website at rogerasmith.com.

Acknowledgments

I want to thank the many people who have supported me during this journey.

- The Brewster Writers Group for sandwiching criticism between praise and for helping me tinker, improve, and appreciate nuance.

- Fellow authors at the Cape Cod Writers Center for sharing their wisdom, hard-learned lessons, and contacts.

- Sid and Margaret of Two Step Approach, developmental editors who made the macro-comments I needed to hear.

- Katherine Talmadge Sallé, copy editor extraordinaire, who was the last person to polish *The Blackmailer* before I sent it off to Sunbury Press.

- My beta readers—Jeff Drake, Christine Jenkins, Bailey Spencer, Bob Spencer, and Ted Spevack—for their time, perspective, insight, praise, and criticism.

- Mel Bornstein, for helping me wrap my brain around what the Panic of 1837 would feel like to Otto Krieger and other business leaders.

- Ted Spevack, for lore about all things medical, in this case, how to get a chunk of wood out of a person's eye.

- Jake Wanamaker, Alex Meyers, Hayden Berg, Maureen Osborne, and Rikki Bates for assistance and perspective on transgender issues.

- Michael Townsend, who escorted me through accessible parts of the Sparks Shot Tower and showed me historic architectural drawings and photographs. Jen Cox and the rest of the staff of the Shot Tower Recreation Center, who were very gracious to me during their busy workday.

- The staff at Sunbury Press:
  - Publisher Lawrence Knorr, who believed in me and the importance of Rian Krieger's Journey.
  - Assistant Editor Sarah Peachey for correcting errors, catching inconsistencies, and prodding me to rework passages that needed attention.

- Cover designer Ashley Nicole Walkowiak, who conceived of the sequence of damask backgrounds that will grace all the books of Rian Krieger's Journey.

- Book Designer Crystal Devine for that final bit of polish.

• A treasured community of friends, fellow members of the First Parish Brewster UU Church, former students, fellow authors, and former colleagues who give encouragement, help me make connections, and send me books, articles, and factoids of interest.

• My family—Susan, Matt, Alecia, Alex, and Courtney—for their constant support and encouragement. To Susan specifically for lore about all things planted.

About the Author

Always fascinated by railroads, canals, the antebellum era, and social justice issues, Rog naturally gravitated to his first career as a high school history teacher. After ten years of inspiring young people, he yielded to passions for which he had no formal training: co-owning a summer camp, farming, founding a participatory science museum, co-owning a wilderness expedition program for teenagers, teaching entrepreneurship at the college level, woodworking, and leading a rural arts organization.

As an author, he draws lore and wisdom from all those professions, and joy from the thought that he is once again making history come alive to his constituents.

Rog and his wife lived and worked on a farm in Central Pennsylvania for forty-one years. They currently reside in Massachusetts with their Great Dane and cat. They have three adult children and two grandchildren.

www.ingramcontent.com/pod-product-compliance
Lightning Source LLC
Chambersburg PA
CBHW011757010726
47497CB00013B/3243